Mary Lowe Dickinson

The Temptation of Katharine Gray

Mary Lowe Dickinson

The Temptation of Katharine Gray

ISBN/EAN: 9783743403598

Manufactured in Europe, USA, Canada, Australia, Japa

Cover: Foto ©Andreas Hilbeck / pixelio.de

Manufactured and distributed by brebook publishing software (www.brebook.com)

Mary Lowe Dickinson

The Temptation of Katharine Gray

PRELUDE

It is useless to try to make a story out of anything that is not worth telling for the story's sake alone ; and that only is a real story which tells itself, or in which, in other words, the characters live their lives out and beguile us into living with them as we read. There may even be a true story with little plot, few exciting episodes or startling events, no elaborate descriptions, and no analysis of human nature. All these are important but not essential factors in fiction, as they are important but not essential factors in life. There may be a genuine story or a genuine life without any one of these ; if it retains the one essential and virile element of reality, it will be a thing altogether alive.

Whatever may be lacking in the nature of Katharine Gray, we hope that this essential element of reality and vitality is strong enough to beguile the readers into living her whole life out with her after they have once been admitted to the arena of her struggles, successes, and defeats. Here was an ordinary woman, without extraordinary environment, swayed by the passion of a mighty mother-love, dominated and held captive by that love, and yielding to the temptation to commit a wrong because of care for one beloved. It is no original or unusual type. The world is full of women who would do anything and dare anything that is right for the sake of a beloved child. The question, whether the love that makes a woman do wrong is really a greater love than that which simply suffers and endures, is one that this story aims to answer.

To live and suffer and toil and endure for the sake of a beloved child, that is a noble but not uncommon type. To dare all things and defy all things for the love of a child, to do wrong for its sake until, under the slow deteriorating process by which the convictions are deadened, one comes to choose wrong-doing for one's own sake, and to cling to wrong-doing until its mark and ·blight is upon everything one touches, is a form of woman's development that few, except students of human nature, would ever care to trace, however dramatically presented. Yet, once having entered into the secret of the life of Katharine Gray, we are convinced few will fail to go with her to the end.

In her life we trace the progress of a human soul loving much, willing to labor, willing to sacrifice, choosing much that is good, yet always hiding a canker-worm at the very heart and root of the life. And the story shows how the very lack of conscience and the lack of right motive may not only be like a worm at the root of the personal life, but that just so far as that spirit permeates any or every good work undertaken, it poisons and destroys. It shows how philanthropic work, reform work, attempts to lift the poor and degraded, efforts to advance the progress of women in every line, may all be outwardly prosperous and successful, and yet for lack of right principle be destructive instead of helpful.

The whole record is one long illustration of the futility of building houses upon the sand, of making bricks without straw, of attempting to do noble work in any of the world's fields with the brain or the hands, without purity of heart and honesty of purpose; a lesson of the value and importance of an active religious principle moving in the innermost life of every woman who longs to be a blessing in her home, and to take her share in alleviating the miseries of the world.

This book is sent forth therefore in the hope that whatever other mission it may fulfill it may deepen the conviction of the utter uselessness and folly of attempting to upbuild life and character on any superstructure except that of absolute honor and unselfish adherence to "whatsoever things are true."

M. L. D.

New York, October, 1895.

THE

TEMPTATION OF KATHARINE GRAY

CHAPTER I

"IT is not that I will not, but that I cannot, Robert. You took the money that came from my last work, and for this I have not been paid."

"It was only a trifle, and I did not take all. What have you done with the rest?"

"Used it for fuel and food; most of it for you and the child. There is not enough to pay the rent of this wretched room. Would you have me put my child in the almshouse, that you might have more to spend in gambling and in drink?" and she cast upon the man such a look of scorn as caused him to pause in his angry stride up and down the room, and brought a muttered curse to his lips.

They were still young, this wretched pair, he not over twenty-seven, she some years younger; but dissipation had taken all true manliness out of Robert Gray's face, as sorrow and irritation had taken grace and charm from the once lovely features of his wife.

The room was high up in a tenement house in Brand Street, a thoroughfare in one of the poorest sections of Chicago.   It was cheerless at the best, and only the lack of dirt prevented its being squalid. Katharine Gray, as she sat close under the window, stitching steadily at a half-made garment, never stopping her work even when she gave back some cold reply to her husband's querulous demands, set one thinking of a dark summer flower suddenly winter-killed ; certainly the warm currents of happy youthful life had been chilled into bitterness and scorn.

She married Robert Gray much against the wishes of her parents.   Dazzled by his good looks, his father's wealth, and his brilliant prospects, she tried to deceive herself into the belief that love of them meant love of him.   Her reaping time followed all too swiftly upon such willful sowing, for no sooner was her husband sure of her than he cut off all communication between her and those who had ventured to disapprove of him.   He began almost at once to pursue such courses of willful pleasure as alienated him from his own father who, while he refused him money to nourish his vices, yet blamed the young wife for not being able to hold them in check.

Yet Robert had not been altogether an evil lad. He was only the natural product of unlimited indulgence in his childhood and almost unlimited money in his youth.   Every one who had loved him had furnished him with funds, until he came to value father and mother and, when their supplies failed, even his wife, according to the measure in which she was able to supply his constant need.   Sometimes he was fortunate at the gambling table, and then he was lavish as lucky. But little by little they had come to where occasional "luck" could not be depended upon for constantly recurring need, and upon Katharine had now for a long time fallen the support of herself and her child ; and small as her earnings were, she never knew when her husband might come and by violence or threats take the last dollar from her purse. Sometimes she pitied and was kind to him. Sometimes she was in such desperation that she gave him what she had, in the hope that he would win ; for the conscience that would once have revolted against money so won, had lost its fine sensitiveness under the awful friction of rough necessities.

There were times when she almost hated Robert, and then she gave him money to get him out of her sight ; and sometimes, as to-day, she would not give it to him at all. One threat alone moved her, though she was careful that he should never see that it did ; and, failing of other means, he tried that threat to-day.

"I tell you what it is, Kate, I'm not going to be told all my life that I can never have anything I want because of that child. I have plenty of rich relations who would be glad to have her. My father would take her, if he could only be sure I would go away and never show myself again. But mind you, Mistress Proud-face, he wouldn't allow you to come near her either."

"I don't believe he would touch the child, Robert, so you might as well cease to harp upon that string. And if he would, he shall never have her while God gives me strength to earn her bread."

"But he would take her; he has told me so more than once."

"When?" she asked, sharply, turning upon him.

"Never you mind when," he answered, surlily; "whenever I ask him for money to take care of her."

"You seek for money to take care of her? The child would have been in her grave if keeping her from starvation had depended upon you—and you know that very well," she answered with unmeasured scorn. "And you know very well too, that if I have not taken care of her it has not been because I could not. I earn more than enough for us two."

"Take care how you provoke me," he answered, "or I will show you whose child she is, and whether I can provide for her or not."

She tried to steady her voice, trembling with rage, while her heart owned to a deeper tremor of fear.

"God knows how glad I would be, Robert, if you would show that you could take care of us all."

"Give me the money then, and let me have a chance to-day."

"I cannot."

"Which means that you do not choose. Then the consequences be on your own head," and he angrily closed the door upon her. Then for the first time, she dropped her work, and rushing to the bedside, threw her arms over the sleeping form of her little girl. Burying her face in the pillow she gave vent to uncontrollable sobs. All her bitterness and hatred and scorn, all her impatience at the suffering which her blinded eyes could not see was the result of her own choice, were lost in one rush of terror lest the exasperated man should fulfill his threat, and take her child away.

That night so possessed was she by nervous dread, that she lay long awake, quivering at the sound of every footstep on the stairs; but the slow hours passed, and her husband did not come. Unrefreshed by slumber she rose before the dawn, moving about softly lest her darling should awaken, and making the little fire, prepared breakfast for the child, tasting no morsel herself, and casting frequent nervous glances toward the door. She went aimlessly about, opening closets and looking into the drawers. Once she paused and took down from a hook a worn traveling bag, and stood absently gazing into its empty depths, as if unable to decide what step to take. Then her bewildered purpose clearing she seated herself at her table and began to write. It was not a long letter, but was written with a troubled face and slow tears stealing down and blotting it here and there. When it was done she placed it carefully in her pocket, and turned with a heavy sigh and a hard, set look upon her face, to the night's unfinished work.

Hardly had she begun when a baby voice called "Mamma," and a little sunny head lifted from the pillow, and, in a moment was performed for her that oft-repeated miracle that changes the hard, injured wife into the tender mother, under the magic of child-arms about the neck and rosy lips melting the heart with kisses. She looked almost happy as she bathed the white limbs and brushed out the tangled hair, and fed the babe upon her knee.

The child was called Gretta, for the mother whom

she had not seen since the day she turned her back on all her love and prayers to follow Robert Gray. As she caressed the little one her hand dropped upon her dress, and she felt the letter in her pocket. Drawing it forth she looked long at it and at the child. Should she send it? Was it fair to take her away from him because she feared he would take the child from her? Suddenly the little girl reached up her baby hand, seized the letter, and lifting her laughing eyes to her mother, toddled as fast as her little legs could bear her toward the fire. Her mother started after her, when the door opened and her husband staggered in, in the savage state of semi-intoxication that usually characterized these early morning returns.. Embarrassed for the moment she slipped the letter under her work on the table, thinking he had not seen it; and when he ordered her to get breakfast for him, she tied Gretta into the high-chair, and ran down to the store in the basement of the building for a little coffee and a couple of eggs. She was not gone long, but the stairs were steep and high, and there was time enough for Robert to read that letter and to slip it into his own pocket. It said but few words, but enough to exasperate the man, though, contrary to his usual custom, he did not storm at her, or betray by anything beyond a drunken sneer that he had seen it. It was written to her sister in her far-away home in Massachusetts, and it told her that life under present conditions had become insupportable, that she had resolved to live it no longer, that all these years she had been held back from writing, first by Robert's reluctance, and later by her shame at the result of her marriage, of which she now repented with all her soul. It did not mention her child, but it told her she was going East at her first opportunity, and begged for one word from her sister telling her that she should have a welcome, and asking to come to her until she could find work.

Sobered by the strong coffee, Robert went away without a word. In that letter, proving that his wife meant to forsake him and to rob him of his child, his muddled brain saw that he had a plea to use with his father, who could hardly fail to consent to save his grandchild from such a mother. Once in the old man's care he would take his chances of the child's winning her way to his affection. And once securely installed in the old home he would trust farther to be able to win his own way back to his father's heart, which would all be on the way to his pocket, which pocket was the ultimate destination of his desires.

So long as his wife loved or feared him he could impress her with his need for money, and rouse her to great exertions for its supply. But this small resource was fast failing him. Her scorn and indignation angered him. To be rid of her and her reproaches would be a relief, if she could not longer be made to minister to his needs. To rob her of the child would be, so he thought, no more than a woman deserved who had no better sense of the duty she owes her husband than Katharine had. Besides, the child was his only avenue to the hearts of his parents. They had money; Katharine had none; and money was essential to his indulgent, imbruted life. So the mind, grown too selfish to consider any interest but his own, and too cowardly for open crime, was yet equal to scheming to rebuild his own reputation on the ruin of that of his wife.

Full of this idea he sought his mother, a woman as weak as she was proud, in her pleasant home on the west side, a substantial mansion surrounded by pleasant grounds, built before Chicago grew so crowded as to make gardens a luxury beyond reach of any but millionaires.

When Katharine Hunt, the child of an unknown and poor New England country pastor, had come to Chicago to visit a family whose country home was among the hills near her father's church, and her son Robert had fallen in love with her, Mrs. Gray had violently opposed his choice. His father had made a fortune in grain, and her boy was therefore justly entitled to an alliance with another fortune, and Kate's father had not the faintest prospect of making a fortune in godliness, which was his only stock in trade. Treasures in heaven were well enough, according to the Grays' unspoken creed, after people got there to enjoy them, but would not serve in this world instead of silver and gold. So, though after a time she forgave her boy for marrying Kate, she never forgave Kate for marrying her boy, and quite naturally had held her responsible ever since for the growth in his nature of the tares which her own mother-hand had planted. And her husband, astute among men and able to see Robert's faults and to resist his constant demands for money, yet, as is not uncommon, saw all other women through the eyes of the one woman who was the light of his own, and was quite willing to find Katharine in everything at fault. And she, who was not overburdened with any tendency to self-effacement, and had never even tried on the recommended "ornament of a meek and quiet spirit," would not pretend that she did not think herself good enough for Bob. And so the proud old woman and the prouder young one never came nearer than at first, and gradually drifted farther and farther apart.

It was not hard, therefore, for Robert, shorn and shaven and pale, with that letter in the pocket of his threadbare coat, to confirm his mother's long-cherished faith in the unworthiness of his wife; and to make her feel that Katharine gone, and the child once in her own care, she would soon have her petted boy reformed and reinstated in her home.

It was a long interview between mother and son, ending in all good promises on his part, while on hers she was to try and induce his father to allow the child to come. She wisely avoided the subject until after dinner, when the lamp was shaded, the slippers warm, and the generous glow of the glass of wine which his boy had learned to sip at his own table was still reddening the old man's face.

"Robert was here to-day," she said, with a side-long glance at his flushed forehead as she passed him the evening paper. But her only answer was an indignant "Humph! wanted money I suppose? It's about time he tried his wheedling ways on you again. But I told you I would not allow it," he added, suddenly growing excited and very red to the top of the shining bald spot on his head. "I will forbid him the house, and cut off your allowance and pay every bill by check but what I will put a stop to his extortions."

"You need do nothing of the kind, John," said Mrs. Gray, growing red in turn. "He never asked for money, poor boy, and I have given him very little since you forbade it, though he was so pale and thin and threadbare, and no overcoat this stormy morning."

"That's all a dodge, I tell you. It is not a fortnight since I paid a bill for him at the tailor's. He has always gone on as if he were a boy, ordering whatever he pleased, and I, like a fool, have gone on paying, trying to keep the scamp respectable on the outside anyway. He spends more on clothes in a year than I do in three, and I pay for them, and he pawns and sells them, and so gets the money out of me to gamble with. Then he comes to you threadbare."

"But, John, John, don't get so excited. You know he has a family to support."

"Nothing of the kind. I don't believe he does it at all. I am beginning to have some sympathy for the poor woman. I hear she sews for Todd & White's clothing store. Now he has always wheedled money enough out of me to support them. If he had done it she wouldn't be doing that work."

"But what can he do with the money, John?"

"What can he do?" repeated the irascible old man. "Are women all idiots? Spends it on himself, of course. I tell you I have tried that fellow with every sort of a chance, and he won't work, and he will drink; and it's no use to talk to me, madame.

I never mean to do another thing more for him until he reforms."

"But, John, you are so unreasonable. I do not ask you to do anything for him. He did not ask you or me. He is in trouble, and he is your own flesh and blood," and her handkerchief, which could be very effective on occasions, went pathetically to her eyes.

"Humph! in trouble; well, out with it, and do not cry," and the old man settled back in the chair to the edge of which he had fidgeted himself in his talk.

"I know he has his faults, John," she gasped between her sobs, "we all have; but, John, think how unfortunately he married."

"Not so sure about that," he answered, gruffly. "But what's the trouble, and what does he want?"

"Wants us to take the child. Here, read this letter." And the old man adjusted his spectacles and read the letter Robert had left with his mother. "You see she means to forsake him and the child."

"Nonsense, I don't believe it. It is neither natural nor probable. Wouldn't blame her if she did leave him though."

"But the child? You see she never mentions taking the child."

"Do you mean to say she consents to let us have the child?"

"Oh, no; Robert says she would starve herself to feed it first."

"That doesn't look as if she meant to forsake it." Then, as if a sudden thought struck him, he asked, "How did Robert get this letter?"

"He found it on her work-table."

"Did she know it?"

"No, I think not; he certainly had a right to take and keep any such proof of her intentions;" but she paused suddenly, for her husband, with a glowering frown, deliberately tore the letter in half, and tossing it upon the fire, adjusted his glasses and took up the evening paper.

Now indeed the handkerchief came into service, and from behind its folds an agitated voice gasped, "I don't know what I am to tell Robert."

"Tell him, the rascal!"—and Mr. Gray almost bounced from his chair—"that I like a man, and I hate a sneak, and I'll take that child any day when its mother consents and its father promises to keep away from her, though heaven knows I've no desire to bring up or even ever to see another child. But I'll never be the party to any child-stealing, and I'll never do one thing for the support of the father till I see him buckle down to an honest day's work," and the old man rose and marched away to the smoking-room, leaving the cambric handkerchief to waste its pathos on the fire.

CHAPTER II

OF course Robert had to be told, and in the course
of the morrow he received his mother's message, telling him of the destruction of the letter
and of the unexpected mood of severity which her
appeal had aroused. Still she did not wish him to
despair, nor did she doubt that ultimately his father
would relent if Kate should consent to give the
child up, or if her desertion of it should prove that
Robert's fears had been well grounded.

All this was far less bearable to him than it would
have been if the letter had contained a banknote,
which it would surely have done if his mother had had
time to recover fully from the effect of her husband's
unaccustomed wrath. So the threadbare coat had
been wasted on the old lady, and the only satisfaction
to be had from that failure, was to get of Katharine
the money that took a better one out of pawn. This
he did by refusing to leave the house again so thinly
clad, and sitting persistently about, teasing the
child in a half-boyish, half-brutal fashion, and pouring an incessant stream of complaint and fault-
finding upon the head of his wife, whom he chose
to hold responsible for all his discomforts and woes.
He tried to make her talk of the letter, exasperating
her with the taunt that she never meant to go, had
not the courage to go, and that it would be the best
thing that could happen to him and the child if she

did go. The varied efforts to torment her were not without effect, for she sent him for his coat, and availed herself of the time he was gone to write a second letter to her sister, which she took good care to place in the post-box on the corner before her husband's return.   .

She had no trouble in understanding his taunts, had not much doubt as to the use he had made of her letter, and knew it would stand to his parents as another indication of her unworthiness ; nor had she any longer doubt as to his purpose to force her, by every abuse and neglect to the very step by which her condemnation and his own condonement were to be secured.

The outrageous injustice of the whole scheme, for scheme her sore mind called it, in which mother-in-law and husband were leagued to drive her away, stung her proud spirit. She meant to go and they could have back their precious son if they would ; but her child, never, while hands could labor and feet could crawl. Her spirit, undisciplined by sorrow, burned like a smouldering volcano in the bitter weeks that followed, weeks in which Robert was at his worst. She gave to him no sign of any change in purpose or desire. She worked day and night with a feverish energy, and could hardly spare time from her work to watch her baby at her play ; and when some mother ministry called her to the child, her eyes looked hungrily at it as if she could never gaze enough, and she seemed trying to feed her heart with the little one's kisses before she would put her away from her arms.

And thus three weeks went by, and an unusual

amount of work waited to be taken home to Todd & White, wholesale and retail dealers in clothing for boys. One of Katharine's trials was the going to and fro with her heavy parcels of work. It was not alone the weight of the bundle, but the contact with the overdressed and fat and frowsy fore-woman, a creature of "frizzes and bangs," who made her feel it a favor that she was given the work at all, and constantly reminded her that it was better for the firm to have it done in its own workrooms. If madame was in haste or out of humor work was rejected which was quite satisfac-tory at other times; so that Katharine, nervous and overworked, and never having learned not to "talk back," always dreaded the test and never knew what to expect.

But this trial was light in comparison to that of leaving her child. Robert would not carry the heavy parcels; but if asked at a good-natured mo-ment, would sometimes promise to keep the little one from falling out of bed or crawling into the fire. But on one such occasion he went out for a moment and forgot to come back. On another he went to sleep, and Katharine found him sitting in smoking clothing, lighted from the cigar that had fallen from his hand. So she feared to trust her treasure to the mercies of a man who seemed to have such a tendency to make a whole burnt-offering of him-self, and sought the services of the only neighbor with whom she had anything to do. This was a certain " Widow Bridget Burke," who lived on the top floor, and was always at home scrubbing like the round roly-poly washing-machine into which she had developed, except when she was on her "bit av a roof " drying the garments of the " gintlemen and ladies " who patronized her laundry, which laundry consisted of two tubs and three flat-irons and a very refractory cook-stove.   She had no need to go to and fro herself with what she called " ayther durthy or clane," for her boy Ted, whom she kept scrubbed as if she were paid a large price for it, fetched and carried for her, as he would have done for Katharine also, except that her pride would not subject her brawny little neighbor to the comments of the forewoman while her work was under inspection, or run the risk of his returning with a rejected garment.

But once, when she was too ill to go, she was very glad to get the widow herself to take it, though somewhat startled at the attire in which she arrayed herself for the occasion.   The Widdy Biddy, as her irreverent Teddy sometimes called his mother, had donned her largest cap with its widest ruffle, out of which her round face shone like a full moon.   She wore a short yellow gown, starched till it stood out with an alarming rotundity, and a red and green plaid shawl crossed under her arms and tied in a bouncing knot at the back.

But the dear old soul's spirit was as radiant as her attire, and Mrs. Gray could not bear to shadow her pleasure by any of her own misgivings.   Biddy returned in high glee.   " Dade and its meself that's goin' ivery toime by yer lave, ma'am ; but it's to confission I'll have to be goin' behind and before, and betwixt and betwane ivery toime I visits me leddy at the shtore; for its lies a plinty I've towld her

to-day to keep me sowl in purgathory a couple o'
wakes, and all the saints won't be enough to git
me out if I have to tell her as many agin."

"Lies! Why Mrs. Burke!"

"Widdy Burke's me name since iver me Mike—
that's Teddy's father, me dear, God rest his sowl—
got blowed up in the mine and come down dead.
It's Widdy's me name, me dear," and she crossed
herself devoutly and lifted her eyes to heaven.

"But, my good woman, I. hope you did not have
any trouble with the forewoman."

"Faith and I did thin, a plinty. Afther blarneyin' wid the clerks till I'd find out the shpot
where her leddyship was waitin', I wint wid a noice
young man into a bit av a cupboard loike. I wint
all nice and quiet and sated myself aisy on the sofa
wid the noice young gintleman guardin' the door and
shmiling at me cap, whin, howly saints alive! the
cupboard rose up on its feet, and up, up it wint,
thro' the air, wid the boy shmilin' and me a
scraachin' at the top o' me wind.

"'It's all right, it's an illivator,' says he.

"'But I'll illivate meself by me feet,' says I.

"'All right, get out,' says he.

"'Shtop yer horses thin,' says I. And thin he
went aisy loike until it shtopped, and I took to the
shtairs, and whin I got to the top, I was that red in
the face with the puffin' that no wonder her leddyship
said, 'Was I a peddler?'

"'Indade and I ain't,' says I, 'I'm a dacent
widdy and me husband was blowed up into forty
smithereens, pace to his ashes, and I've brought
home your clothes made by a sight grander leddy

than I've set eyes on here this day'; and I gave the fat one a look that made her kinder wither up as if I had brought her an invitation to attind her own wake," and Biddy's round sides shook with the recollection.

" But, my dear woman, how could you talk so? It would only anger Mrs. Smith."

"I did it to aise my moind loike. Isn't it I that's seen ye whin ye come back from there so pale and wakelike, and lookin' as if ye hadn't had a kind word for a month? And as soon as I looked at the cold round eyes of the crayther, I knew she was ayqual to the batin' of ye with her tongue, and I gave her no blarney, not me, ma'am."

" Did she find fault with the work? "

" Dade and she did, and I towld her ye was a leddy born, and it wasn't right to expect it of ye to be givin yer moind to it as we would of the loikes of hersilf.

" And thin she asked ' What was I to you,' and thin the divil he coom over me shoulder before I could make the sign, and I towld her yez was an illigant leddy, and I was proud to be yer sarvant, and that I had the delight of working for yez and nursin' the child, and my son, that's named Theodore—catch me callin' him plain Ted—I said, ' was niver so proud as whin he was a waitin' on ye.' "

"Oh, Biddy, Biddy, how dreadful! What can I do about it ? "

" Now be aisy, honey. It's not your shtory at all, at all, and its meself will shpake a word to the praste ; and indade its a bit thrue after all. It's Ted says to me in his funnin', ' Widdy Biddy, its oursilves ought to be taking care of the lady below, and the child is swater than hay.' Once, ye see, Ted wint to the country with the Frish Air Band, and iver since he says ivery swateness is 'swate as the hay.' And isn't it he that's a watchin' always to git a wink at yer child? And don't you lave me to mind it a bit onct and agin whin ye go out? and ain't it me scrubs and washes for ye? Faith its yer Biddy I am, and niver a story at all."

And Katharine had to let it go, and even fancied afterward that Mrs. Smith was kinder to her for thinking she was not utterly desolate and alone.

After such an exhibition of devotion she was quite ready to ask Mrs. Burke to stay with the child on the occasion when she went home with the work, the payment for which would, she hoped, make up the sum that would be needed for her flight. Biddy cheerfully consented, and wrapped as warmly as her scanty wardrobe would permit, Katharine went forth to face the cold wind blowing from the lake, and the colder human throng of men and women, hurrying home to happy firesides,—a throng in which she felt herself to be utterly a stranger and alone.

Robert had been gone all day. She did not know where; he would not tell her if she asked, and she had learned not to ask. She knew he had won a little money, and one night's luck usually meant a three days' debauch. If he was in the midst of one to-day, she could only hope it would last until she could be gone. There was nothing now to wait for except her sister's letter, which she hoped might come to-night. If it held even the shadow of a welcome she would turn her steps at once and forever away from the life she loathed.   As she walked along with bowed head, burdened by her heavy load, and turned the corner of the street to the entrance used by the employes of Todd & White, she caught sight of a man and a woman emerging together from the front door of the store.   It needed no second glance to show her her husband and his mother.   Robert was in a new overcoat and gloves, evidently the result of their visit, while her own hands were bare and red with cold.   Her first impulse was to shrink from sight, as they approached Mrs. Gray's carriage; but all the old spirit of rebellious scorn rose, and she tightened her arms about her burden, and walked resolutely forward. At the door of the stylish coupé they met.

"You here?" said Robert, with an added oath under his breath, as he tried to jostle her aside that his mother might not see.

"Yes, I am here," she answered, calmly. "Why not?   It is the proper place for mothers to come for clothing for their children; I am here that my child may be clad.   We have different ways of doing it, that is all.   I see your mother's is an easier way than mine," and with one look of contempt that swept Robert's attire from top to toe, she entered the building and tottered up the stairs, while her husband with a muttered curse followed his mother into the coupé.

"How dreadful!   How painfully mortifying and uncomfortable!" moaned Mrs. Gray, with a shiver; "and one is liable to have such a shock as that any day.   It is, really it is, quite too much for my nerves."

The money for the work was paid, but not without much irksome delay. It was late when she came out ; it was now dark ; there were many little purchases to be made, and many of the stores were closed. Hasten as she would, her progress was very slow. As she hurried from point to point, there was constantly before her mind the picture of her husband, comfortable, well-clad, petted, looking at her with a threat in his eyes, cursing her under his breath, putting forth his hand because he was ashamed to have his mother see the forlorn creature his wife had become. If this was the last time, as she hoped, if she never saw him again, she had gathered fuel enough in that hour to keep the fire of her hatred glowing many years.

Then the picture would fade for a moment from her mind, and in its stead she saw the dingy room where she had left her babe before the scanty fire, with Mrs. Burke's round face shining and her cap border flying, as Gretta, half undressed, lay on her lap with her pink toes in Biddy's fat hand, while she crooned :

> " This little pig wint to market,
> And this one shtopped at home,
> And this one got all the shupper,
> And niver a bit this one."

And the last picture gave her strength to go on.

Fearful that a letter might come from her sister in her absence and fall into Robert's hands, she had ordered her mail directed to the post-office instead of to the house, but told her if necessary to telegraph, to send in care of Mrs. Burke. When all else was done there was barely time to reach the post-office before the hour of closing. A trembling hand received the letter which she had felt sure would come to-night. She went forth hastily, with a strange sense of having found a hope once more; but it was not until she reached the nearest street lamp that she looked at the precious missive, and saw, not the hand of the long-estranged sister, but a stronger, strange hand which she had never seen before. Hurriedly she broke the seal and read:

MY DEAR MADAME: The receipt of your letter has given to your dying sister an unexpected hope of seeing you once more. She is, we are sorry to say, hopelessly ill, but may linger some weeks yet. I think best, as her physician, to urge you, however, to lose no time after the receipt of this, as she, a widow with one little child, has much to say to you, and many matters, which now she has found you, she is willing to confide to no other care. We will do our best to keep her till you come; but her anxiety to see you is one fact that makes her lingering doubtful. Let me beg you to make no unnecessary delay.

Respectfully yours,

THOMAS NEWMAN.

Overwhelmed with this new trouble, following so sharply upon her hope, Katharine staggered forward, resolved to lose no time in starting for her sister's Eastern home. It was very late when she reached her lodgings, and she was not surprised to see no light in the window, for Biddy's economy would make her sit by the sleeping child in the dark.

Wearily she climbed the stairs, and pushed open the door, which stood ajar. The silence burdened and oppressed her.   She called Mrs. Burke; but Biddy was evidently too sound asleep to heed. She groped for the candle, and lighting it, hurrried toward the bed. It was tumbled and tossed, as the little hands and feet often made it; but no golden hair bathed the pillow, no little rosy mouth waited for her kiss.   Upon the bed lay a satchel in which she had packed, in preparation for flight, the clothing of her bairn.   It was quite empty, and with a cry of horror, she threw herself across the bed. Her little one was gone.

CHAPTER III

AS consciousness returned, after the deathly swoon
into which the sudden knowledge of her child's
absence had thrown her, there broke upon her dim,
bewildered sense of loss and pain, the angry voice
of Widow Burke, who was urging her panting pon-
derosity up the staircase, puffing and scolding with
every breath. "And where is it ye are thin, ye
dirthy, desayvin' craythur? Give me two hands the
howlt er ye, and I'll dip ye into me washtub, and
wring the lies out of ye, and hang ye up to drip,
the durthy rag that ye are!" and she burst into the
room to behold Katharine sitting on the bed, clasping her head with both hands, and gazing at her
with speechless questioning. At sound of Biddy's
voice a sudden thought of hope had pierced the
dense misery that seemed paralyzing her power to
act or think. Could Biddy, her faithful creature,
have yielded to the temptation of the corner saloon
and taken the child down to the shop or up to her
own quarters?

At sight of her, Biddy had stopped short in her
tirade and answered at once to Katharine's half-
whispered, "Where is my child, Biddy?"

"The child! Indade, and haven't ye got her
there behind yer own back in the bed?"

Katharine threw back the clothes.

"Biddy, Biddy, are you drunk or mad?"

"Naythur," broke in the woman, with an indignant toss of her cap border.

"Then where is my child? Do you not see?"

"Gone! Gone is it? Thin it's the divil has got it, ma'am, and it's me, the big blarneyin' fool of a widdy that left him to do it. But how's the loikes o' me to know that a man would be thaving his own flesh and blood? Mighty quare koind of a faythur, ma'am, savin' yer prisence, to be shtalin' his own baby. Whist, now, me darlint, don't ye be troubled. He's but taken it a bit 'round the corner to the saloon. There's a dale of fiddlin' and a dancin' and a singin', and it's but to give her a bit av the world, and to show her off to the men that's got no such to be braggin' aboot. Rest aisy, ma'am, it's meself had her all nate and snug in bed, and hushin' her to sleep wid singin' a nice quietin' little story that me Ted's fond of—

> " A swate little story 'bout Michael McGlory,
> Who wint in the woods and murthered a tory,
> And broke his pitcher and spilled his wather.
> And married his wife and kissed his dauther.

"And Ted was always for askin' me whin I sung it, if it was the tory's dauther that Mike was married to, and niver once could I seem to make it clear in me own head. But your child, ma'am, she was too small to be botherin' me wid questions, and joost crowed along wid me, and tried to say it herself, till I could think of nothing but her and me swate little twinklin' mornin' stars a singin' together."

"Stop, stop, Biddy. That does not comfort me. Where is my child? Did you see her father?"

"And isn't it that I'm tellin' ye all the time? When she was aslape I was joost stirrin' the foire, thinkin' I'd run and git ye a bit of a chop from above in me rooms, ma'am, and make ye a pot o' tay and a bit of toast whin ye come in from the dreary weather, whin in walked yer husband, ma'am, all in a flurry like, wid a plinty of nice new clothes on the wicked bones of him, beggin' yer pardon, ma'am, and he said to me, says he, 'There's a crowd down at the crossing, Mrs. Burke, where the train runs over the strate, and a boy's run over and hurt, and as near as I could find out, it's your Ted.' And indade, ma'am, wid me husband blown into smithereens, ye wouldn't be having me wait to make the tay and mind the bairn. Moreover, he told me to run, and me wid me two hundred pounds and hardly breath enough to tell me beads. I did run. And whin I got there I see'd no crowd, and I asked every crayther that passed, and one said, 'Moist likely 'twas Ted,' and another said 'It wasn't Ted at all, at all,' and another one said ''Twas his legs was off,' and another that 'his legs was all right for he saw him walkin' home, but he hadn't never a sign of a head to his name.' And I was that mad at this taising a poor lone widdy, with only one boy and his father blowed high as the sky, that I wint straight to a policeman, and pointed the laughing blackguard out. But he said, 'Niver you moind; I suppose he thought you were drunk or crazy.' And no wonder, indade, wid me cap down me back and me bald head a shinin' and the wild ways of me, scraachin' for me boy. Thin he towld me if a boy had been hurt he would have known it, for the crossin' was on his bate, and that somebody had been foolin' me. And thin I come home again to find the craythur who did it, and indade, ma'am, I'm ashamed to tell yez, but I was that overturned whin I saw my Ted just shtalin' into the candy shtore below, that, haythen that I be, I took him by the ear and walked him into the hallway, and took him over me knee, and sint him shmartin' up to his bed. To think o' that, ma'am, a batin' me own boy because he wasn't killed afther all, whin I gave him the money myself, and told him he could have some candy with me own lips, bad luck to 'em. Ted's a heavenly angel, he is, and his ould mother's a baste."

And all this time, heeding only enough of the old creature's tale to confirm her own suspicions, the poor mother sat with her face buried in her hands. It had come. He had proved too quick and too strong for her. She had now to face the fact that his only desire and purpose was to rid him-self of her once for all. For him, hereafter, luxury and ease; for her, heaven only knew what, but surely hardness and toil. For him the sight of his child's face, and for the child all comforts and a life in which she would grow up if not like him in other things, yet like him in despising her mother. She had no doubt that the baby was with Robert's mother now. Should she leave her? Not for a moment did she waver on that point. Not for a moment, I am sorry to say, did her struggle take the form of a question as to what might ultimately result in the greatest good to her little one. Not for a moment did her heart rise in prayer for guidance or help in any work or plan.   Willful from childhood, finding the religious restraints of her early home most irksome, outwardly correct, inwardly wrong, like many another soul she had always chosen the thing she liked to do, instead of the thing that was absolutely right.   Even now, she could not see in her suffering the natural result of her own choice of life.   She called it the hard luck that pursues the unfortunate. Life had said no to her ambitions and wishes, but her fierce love does not propose to be denied her child or her fierce hate to relinquish her purpose to baffle and defeat the man who had made her miserable.   And the love and the hate together were strong enough to bring back to her stunned and exhausted body the power and the will to act.

Slowly she began to move about the room like one in a feverish dream.   Nothing was disturbed except the child's clothing.   What could he have wanted of her scanty attire if he had taken her to his mother's house? All dainty things would clothe her little limbs if she lived there.   Slowly she gathered up the cloak that had fallen from her shoulders, as if to go out.   Drawing from her pocket the money just paid her and the letter written by her sister's physician, she proceeded to place both in a little bag which contained a few things already prepared for her journey, and in which she had been careful to hide all the money she had from Robert's sight.   But he had found the purse, and when she opened it to add what she had just received to her little hoard, every cent of it was gone.   Burning with indignation at the petty meanness of this theft, she turned to go out.

"Indade, ma'am," said Biddy, who having vented her own emotions was silenced by the sight of this speechless intensity of feeling, "ye'll not be going out alone the night?"

"I must, I must, I cannot wait till morning."

"But ye'll not find her in the night, ma'am."

"Yes, I think I know where she is. He has taken her to his mother."

"Faith thin, but her own lawful granny 'll be good to her own kith and kin. Don't go, ma'am."

"I must," answered Katharine, impatiently.

"Then ate a bit, there's a dear; just a bit o' this toast I've been a nursin' for ye, and coaxing it not to be too dry. No? Thin it's meself is too weak, wid all me worry, and the loss of the cherub, and slappin' me angel boy, and shrakin' in the strates, to let it be wasted, and if ye don't mind, dear, I'll just take it up to me Ted. Wait a bit, ma'am, if ye're goin' I'm goin' wid ye."

But Katharine did not wait, and when Biddy came down and found her gone, she bustled back again, and hustling her sleepy son into his clothes, told him in emphatic brogue that "the thafe of a fayther had been shtalin the baby below," rousing him to such an excitement of indignation as made him double his fists at an imaginary antagonist, while his mother struggled with the button in his collar.

"Whist, now, sthand still wid ye. Ye must be decent aven in the dark. Now run wid all your legs, me boy. Ye'll get close behind her before she gets to the cars, and if she takes the car get on behind and kape in hidin' if she goes into a house. But if she comes out wid the baby, ye just walks up and relaves her like a gintlemin that ye are. And oh, Tiddy, Tiddy," she broke out, as he was half down the first flight of stairs, "don't go and get killed no more wid the crossin', for moind ye, ye'll get a harder whoppin' the next toime if ye do." And yet she followed him down to tidy up Katharine's room, muttering, " Bad luck to me if ever I puts the tip of me finger on him again."

Away through the darkness the little champion sped, and away on before him he caught a glimpse of a woman's figure hastening forward to the cars that would take her to the avenue where stood the mansion of Mr. Gray. When she entered the car, Ted jumped on behind, and if his little honest heart could have kept quiet, she would never have found him out. But he admired her so and loved the baby so that he could no more resist flattening his freckled nose against the glass than he could have resisted the buttered toast with which his mother made atonement for his smart.

Katharine saw and beckoned to him to come in, and blushing and much abashed, he took the seat at her side.

" Where are you going, Theodore ? "

" Wid you, ma'am."

" With me ? What for ? "

" To bring the child, ma'am."

" But I may not find her to-night, Teddy."

" No matter," he answered, sturdily, " I'll find her for you some other day."

" You ? Do you like the little one, Ted ? "

" Dade an I do, ma'am."

“And you will keep on looking for her, will you ?”

“Dade an’ I will, ma’am.”

Near Mr. Gray’s house they alighted. It was eleven o’clock, but the lights were still burning, both in the upper and lower floors. Katharine glanced upward. In which of those luxurious rooms was her child lying asleep? Her ring was answered by an old servant in faultless attire, who had seen her more than once in other days. He started back in astonishment.

“Let this boy wait here in the hall for me, Joseph,” she said as calmly as she would have done in those days of her early marriage, when she went in and out as one of this household, “and show me in to your master.”

“Mr. Gray is in New York, ma’am, and Mrs. Gray has—I think she has retired. She went to her room early, and begged to be excused to any one who called.”

“I must see her Joseph,” and she entered the library and seated herself before the fire. “Wait a moment ; say to Mrs. Gray that I will not detain her long, that I will come to her room if she is not able to come down, and that I shall be here early in the morning, if I fail to see her to-night.”

The message given left the woman “with nerves” no choice. If she refused to see her now, she would come again and again, and there would be talk among the servants. So Joseph went back with permission to conduct the lady to Mrs. Gray.

Bent like an aged woman, she dragged herself up the stairs. For the chance of a home like this she had stifled the best life of her youth, married a man of whose weakness and vices she was not ignorant; and she had done it not from pure love or from a purpose to uplift and save him, but simply to be the sharer of what comfort and luxury were his.   She had played a little game of expediency and failed, and felt it vaguely as she went on to meet the woman who had denied her the place a son's wife should have held.   And the thought gave an added bitterness to the voice and manner with which she greeted Mrs. Gray, who, enveloped in a soft wrapper, reclined in a large easy-chair before the fire.

"I have come for my child, Mrs. Gray," said Katharine, hastily.

"Your child.   And why, may I ask, should you come to me for her?   I know nothing of your child. I have never even seen it yet."

For a moment the room swam before the mother's eyes.   She had been so sure her child was here.   "Not seen her!   Then what can he have done with her?   He told me you would take her. He tried to make me consent to give her up.   He took her away to-night after I met you, before I reached home."

"He told me of your plan to leave him and the child," said Mrs. Gray, coldly.   "It is not strange that he should have wished to provide for her, but he has not brought her here, nor do I know where she is, or of his intention to take her away."

Too much startled and frightened to reply, Katharine only said, "I was not going to leave her. I did feel that I could not stay with him, but I meant to take the child.   I cannot give her up.

And, oh, Mrs. Gray," she burst forth, no longer able to control her fears, " I cannot wait, I must go on and look for her. If he brings her to you, remember I must have her again."

Once over the dread of the meeting, Mrs. Gray would have gladly prolonged it, and have tried to bring Katharine to see what would be, in her own eyes, the good of her child; but the strain of excitement and anxiety had been too prolonged. It was true that Robert, seeing Katharine on the street, and knowing that she must be some time in returning, had, after leaving his mother, secured a cab and driven hastily to the house of a former nurse in his mother's family. He told her his wife was going East, and asked her if she would receive and care for the child till her return, or until his mother could receive her. She was a decent, hard-working woman, not averse to such a task for the very liberal sum offered. And he had taken the little girl at once to her, trusting to his mother's tact to induce his father to let the child come home, as he believed he would, after he found that her mother had really forsaken her.

But not even the fact that Robert's mother was evidently innocent in this affair, could induce Katharine to wait or to talk. She hastened forth just in time to secure the midnight car, and Teddy, sitting or walking beside her, found himself hushed into unwonted solemnity by the set, hard look upon her pallid face. Only once she spoke to him, and then as they climbed the stairs she said, "I did not find her, Theodore. Remember you promised to find her for me another day."

"Indade, and that's what I be going to try, ma'am," he answered, with a little grab at his woolen cap.

Inside the door the "Widdy Biddy" met her with open arms. All her excitement had subsided, and the kind motherly heart was itself again. "And so ye didn't bring her to-night, dear? Well, it would have been a pity to wake her out of the shlape. Sure and all the saints in heavin is a watchin' her, ma'am. Niver you doubt o' that. And here's a yeller letter come to ye, ma'am. I'm sure it's to tell ye the child is aisy and safe."

Katharine took the telegram in her trembling hand. After all Robert had been merciful, and had sent her a word of hope. She opened it and read: "You must not lose a day if you would see your sister alive. Take the earliest possible train."

CHAPTER IV

IN the haggard creature waiting on the outskirts
of the crowd that surrounded the ticket office
at the Michigan Central Station in Chicago the
next morning, one would hardly have recognized
the erect figure and proud defiant face of Katharine
Gray. The nervous trembling voice in which she
asked for her ticket to Walden, a town among the
Berkshire Hills in the old Bay State, sounded
strange, even to herself.

"Can't ticket beyond Springfield, ma'am," and
her lips had parted to say " Springfield, then,"
when a kind voice at her elbow said, " Cost you no
more to take a ticket straight through to Boston,
madame. Better take unlimited ticket to Boston,
and stop off where you please."

Ordinarily she would have weighed any such
gratuitous information, and stopped to consider if
she had any need to go to Boston ; but she raised
her eyes to the speaker, an old man with a closely
shaven face and gray hair combed behind his ears,
falling in straggling locks upon his velvet collar
of ashen gray. A broad-brimmed, soft gray hat
framed a face at once so gentle and so strong, that,
without knowing why, she let herself be guided by
it, and said, " To Boston then." " Twenty, seventy-
five, and pass on, please ; do not keep the others
waiting," and gathering change and ticket in her

trembling hand, she turned to thank her informant, but he was nowhere to be seen. He saw her, however, and touched by her evident suffering, was slowly moving behind her, keeping his eyes upon her in the crowd, when something round and heavy came bumping against his traveling bag, and his view was cut off by Biddy's full-moon face and the flapping frills of her cap.

"The saints defind yer honor," said she, giving him a backward glance over her shoulder, "but it's me that has lost me leddy, and niver a bit did I remember who was behind me when I got a look at her before, so white and spachless, and crying all the while for the child. It's a bit of breakfast I've got in the bucket here. It's not a bite or a sup that's crossed her lips since ever the thaving crayther wint off with the baby, makin' no mintion of the money and the clothes." By this time they were at the cars, and, pushed along by those behind, Katharine had entered and passed from sight. The long-coated old gentleman was climbing the steps when Biddy was stopped at the gate for want of a ticket. In her despair she called out, swinging the little tin pail under the very nose of the guard: "Shtop, yer honor, you wid the long hair and long-tail coat. Its one o' the Lord's dear saints ye bez, sure," she added in her most blarneying tone, as the old man walked slowly back. "Indade, ye nadn't dishpute it, for didn't ye shmile whin I bounded inty the middle of yer stomach wid mesilf, whin any mortal sinner would a shprinkled the air wid bad words. Take it and make her ate it, for she's that full o' the trouble that she hadn't an

inch lift for the victuals, and she do be needin it
sore. Do take it. And long life to yez ! And may
ye niver die. And may the saints give ye the finest
kind of a wake !"—and before he could ask a
question, she had thrust the pail in his hand, the
conductor was crying "all aboard," and there was
just time for him to scramble on as the train departed, but no time to see Biddy's grateful grimaces
between the bars of the gate, or to see Teddy, who
farther down the station, was half-way up a post,
trying to get a last glimpse of "the leddy," whose
true knight the loyal little Hibernian had become.

Katharine did not see him, but his mother did, as
she came trundling down the platform, and before
he saw her his convenient attitude upon the post
reminded her that she had sent him in quite a different direction for a basket of clothes. Hurriedly
wiping her eyes, weeping in sympathy for Katharine, she stooped, removed one generous slipper,
and lifted it for an attack on Teddy in the rear.
But some inner consciousness of her approach
must have come to him in that final moment of
grace, for he suddenly slid into her very arms,
and twisting himself in her voluminous gown, he
whirled her around and around, dodging her in-
effectual dives at him with the slipper, and laughing until she forgot all discipline, and her round
sides shook with the fun.

" 'Way wid ye," she said, shaking him off finally,
and restoring the slipper to her broad foot, " and
mind if I foind ye goin' wan way whin I'm sendin'
ye another, ye'll find yerself like a puddin', with
niver a bone lift in yer body."

"It's to shpake to the leddy I came, 'Widdy Biddy,'" he answered, keeping himself wisely just beyond the reach of her hand. "It's to ask her will I bring the baby to her whin I finds it, or will I lave it at home wid yerself?"

"Well, it's me that'll be tachin' ye what to do wid the choild, me man. Lave me be seein' ye foind her furst."

"Dade and I will," said Teddy, and away he went on his errand, while his mother went home to her tubs, into which more than once she spattered a rain of tears.

As for Katharine, she felt and seemed like an aged woman as she sunk wearily into the seat. She moved as near to the window as possible, drew her veil between herself and her fellow-passengers, and gazed out upon the city that seemed like a great grave in which her hopes had all been sunk ; and upon the prairies where the greenness of the grass had changed to a leaden gray. All the life and glow and color had gone out of the fields, as it had gone out of her life that was as fresh and full of promise as the springtime, when she brought it here so many years ago. She remembered it all, and, seen through the haze of to-day's misery, it seemed only a fair background for a pictured tragedy of horror and pain. She wondered at herself that she did not cry out and startle all those comfortable indifferent people near her out of their novels and their lunches and their careless chat, and send them shrieking up and down the wide world that she had lost her only child. She wondered how long she could go on and on, drawn by the restless fascination of a dying face on its far-away pillow, and yet keep so still, so very still. As soon as it was dusk she found herself staring at every lighted window, as they flew past villages and towns, as if in some one of these homes she might get a glimpse of the little face that she knew somewhere would be wet with tears for her, as soon as the night came down.

Sadly the day wore on to the poor half-crazed woman, whose sowing to the wind had been so carelessly done, and so in accordance with the world's ways of doing, that, seeing her anguish, one was tempted to forget that sowing and reaping are ever of one kind. At times the impulse to return and the regret at having abandoned even for a few days the search for her child, was so strong that all the force of her will was required to keep her in her seat whenever the train stopped. As night came down the conductor asked her if she desired a sleeper. She never turned her face from the window, but answered faintly " No." Then in the shadows she heard the same kind voice that had spoken to her in the station saying, just at her side, " Doesn't thee think thee'd better take the sleeper? The night is long, and thee must be tired." She lifted her eyes, and he placed the little tin pail in her lap. "This must be for thee, I think. Thy servant, a little round woman in a white bonnet, brought it to thee, and was too late to reach thee with it on the train."

" My servant ! I have no servant," she answered, in surprise.

" It was thy friend then, one who loved and

would serve thee," he answered gently. "I will share it with thee, if thee lets me come back after I have told the conductor to save thee a bed," and he went on, leaving her no alternative but to see what Biddy had brought. He was a very wise old man evidently, for he seemed to know that the only way to make her take food was to make her for the moment his hostess, and while he sat beside her, talking as if it were the most natural thing in the world, she forced herself to swallow the food, lest he should see the grief that made it hard. And then he went away, and the conductor came and showed her a berth where she could hide her misery away in the dark, and weep her tears with no fear that any one would see. And all night long, amid the rumble of the cars and the heavy breathing of the sleepers near, she lay and struggled rebelliously against her life, strengthening her hands and heart for war. She would hasten to see her sister, and then go back and live to find her babe, and take her so far away that no such cruel thing as this could ever touch her life again.

Once a child cried in a compartment at the other end of the car. She sprang up, and before she knew it, was half-way down the aisle. Then she crept back again as if caught at something wrong, without seeing the mild blue eyes of the old man, who peered at her from behind his curtains, and then lay back, whispering to himself, " Poor thing, poor thing, the sorrow of the world has overtaken her."

In the morning he smiled at her as he passed by, but did not come near until they reached a station, from which he ordered a cup of coffee, and telling the boy to wait for the cup, went away to his own breakfast. Beginning to feel that she was in danger of arriving ill at her sister's bedside, Katharine took it and ate some bread from Biddy's offering, and, calmer than yesterday, tried to control her anxiety and to think only of the time when she would have her little one once more within her arms.

Once, toward night, the old man came and sat opposite her for a few moments, and as she tried to speak cheerfully of the country through which they passed, he said : " Thee needn't talk, my child. Thee is too sorrowful to talk. Thee is like Rachel weeping for her children. Tell me when the Lord took thine away from thee ? "

" The Lord never took her," she exclaimed, with a sudden flashing of scorn. " It was the devil's own task. The Lord had nothing to do with it."

" Ah, is it so ? " he asked, soothingly. " Then, perhaps if we ask him the Lord will restore. If he was not in the taking, he will be in the giving back. He must be in the lives of all little children somewhere, I think, for he loves them so dearly."

Katharine opened her eyes wide, her astonishment for the moment overcoming her grief. It was the first time she had ever been reminded that the child had any one but herself to love it. The instinct of motherhood had claimed it for herself and herself alone. That God loved the child, that it was his to care for and watch over, was as foreign from her daily thought as if her life had been lived in a pagan land. Unconscious of this, the old man talked on gently, and, gradually softened more by his tone and manner than by his words, she would gladly have told him that a far more cruel hand than that of death had taken her baby away. But whenever her lips opened to speak the words, some sense of womanly shame and caution sent them back, and she unfolded little beyond the fact that her child was still alive, though separated from her by cruel circumstances that made its restoration a matter of serious doubt.

On the second morning of their journey he approached her again as they were nearing Springfield, and, after a mild attempt to induce her to trust more fully in his kindness, he helped her from the train and pointed out the one which would bear her to Greenfield, from which point she would go by carriage to her sister's home. As he left her he handed a card to her, and with a solemn " The Lord bless thee," returned to his place on the train by which they had come. No sooner was he out of sight than she read the card, which said : " The Community of Shakers at Loriston, in New Hampshire, will receive any orphan child or children, or any tired mother who may choose to come to them for comfort and rest. Its home is wide and open to the weary and to the little ones of God. They believe His words who said, ' Whosoever receiveth one such little child in my name, receiveth me.' "

With soft tears quenching the fire of trouble and anger in her eyes, the weary woman gazed upon the hills, familiar and yet as strange in their outlines as though all memory of them had been buried under the crowding events of the years.

From the cars she passed through the new and rather imposing brick station that had taken the place of the little wooden building where her father used to meet her with the low carriage and brown pony familiar to all the country as it took the pastor on his visits to the sick and the aged among the distant hills. She almost found herself looking for him, though she knew his white hair had been under the greensward these many summers—passing all the more swiftly and sorrowfully thither because of her, though mercifully she did not remember that. The brown pony was gone, but there was the same old lumbering open coach, with old Job Tuttle, the same wheezing, asthmatic driver who had been there for a generation, on the box. Into this wagon the tired woman climbed, and was soon jolting along the road that led to Walden, the town where her father had dwelt as pastor, and where her sister's husband had succeeded him in the church and in the hearts of his people.

Old Job, whose head was so muffled in the big woolen scarf that he called a " comforter " as to leave only two twinkling eyes visible beneath his ragged soft hat, suddenly turned upon Katharine with a nervous little nod. " Some folks tells me where they're goin' to git off and some folks leaves me to guess. Neow I'm ruther fair at guessin', and me and my off-horse hit it poorty near, as a gineral thing. Fact is he's kinder ketched a trick of guessin' from me. Folks did uster say when I was young— I've been drivin' this ere team nigh 'beout thirty year come Christmas—that I was a reg'lar Yankee for askin' folks questions, and deown to the store they said I jest asked folks so many questions that I didn't take time to breathe in between, and so that's the way my breath begun to give eout and I got the asthma. There weren't an atom o' truth in 't, not an atom, fur I only jest took an int'rest, and most folks is glad to have somebody take an int'rest. But anyway I got kinder riled arter one spell deown to the store, and I jest said I'd bet my yaller dog agin a Thanksgivin' goose that I'd run this coach six months 'thout askin' one pesky question. And you better bet I got thet goose. And when I got it I told my wife to cook an extry lot of onions with it, for I didn't care if they smelt 'em from the meetin' house to the store. Fact is, I airned every scrap of that goose, tail feathers and all."

Katharine laughed, in spite of her heavy heart. " It could not have been easy," she said, as he paused, evidently thinking this a proper point for encouragement or applause.

" Well, I reckon not. Fact is, them fellers that made the bet and the town folks gin'rally, I didn't need to ask them nothin', fur I knew where they lived ; but I used to think some on 'em actilly writ their relations not to tell me where to take 'em when they come to town, for it seemed 's if every aggravatin' soul on 'em waited for me to ask. Then I tell you I larned what ain't deown in none er the appinted school books, that guessin' is the highest kind of larnin'. And my old horse larned too, for once or twice what d'ye think he did ? He jest took a squint at old Deacon Popdyke's red nose as he was climbin' in, and I jest let the reins hang loose, and instid of takin' the deacon home, he jest turned up and stopped front of the worst drinkin'-place in town, and looked round with a real kind of a wink as much as to say, ' This is the place for the deacon.' Fust-class total abstinence man too, won't raise apples cos' apples has got inside of 'em the iniquity of cider; but my horse wasn't eddicated enough to know a whisky nose from the arrysip'lus nose, and I dun know's I was to blame for that.

" Nuther time, Squire Putney's widder, she's ruther strong on trimmins and real fat and dressy, she wouldn't say where she's goin' and I wouldn't ask her, and the horse took her like a streak round the corner to. the Old Ladies' Home. My, but didn't we ketch it ! 'Twa'n't my fault. Fact is, not having nothin' to say, I was meditatin', and while I meditated the horse kinder took advantage. Then the horse I expect must ha' told it to the yaller dog, for the dog watched folks mighty close, and whenever I was in danger of meditatin' too long would dart up to the gates and bark, and wait, waggin' his tail, 's if waggin' would win the bet.

" Neow I don't see, sence the goose is won and eat, and plenty of onions and apple sass with it, why I need to hold my tongue still, more than that yaller dog need keep his tail still. Yet if you'd ruther I'd guess, I'll leave you at the parson's," said he, with a triumphant crack of the whip, as he drew up before the gate of the old home.

CHAPTER V

THE gate creaked upon its hinges. Her own steps sounded unevenly upon the gravel walk, but she did not hear. The "yaller" dog lingered behind after Job drove away, and watched her as if with a dumb kind of comprehension that she was in trouble. She did not heed him. Her hand brushed aside a dead vine that hung dejectedly from the porch, but she did not feel its touch.

Here at last was the rambling old house, with its broad staircase, on the landing of which she had sat with her sister in long-ago summer afternoons, petting their joint family of infirm rag dolls. The front door was ajar. She entered; a light gleamed from a room at the head of the stairs. Following its gleam, she scarce knew why, she mounted slowly, seeing as in a dream the little sister sitting there at the top, hugging an invalid dolly in each fat arm. Instead here was a wide-open door, an invalid chair, a wasted figure reclining on its cushions, a white, wan, waiting face, toward which she tottered and over which she bent, while her hot tears fell like rain.

"So many years, so long, so long," whispered Eunice, winding her arms tight around Katharine as she knelt, and laying her head upon her shoulder, "and now you have only come in time to see me die."

"No, no, I have come in time to see you grow strong and well. I have come to nurse you back to health," but her sister shook her head and smiled faintly.

"You must take her away, Deborah, and take care of her," she said to an elderly colored woman, in a long white apron with a gay kerchief twisted turban-like about her head, who came gently in from the adjoining room; "my only sister, my precious sister come back to me once more," she added, caressing Katharine's cheek, as if she could not bear to let her go.

Mechanically she followed the nurse, and stood almost helpless while the kind Deborah removed her wraps and led the way down to the old-fashioned parlor, where she left her alone. Alone! Here was her father's portrait, taken when he was a young man with a book in his hand that confined three fingers within its covers. Katharine remembered often wondering what book that was, and what passage the fingers marked. Here were the portraits of herself and her sister, painted side by side, with five-year old faces and very short frocks, and very long white pantalettes. Here the bookcase full of old books, and another full of newer books, probably belonging to her sister's husband. There was the old hair-cloth sofa on which they used to bounce and play when no one saw them, and the wide fireplace where, as Deborah said, " De fire jes done tired heself out spectin' Miss Katharine to come."

So far from being alone, too many old faces haunted her, too many long dead voices sounded in

her ears.   In her overstrained and exhausted condition she stood among her new impressions of her
dying sister, and her recollections of those long
gone, helpless and unable to grapple either with
memories or fears.   Debby's return with a tea tray
was a positive relief.   "There now, honey," she said,
placing it on the marble-topped table, "I'se boun'
to leave yer now fur to git Miss Eunice inter bed.
S'pose you know the old house same as me, for missis
she tell me heap 'bout you'n she chillen togedder.
She never git beat out talkin' 'bout you, and I'se
mighty glad you'se come.   My sakes and bones,"
she added, waxing animated, "eber since Doctor
Newman said you'se comin' pears like Miss Eunice
kep a breathin' a purpose to be on this yarth when
you come.   And we's prayed de Lord to hurry up
dem kears, and sho' nuff here you is.   Now don'
you go to be lonesome while I'm gone, kase I'm jest
up top dem stairs takin' keer of missis, and jes next
chamber dere's the baby fast asleep."

Katharine started.   "The baby, whose baby?"

"Yer sister's, honey, and Marse Lawrence Wild's;
jest like him too.   She is got de fambly nose.
Reckon I know, for I was his mammy's nurse down
in Washington, and when Lawrence he got married
way up Norf his mother, my old missis—she dead,
poor dear—she sent me to fotch his chillun up.
Lord knows I've done my best; I took the baby in
my bed right soon, and keep her dar eber sence, so
Miss Eunice she neber get done out her sleep.
Years ago I used to nuss Marse Lawrence, and de
sperrit of de Lord'd say, 'Deborah Dangley'—
dat's my Christian name—dat ar chile he gwine

preach de gawspel and magnify de Lawd.' And when he come Norf to college, and old missis fret herself, fear de debble play some shines on him, I say, ' You jes' don't fidget Miss Calline ; de good Lawd he's more'n a match for de debble, and he don' go back on a poor colored woman. Now don't you go upsettin' de plans of de good Lawd by on-believin', cos ye can hender him jest as if he was folks.' And sho' nuff she did hender, a worritin' and worritin', and for quite a spell de debble did seem to be gettin' the upper hand. But I wrastled and wrastled, and bime by at de suminary de blessed Lawd put his hand on Marse Larry, and showed him de quick road into the kingdom. And he got mighty pious, and den he got your sister for to marry him, and I lived to see him pitch into de debble like all possessed, jest in that same old church that used to belong to your pa. But mercy me, I declare I done most forgot Miss Eunice. You g'long right in to the south room and see the baby if ye git lonesome fo' I gits missis ready for to have you set by her."

Hardly had the shuffling old feet ceased to sound upon the stairs when the tray was pushed hastily aside, and with light footfall Kate made her way to the old south room, It was the one sunny room, the " sitting room," dearer far in the olden time than the stiff parlor sacred to week-day company, to Sunday prayers, and occasional wedding ceremonies, when bride and groom, mutually nervous and miser-able, stood before the corner whatnot under the hair flower-piece, and were joined in holy matri-mony. At these weddings her mother occupied the middle of the hair-cloth sofa, with a little girl on either side of her, brought in more to keep them out of mischief than to add to the impressiveness of the occasion. Katharine remembered a day when a raid was made upon the glass jar of company ginger-snaps during one of these weddings to which she had not been invited for lack of time to comb her locks and put on a fresh white apron. With hands and face well smeared with the sweet and sticky compound, she had rushed in upon the moment of prayer, causing the young bride to giggle convulsively and the groom's efforts at self-control to end in a wild snort of laughter, and her reverend father to lift his prayer-shut lids and regard her with a mild and helpless horror. As vividly as if they were of yesterday, scene after scene swept before her, and the haunting faces followed her into the old south room.

The house had never boasted a pastor's study, but the old mahogany desk in the corner, where the sunlight used to fall upon the shiny bald place on his head, was her father's favorite spot. Here the sermons were written, and here the children, if not allowed to run and play, might have a story-book in the window seat, even when father was at his work. Here too, in the low rocker, the mother sat, with her basket of mending, because father fancied he worked better if she was near ; and here, when the work was done, was the round table and the evening lamp, and the place that, more than any other, was the home.

And after all the years it was not much changed. There was the old desk, the faded carpet, the wide lounge where the father used to lie while mother read the church paper aloud. There too, in the dim shadows, though no one but Katherine could have seen them, were the sweet mother face and the father's white head, bent over its accustomed task, yet neither lifting for a moment with a smile of welcome for this wandering and prodigal child. Why not? Why not? she asked herself, as her overstrained nerves shrank from the loneliness and silence. And then suddenly it all came clear to her. For these, her dear old parents, her return and her sorrow that she had ever left them had come too late. Indeed, as she stood there in the solemn stillness and gloom of this truly haunted home-room, there came a little faint gleam of the truth—that her impatient regret at the outcome of her folly had not one touch of real repentance for the sore grief of these two hearts that had loved her and longed for her return. For one moment she saw that they were not more uncomplaining, now that the grave-sod lay over them, than they had been when only the mantle of daily duty and patient toil helped them to hide their pain. For one swift moment too, there came a memory of the One Great Heart of Love, of whom they had taught her, and who would have kept her had she not chosen for herself the way that was not his way, but her own. For a moment "the Light that lighteth every man" shone in upon her, and with a new sense of justice she lifted the blame from "fate and luck" and God's neglect, and let it rest where it belonged, upon her own self-seeking and willfulness and lack of filial love. For a moment there bent near her the white wings of the angel of penitence; but there came a little rustle and stir in the gloom, a fluttering movement on the pillows of the wide couch, a little quivering drowsy cry, and all the fierce mother-love stirred in her to a tempest of passionate longing. Here was this child, this little girl, as young as her own, and as fair and sweet, lying here with moist, sunny curls and sweet mouth smiling in dreams. She was safe, sheltered, her soft limbs daintily clad, while her child, with face as fair, with little restless baby hands that reached up even as these to find the mother's face, her child was—God only knew where! And yet God had seen who took her, God had known all about it, and had let that awful thing be done.

Then as if her passion of resentment at the cruelty of it all yielded to her heart-hunger for her own, she bent yearningly over the sleeping child, and hot tears rained upon its face. The baby stirred restlessly, and as if trying to cheat her own heart, she gathered it in her arms, and pacing swiftly up and down the floor, hushed it with tender touch and tones that were more sobs than words.

There Debby, entering silently, found her and heard the murmured broken utterance in which she crooned, " My baby, my own poor, lost little baby ! Mamma's little, white lost lamb ! " and with instinctive delicacy she stole back again to the invalid's room where, propped upon the pillows, she was waiting for her sister to come in.

" Where is Kate ? " she asked, feebly. " I must talk to her to-night."

"Wait till mornin', honey, fo' de Lawd, I do bleeve she's done beat out. Every bite dat nice chicken waitin' dar on tray ; every drop dat tea-pot fresh tea. Eat nuffin, drink nuffin, jest take on and take on."

"What do you mean, Debby, where is she ? "

"Mean she just done up over our baby, po' chile. She's got dead baby her own in de grabe-yard some place, sure. She jest lovin' and snugglin' our baby, and cryin' bout her lost baby. You wait till mornin', honey, and I'll go and take our baby, and make your poor tired sis eat suffin, and get her to bed ; " but before she could carry out her kind intention, Katharine came in with the little one in her arms.

" Here, Debby, you must get her to sleep again," she said quietly, placing the child on the nurse's lap, and turning to Eunice, whose eyes were fixed in tender solicitude upon her own white face.

" It is a lovely little daughter, sister," she said, as Debby carried her from the room. " She will be such a joy to you as you grow old."

" Not that, Katharine. I shall never grow old ; but she has been a joy to me every hour of her little life. I want to talk to you about her, about "— her lips quivered—" about the days when I am gone, but Debby tells me you are quite worn out. I see it too, and must not be selfish. Yet it is so good to get you, so good to have one's own to talk to. We will leave it all till to-morrow, all," she added, seizing her sister's hand, " except this ; Debby tells me she heard you sobbing over my little one. Tell me, sister, have you lost a child of your own ? "

Katharine's head dropped upon her breast. The white lips moved as if she would speak, but no words came.

" I see, poor dear, poor dear," said Eunice, stroking her sister's hand gently. " It must have been so hard, darling, but though I am so sorry for the loss, I can hardly help being glad you have known what it is to be a mother ; and I want you to promise me you will take my little one and bring her up for me as if she were your own. You needn't say one word," she added, as Katharine seemed making an effort to speak, " not a word. Kiss me, and I shall know you will love her. You will not need to work and struggle for her Katharine. There is enough and more than enough coming from her father's family. Our dear father did not know where you were," she added, " and he left all the little he had saved, and all that came from mamma, not to me—I think he remembered you and could not bear to leave you out," she said, as she saw the swift look of pain cross Katharine's face —" but to me in trust for my children. It will come as a trust to you, Kate, and indeed," she added, eagerly, " I wish he had left it to you or to me outright ; for if it had come to me, I would have willed it to you, for I know that you would do all for my child that I would do for yours. Or I would care for you out of my husband's property ; but that, alas, did not come to us until after my Larry's death, and so went directly to his child, and not to me. It all seems unjust and wrong, Kate," she added, as the white face dropped lower and lower, until it was hidden from sight in the pillow, " but I do not know how to make it right. Perhaps we can find a way together. Of course, the estate must care for you if you care for my child, and her home must be your home also.

"But all this is not what is most important to me, Kate. Let me tell you what is." Her voice dropped to feebleness, but her hands never ceased to pass caressingly over the bowed head. "You know the faith in which we were reared, dear? It was my husband's faith also, and," she added gently, "the faith of our father and mother. Though you went away from us, Katie, I never believed that the vows taken at my side when we were young girls together could be less to you than to me. To me the Christian life has grown more real and more vital every year. The Christian principles seem more and more to me to be the only safe and sure principles on which to build a character that will stand the test of life. I know you feel as I do, and I want you to promise me to take my child, my one great gift, and to rear her in the faith her mother loved and tried to live."

She paused suddenly. The thin white fingers found their way to Katharine's face, hiding its pain and envy and shame from the eyes that were gazing already into the life where the hidden things shall be revealed. Slowly the white face lifted. Behind it the soul, of which it was the mask, was saying, "All that was left by both her father and mine to go to this child; for my child nothing. For this mother, heaven and love and joy; for me, poverty, pain, cursing, and toil. For them, faith of soul, peace of mind, love of each other; for me, desolation, bitterness, strife." And yet the lips did not utter a word of it all, and the sad eyes, dim with weariness and sorrow, gave no sign of rebellion or envy or scorn. And the gentle face on the pillow lifted itself feebly toward her own, and the spent voice whispered, " Kiss me, sister, and I shall know you promise all." One long, slow shudder of the soul shook her body like a wind-swept leaf, and yet she laid upon those waiting lips the kiss—that was a vow.

CHAPTER VI

ALONE at last, with the door closed against
Debby, whose kind heart could not refrain
from urging her to eat and sleep, she passed such
a night as added new and deep lines to her haggard
face, and made her feel as if years had been added
to her life.

It was the same room she had shared with her
sister all through her happy childhood. All night
she tossed and turned upon the same bed whose
bright pink hangings, now faded to a dingy white,
had shaded her sleeping face before the rosy fresh-
ness of its beauty had taken one trace of care. She
was alone at last, and yet she was not alone. Close
her eyes as she would, she yet could not escape the
haunting eyes that pleaded and questioned, and
would not be turned away. In them she saw the
reflection of her own thought. They asked her of
herself, of her innermost purpose and principle and
motive; they looked as if they doubted her truth,
and yet it was her own soul that had not faith in
itself. They asked her of her child, where was it?
how should she find it? what would she do with it
and for it? what share could it have in the life of
this other child? And she shivered and shrank
from these questions, even though she knew they
were but the echo of her own heart, asking itself
over and over again how it could compass its will.

Most of all she felt that the eyes questioned her of her faith, and forced her to answer that she had no faith. In vain she pleaded angrily that it did not matter whether she had or not; that some of the noblest souls and truest helpers of humanity had had no faith; that justice and truth were what the world needed, not dogmas, not personal allegiance to myths, however fair. And while she muttered this in her feverish tossing, still the fading eyes clung to hers, and still they questioned if she, lacking faith, had justice and mercy and truth to teach this little child? If she had lost their mother's faith, had she their mother's heart of tender love? And then the haunting eyes grew troubled with a trouble she could but feel. They had reached her heart at last, for they burned with an anguish that her own had known. Out of them passed all at once the sweetness and the trust. They were wild with the same anguish she had felt herself when she had thought of separation from her child. Ah! this was a pain from which she could not turn away. With a shudder that shook her like a leaf, she turned her face in the pillow and sobbed, "It shall be as you wish. Your child shall be safe. I will make true the promise of that kiss. I will teach your child to be like you and like our mother, and I will learn to be like you myself." And with the coming of the inward impulse to open her heart fully to her sister in the morning, it was as if swiftly the accusing presence departed, and another —radiant, peaceful, strong—stood suddenly in the midst of all this conflict; and, like a worn-out, over-wearied child, she sobbed herself to sleep.

And while this battle between the life-hardened woman and the tender mother went on in that upper chamber, the Angel of His Presence had come gently, silently to that lower room where one lay sleeping, and on the lips where lay the kiss that was a sacred vow, and on the close-shut eyes had placed the seal of silence that would never be broken to answer even a penitent heart's confession, or a motherless infant's cry.

Debby, faithful and loving watcher as she was, was not young any longer, and her old bones wearied under the duties of nurse for both invalid mother and infant child. She was unusually weary to-night, and fell asleep on her couch, drawn close to the bedside of her mistress. The silent messenger did not waken her, nor did Debby waken Katharine when, in the early dawn, she found the Angel of God had come and gone, and that a sweet young life had escaped at last from its long imprisonment of pain. And Katharine, overcome by fatigue, slept heavily and long, taking gratefully the fragrant coffee and toast from the tray which Debby placed noiselessly beside her bed, departing without a word. Refreshed and strengthened, remembering much of the night as a troubled dream, she went down to her sister's room. She found the morning sunlight stealing in through half-shut blinds, the white bed empty, the invalid's table with all its medicines and signs of illness gone, fresh flowers from the garden on mantle and window-seat, and the door wide open into the dear south room, where on the wide old couch, in a soft wrapper of white, as if she had just thrown herself

down to rest, lay her sister, the face so young, so
sweet, so unmarked of pain, that her heart at first
gave a great bound of hope. It was as if she had
been healed and given back in a night her birthright of youth and joy.

"I'se sure the baby will 'member her," said
Debby, "and I want her to done forget eberyting
that look like she's daid and gone; jes 'member
only her pretty mamma all smilin' in her sleep."

And so they left her while the neighbors came
with kind offers of help and departed, astonished that
there seemed nothing left to be done, and that they
did not even wish to have the little child taken out
of the way. And still more to their astonishment,
they left her lying there, with the flowers bright
colored as well as white, smiling around her during
the short home services, which were all that Katharine desired to have. "She is all my own," she had
said to the kind pastor. "I cannot bear to take
my sorrow before the crowd in the church, or to
think of her lying there for every careless eye to
gaze upon."

"But you forget," he said, gently, "that she is
the daughter of one pastor and the widow of another. The church claims its right to mourn her
as a part of itself. She was a child of the church,
and," he added with a touch of severity in his tone,
"she has loved it and clung to it through all her
life."

"Why could not the people come here?" asked
Katharine.

"So they can and so they will, but the house will
not hold them. Have your own service here if you

wish, and let those come who knew her best; but after it is over, let her lie before the pulpit where her father and her husband ministered in life, and where they rested in death. The people loved her, Mrs. Gray."

And so they did, though had Katharine heard poor old Matilda Todd, the town tailoress who knew the "ins and outs of every house in town," she might have felt that even such neighborly love as theirs had its mixture of alloy.

"I call it downright pagan, I do," Tilda confided to her particular crony, Widow Jones, who earned her living going out nursing, and felt just a little "hurt" that one who belonged, so to speak, to the parish should have departed this life without her professional assistance.

"Well, I don't know's I'd say pagan, for after all I don't s'pose Katharine would bow down to wood and stone, 'though they do say she married a friv- 'lous kind of a feller jest because his folks had money. Worshipin' gods of silver and gold ain't true religion, and won't stand in the day of jedg- ment. But to go and lay anybody eout right on the fam'ly sofy, where everybody sot and sot, and put over 'em a blue afghan with a streak er yeller in the border, and red and yeller flowers instead of white—well, 'tain't accordin' to Scriptur, anyhow."

"'Tain't accordin' to no fashion for fust-class funerals that ever I see," answered Tilda, sorrow- fully, "and for one I'm sure I felt 's if she was layin' down there kinder beat out, jest tryin' to take a nap."

"But that Katharine Gray is goin' to have her

own way every time," said the widow. "She never did care nothin' what folks said, and all creation couldn't stop her if she got a notion in her head. I s'pose she thought she would look more natural, but to me she only looked as if she didn't belong here, and hadn't been pervided with any way to get away, and it's my opinion, if she could speak, she would ask to be comfortably put in her coffin, like other folks."

Yet, notwithstanding this minor strain of dissent that ran through all the sad preparations, a protest that she felt if she did not hear it, Katharine held to her plan, only consenting at last to have the service at the house precede a later one at the church. And when it was over—the soft light, the sweet music of the church choir, the kind pastor's fatherly words—and they had borne her sister to the church, then and only then Katharine knew how hard it was for her to pass within that old familiar place. The old family pew where she had sat as a child, clinging tightly to her mother's hand, the pulpit where her father preached and before which she took her early vows, the place where they both lay in the sleep that knows no waking—these all filled a cruel hour full to the brim of sorrow and of pain. Memory, that had seemed numbed and dead since that first troubled night, waked again to life. At the open grave in the old familiar churchyard it was harder still. If from the grassy mounds before her had risen the two who had loved and prayed for her through all her wayward youth, to chide her with the patient look and smile she never could forget, they could not have seemed nearer than they did in this hour when she saw the new mound made beside the others on which the grass was growing. Vainly she tried to hold herself still and tearless before all these neighbors lingering about the gate, watching her white face as if they would read therein every trace of the life since she went out from among them so long ago. Vainly she tried to be strong, to bear their looks and the pastor's harrowing words. Quietly she went back to the carriage, but when it reached the door they had to bear her, as if she too were dead, into the house, and lay her on the wide couch her sister had just forsaken for the narrow bed beside her best beloved.

After these days the stillness that settled down upon the old parsonage was too solemn for a soul at war with itself. Black Deborah's garrulous old tongue was silent as she went dejectedly about setting the house in order, sighing audibly as she gathered up and put out of sight the belongings of her dear young mistress. Even the cradle-songs crooned in the low, sweet minor of her race no longer answered the cooing or crying of the orphan child. For old Debby was stricken to the very heart by a new sorrow, heavier to bear, if that were possible, than the old. She had lost master and mistress, and now she was to be separated from their only child. Mrs. Gray had willed it, had planned it, her own heart aching all the while, for none knew better than did she what it meant to be parted from a child beloved.

Sometimes at twilight or in the early dawn, looking out across the churchyard from the south-room window, she shuddered as if from the grave near the ivy-grown gate she feared to see a form arise with outstretched arms and reproachful eyes, demanding that she give back the child, restore the trust that had been committed to her hands. At such moments, an almost uncontrollable impulse urged her to flee, alone and at once, back to the place where her own little one was hidden, leaving this babe to Debby's cherishing care. Why should she not? Debby would take her to her father's Southern relatives. To them she could pass over her own responsibility and her control over the life and fortune of the child. She would be safe with them. No counter interest could divert them from her care. No other child was tugging at their heartstrings, reminding them that for her there was no chance, no means, no kind provision for her needs and care. True she had promised her sister to keep the little one with her, to guard her interests as she would her own; and that promise would in the eyes of the world justify her in sending Debby away, and taking the babe into her own sole keeping. But in her inmost soul she knew that from that promise she would have been absolved before her sister died, had Eunice known the truth. Somehow she could not shake off the feeling that she knew it now, and that the dead mother's heart-protest was as strong against her keeping the child as the pleading to take it had been.

No wonder, with this inward conflict raging night after night, that she longed to be free from the sight of Debby's jealous, watchful eyes, jealous lest Katharine should not love the baby enough, and lest the babe should come to love Katharine too much. It was a great sacrifice in one way to let Debby go; but, on the other hand, how could she take her to Chicago? How could she find her own child and rear the two together, one in poverty and one in plenty? How could she spend her heart's love on one, and give the fragments of that fierce mother-love to this other child, as she knew she would, and yet have Debby's reproachful face forever in her sight? No, Debby must go back to the old Southern home. Katharine would bring the child to the Southern aunt often, but now, just now, she must fulfill her sister's wishes, and keep the baby in her own especial care.

In the solemn night hours before her sister died, the powers of darkness and light had made a battle-ground of her heart, and the light had almost claimed the field. Now, again the roads divided. On one hand, poverty, honor, principle, return to duty and absolute truth of character and to life-long struggle to protect and rear her own. On the other hand, who knew, who could say, if she kept her sister's child, what might open out for her own? And, after all, was it more than justice to her own that she should share that which had been withheld from herself, and which should have been divided between the two instead of having been all bestowed on one?

And so the battle waged, and the angels, if they hover about human lives as they are thought to do, waiting to bear the news that makes great joy in heaven, must have turned back often with drooping wings and downcast eyes into the presence of God.

And all these days the outward tasks went on, and Mrs. Gray's hard experiences in the use of her own hands made rapid work of setting in order all that pertained to the house, and the quick brain that had worked so long at her own problems, was equally ready in grasping the business left in her care.   Indeed, all this had been wisely and carefully adjusted both by her father and by the husband of her sister, Lawrence Wild.   By her father's will all his savings and a few thousand dollars that had come to him from her mother's family had been left for the use of Eunice, the younger sister, during her life, and to her child or children at her death. No mention was made of the elder sister except the hope that, should she ever return in need of a home, the old parsonage might be her shelter as long as she had use for it, even to the time of her death, when it too, should revert to her sister's child.

True to this suggestion Eunice had left this home-place to Katharine and had made her the guardian of her child, with full control of all this inheritance, as well as of that much larger estate that came to her from her father's Southern relatives, and the promised inheritance that was to come on the death of the relative now passing her declining years in the Washington mansion that had been beloved by all the family.

Left widowed and wealthy while still young, Marion Wild had resisted all attempts to induce her to form new ties, because that which bound her to her younger brother Walter was one of special tenderness and strength.   They had grown up to-

gether on the North Carolina plantation where
their parents died. For Marion there had come
the early marriage to Roger Maitland and the life
in a foreign capital. For Walter a brilliant career
in a Northern university, a rapid and deserved pro-
motion at the bar, and an early and repeated election
to Congress.

Coming back to her brother after the death of
her husband, Mrs. Maitland found the plantation
life had given place to that of Washington, and it
was she who built the home into which the brother,
of whom she was so proud and fond, brought the
gentle Northern girl who was his wife. It was she,
stately, gracious, cultured, whose warm Southern
heart made home for everything her brother loved,
whose dignity and grace of bearing gave that home
its tone and character, while her nobility of nature
and Christian spirit made it a social and religious
center for the best that Washington could afford.
More and more the Southern plantation called
" Beechlands," grew to be like a winter retreat for
the household, while " Wildholm," the Boundary
Heights mansion became more and more the family
home.

Here Lawrence, the husband of Eunice, was
born. Hither Debby was transplanted for the comfort and the care of the child. Remembering his
own college life, Mr. Wild had sent his son to his
own alma mater, and remembering the sweet
woman he had himself brought home to Washington from the Northern college town, he was not
disturbed when Lawrence made choice of a country
parson's daughter and a country parson's life.

Concerning his son's ability to prove himself worthy, in time, of the largest field in the profession he had chosen, he had no question, but he had seen too much of public men and public life to undervalue the discipline of years of honest hard work and simple living, for a brilliant fellow at the outset of his career.

In the midst of much in his association that was quite the opposite, Judge Wild had preserved an ideal and a standard of Christian manhood none too common in the world's high places. How much of his power to maintain it was due to the two good women, his sister and his wife, he did not realize, and of their unconscious influence they never even dreamed. Utterly unlike in character and culture, the Southern woman of the world and the daughter of a truly Puritan professor of theology were yet one in the value they placed upon Christian integrity of principle and life. That Lawrence should be grounded in these particulars was more to them than any honors or successes that might crown his later years. That Debby's prophecy that " he should preach and magnify the Lord," had been fulfilled, was the comfort of his mother in her dying hour. And when, not long after his mother's departure, there had followed the shock of Larry's sudden death, the aged, stricken father found a consolation for his sore grief and broken ambitions in the thought of the lowly service that had claimed his boy's young life.

And when within one year he too went on to join his wife and son, and Marion Maitland was left alone in the home, it was not strange that her desolate heart turned tenderly and longingly toward Larry's only child. It was she who had brought Debby again from the old plantation, whither she had returned to dwell among her kindred. and to aid in the care of Beechlands, and sent her to Walden, to be the nurse for Larry's little girl. After Larry's death she had written, urging the mother to give up the parsonage home and come to her; but already the influence of weakness and pain was creeping upon her, and she had waited, dreading to sever the old ties, or to leave the house which had been the only home she ever knew. And while she lingered, the enemy stole nearer and nearer to the citadel of her life which had gone out at last, without her ever seeing the face of the woman God had provided to be her strongest protector and her truest friend.

And to this woman it was that the heartbroken Debby went back one late spring morning. She had arrived at daybreak, and the servants—her fellows, some of them, in the past plantation days—yielded her at once her old place as the special care-taker of "Miss Marion," who opened her eyes to find her standing there, tray in hand, as if she had never been away.

"Why, Deborah, dear Aunt Debby, how glad I am to see you! How glad I am to have you come back to me!" And the white hand grasped the dusky one with the warm clasp of a friend.

For a moment Debby kept the quiver out of her wrinkled old face, and bathed the forehead of her mistress as tenderly as she would have touched a child. "Don't do that, Debby. You must not begin to spoil me," said Marion, as Debby reached out to bathe her hands. "You may pour my coffee, please." But the effort to turn aside the tide of emotion that was swelling the poor woman's heart was useless.

"Don't you turn 'way now, Miss Marion. I jest mus' take care somebody, chile. I'se poor—no 'count, old Debby—I is, but somebody done got have me roun'." And throwing herself by the bedside, she buried her gray head in the coverlet and sobbed and cried. "You's my fust baby, Miss Marion, and I toted yer day and night for yer mammy. And I toted your brudder Walter when he was a little tot, and walked the floor with him many and many a night. And I toted Massa Larry, and Massa Larry's baby too, and I nursed Miss Eunice, jest like she born one er the fambly. And now they's gone, they's all gone, and I'se got to tote somebody, Miss Marion, I'se got to have somebody to tote." And she held up her empty arms to the air with such a look of despair as revealed even better than words the hunger of her heart.

"That's true, Debby, that's true, and you shall take care of me now. I need you, Debby. I'm getting old and like a child again myself, since—since they all went away." And she passed her hand soothingly over the bowed shoulders. "Come, Debby, you must help me now. See, my coffee is all cold. Run and bring me a fresh cup." And she followed her with pitiful eyes as she shuffled away, hanging her head as if ashamed of the sudden outburst of distress.

"Why did not Mrs. Gray come this way with the child, Deborah, as I invited her to do, when she wrote me she must take her to Chicago, and send you back to me?"

"I dun know, miss. She done tol me she gwine write you she mus' go to Chicago mighty fas'. Mighty curus, 'pears like; but Miss Gray she nice and kind and good to me, powerful good, but she ain't been brought up like we have, and somehow she didn't seem to sense it that *we* was the fambly. She work all day twice as hard as me, and all night too. I hear her when I couldn't sleep for thinkin' 'bout leavin' the chile. She jest work and work to get all ready; she in such powerful hurry. Reckon she couldn't wait no more days, nohow. She took it hard, her po' sister's goin' right off, fo' she had time to tell her none her troubles. Shore enough she had troubles. I knows it, though she's that kind as never tells a word—no, not even if it killed her she wouldn't tell; but I pitied her, pore thing, and reckon if her sister had lived, she would have jest loved her into cryin' it all out. I tell ye, Miss Marion, she looked—well," and she drew nearer and whispered out the words, "she looked haunted; she used to moan and cry in the night, when she tho't I was asleep, and in the morning she jest looked—I don't know how to call it—haunted."

"Poor thing, I have no doubt she has seen much sorrow," said Mrs. Maitland, gently, "and her sister was the last of all her kin. I wish she had come this way and let me see if I could not be a friend and help her in the care of Larry's child." And she gave a disappointed sigh.

"Not she, Miss Marion, not she; she was nice and good, Miss Marion, and very sorry, she said, to part with me; but she had lost a child of her own——"

"How do you know that?" asked Marion, quickly.

"I found her hugging and kissing our baby, and holding it tight, and crying all the time, as if her heart would break: 'My baby, my poor little lost baby!' I reckon, miss," and the voice sank again, "that she wanted our baby in place of her baby that was dead. She was 'feared she would cling to me if I went along, or that you would want to keep her if you once got her home."

"Indeed I would," said the lady, fervently; "and yet her sister placed the baby in her care, and she is young and strong, and could do so much better for her than I could. And yet, and yet—well, no doubt she was right and had good reason to hasten back to her home. She wrote me she would bring the child here before long. If I were not so feeble and so old I would go to Chicago to see her."

"*We* isn't too old, honey," said Debby, promptly. "I could take keer of ye, chile."

"So you could, Debby, and if she does not come before long we will try to go together."

"You won't wait till the baby forgets me, will ye, miss?" said Debby, her dark face brightening.

"No, indeed, Debby, and perhaps if she promised her sister, as she writes, that she will not be parted from the child, she will come here and live with us, and then we can all have the little one as much as our hearts desire." And comforted and cheered, old Debby took back into her heart a hope.

CHAPTER VII

AND while this talk was going on in this wide fair chamber, with the fragrance of the spring blossoms drifting in upon those two whose hearts mourned for a lost child, another heart, younger than either by a score of years, and older far because of lack of love, was watching in the upper chamber of a Chicago tenement house beside the cradle of a sleeping child. It was not the same room, though almost as poverty-stricken in its appearance as the one in the house with Mrs. Gray's only friends, the Widow Burke and Theodore, her son. Nor was it the same little child, nor was it the same woman, though features and form were unaltered, and the pale, hard face gave little sign of the subtle inward change that had overswept the soul. She sat silent, her pallor deepened by her black dress, one foot upon the rocker and one hand supporting her chin, while her eyes were fixed upon the small cold bit of gray sky, fast deepening into night, that could be seen through the upper window-pane.

In their look of concentrated resolve, her eyes were not unlike that lowering, darkening sky. She had traveled all the long way in silence, except when she answered soothingly the cry of the tired and fretful child. She had tended it with utmost watchfulness and care, but with never a smile and hardly a kiss, though she hushed it with her lips against the soft hair as she held it against her breast. She had parted from her fellow-travelers— kindly, commonplace people who shrank, she fancied, from her pallid face—with a silent nod, and walked forth from the station into the darkness and the rain. She had gone straight to an agency and asked for a list of thoroughly respectable furnished rooms with honest people, who had only first-class lodgers. She chose one just around the corner from Brand street, for in Brand street lived Mrs. Burke and Theodore, her only and faithful friends. She would not go back to the old room, lest her husband should seek her there, and, moreover, though her lonely heart would have welcomed a sight of Biddy's honest smile, she would not seek her until she "had made up her mind."

For all this time of weary days and haunted nights she was tormented by conflicting temptations, but no one of them all was like the torment of her indecision. One maddening purpose to find her child and to keep her for her own, stood like a rock in the tossing sea of her other shifting plans. When she had found her, what should she do with her? What with the other child? Where should she flee to be beyond the reach of her husband's wrath? How support her own, if she must have the care of another little one as well? How repay to the fund that had been placed in her hands by her sister's lawyer, that which she was already using to recover her little girl? How rear them together, one in plenty and the other in poverty, when one was her own very heart and life.

All these and more were part of the torment that was hidden behind her silence, and as she sat there with no conscious decision to consider her child before she considered her duty, she yet "made up her mind." Once decided, she waited no longer. With a last look at the sleeping babe, she locked the door, and taking the key, hurried down the stairs and around the corner, and in at the door of Biddy's dwelling. As she paused in the familiar passage, a clattering step came down from the rooms above. She knew it, and it did not need the gleam of Teddy's red hair flashing across the dimly lighted entry to show her that her friend was really there. As he darted forward she thrust forth her hand. He paused suddenly, gave a little exultant whoop, and his Hibernian legs began to shuffle and caper as if determined to dance in spite of his sense of propriety. After a breakdown of a quarter of a minute, his excitement subsided as suddenly as it came, and he stood before her with hat in hand, his eyes cast down, waiting for his commands.

"Come home with me, Theodore, I want you," she said, and giving one glance upward as if he heard the sound of Widdy Biddy's slipper on the stair, he said, "Will I fly to the top and tell me mother, ma'am?"

"Not now, Teddy, perhaps by-and-by. I will tell you where I am staying, and you can bring her in the morning; but now I want to see you quite alone. You must come to my room, Teddy, for I have brought back with me my sister's little girl, and I am not willing to leave her a minute alone."

When once inside the door, she took the lamp and held it so that its light fell upon the sleeping face. The baby moved uneasily and smiled. Teddy had tiptoed close beside her. "Faith and its another almost the same as me own," he whispered.

"Yes," she answered, "they are much alike, and about the same age, and I want you to be good to them both."

"Dade and I will that," said he, proudly; "but its your baby, ma'am, that I be lovin' the best; and the Widdy Biddy, that's me mother, and me, we spakes of her iver as 'me own.' Its lookin' for her ivery day, I am;" and he drew near and added in a tragic whisper, "and it's me that's afther findin' her for ye, ma'am."

"What!" she caught his arm, gasping. "What! You have found her? Oh, Teddy, where is she? Come with me at once and get her. I must see my child. Take me quickly, Teddy, I cannot wait."

"Not to-night, ma'am, not to-night. It's the father of her goes ivery night and stays shlapin' in the same house wid her. It's a dacent house too, and a dacent woman kapes it, and she takes good care of the child, and rints her rooms to any one that's wantin'."

"Take me there, Teddy. No. I must not leave this little one. You stay here and watch her for me, and I will go myself. Tell me which car to take and the very shortest way," and, too restless to pause for an answer, she stood impatient before the startled lad. But Teddy's wits, suddenly put to flight by her vehemence, were not slow to rally.

He knew the uselessness of trying to make her wait; he knew the worse than uselessness of her going on such an errand at night, and the danger of her meeting her worst enemy face to face if she tried to enter the house where her child was. He knew also how impossible it would be to hold her back from a sight of her babe, if once she stood before its hiding-place. There was only a moment for thinking, but in that moment the boy seemed to become a man. If she must go, she must. He would not think of controlling her, but she must not go without him.

"Lave me run for me mother, ma'am, to sthop wid the babby here, and thin I'll show ye the way."

"No, no, I will not wait, and I do not want you with me, Teddy. I will not have you."

"Will ye promise me thin that ye'll not make a rap at the door to-night? Sure as ye do, the woman will call the father, bad luck to him, and they'll not give ye the child, and they'll call the perlice, and he'll drive yez away, and they'll say ye are mad or ye're drunk, and before ye get out er the station house in the mornin' they'll be bringin' the baby away, and I'll niver be able to find her no more."

Suddenly conscious of his long speech, he hung his head. His face flushed, and he turned quickly to the window to hide his quivering lips and the merry eyes clouded with tears.

"And who are you, that should tell me what I may or may not do? Who are you to stand between me and my own child?"

"Only Teddy, ma'am, only Widdy Biddy's Ted;

and sure yez wouldn't be givin' the thafe of a man
the chance to be off wid the baby again when I
found her for yez the onct?"

"I do not care for the man I tell you. I am
going to claim my child."

Teddy's tender pleading eyes suddenly darkened
and glowed.

"Tell me where to find her," she ordered.

"Niver a word," he answered, "till ye give me
yer promise. I'll not have her stolen again."

And, silenced by the boy's dogged resistance, she
promised, and taking from him the street and num-
ber, she almost flew out of the house. Hardly had
her steps died on the stairs before he was after her,
in his arms a squirming bundle of about equal quan-
tities of blanket and baby. Round the corner, up
the staircase—bursting into his mother's room—he
paused, panting, while she, springing from her knees
where she was devoutly telling her beads before a
little pictured crucifix pasted high against the wall,
confronted him with a quivering cap-border and for
once a silent tongue.

"Don't ask me a word, mother darlin', it's an
angel that ye are. Take care of the new baby for
me, that's a darlin'. Give her plinty of milk,
mother, and I'll be soon back with a shtory to tell
that'll knock your cap off wid the shtandin' up of
ivery hair that's on yer blessed old head."

"Tiddy, Tiddy," she shrieked, "are you gone
crazy, Ted?" as he rolled the squirming, crying
bundle into her arms.

"Not a bit av it; but I've found the baby, our
baby, and if ye kape me here to talk I'll be losin'

her once more as sure as me name's Ted." And before she could protest, he was scampering down the stairs. He knew a short cut and he took it, captured a car and running a few blocks reached the corner, where he had told her to leave the car, in time to see her come. He slunk back out of sight behind a pile of lumber in a vacant lot opposite the decent three-story house, and watched her as she paced restlessly up and down, gazing at the windows, behind whose shutters faint lights were gleaming. Would she go in? Would she resist? Would she, his faithful young heart kept asking, would she keep her word and stay on the high pedestal where he thought she belonged, so far above him, above his mother, above any one he knew, the ideal and the idol of his boyish heart that had never yet seen anything sweeter than this woman, who seemed to have come to them out of another world?

Would she stay there, high up, like the Mother Mary, or would she come down from this exalted place, and like other people forget a promise and tell a lie? He did not know it, but his young soul was not more afraid of trouble to the child, than of wreck to its ideal. Already she had shocked him with her anger, her willfulness, her lack of reason, but it was not strange that she should be "unraysonable." "The Howly Virgin herself," he muttered, "might aysily be wrathful wid a little sphalpeen of a Ted like me." But still he watched, every nerve strained, while that restless figure went up and down and to and fro, now nearer, now farther, and then his heart went down, down, down, as if every step of her foot crushed something sweet and good within him, as she crossed the street and deliberately applied the knocker to the door.

Before her hand had reached her side his hand had seized it. " Whist now, me leddy dear, run round the corner, quick. The car is comin'. I hear the bell. Run, now, for yer husband is just comin' from the other end of the block. I saw him meself. It's drunk he is. Hurry now, it's yer one chance of not losin' yer child," and waiting no longer, he hustled her down the steps, around the corner and into the car. As it passed she saw the house door open just in time to admit the half-tipsy man, who staggered up the steps and passed in out of sight. And as the horses' hoofs clattered over the stony road, and the bell jingled, and the people passed in and out, these two, the strange boy and the strange woman, spoke not a single word. She was wrathful toward him ; he grieved for her. She must wait a little longer to get back her child ; but unless God's watching angels were pitiful there was no one to pity him—and he had lost what, search the wide world over, would never come back to him, his faith in a woman's absolute tenderness and truth. And, in the day when God's light should flash down upon the sins of her soul, she would see that not the least among them was counted this hurt to another soul, that, believing in her, believed also in love and truth and God.

At the door of her lodging he ran before her, darted up the stairs, lighted the lamp, and had time to give the fading fire a vigorous stir with the poker before she wearily climbed the steps.

" Rist aisy a bit now, while I run for the baby.
I carried it out to me mother," but as he rushed
forth she followed.

" No, no, Teddy, let me go to her. I do not like
to be left alone," and, utterly defeated and weak,
she went with him around the corner, and struggled
with aching feet up to the chamber under the roof.

" And is it back again ye are, wid yer blessed
saint of a face shinin' on me old eyes? Indade,
but it's swate of ye to come, for it's that distracted
I am wid the monkey shines av that Ted of mine
that I don't know me head from me feet."

" The head is the place for yer cap, Widdy
Biddy," said Ted, picking it from the bedpost, and
replacing it upon her shining bald pate. " And the
fut is the place for yer shlipper," he added, pushing her broad flat shoe toward her.

" Ah, it's me cap that the babby ye brought me
was a-scared at, and whin I put it on the bedpost,
away she wint off to her shlape. And as to me
shlipper, to wear 'em out aven, there's nade for me
to go one fut barefut. I'm savin' that shlipper for
Ted. It's me that's brought him up not to be
racin' the street o' nights, and I towld him I'd bate
him for ivery night he wint out whin I told him to
be in. He said he was hunting the baby, and he'd
go laughin' at me shlipper, and sayin' he'd take all
the beatin' to wonct if at the ind of three wakes
he didn't find her. And when the three wakes was
up, ma'am, in he comes to me all noice and swate
on Saturday night, just out of his bath in me big
wash tub, bringing me the strap av me trunk that
I brought me things in out av the old country, and

saying to me all smiling, 'I didn't find her yit, Widdy Biddy ; and it's three wakes and more, and I have brought yez the shtrap, for it hurts a dale harder nor the shlipper, and I'm a big boy now and the shlippers is for the little chaps that don't work, and don't hunt for the childer. It's not very bright I am, ayther,' he said, discouraged like, ' or I'd not be goin' on three wakes widout findin' her, and I'm thinkin' it's a good beatin' I need. If yez makes me shmart, maybe it'll make me shmarter.' ":

" But you didn't hurt him, surely you couldn't ? " said Katharine, drawn away from herself and her trouble for a moment.

" And didn't I cry over him, and beg to be let off, and didn't he cure me of me promisin' him a whippin' foriver more, by howldin' av me to me word ? ' If it's no beatin' ye give me the night, it's tellin' me a lie it is, mother, and it's breakin' yer word it is, and it's deservin' it I am for bein' so stupid. I couldn't find her yit, and in this family, mother, the promise must never be broken.' "

Katharine winced and turned away, and bent over the child sleeping on Teddy's bed, while Teddy violently gesticulated to his mother to have done with her yarns.

" Teddy won't let me finish, miss, but I had to keep me word, but I kept it moighty aisy, and whin I had cut his hands a bit with the strap I dropped on me old knees, and vowed a vow to the Virgin that if he moinded, or if he didn't moind, if he drove me crazy, or lift me my sinses, I'd niver raise hand to him again. And now whin he's bad, I just threaten him, and he says, ' a promise is a promise, mither.' And thin I tell him I promised niver to raise me hand. I didn't promise for me shlipper, and he laughs and says, 'the shlipper won't lick him itself.' So now he thinks he's the man er the house, and can bring me all the babbies he finds."

"But this is my sister's baby," said Katharine, glad to stop the flow of Biddy's words.

"And, indade, I'm not a goose. Didn't I read it out for meself, though Ted wouldn't shtop to tell me the tale. Isn't she as like the ither wan as two peas? Sure and I think ye'll be bringin' em up for twins. But what are ye doin', Teddy, wid the tay-pot and the frying pan?"

"Going to have some supper, mother."

"And why wasn't ye home to ate it at the proper Christian hours?"

"Off wid me leddy after her baby. Didn't I tell yez I found the baby, mither."

"Found her, is it, and whin and where? And why didn't ye tell me ivery day as ye wint along?"

"If I told ye I was watchin' the house of the grandfather ivery night till I saw the father come out, and that I followed him to saloons and gambling houses, ye would have come howling after yer boy. But I did it till I found he used to go and shlape at this house in B—— Street, on the north side. And thin I watched till I found out the rayson why. He came to see the baby was safe, and I was jest hid by the area door whin one night the woman wouldn't let him in because he was so very drunk, and I heard her say to him : 'I'm not goin' to keep ye, Masther Robert, much as I loved yer mother and yerself whin ye was a swate little choild. Ye disgrace a dacent house, comin' in that tipsy way, wakin' the neighbors wid the noise; and I'm not goin' to kape the choild ayther, if ye don't pay me as ye promised. I'll bring her to yer father's office or yer mother's house and lave her there.' So thin I knew he hadn't paid for her."

While Teddy talked, his mother had relieved him of teapot, toasting-fork, and saucepan. She stirred the fire, and soon placed on a tray the tea and a slice of toast, on which rose a little golden hillock of scrambled eggs, and Katharine, who had not known how exhausted and hungry she was, ate every bit of her portion, not however without look-ing over to the oilcloth-covered table, on the end of which a like repast had been laid out for Ted. And as she looked at the mass of yellow curls, the broad white forehead, the honest gray eyes, she forgot the freckled face and foreign brogue and shabby clothes, and remembered his mother's tale of how he had kept his word to find her child, and in her soul she recognized that here, in all this strange environment, was the heart and courage of a man. She had failed him, suddenly she realized it with a little flush of shame, but she could trust him now and forever, and he was worthy to be her friend. As if some subtle spiritual insight told him this, he suddenly lifted his eyes. Springing up, he came and lifted the tray from her lap, and with a look that had in it all promise of knightly service, yet nothing of the servant, he smiled brightly, and said: "Ted's going to get her for you; don't you be afraid."

Yet, she was afraid—afraid herself to go straight

back to the old nurse and offer to pay for all arrears in the child's care and to claim her and take her away. If the woman was loyal to the family she had served, this move would avail nothing, and would, she feared, incite her husband to take such steps as would, if backed by the name and influence of his father, deprive her altogether of the child. She could not go to her husband's parents and plead with them against his cruelty; there was nothing to be hoped for there. She knew nothing of the law, which seemed to her only an agency for making the poor and oppressed pay for continuance and confirmation of oppression. Even the money now at her command would be as nothing against the money of Robert's father. No, there was one way only, and that was the way Robert had taken. Too full of this problem to heed much of Biddy's constant talk, she was glad to get back to her own room and to wait for the slow-coming dawn.

When morning came, her mind was once more alert and clear, and her heart could not help being buoyed with hope. She went to Mrs. Burke at once, and forcing the warm-hearted old creature to be quiet by first consenting to drink the cup of fragrant coffee she had prepared, she laid before her her hopes and plans.

"I want you to go East with me when I have my little one again," she said. "I cannot take both children. It would arouse suspicion, and if my husband tries to follow me, I should be too easily traced. You once said you were my servant. I want your service, but you are and must always be my friend. Give up the laundry. Come into my employ. We will live in the East, perhaps even go over the sea, and you can see the old friends in Ireland."

At this hint Biddy could hardly be made to sit still to hear the rest.

"Take my sister's little girl now, and care for her for me in these days that I must be absent so much, watching for my own. This little one will feel at home with you then, and you can bring her to me in the East. I have a home there now, and you can take care of it and help me with the children. I shall not be rich, but it can be made better for you than the hard work you are doing now,"

"And Teddy?" asked the widow, her face all aglow with the prospect. "Me Teddy's me life, me leddy."

"And Teddy shall come too," said Katharine. "And, since we must be ready to go at any moment, I want you to be doing everything to get ready."

"And phat'll I do wid me tubs and me furnitoor?" asked Biddy, looking about her clean, scantily-furnished room with honest pride. "It's not that I mind lavin' it behind, for it's not like it was whin I left Ireland. Thin, every stool and table had on it the touch av me mother."

"Then you better send what you do not want to the salesroom," said Katharine, "and the things you want begin to pack at once, so that we may go by the very next train after I have my child."

"And couldn't I go before ye, ma'am, and be gettin' the place in order?"

Mrs. Gray hesitated a moment. Why not? It

would simplify matters to have only herself to get off. But a second thought of the probable effect upon the old neighbors in Walden of Biddy's advent at the parsonage in charge of the child sufficed to check the temptation to haste.

The morning was spent in completing arrangements for sudden flight. She would go by the Grand Trunk road, Biddy by the Michigan Central, and they would meet and go on together from Detroit. This decided, she hastened away to B—— Street once more, driven by her eager heart, even though she did not know what to do there, or that she could do anything at all. After her lesson of the night before, she was surprised to find that lack of confidence in herself, and dread of making matters worse by premature action had taken the place of her fierce courage and for the time being paralyzed her powers. Still she went, and walking slowly on the opposite side of the street, wondering behind what window was hidden the baby face, she suddenly saw the side door open and a little wicker carriage pushed forth upon the walk. Her heart gave a great bound, but she was wise enough to resist the desire to rush forward. Instead, she halted, partly hidden by the pile of lumber placed in the vacant lot. Carefully the carriage, with its faded blue cambric parasol, was backed out at the door, and her heart almost stopped beating when she saw that the curly-headed, freckle-faced boy who was pushing it was Theodore Burke, the Widdy Biddy's Ted.

Glancing hastily up and down the street, as if fearing the child's father might appear, he caught sight of Mrs. Gray, and trundling the child quickly past her, never paused a moment except to lift his eyes and say under his breath, " Don't follow me, lady, don't follow. Go the other way round by the church," and, catching his thought, she passed him with one look, just one, at the sleeping baby face, and one tight clenching of the hands to keep them from obeying her wild impulse to fold the little form to her heart.

The church was three squares away. The service was going on. There floated out to her ears the organ's notes and the boy voices singing the words of an old hymn that she had often heard at the family altar and in her father's church at home. But when she reached the church door and waited for the little carriage to come from the opposite direction, so intent was her mind in watching for it to appear that the hymn came to her like something heard in dreams. As she stood there her hands were so tightly clenched that the nails cut into the tender flesh. To the day of her death she never forgot those distant floating sounds, the gray church tower, or the swaying of the ivy, just putting out its leaves of tender green under the soft spring wind. For a long time she never lifted her eyes to the sky without remembering the mottled, feathery look that it wore in these moments, in which she lived whole nights and days of longing and expectancy and pain.

As she waited, her fear, lest after all something should come between her and the child, grew into a positive terror, and hardly knowing that she prayed, yet she prayed, dimly recognizing as she stood there in the shadow of the sanctuary, that God was in the midst thereof. Swiftly her agonized sense of supplication passed over into the fierce feeling that she could tear Ted and the little shell of a carriage into shreds if only so her hands could grasp the child. But as her fury grew she saw him coming. It was too late for caution. She had borne enough. When she swept him aside and gathered up the child against her heart and walked on, he knew better than to urge her to stop, or to take that time to tell her the story of the day when he came to the house to which he had traced the child, and asked for any small job of work. As it chanced there was coal to put in, and the lad was so quick and so tidy about it that he got not only his money, but a bit of dinner, and a sight of the little child, though he dared not show he knew her. Baby that she was, she knew him, and laughed when he rattled the tin pan of clothespins, with which the old nurse was trying to have her amuse herself that she might get time for her work. She was old and stiff with rheumatism and overworked and poor, and it pleased her to see the child pleased. And when he asked for more work, she told him he might come and clear up the back yard, and he came. The next day there was the cellar to be swept, and a bit of the back fence to be mended, and kindlings to split, and the wee border to be dug up for the flowers. And every day he saw the child, and lately he had been allowed to take it out to ride, borrowing the carriage of the grocer on the corner, whose baby had outgrown it and who let him have it for a nickel an hour.

Dropping the curtain of the carriage that no one might see the baby was not there, he followed the mother as she strode off in the sunlight, so strong in her new sense of triumphant possession that it mattered little whether the boy who followed her was friend or foe. Let them come, all of them, now; her husband, his father, his mother, yes, even her dead sister, with her pleading, questioning face and sorrowful, haunting eyes. All these had had their hour. Now her hour had come, and in the fierceness of her joy, she was dauntless before sting of conscience or memories or fears.

Ted watched her until he saw her hail a passing cab. She waited a moment as he pressed forward to her side. "Come in quickly," she said. "Leave the child's wagon and come."

"I cannot, miss," Ted answered, falteringly, divided between his fear of dishonesty and his fear that she was going away with the child where he would never see them again. She looked so fierce and strong, there was no guessing what she might do. For one miserable moment he halted. Then he said, falteringly, "I must not, miss, I must not. I have hired the wagon. I must take it back and pay the man his money."

She gave him one withering glance. "Go on," she said to the driver, and the poor little disciple of honesty and honor stood and watched the cab out of sight, with eyes full of disappointed tears. Then, trundling his little wagon back to the grocer, he paid him his nickel, and with a curious look of age upon his bright, boyish face walked slowly away to his home as dejectedly as if he had found life not worth living, since out of it had gone what gave it its sunshine and its joy. Yet he had been working weeks to bring about what had happened, to find and bring her back her child. Why should he feel defrauded now because both had gone out of his life? Yet, might she not have remembered to look back once, recognizing that he too was bereft?

He heard that organ music too, as he went back alone and caught the last strain of the hymn, and lifted his eyes a moment to the cross on the high church tower, and made its sign on his faded jacket. Brave, tender boy soul! It had truth and honor and honesty and love enough for sacrifice, and so it was a living temple, a sanctuary, and "God was in the midst."

CHAPTER VIII

WHEN Ted reached home he found the house in direst confusion, and his mother in a state of almost hilarious excitement. In other days she would have fallen summarily upon the lad in penalty for his long absence, making his legs tingle with a switch and his ears tingle with the lashings of her tongue. But she had learned her lesson, and tempered her reproofs with kindness, though she broke forth with, "It's aisy enough for yez to go and play all day in the strate and lave yer old mither to be prancin' early and late to impty the place."

"But what does it mean, mother?" he asked, as he lifted the child from the washtub, in which the ingenious woman had deposited her to keep her out of harm's way.

" Lave the baby alone, lad, and give me a lift wid the work. Bad luck to yez for gittin' oot er the house before iver me lady came with the good news. It's goin' to live in the country we are, and there's grass and plenty of buddin' things, and chickens and ducks, like in Ireland ; and I'm to be cook and maid of iverything, and we're goin' as fast as iver we can, and niver comin' back from the swate smilin' country to this wicked old city no more. And there's a garden, lad, and pertaties to grow, and niver no more thavin' craythurs around a stalin' of babies.

And ye're to go too, Ted, ye plague av me loife. There's no gettin' rid of yez, ye bad pinny. Off all day and me that fond of ye that I've no heart to give yez a shpankin' or ask ye wheriver ye wint. Howly Pether! spake a word, boy, can't ye? Ye make me feel all quare-like, as I do whin the Sisters comes shtalin' in so still, wid the white bands on their heads, as if they was jest let out er their graves to ask we poor widdies for money."

But Ted put down the baby, and met her excitement with his boyish face so pale and grave that her overflow of words stopped suddenly in the midst.

"I see, mother; Mrs. Gray is meanin' to lave all at once now, and ye are meanin' to go wid her."

"And yerself too, Teddy; I'll not lave me darlin' only blissin'."

"Yes, I'll go with you, mother. Maybe I'll find work near you. Niver mind now," he added, as she held out her arms, suggestive of motherly hugs. "I'll be off and do what nades to be done."

And though it was true that his mother had "pranced" to and fro all day in the midst of her household gods, it was Ted who made his mother take the child and go over to Katharine, telling her he knew she needed to be taken care of, and that only Biddy could do it. "Kindle the fire, mither, and make her a bit to ate."

"But how'll I be lavin' me duds here?"

"Lave it to me, mither."

"But ye'll get no bit or sup for yersilf."

"I'll not be neglectin' me own flesh and blood. If ye don't go ye'll be losin' a sight of our own baby, mother.   She'll not be shtoppin' in town now she's got it, I tell ye shure."

"Ye decavin' thafe of a son.   If it wasn't for me promise on me beads, I'd not lave a bone in yer body.   Why didn't ye tell me she had the blessid angel back again?" and taking her fiery plaid shawl on one arm, and the little child in the other, she was off downstairs in a minute.

With the kind-hearted voluble old creature out of the way, Ted showed the stuff that was in him. He flew downstairs, into the baker's and the grocer's, with an order to send quickly a few supplies to Mrs. Gray's room.   Seizing an old bit of carpet, he wrapped the little oil stove, and placed it in the bottom of a box with the teapot, a few utensils, and on the top one dainty cup and saucer for the lady.   A nickel or two to a lad from the street to help him carry the burden, which, deposited at Katharine's door, he was off again.   Some instinct of loving kindness revealed to him that the poor woman must be brought down from her exalted state of excitement and be made conscious of common needs, and he felt intuitively that the sound of his mother's talk, and the sight of the other child would help to bring this about.   Feeling too, that the fewer people who knew of the children's presence the better, he desired to get his mother away before he brought a man from the second-hand shop across the street to set a value on the household effects that must be left behind.   Anxious to secure every dollar possible for his mother, he yet put an end to the haggling over the price for each old tub and chair, by offering all together at a very low rate, provided the man would send his wagon and have everything out of the house in two hours, except the beds, which he thought might be needed for the night, and which could be given up with the oil stove in the morning.

Two hours later the rooms were cleared and swept, the boxes packed to go ; his best suit, his mother's Sunday gown, and such other things as he thought a journey needed, ready, and the bed waiting for Biddy to rest for one night more. Then after an old-fashioned scrub, and a vigorous brushing of his curly hair and his clothes, he went over to see the "family" which seemed to have fallen into his hands.

As he hoped, without really knowing it, the atmosphere was less tense and strained, the little girls both fed and fast asleep, looking enough alike as they lay on the bed to have been the children of one mother.

The remains of the rolls, and jelly and eggs, and the jar of potted meat were still on the table, and the little oil stove was burning to keep the coffee hot for him.

Katharine was very quiet, though the intense light still burned in her eyes, which, even while she worked, turned constantly to the bed, as if to make sure her child was really there.

If Theodore had been a tender woman he could not have been more tactful or self-effacing in this long day's work ; if a strong man he could not have been more prompt, practical, and efficient ; but in the way that he now fell upon his supper after he was assured that Mrs. Gray and his mother had been fed, he was simply and only a boy. The things that were dearest, that he thought might go out of his sight forever were here, and on these he feasted his eyes and his heart. As for his tired body it enjoyed the supper as he never remembered to have enjoyed a meal before.

Exultant and excited as she was, Katharine had been very cautious in her preparations. She had been driven straight to the railway station and dismissed the cab. She had made all inquiries and purchased tickets, and then made the way back by the street cars to her lodging, where Biddy found her sitting, dumbly gloating over the child. But Biddy's voluble delight and noisy preparation of the supper seemed to arouse her, and she went on hurrying things into the trunk, gathering and folding with one hand while she kept the child constantly in her arms as if she feared she might disappear if, even for one moment, she let her go.

"There's one thing more to be done," she said, pausing suddenly in her restless walk about the room.

"And what is me Teddy made for but to do it for yez?" said Biddy.

Teddy sprang from the table, and seizing his Scotch cap, stood before her, twirling the ribbons in his fingers.

Up to this time Katharine had not met his eyes. Under all her pain and triumph ran a consciousness of shame at having taken her treasure from the hands of this lad, and fled away with not so much as a thought or care of what might be the result to him. But now his clear eyes smiled up to her with such forgiving eagerness that she forgave him too, for the prick of conscience which his very presence brought. He loved her, brave little faithful soul, and for one moment she was enough like the woman she ought to have been, the woman God meant she should be, to recognize the beauty and nobleness of such a love and to wish that she herself could love something besides her own will and way and the child that seemed to have absorbed the power to recognize the claim of any other human soul.

She answered Ted's eager look by sending him to the office for letters. She had received some funds from her sister's man of business before she left. She expected more. She expected too, a line from the aunt in Washington to say if Deborah had arrived safely. And Ted came back with these, but with another letter also, from her husband's mother, Mrs. Gray. She knew, of course, the place of Katharine's early home. She had read the letter to the sister, which her husband had committed to the flames. She knew, because Robert told her, that Katharine was gone, and her natural inference was that she had gone to the sister's home. If she could only be made to stay there. In this hope she had written.

"My son has told me of your departure, without his knowledge or sanction, for some place unknown. Naturally I infer, indeed I hope, you have gone to your own relations, and therefore I shall send this letter to your early home.

"Your husband tells me he has been forced to

place his child under proper protection, since your desertion of him implies desertion of your little daughter also." Katharine's lips curled and her eyes blazed angrily as she read. " Robert could not bring the child here, as his father would not be willing to receive her, neither would I, indeed, unless you would agree to relinquish all claim upon her, and allow us to bring her up in our own home and as our own child. If you will consent to this, we will have her come to us at once, and you need have no further anxiety as to her proper rearing or support, or as to an ample provision for her in the event of our death. My son Robert, notwithstanding the unhappiness of his married life, which has told terribly upon his health, will agree to relinquish all claim upon your future consideration if you resign the child to his care. He is to leave in a very few days for San Francisco, and will take a voyage around the world to recover his shattered health, and to find, if possible, in change and travel some consolation for his broken life. His father has consented, in view of all he has suffered, to give him the opportunity to travel for his firm, and I have no doubt he will be able to support both himself and his child. He agrees with me that you would be wise to consent to this plan, since it would be useless for you to expect or attempt to find or to gain possession of the child."

Katharine's face added a sneer to its look of scorn and rage, but she read the letter all through and then said quietly, " Teddy, I intended to wait till morning, and leave at the same time but by another train than that which would take your mother and yourself. Now I have decided to go to-night by the Michigan Central. You will come in the morning by the Grand Trunk. I shall join you on the train at Detroit, and we shall go down through Canada together. You are not to look for me ; I shall come to you on the train. I shall put the money and tickets in your care, and you will bring your mother and the child safely ? "

There was no time for many or tender farewells. She came back once from the door and bent a moment over her sister's child, and in the dim light it seemed to her overstrained imagination like her sister's own white, pathetic face, as it gazed up to her own from the pillow the night before she died. "Take care of her, Theodore," she cried. "I ought not to leave her, I know, but I cannot, I dare not wait another night. They will miss my child and take her from me before I can get away."

"And why wouldn't we all be comin' along wid yez ?" asked Teddy, as the old terror lest the two should go away beyond his reach came sweeping back in full force. "I could bring both the childer for yez."

"But that must not be. We should be followed and traced more readily if we were together. If I am pursued it means — " she paused and her voice choked—"it means—death to me or to—. some one else. If you are followed no one can hurt you, for no one wants to take away that child ; but you will take care of her for me, Teddy, as if she were my own."

And two hours later Katharine lay with wide-open, staring eyes, behind the curtains of her sleeper, with the window shade raised high, so that in the moonlight she could watch the spectral shadows of the trees and rocks, as they swept in swift procession across the face of her sleeping babe.

And two hours later, as Biddy lay sleeping in her own bed, with a child beside her, and Teddy, tired with such an exhausting day as he had never known before, lay fast asleep, rolled in the remnants of an old quilt, there came hurried and heavy steps up the stairs, and a pause on the floor below, the floor now vacant, but that had been the home of the Gray family before Katharine went away.

Stupid with sleep as he was, the lad heard it, and raising himself on his elbows, his eyes shining like stars, he listened. He had heard Robert Gray's step on that staircase, as he came home more or less tipsy, too many nights not to know it now. The other step was new, but the voice, yes, it was that of the policeman who knew them all, and who had helped Robert home to bed more than once long ago. In a minute Teddy saw the situation, and chided himself for letting his mother come back there to sleep. But Biddy had wailed that it was her home, and the last night she iver would see it, and she would trust no boy, "not aven Ted, . to 'see the last of it, and make sure that all was not behind that should have been attinded to before.' I'll not be lavin' it all ends fustward, Ted. Its dacent and clane I lived in it, and dacent and clane I'll lave it." And so, much against his will, he had brought them home to sleep. And here they were, and he was to be arrested for "shtaling" a baby, and here was the baby to prove it, and he would be sent to prison, and the two childer, for wasn't his mither just anither baby whin it came to good sinse, to be left to the cowld world, and Katharine gone, and his own swate baby gone out of his soight intirely. He crept out of his quilt and stood with the door ajar. The door below was open and the voices loud.

"You see there's no one here, Mr. Gray," said the policeman.

"But the boy brought the child here," said Robert's voice. "It's all a plan. The mother is in the city, she sent the boy to steal this child. He brought a child here to-night. He has it upstairs now."

"But I tell you the old woman and the boy are gone, and all their goods gone too, packed off this afternoon."

"I'll go up and see," and the tread, uncertain, unsteady from drink, moved through the lower hall.

Quick as a flash the boy lifted the sleeping child from the bed to the tattered quilt, and holding her tenderly, he sprang to the window that opened from the tiny kitchen on to the fire-escape. Holding fast with one hand, he descended backward iron step after iron step, to the landing below. The window there was unfastened. He listened—the steps were already on the upper stair. A second more and they would rouse his mother, who had the power of sleeping through a cyclone. There would be a noise he knew, and in a minute it came, a whirlwind of angry talk, and under cover of it he softly lifted the window and passed in and through Katharine's old rooms and out and away down the stairs. She had bidden him take care of this child, and he had said nothing, but had taken the new trust as he had taken the old. He would put her in a safe place and be back again in a minute to help his mother, though she had stolen no children, and even if they cared to arrest her, he could trust to her making it a very slow process to get her away. Full of these thoughts, he ran out into the street and around the corner, into the other house and up to the room vacated by Mrs. Gray. The child had awakened but had not cried until now. Now she fretted, and poor little Ted had the worst twenty minutes of his life between his longing to get back to his mother and his desire to soothe the little motherless thing that clung to him, yet would not be trotted or rocked or coaxed or sung to sleep. He felt little enough like singing, but he sang, and little enough like whistling and little enough like dancing, yet he whistled and danced, but all of no avail. The child was happy in his arms, but cried if he put her down ; yet over yonder was that other gray-haired child fighting tooth and nail no doubt, probably telling all she ought not, and wild with loss of himself. As he was about to start back again, baby in arms, to face the worst, he saw on the table the remains of his supper. Oh, happy discovery ! Here was milk and bread. In two minutes he was pouring the milk in most unhygienic haste down the child's throat, and joyful result, the little thing seemed satisfied, and cuddling down in his arms, let herself be rocked and sung to sleep.

Ted never knew how he got around the corner, but he found his mother sitting on the bedside in her red flannel short-gown and petticoat, nightcap awry, her round head shining like a billiard ball, a broom in one hand and one of her broad-soled shoes in the other. Instead of wailing for her lost boy she was laughing till the tears streamed down her cheeks.

"And is it alive ye are?" said Ted, rushing to embrace her.

"Alive it is, me boy? It's alive and that aisy in me moind. I've done what I've wanted to do this mony a month, and what his own mother ought to have done whin he was a boy. Sure enough, would I lave him alone whin he came tumblin' straight over me knees?"

"Mother, mother!" said Ted, "are you crazy? What has happened? Did Mr. Gray and the policeman come here?"

"Dade and they did, intered without aven knockin' at the door and sayin' 'by yer lave.' I was a shlapin' and a snorin' whin the officer he said he had come to take you and the baby. And I rached me hand down onto the place where ye was by me side whin I wint to slape, and ye wasn't there at all, at all, and I whopped me arm over to the place where I left the baby, and the baby wasn't there aither, and thin, Tiddy, ye think yer mother's got no sinse, but if I've none its because, bein' me only son and yer poor father blowed into smithereens, I've bestowed me extra sinse on yerself.

But I'd enough not to howl and scrache for yez for
I knew what long ears ye had me darlin' donkey of
a Ted! And I was sure ye heard 'em a comin' and
had scud away yerself and the baby, lavin' yer ould
mother to fight it alone."

"No, no, mother," Ted began. "I was coming
again——"

"Howld yer whist noo, Ted. That baste of a
Gray man, he shwore, he did,—and I never could
abide shwarin' in the prisince of a lady,—and he
said he would have ye in jail for child-shtalin' and
he would have the child, and he made a clutch at
the bed rachin' over me fut as I sat on the bidside,
meanin' to grab the child that wasn't there. And
bein' top-heavy with the drink he just tumbled over
me fut in the way most convaynient, and the saints
forgive me, I sayzed me shlipper and I hild him
down there wid my hand that's so strong wid
wringin' the clothes, and I gave him such a
shpankin', and he a howlin' and a twistin' and me a
layin' it on till I think the shlipper has a big blister
on it if it hasn't lost its sowl intirely. I don't
know but I've lost me own too unless they bees
aisy on me in purgatory, rememberin' that time
the blackguard sint me out in the strate crazy, be-
lavin' ye was killed. Oh, but it was a picnic, and me
a laffin' and a laffin', wid the tears runnin' down me
face and the perlaceman sayin', 'Lave him go, 'twas
'salt and battery,' and me pretindin' 'twas his at-
tackin' myself in the bed that was assault and battery, and then layin' it on to him again. And thin
whin I let him up, and his eyes a poppin' wid rage,
didn't I look that surprised and say 'How would I

know whin they come into me-room in the dark of the night like burglars, and me ashlape that it wasn't the perlice bringin' home me Ted?' And I tould him how it was a rule av the family iver since ye was a scrap of a lad that ye'd go to bid shmartin' if ye stayed out to the middle av the night. And the perlaceman wouldn't arrist me, for all the shpluttering blackguard of a Gray, for makin' an innocint mistake and shpankin' the wrong boy. I'm aisy in my moind now, Ted, and I'll go to the end of the airth with me leddy;" and she wiped her eyes and settled her cap. "And the perlaceman he asked me where was me leddy? And I said, 'I don't know now. She went aist.' And, where was her little gurl? and I said, 'I don't know that nayther, she wint aist too.' And he said, where was Ted? and I tould him I lift ye ashlape, and ye must have shtole out after ye heard me shnorin', and if it wasn't for me promise, I'd have tould him that most likely ye'd get the other shlipper when I caught ye again. He was askin' me phat for was I movin' all me things awa'? and I towld him I was goin' to service. I was tired of the suds, I'd been long enouf thryin to make a dirthy old world clane and to straighten up the men folks wid starch, that couldn't kape themselves straight for want of a bit of back-bone. And thin he said, 'hould me tongue and get out av the neighborhood, and that he couldn't answer for me or Ted, if Mr. Gray caught us aboot.' And I said, innocint-like, I hoped he wouldn't again till I got me shlipper mended, and away he wint shakin' himself wid laffin' till I think ye'll foind his buttons all along the shtairs."

Notwithstanding this signal triumph Teddy felt the importance of hastening their departure, and if he had known that Robert Gray, thoroughly sobered for once, and on his way home to his mother, white with rage, had engaged a detective to watch their every movement, he would have waited till morning with much less peace of mind.

As it was he knew no rest until the train had left the bustling, noisy city far behind, and he could see the wide prairies stretching on and on until they touched the bending summer sky. Then there took possession of him a growing sense of freedom and the long strain of weeks relaxed. He dared to let himself, boy-like, look forward to his meeting on the morrow with the two who filled so many of his dreams.

The Widdy Biddy seemed to be in a state of inward satisfaction, with a gratified sense of importance. She was most assiduous in her attentions to the child, and her air to Theodore would have become a great lady traveling in grandeur, to her courier or *valet de place*. She kept him so busy as to hardly allow his little soul its look at the sky and its daydream of what was yet to come. In those dreams was always Katharine to whom the little fellow had transferred all he had been taught to feel toward Mary, the Mother of Sorrows. And there was foremost always, the child that had come to be the object of his first boyish chivalry. And here was this little motherless stranger to whom his heart went out pityingly with a full acceptance of the fact that he must care for and protect her too. His love and loyalty to Katharine were unbroken, but his faith had had a blow and he knew far more than she ever could guess, her real feeling to her sister's child. While he amused the little Margaret by letting her have his tangle of yellow curls to pull as hard as ever she liked, one would not have guessed that under that tossing hair was already growing a consciousness for which he had no name and which he could not have defined, but that became a conviction that he must be the one to stand among them all, and see that no injustice and no harm should come to any one. And all this time there hung such a shadow of harm over this little life as he could not see and as his whole life, however freely given in sacrifice, would have no power to avert.

"Watch them both, the boy and his mother," said Robert Gray. "Get some one to follow them both, if they go different ways. If, at any time they are seen with a child in charge, capture that child at all risks. I am called to San Francisco, but recover the child, take it to my mother, Mrs. John Gray, No. 194 Gray's Terrace. She will see that the reward agreed upon is yours." And then he had charged his mother to be ready, for he did not think it wise to delay his own departure lest his father refuse to receive the child and withdraw his consent to send him abroad, which had only been granted in response to the importunity of his mother. The indignity he had suffered at Biddy's hands was only a new score against his wife. He wanted the child before as a means of renewing the tie with his parents. He wanted her still, but chiefly now to make its mother suffer. He did not know Katharine had been in Chicago. He had been informed by the old nurse of the child's disappearance; he had known the boy from the nurse's description; had refused to pay the good woman for the care of the child; and had concluded, notwithstanding the seeming solitude of Widow Burke, that the child and her son were in hiding and that all would go away together. He would not delay his own journey. Indeed, he preferred to have the child come when he would escape discussion and conditions with his father. He had accepted one condition, that he should travel, and work while he traveled. If he failed to do the work by any " bad luck "—he always called his troubles " bad luck "—why the child would be in the home when he came back to make such a welcome for him which he might not be able to make for himself.

And even while he was beguiling himself with thoughts like these, his plan was working, for the man who had taken his seat on the train behind Theodore, the man with a bald head and a heavy mouth and narrow black eyes half hidden under drooping lids, was one who meant to earn the generous reward which Robert had promised readily, since it was to be presented to his mother for collection.

And the day waned slowly. At many stations passengers came and went. Ted jumped off with the little cup and ran to the restaurant for fresh milk and always brought back something for his mother and held the child while she rested, and got bits of time for thinking his own thoughts between. His mother was nodding in her seat, the child was dozing in his arms, the boy's eyes were fixed upon a mass of white clouds piling in castles and towers against the western sky. The train was sweeping around a long curve and on to a lovely bridge whose slender span swung in midair above a brawling river sixty feet below. At one end a high trestlework swarming with laborers showed the bridge was undergoing repairs. There was no time to wonder or to fear. For one second the train trembled and quivered like a living thing in a mighty spasm of horror and of dread, the next it shot forward like lightning. They were on the bridge, and the only chance with the trembling swaying structure was to put on all steam and fly, as through the air itself, to the other end. An awful shriek ran for one breath through the car, the next breath was held in speechless horror while parted lips tried in vain to utter another sound.

The engine passed safely, the baggage car was over, and the next was one-third its length upon the solid land. The man in the seat behind Teddy had rushed to the door. Close after him crowded Ted, the baby in one arm, dragging his frantic mother forward in spite of maddened men and women who would have trampled her under their feet.

The detective sprang to the ground and with the impulse of fear turned to flee. Teddy could have followed with the child, but no, his mother, knocked and jostled, had been thrust aside, and two strong men were between. Quick as a flash he shouted to the man staggering yet from his jump:

"Quick! hold up your arms—save the child."

He turned and the child came gasping and screaming against his heart. Half paralyzed with horror he fled again, and Ted, fighting madly for his mother's life, sprang between the men, and seizing her, by main strength pushed her forward. The men got off before her, but Ted pushed her, and as the car, drawn backward by the weight that was making the bridge sway and swing, went down, down into the whirl of waters, Ted saw his mother, unconscious perhaps, but lying upon the solid ground.

They were saved; they were all saved, all his dear ones; what matter if he died? But the question found no answer. For one instant only, like a flash of golden sunlight his young head glanced downward through the air. For one instant a bright spot glowed on the surface of the now turbid river and then the black waters closed over it, and in the crowd that gathered above to look down upon that awful wreck there was no one to miss it or to watch if it ever came up again.

CHAPTER IX

BIDDY, greatly bruised otherwise as she fell, had also struck her head against an iron portion of the bridge and lay quite unconscious on the ground. Nor did consciousness return even for a moment, and after the physicians arrived they ordered that she be put upon the train and taken to the hospital of the nearest city. Of all the people who had succeeded in escaping from the forward end of the car, one man only reached the ground uninjured. In his arms he carried a little fair-haired frightened girl, who repelled, with every sign of resistance that her infant powers could command, his clumsy efforts to soothe her. Around the station was great confusion and crowds flocking from every direction. There were no ears for anything but the cries of the wounded, and no eyes for anything but the tottering framework of the ruined structure, yet swaying in midair. Crowds rushed down the steep embankment at every accessible point. Boats approached as if by magic on every side of the wreck, their occupants anxiously watching the trembling remains of the bridge above, lest it fall and bury still deeper the wounded human beings yet alive under the broken train. All hearts were bent on rescue, and a great cheer followed every boat that sped away toward the shore with its freight of the living or the dead.

The man with a child in his arms was hardly noticed by those hurrying toward the wreck, and when
he took his seat in the relief train sent on from the
nearest town, and the porter asked if he was among
the injured, he said, " No, I wanted to get the train
the other way and will catch it at the junction."
And that he did, dropping out quietly without admitting that he had any part in the awful disaster,
and taking a place on the night train to Chicago.

Safe on the cars, though the danger was over,
his trial was not by any means at an end.   The little creature, tired, rudely handled, and sleepy,
fretted and cried incessantly.   To ferret out crime,
apprehend criminals, and beguile them from their
hiding places in the world's dark holes and corners,
this was work from which the detective never
shrank, and in which he very rarely failed.   But
this child was more than a match for all his inge-
nuity and skill.   Not a little shaken up nervously
himself by the danger and the narrow escape and
the awful vision of the crashing train, he longed for
relief from the crying child, or for a respite long
enough for one good soothing pipe in a corner of
the smoking car.   Gazing helplessly about while
the little one squirmed and protested as only stif-
fened baby backs and flying baby legs can protest,
against his efforts to soothe her by trotting her
hard enough to set her into fits, his eye fell upon a
boy about twelve years old, with bright yellow hair,
asleep in a seat near him.   Almost in despair, he
held the little girl so that she could see him, when,
with a wild struggle of hands, feet, and squirming
body all together, she scrambled out of his arms, and

toddled over to the boy, laid her head confidingly against his knees, and gave a triumphant little chuckle that, when the stranger would have drawn her away, changed into a defiant howl.

The man lifted her to a seat beside the lad, but she pulled away from him with all her little might, and clung to the boy's jacket. The little fellow stirred uneasily, and then as if some pleasant dream had come over him, put out one arm and laid it gently over the little girl.

" Blest if I don't believe the little beggar thinks it's the other boy, the boy she's used to," the man muttered to himself.

From her new shelter the bright eyes watched him suspiciously. He kept very still, and soon the lids began to droop, and in a few minutes she was fast asleep. Now was his chance, and he was not long in making the best of it. A good smoke, yes, and a bit of a nap, just forty winks, no more, he thought, and he would be back again.

Both were awake soon, and the child astride the lad's knee, was tugging with both hands at his yellow curls, as she had tugged only this morning at the bright young head that had gone down under the waves.

The lad had waked to find the little thing clinging to his side. " She belongs to a gentleman who has gone in the smoker. I fancy she's used to being with children at home," so one of the passengers had said ; and when the detective came back to claim her, she cried and resisted, till he was glad to let well enough alone. Not caring to emphasize too strongly his presence with the child, and seeing the importance of concealing the fact that they had been on the wrecked train, he took the stateroom and asked the little fellow to come in there and sit with them. From the boy's hands she took the bread and milk brought in from the restaurant of a station, and all went well until when, on reaching Chicago, he put the little girl on the seat of the carriage, when she shrieked and cried as if her little heart would break.

"Let me go too, sir. She's crying for me," said the little man, standing hat and satchel in hand at the door of the cab.

For a moment Mr. Morrow hesitated, then the detective got the better of the man and he said, "No, shut the door will you," and when it was shut, something rang on the pavement. It was a silver dollar. For one second, while the driver was climbing to his seat, the lad's heel came down upon it and ground it into the dirt. He didn't want the dollar; he wanted to go. The next second he had the dollar in one hand and with the help of the other had swung himself up behind the cab as it drove away, and there he sat until it turned in between the stone pillars at the entrance of the grounds belonging to the mansion of Mr. Gray. From behind the pillar a boy's face peered out when the cab drove away, and he knew where the little girl who clung to him and cried for him had found her home.

Robert had not gone away without sharing with his mother all his hopes and plans for securing the child, nor had she been idle in her efforts to bring her husband's mind to receiving it. She had persuaded him to give Robert another trial, partly by the fact that it would take him away for an indefinite time. She had used skillfully the fact, as she believed it, of Katharine's desertion of her little daughter. She had gotten his consent to write the letter that offered to take the child, but she had not told him of the fact that no notice was taken of the letter or of the plan for the little girl's capture. At heart, the old man's outraged sense of honor and honesty was strong. He would take the child if he must, if it was true the mother was not fit to care for it. In the father's fitness he had no confidence whatever; but he would have no underhand dealings, no taking of the child by strategy or force. He justified Katharine in her efforts to get the child, and her desire to do so was to him an evidence that she had never meant to desert it. Mrs. Gray knew the stubborn nature she had to deal with, and knew better than to tell him the whole truth. She only told him that Robert's wife had resigned the child to the care of an old woman who had met with an accident upon the railway and could care for it no longer, and that Robert had arranged before his departure to have the little one delivered to her care. Katharine had not indeed, written that they might have her, but had really left her with those who could no longer care for her. And with this half truth the old man had to be content, though he had grave doubts of any transaction in which Robert was concerned. But he was glad on the whole to know that the child would be cared for, and gave his wife money to pay just charges, though not the sum Robert had promised. Still she dared not ask for more, but added to it from household and personal funds, and so was, at last, in full possession of the blue-eyed, sunny-haired little girl.

And while, that night, the little traveler who, since her mother's death, had been passed from the care of Deborah to Katharine, from Katharine to the Widow Burke, from the widow to her son, from Ted to the detective, and from the detective to Mrs. Gray, lay sweetly sleeping in a luxurious little room, her dimpled limbs softly wrapped in dainty garments; while Biddy's bald head was resting on the hospital pillow in the unconsciousness that was so much like death that they doubted if she would ever wake again, and Ted's bright curls were resting no one knew where; Katharine turned restlessly on her pillow in the sleeper of the train going eastward from Detroit. She was very weary, for the long tension of weeks over, the desire of her heart satisfied, her whole nature relaxed and sleep kept coming, even when she had resolved to keep awake. Starting up suddenly her hand groped always for the child, to be sure she was still there, and then busy thoughts began to burn in her brain and the noise of the whirring wheels to repeat itself over and over in her head. This was the train on which Biddy and Ted and the little Margaret were to come. She had made a mistake, as she saw now, in telling them to stay on the train and that she would join them there. She had done this partly on account of her certainty that they would be watched, and that it was not well to have the two parties meet in the station. She had kept herself close in her room in the little hotel on the Canadian side, that she might not attract observation, and had arrived just as the train was about to start. Taking her place at once, it was not till they were speeding fast out of the station that she was able to secure the attention of a porter. He called the conductor, who told her he would look for her friends, a nurse and a yellow-haired lad with a child in her charge. He was long in coming back, but she was not troubled till he returned with the news that there was no such party on board. "But then," he explained, "this train runs in two sections sometimes, and when the day train from Chicago is late, this first section goes forward and the other comes on as soon as it can be made up. It will overtake us at Toronto."

And with this she tried to be content, though she was now very anxious about all three, and in the solemn night-time remembered all the devotion and service of Biddy and the absolute self-forgetfulness of her noble boy. She remembered even old Deborah with tenderness, and her sister, with a great hunger to see her once more and tell her that she would be faithful and true forever to her child. All the terrible hardness that had possessed her when she was deprived of her own, seemed to vanish now that the breath of her child was on her cheek and the little hand lying like a blossom cool and sweet against her heart. For this night at least the good angels were hovering near, and love and gratitude made her less like some wild creature robbed of its young, and more like the woman tender and true that it must have been God's wish that she should be.   In this softened mood she blamed herself for having been so absorbed in her own trouble, and she longed to have again her sister's child, and rejoiced that Ted was coming that she might show how much she loved them all.

And upon this mood, as she sat in her seat in the car, broke the news that the second section would overtake them at the next station.   But when it came it brought no Biddy and no Ted, but instead the news of the terrible wreck, a confused list of the lost, and among these "an Irish nurse having a little girl in charge, and a bright-haired lad who might have been a brother of the little girl.   The passengers had heard the nurse call the boy Ted.   Nothing had been seen of either. They were doubtless lying with many others at the bottom of the river beneath the ruins of the train."

Benumbed, dazed, she sat and stared at the paper. She hardly knew it when the train moved out. She had not thought what she should do, whether she ought to go back or if she should go on.   Before she had begun to think or to do anything but feel, she was far on her way eastward, she and her child, her own child.   For one moment her heart revolted at her utter self-absorption in her own. When Debby had wanted her sister's baby, and she had wanted to use the funds the child's care would place in her hands, she had told Debby she must keep her promise to her sister not to be separated from her child ; but when her own was to be considered, she had not heeded the promise, but had left her to those far less experienced than Debby.

For one brief moment God gave her a glimpse of the true significance of this act, and she cowered and shivered as she muttered in her anguish of spirit, " I did it. It was my selfish, wicked desertion of them all," and, like Peter in the garden, she buried her face in her hands, and "wept bitterly." And yet so subtle was the serpent of self, that not many hours passed before it ventured like an evil spirit to whisper in her ear that now her own child had a chance of a future like the rest. The suggestion made her shudder, but she shut her eyes and let it be whispered again. There was no question now of anybody's sharing with her little daughter, all would be hers alone. All? No, certainly not all. Lawrence Wild's property would go back, in case of his child's death, to his family. The old aunt, Mrs. Maitland, would have it, and that which was to come from her of course would never now pass through the hands of Mrs. Gray. And the little that was left by her own father— that was so very little for such a life as she meant her child to live.

Ah, once more the good angels, so near in all these last hours that it seemed as if they might be striving again to find in her heart a home, turned away in sadness and in tears. Once more the temptation to deceit and injustice swept over the soul, and before the maddening whirl of the wheels stopped and they had come to a resting-place for the night, the tempter was saying, "It was not your fault. If it had not been for that cruel letter from Robert's mother you would have stayed with them. Why tell anybody at all that the child that is gone was not your child, and that this one is not the child of your sister and the heiress of all that was waiting for her? Who will be benefited by her being deprived? Mrs. Maitland has wealth already. Why condemn this young, sweet life to poverty that the old worn life may have still more?" And again and again the evil spirits whispered it, and though she knew she was incapable of such a deed, yet she let herself dwell for a little upon what life might have been for her own child if wealth like that had been bestowed on her. That night she could not sleep, but by morning she considered no longer the question of returning to the scene of the accident. Why should she harrow her spirit more? Already she was nearly crazed with trouble, and somewhere, somehow, her nerves must find repose. Yet, as she neared the Massachusetts home, her courage failed her. How should she meet the kind inquiries, the neighborly offers of company, the tongues and eyes from which there would be no escape, and, stronger reason still, how could she bear to live again in the old house, going through the days with eyes bent downward, lest from the windows she should see the gleam of the churchyard stones? On the other hand, she had already spent more money than she had thought to spend, or than would seem to any one compatible with the care and comfort of a child. She had taken from her sister's man of business a larger sum than she had supposed she would need, but she had used it and more. By-and-by she would have matters fully in her own hands, but just now she did not wish to subject herself to comment or to create any question by making further demands. Surely it would be better, for a time at least, until her child was older, to be beyond the reach of questioning eyes and inquisitive tongues. She was weary, heaven only knew how weary. There was the kind old Elder of the Shakers who had bidden her come and rest ; and the next night, just as the sunset was lighting the western sky with glory, she sat in the parlor of the Community with her child in her arms, and heard the word of welcome repeated and the kind orders given for her security and comfort and care. It was all so genuine, so simple, and yet so sweet. The old voice was like a benediction, the blessed stillness of the place was like a prayer, and, but for the evil guests that had made their home in her heart, for the first time in many years the tired woman would have rested and her spirit tasted peace.

CHAPTER X

THERE was no lovelier spot in all New England than that chosen for their home by the Shaker Community of Loriston. Wide, green valleys, sloping hillsides, great stretches of woodland and fertile fields, perfect roads, well-kept hedges, and all that made the fairest environment for a village of long, low, unpretentious buildings. Thrift and plenty and neatness were everywhere, nowhere a single trace of grace or adornment. Not a dainty bit of muslin at the polished windows, or a vine climbing over a lattice, or a green thing growing indoors as in the common New England home. Not even a cluster of clover blossoms or buttercups to break the monotony of the long rows of shining forks and spoons upon the well-filled board. The work indoors and out moved in orderly routine, and the people seemed like parts of a great smooth-running machine. The various groups of men off to the fields with their shovels and hoes, or of women filing away across the yard to the laundry laden with piles of linen, or to the dairy bearing the shining pans of milk, reminded her somehow of lines of ants scurrying away, each bearing its burden of sand. To her it seemed a community of labor with no communion of laborers. As the dull days wore on she became conscious that behind this uniform garb of blue overalls and blouse, or calico gown, fashioned so as to take away all grace that might once have marked the form beneath, the high apron of the child, intended to save the dress all soil and tear, were real, living men, women, and children, with an individuality even more marked for the uniformity of personality and monotony of life. She came to know the kind voice with its ring of human interest, from the apathetic voice that had said long ago in some past and dead life all it had to say in any human ear. She learned to see the twinkling of humor and sunny good nature under the drooped lids of some of the most devout. She felt her way, without a word being said, to the recognition of those who were there because it was better than the poorhouse—those who hated it but would equally have hated any other place because of the hate in their own souls— those who, like herself, carried such a heart-burden that they rejoiced to be where it did not matter, if, week in and week out, they never uttered a word. It was a place where human souls let each other alone. No conventionality required the utterance of one unfelt word, the giving of one unwilling nod or smile. If the daily task was done, the times and seasons of work and worship regarded, no soul took heed of what another thought or loved or felt. They were like an army of prisoners, each one his or her own jailer, shutting their real selves out of sight altogether, or revealing as much or as little as they would. The demand that in the outer world had made life artificial, forcing them to seem bright if sad, agreeable if disagreeable, something other than themselves at their best or worst, in this place ceased to exist.   There were some strong minds there who had chosen the life because they could be free to think their own thoughts ; some strong souls glad to be free from the unconscious tyranny of smaller souls.   These dwelt in common with the crude, the coarse, the sordid, or the selfish nature, and yet they dwelt, each on its inward height or in its inward depth alone, and the atmosphere around felt the tonic of that upper or the depression of the lower air.

Into this peopled solitude, into this orderly routine Katharine came, out of the strain and shock of the moral and emotional conflict of her recent life, and for a little time it seemed as if there had settled upon her the apathy that could not again be roused to hope, to struggle, or to fear.   They tried the method of healing that is better than medicine for the sick or tired heart.   They let her entirely alone, to do in every particular exactly as she pleased.   They even set aside the rule that forbade using the home as a hotel except for a temporary or an invalid guest.   These for a limited time might pay in money for their care, but the usual hospitality was for those who, sharing its shelter, would also share the common outward life and take some small portion at least of the daily burden of toil.

Little children coming with invalid or tired-out mothers were ordinarily consigned to the care of those among the women who were healthy and gentle and loving and not too old, while the mothers were being built up to a point of ability to share the household tasks.   But for Katharine there was never even a hint at separation from her child. The old man at the head of the Community understood her condition too well to urge anything against her will. He knew a day would come when she would desire for her child the companionship of the little playmates, and trust her little by little to the gentle nurses and teachers who had the other children in their charge. He knew too, that her restless soul would drive her soon or late to desire bodily occupation, and that there were motherly women there to give it when most needed. And it came about as he had foreseen, though for a long time she stayed in the place where guests and invalids were entertained, coming out gradually to where her intelligence and practical knowledge, her dainty deftness of hand, made itself felt among the women who allowed her to guide and help, but who never, one of them, came near enough to overcome the reserve that, under no circumstances, ever spoke of herself. This reticence was not born altogether of her distrust of those about her; it was in good part her distrust of herself lest, if she yielded in the least to the natural human desire for companionship, she should be brought to some betrayal of her inward purposes and life. In common with other guilty souls, conscious of something to be concealed, she fancied that her secret was suspected, and watched for consciousness of it in other faces; fancied she caught a sound in other voices that echoed the pleadings that were ever and ever ringing in her heart.

She knew that other torment also that comes

only when souls in sinning outrage holy memories, saintly teachings, and the knowledge of good that makes choice of evil a doubly deadly thing. She had chosen evil, but it was not in her power to ignore or forget the good. As long as she lived she might go on so choosing, but she would also go on loathing her choice and herself and striving feebly and probably vainly to cast the evil off. Even in these months, when she was too deadened in spirit and will to question much, or to care as to who else might be dead or alive, she had sometimes to hold herself with all her will from going back to the scene of that accident and searching for some surer knowledge of the three who had failed to come to her that fair June day. There were others, half a score or more, of whom there was no record save "missing." The river was deep and wide and had not yielded up its dead. And, horrible as the thought was, strive to drive it away as she would, the tempter kept saying to her again and again and again, that it was better for her daughter if they all, yes, all, were gone. And she answered every time she listened, that she had nothing to do with their going, and should never profit by it; and yet she continued to listen whenever the vile thought came. A better voice came too, sometimes in the stillness of the night, asking if she could not have risked one night more and defied her husband if he had come to claim her child, and not have fled, leaving her sister's little one and the faithful old woman and the devoted boy, inexperienced as they were, to take their risks alone. It told her she *had* had something to do with it then; and yet, though her conscience whispered that it was really murder in her heart that kept her from grieving that they were gone, yet, except in rare moments, she could not and did not grieve. Yet, all this time she never said to any one, not even to the dear old man who had befriended her, that the little girl was her own child. When she came it was as if from her sister's home, and she told him that when he was so kind to her before, she was on her way to a sister who had since died and left her only child for her to bring up as her own. She said nothing of the recent Western journey, and when he asked her if things were better for her than when he saw her first, if she had recovered from the sorrow that was pressing on her then, she answered:

"There is a sorrow for which no help can ever come, and my only chance of bearing it is never to speak of it;" and, with the delicacy born of true sympathy, he not only never questioned her again, but the curious ones of the Community, who were not altogether above desiring to know something of the new-comers, never heard from him that he had ever known anything save that her sister had left her this little orphan child to toil for and to rear.

And they loved the child, every one of them, old and young, rough men on whose knees she climbed fearlessly as they rested after the labor of the day; aged women who snuggled her in their scrawny old necks that had not felt a child's kiss for many a year: and even the soured and sulky young women, who lived in the Community because they had nowhere else to live and felt the whole thing a hardship, and the orphan children they had to work for the greatest trial of all. Gretta's little joyous, sunny face even brightened the solemn silence of "the meeting," for Katharine would not go without her, and the sunny presence reached to the schoolroom also, where one reward of the children for goodness was to be allowed to sit or walk beside sweet Gretta Wild.

Merry with a merriment that ill suited the grave quiet of the place, her laughter was music to these people who had left off laughing long ago. Nobody chided her childish faults, and the secret of her charm was the exceeding lovingness that could not bear to let the shabbiest old soul among them have a discomfort that she did not try to soothe. Quick to imitate all she saw, she would run with her mimic plaster, or her mullein leaf pressed between her folded handkerchief for a toothache or a "crick in the back." The nearest she ever came to disgrace was when, having been to ride with Elder Osborn, she had seen a young man with a rose in his buttonhole, and on the next day had carried her little apron full of daisies and clover and buttercups right into the silence of "the meeting" and proceeded to distribute them to every solemn man who sat upright on the benches meditating on his own frailty and the goodness of the Almighty. And as the little sunny head went darting in and out among them, many a hard face softened, as if there had been given them a look or smile from some sweet messenger of God. And the child grew and waxed strong while the silent years sped on.

The long day's work for the men in the fields and for the women in the house was over. The

bountiful supper was followed by the evening service of mingled silence and testimony, and the
filing off of the boys and girls to their beds. In
the parlor of the official house of the Community
Katharine sat on one of the high-backed chairs that
were kept from scratching the polished floor by
little knitted socks drawn over the legs. Leaning
against the mantle stood the white-haired, placid-
faced Eli Osborn, whose voice had uttered, so long
ago in Chicago, the first kind words that Katharine
had heard in many a week. She could hear the tones
now, and their kindness made it hard to steel her
heart against his counsel. She let her eyes wander
out on the wide fields of waving grass and away
beyond the blossoming trees to the line of hills
slowly darkening in the summer night.

"I never intended to remain," she said ; "I never
intended that Gretta should live the life of your
people here."

"For the world-weary soul there is no better
rest, my child," he said, gently. "Here is the
cloister's silence and the opportunity for communion
with God that leads to true knowledge of one's
self." Katharine winced, but did not take her eyes
from the slowly blackening hills.

"And the soul needs all that sometimes," he
added, "and this place gives solitude of spirit without loneliness or that idleness that leads to much
that is wicked or weak. It is, moreover, a life that
need have no care as to what we shall eat or drink
or wherewithal we shall be clothed."

"The last is good," she answered, bitterly.
"Only those who have felt what it is not to know

where the next morsel for a loved one is to come from, know how to value that.   But I did not come here with any thought to stay.   It was a refuge. God knows I have had enough of what you call the world to be glad to hide from it forever for myself ; but this girl must have her chance at life."

"To what good?" he asked, gently.   "It means only strife and suffering and agitation and more of anguish than joy ; and in the end it comes to the same hunger for repose."

"Yes, in the end the longing for repose," she repeated.   "But first it means life—the use of all one's faculties, the training of all one's powers, the being and doing and feeling all that makes life worth living.   No, no, I might stay gladly till I died within the white walls of yonder little chamber that has indeed been to me as much a refuge as ever was convent cell ; but for the girl I must make broader conditions, other associations.   She must have life, and by-and-by when she wearies of it, let her come back if she will ; I know the doors would never be shut against her while you lived."

"No, nor after I am gone.   No child that ever came to us has been to the hearts of the Community what Gretta has been.   There is no one of us who does not love her, and to me," he said, with a little falter in his placid tones, "her coming has been like giving back to my old age the sweet little girl I lost so long ago.   Yes, so long as the home is here, there will always be a place for Gretta and for thee."

"And you will believe," she added, with an effort, for it grew harder and harder for her to utter any emotion of her heart, "you will believe that I do feel deeply all it has been to us to have this shelter all these years, and you will believe I am not ungrateful; that I go for Gretta's sake and not my own?"

"I believe it," he said, still sadly, "and yet I wish that for a few years longer she might have stayed with us. I would have her go out into the world, if she must, after she was rooted and grounded in faith, after she had learned to be guided by the Spirit of truth into all truth."

"I think she is a good child and a true," answered Katharine, flushing.

"Thee is right, friend, but thee must bear with me a little. Good and true she is by nature. I knew her father. He was indeed a man of God, and her grandfather, Senator Wild, a stanch and noble soul." Katharine started, and it was well that the shadows hid her face; he had never before betrayed by any look that he knew the family from which she came. "And I knew thy father too, Mrs. Gray; we were classmates in college, and when thee and thy sister were wee girlies I have held thee on my knee, for I was out in the world then. Of course, I know all the valley people hereabouts for miles, and I knew when Mrs. Wild died, and I drove over to the church that morning not dreaming her little one would ever claim my care. I felt in Chicago that God would send thee to me if I could serve thee; and he did. Thee could not trust me with thy own sorrow, but I know it has been great indeed. Let me tell thee mine:

"Thy father chose the ministry, Katharine—the

Lord's own work, and I chose my own work and my own way. I won money—thy father won souls; I lived to see my child follow her way as I had followed mine. She died in deepest trouble. She had lived a life without a governing principle of duty or conscience. It was your father and your mother who stood by her in her last hours, and heard her repentant words, and brought her message of love to me. They knew God. They knew how to strengthen and console. I was reaping the whirlwind, and that child was all that was left to me. When she died I was done with life; I chose seclusion, humility, service to the will of God at last, with quiet, silent work for his children. Dear friend, it has given me peace, and if I know thy heart thee will find peace nowhere else. I would have kept thee for thy father's sake, and given thee my poor dead daughter's place. I know that Eunice, thy sister, would have thee rear her child to live the life of humble, patient service to God and man. Take her away, but see to it that in all thou seekest for her and would give her, there shall be the presence and the power of God. All else thee will find, nay, thee has found already, changes to ashes on the lips, is worse than weak, is wicked. But 'the Lord thy God in the midst of thee is mighty'; strength, and honor, and glory, and peace are where he is, my child."

Katharine's head was bowed against the window-pane and her eyes shone through a heavy mist of tears. When she choked down the sobs in her throat and turned to tell him "good night," the dear old man was gone. As he passed along the corridor a light step made him pause, and in the

darkness a young girl came close to him, and slipping her hand into his, said hurriedly:

"I was coming to see why auntie was so late. I
have all the boxes packed, and I heard you talking
and I could not help hearing your dear, kind words
about me, and—I must say it—never mind just
this once whether it is proper or not, I must say it,
I love you all so much here, it is the only home I
know. I don't want to go to Washington or anywhere, but if I must go, I want you, dear father, to
know that I mean to be—" her voice broke and
she added softly, "what you told auntie you wanted
me to be; I mean to be good, oh, so good. I know
what you meant by the truth, and being led by the
Spirit, and the life I want is the life 'with God in
the midst.'"

"Bless thee, my child, bless thee," said the old
man, fervently. "Take that as thy motto, 'The
Lord thy God in the midst of thee is mighty,' not
only in the midst of thy affairs, though thee must see
to it that he is there, but in the midst of thee, in
thy life, in thy love, in thee," and he opened his
arms as if he would fold her to his heart, and then
laid his trembling hand upon her head and passed
on. And upstairs, in the little whitewashed room
from whose window she could see the waving locust
branches and the silent stars, the girl knelt and
prayed that in the new life to which she was going
she might be very good. And her mother, a part
of whose punishment it was that she should never
hear those sweet lips call her mother, pausing
silently at the door, felt as if around her child had
been drawn a circle of light across which she could

not pass to gather her close to her hungry, lonely heart.

As Katharine stood there in the dim light, she was again what she had been when she married Robert Gray, a stately and beautiful woman. In the quiet of these years the body had claimed again its birthright of beauty and strength. The traces of the time of exhausting toil, the wasted figure, were gone. The inward fight gave the face great sensitiveness and reserve and pride; but it became her well, and she looked well-equipped in face and bearing to meet the new, strange world into which on the morrow she would go with her beautiful child.

CHAPTER XI

STRANGE thoughts that neither could have told the other stirred the hearts of both mother and daughter as they set forth with abundant blessings and every comfort that could be crowded upon them on the morning of a radiant day. The elder went with them to the station, but his words were few and sad. With the exception of her rare visits to Walden, visits in which Mr. Morse, the business man, found her careful, accurate, and frugal, the years had been those of almost absolute isolation from the world. Communication with Mrs. Maitland had never been entirely interrupted; and the letters on one side were always full of eager expectation of the day when Gretta should be transferred to the Washington home, and on Katharine's part to minute descriptions of the child, such as would be sure to keep the affectionate interest alive. She had been on to confer with Mrs. Maitland several times, and on one occasion, one only, she took Gretta to Washington, and passed a a few days in the beautiful old home when the little girl was at just the age to have forgotten her babyhood and had so changed that Deborah could not, by any chance, suspect she was not getting back her fond old heart's desire.

From this visit Mrs. Maitland was confirmed in her previous opinion that the child was in excellent care, and that it was better for her to be, during childhood, under the quiet, steady influence of this reticent, but intelligent and well-bred woman, than to be spoiled by Deborah's worshipful indulgence and excess of devotion. Satisfied with the promise of future possession, and finding her health greatly impaired, Mrs. Maitland went abroad for some years, and it was the fact of her return that had decided Katharine upon a change of home.

In all these years Gretta's education had not been altogether neglected. She had all that her mother could give supplemented by all that could be gathered from the school and the teacher. And when Katharine wanted more, and explained to those in authority that she must go away and seek elsewhere what could not be provided there, the good elder himself became the girl's tutor and set the tasks which mother and daughter together studied and read, until their knowledge was far beyond the Community standard of woman's need. But for the fact that the entire Community was a unit in the feeling that Gretta was to be denied nothing, the good elder would have found his self-imposed task difficult, but they did not criticise too severely the man who so ably represented them before the world, whose learning and ability and wealth had been freely used in their behalf. Neither did they desire to lose the pet of the people, the one child who had made her place in every heart. And the lack of companionship in study was supplied by the mother, whose life was never free from the haunting, jealous fear of everything that could make a barrier between her daughter and herself. Therefore she insisted upon solving every problem, writing every exercise, studying every Greek root or Latin conjugation, analyzing every plant, in short, striving to think the thoughts that filled the mind of the young and eager girl.

It was therefore no rude or ignorant creature who lifted her eager face for Madame Maitland's kiss, but a maiden so bright, so vivacious and yet gentle, so truly kind in the sweet, simple courtesy of her Community manners; so alive to new impressions and to new kindness that the old heart rested in her without misgiving of any kind. "Just a new blessing sent of God," Madame Maitland said to Deborah, "to make up for all we have lost—a gentle, gracious little woman with the merry heart of a child."

Too wise to expect that the Community life would not be talked over by Gretta, her mother had taken the first opportunity to speak of it to Mrs. Maitland.

"Before you went away you may remember that you agreed with me that a simple country home would be best for Gretta, and I did not like it to be in the old Walden parsonage. That house I gave over for a term of years to Mr. Morse, the lawyer, who always had charge of my sister's and my father's affairs, and in whose hands I have left them ever since. We could have lived there, but it seemed to me wiser to escape the village associations and companionships. I preferred to have Gretta wait to form friendships till she could see more than one type of being and become wise enough to choose for herself.   So I have been staying with her at the Loriston Community, whose leader, Eli Osborn, is my father's early friend.   He is a scholar and a gentleman, and," she added, gently, "a Christian, and he has been our teacher and our friend."   And so reasonable did all this sound that the dear old lady's involuntary criticism was changed to wondering admiration at the wisdom and foresight that had been shown in this unusual choice of a home.

"You have certainly preserved her from all the dangers of too familiar association with other young people," she said, gently.   "Whatever the peculiar views of this strange sect it is evident that they teach the regulation of life by principle, and I know you will agree with me, Mrs. Gray, that religious principle, allegiance to right, is the only foundation on which any life should rest."   She did not pause to note that Katharine made no answer.   If she had answered, and truly, she would have given unqualified assent.   She did believe it, alas !   She did know that all the misery her own life had known had been the result of lack of principle in herself or in others, and yet——

"There are some disadvantages," the gentle voice went on, "however, in too great separation from other lives.   I should think well of bringing Gretta as soon as possible now into every-day contact with other phases of life."

"I have been thinking of school for her," answered Katharine, "possibly some school in Washington."

"Not here," answered Madame Maitland, quickly ; "not the home life, and the social life, and the school life all at once. If I kept her here I should want her so much of the time for myself and there are so many friends, young and old, with whom to share her youth and beauty, that she could not give her mind to books. I love her so dearly already that I must resist my temptation to be selfish. She seems a precious treasure sent me out of the wreck of the past. And I think she loves me too. We seemed to understand each other at once," she added, turning her sweet, aged face trustfully toward Mrs. Gray's, "and she opened her heart to me about her thoughts of life and of God. She said she could not see how any one could live without the consciousness of him in the very midst of every day's work or pleasure. It made me, as I am sure it does you, very happy to feel that, young as she is, she had found the blessed secret of content."

"So you think a school at a distance will be best for her?" asked Katharine, in a voice so sad that Madame Maitland answered, with a smile:

"Ah, that thought pains you! If she stayed here, you would, at least I hope you would, stay with her. If at school, perhaps you could not ; and if the idea of letting her go is painful to me, what must it to be to you who have had her all these years?" and the kind-hearted old lady laid her white, thin hand gently on Katharine's arm. Under the unaccustomed touch of real tenderness and sympathy hot tears rushed to her eyes. For one wild moment the poor heart beat painfully against the bars of its prison house of deceit, and longed to utter, yea, even to cry aloud the truth, for well she knew that nothing but the truth could ever bring her peace. Her throat throbbed painfully, she longed to throw herself on her knees here in the twilight of the dying day, and put her head on this dear saint's lap and tell her everything. True, it would be like death to her to live apart from the face and voice she loved, yet infinitely more cruel was the torturing thought, always recurring, always thrusting itself upon her in the moments when she was most at rest, that this difference in character and in motive was going to force them inevitably apart. The girl loved truth—she herself was living a daily lie. The girl loved God—she was continually defying him. The girl, dwelling in him and he in her—she, outside in a cold world of her own, taking her own will and way. The girl was surely coming in touch with other hearts that knew and loved him too—she was more and more shrinking back into isolation and loss. Surely after all she had suffered this was too much to bear. Strange that her own inherited, innate love of the truth, always rising and chiding and pleading, should be so hard to die! For the moment the child in her, long smothered and denied, pleaded to pour her heart out into this aged mother-heart, and yet, she withdrew her trembling hands and clasped them tightly in her lap, and choked down the sobs and talked quietly about different schools and about her own chance of living in or near whatever school should be chosen, so as to make certain that no day might pass without a sight of her idol's shining face.

And when a few months later Gretta became one of the hundred girls at the beautiful institution of Castleton, within three hours distance from Wildholm,

Katharine went with her, and finding a home in the family of one of the professors who lived with his mother in a charming little house within convenient distance from the college, she gave herself to study of everything that Gretta was to learn, and was able to keep in touch with her life in so far as books could make a common meeting ground. Haunted always by the cruel fear of inward separation, she watched Gretta's every mood, supplied her every need, and never, by any chance, allowed her to become accustomed to living without her.

Gretta's daily visit during the hour of recreation was never omitted, and was always made delightful to as many classmates as Gretta liked to bring. Mrs. Gray was never anything but the rather stately well-bred lady of whose tender care any young girl might be proud, and more than one bright young student, brought in contact with Mrs. Gray, wished that she had aunt or mother who cared as much for her progress as Katharine seemed to care for that of her niece. And Katharine, who had not at first much heart for the other girls, yet became in time comforter in homesickness, the nurse in headaches and heartaches, the helper in difficult lessons, strengthening herself with her own child by making a place in her own life for all that Gretta brought or for which she seemed to care.

And, strange as it might seem, this new atmosphere brought to the silent, lonely woman, hitherto so engrossed in her own cares as to have no room for the outside world, a new life of the intellect of which in her youth she never even dreamed. She could not keep pace intellectually with a young girl's processes of training and not go in reality far beyond them. She could not live a life among books in an atmosphere of growing thought and not find her own thought-world widening. So self-centered and concentrated had been her existence at Loriston, so repulsive her previous contact with human beings, that the reaction in favor of seeing and knowing people was naturally slow. In the past, if she could but have her own child and be let alone in the enjoyment of her possession, it was all she had asked; but now as she accepted the thought that her child's life was to be in a world of living women and men, she resolved not to be left outside, and was astonished to find that, gradually she was becoming glad to be there, and finding pleasure in things she had at first cared for only because her daughter cared.

She had lived too subtly and intensely herself not to be able to feel her way to the real spring and secret of motive in many other lives, and human nature as she found it, if it failed to arouse her pity, did not escape her scorn. And what seemed even more surprising, considering her past deadness to all that appealed to sympathy, pity was often more alive and active than contempt. She lived amid uplifting associations. Madame Maitland's life was nobleness itself. Every one trusted her, and, strange as it may seem, the better side of Katharine's nature vibrated in response. She had felt herself debarred by the inward tragedy of her own existence from the every-day experiences of her kind. Now, to her surprise, she found a warm human element of fellowship that, while it did not make her less a sinner, made her shrink from the loneliness of sin. She found she was not only interested in knowing what people were on the inside, but she was interested in knowing what had made them as they were, and strangest thing of all, in what could make them better. For herself, she knew what had made her as she was. She could make a cruel and cold analysis of temperament, tendency, and circumstance, and follow, step by step, a pitiless process of deterioration that revealed to her how she came to be the woman she then was. Now she found herself doing the same with other people, with a strange addition of an element of charity and tolerance that never for a moment had she applied to herself. She was a sinner, but never yet, by one hair's breadth, did she narrow the sin, in her own view, to a mistake or a misfortune or another's fault. She met it squarely as a sin, her own determined and deliberate sin, and however strong at times might be her impulse to let her own heart break, if so she could rid it of its awful secret, yet she knew for her child's sake, unless she would doubly blight her young life, she must go on and on. There was literally no " place for repentance " anywhere down the long vista of coming years, unless indeed Gretta should go before her out of life; and at this thought always came back all that made her hard and unrepentant and bitter to all the world.

Yet she did not want to be bitter any more; she was aweary of her isolation and of herself. For her all must just go on as now, but for the others— those in error and those in trouble, those for whom life in any particular could be made better—she felt this new, strange softening of heart that would have worked for them; and though she could not pray for them, in her fervent eagerness to have them helped was glad when others prayed. She would even have been glad if by giving herself and her time, all except that needed by Gretta, she might feel that she too was diminishing by ever so little the world's misery and guilt; yet, if some vague, half-formed notion of atonement was at the bottom of her desire, she had not recognized or formulated it as a motive for the change.

In the vacations they were always claimed at Wildholm, and at all other intervals when she could bring herself to be absent from Gretta she yielded to Madame Maitland's pleading that she should spend the time with her. The sweet woman was gradually growing less active, but the eager mind and loving heart could never be robbed of youth. Realizing her infirmities, she had come to look to Katharine as the natural sharer of all her loving interest and the one to carry out her wishes concerning Gretta's future life. And Katharine would have been less than woman if she had not loved her; and in her presence the hardness and bitterness slipped more and more into the background, and the nobler side of the woman pleaded for outlet and expression.

They made a lovely picture one vacation morning as they sat on the veranda—Madame Maitland, her gray hair crowned with the soft, white muslin that Debby liked to fashion into a cap; and Katharine, the soft folds of whose attire of Quaker gray always harmonized with her reserve and gentle dignity of bearing ; and Gretta, flushed from the exercise of loading her arms with roses, her cheeks as bright as the flowers themselves, resting on the steps at Madame Maitland's feet. Debby, in bright red kerchief and turban was on one side, and Beppo, a great, shaggy Newfoundland dog, who stayed as close to Gretta as did Deborah whenever she was at home, was lying at her feet.

"It is so delightful to be here again, auntie," said Gretta, tossing a cluster of the scarlet roses on Madame Maitland's lap.

" Why do you not say delightful to be home again; isn't this home ?"

"Indeed it is, the only real home I ever knew."

" I want you to think of it as home, both of you," said the old lady, seeing the shadow on Katharine's face ; " I want it to be real home henceforth to you both. There's no one else to care for it when I am gone. It will all come to Gretta, and she will remember that I expect her auntie to share it, she has been so good to my own little girl," and she passed her hand lovingly over Gretta's face which rested against her knee.

" She is my little girl too, Madame Maitland," said Katharine, flushing.

" Yes, I know you are even nearer of kin than I am, but really her father was more like my son than my nephew. I was mother to him after his own mother died, and so she seems like my own little granddaughter. And we are very close too, are we not, darling ?" she asked, lifting Gretta's face until the smiling eyes looked into her own.

"The very closest, dear grandmamma," said Gretta, laughing back into her face. "I used to wish at Loriston, when I watched the sweet, placid faces of the white-haired women, that my grandmothers had lived till I knew them, though I don't believe I would have loved them or dared to tell them all my naughty ways as I do you," and she kissed and fondled the thin hand that lay against her cheek.

"I was about saying, dear friend," the old lady went on, as if her mind was too full to pay much heed to caresses, "that I want you to see to it when I am gone that this house is a true Christian home. I believe such homes are to be our country's salvation, and the increasing lack of them is our greatest danger. Gretta is young and she might not realize its importance as you will, but this has always been a Christian home, and I wish it to continue to be so. And, dear Mrs. Gray, Gretta may not care to live here, but whatever or whoever else goes, you must feel it is your home always. Do you hear, Gretta," she added, as Katharine made no reply. "You will not need, unless you prefer it, to make this house your home. There will be enough, with what will come to you from your father and from me for you to make your home where you will; but in case you should not choose this house, I want it to be given for some good work, and I want your aunt to keep a home for herself here whenever she chooses to come."

"Should that good work be for women?" asked Katharine.

"Yes, and not yes. For women or for men. I

have not separated them in my thought of human needs. There will be time to think it out I trust, for it may be years before I go. I am watching carefully the changes that are coming in women's opportunities for usefulness. Some of the so-called " movements " my heart has longed and prayed to see. They come too late for me, but so far as they mean good, that is, good-will to man, I want to see them prosper. I don't believe they can prosper except on one foundation."

" Do you believe then, that no good is done outside the church ? " asked Katharine, a tinge of her old bitterness creeping into her tone.

" No, no, I would not be so misunderstood. But I do believe that the principles of love and unselfish good-will, the willingness to give one's self for the healing and help of the world, as it was illustrated by the life and emphasized by the death of Christ, is the only spirit that is going to avail in any form of work. When we organize and plan and labor, and leave that spirit out, we might as well leave the good work undone. It lacks the only element of power, the leaven of life. We speak of that spirit as Love. To me it is Immanuel, it is all we have of God with us. You remember the passage that says, 'The Lord thy God in the midst of thee is mighty' ? Well, I have little hope for any life, or any work that has not God in the midst. But," she added, with a gentle half apology in her tone, " I need not make you a sermon, I am sure you would feel as I do about the home ; yet——" she paused and the eyes sought Katharine's with a little anxious and troubled question in their depths.

"I am sure we do feel every bit as you do," said Gretta, impulsively springing up to kiss the sweet old face; "but I don't believe I would ever be good like you and want to give the home up. We couldn't bear not to have it for our very own selves, could we, Debby? Yet," catching the black eyes fixed on her with their usual adoring gaze, "we couldn't, couldn't stay in it without the sweetest of grand-mammas; I can't even bear to hear about that for a moment," she added. "Come, Debby, come, Beppo, let's go for more flowers," and the girl hurried away to hide the swift-coming tears.

"The dear child is so happy now she cannot bear the thought that any change can come," said Mrs. Gray.

"And yet I must tell her or I must tell you," pleaded Madame Maitland, "though I shrink from saddening either of you. My remaining years cannot be many, and there is no one but you to carry out my plans."

"What sort of a home had you in mind? I am most glad to hear about it, and I need not tell you most glad to help," said Katharine, her eyes still fixed upon the ground.

"I wish, first of all, the home to be used by Gretta, if she wishes, and I shall leave, aside from her portion, a sum sufficient to support it from year to year. But if she does not want it, I do not wish it made an institution for any one class of men, women, or children—not a home for old men, or old women, or inebriates, or a hospital, or an asylum for any class; but a Christian home, for a man or a woman, old or young, or for little children; a refuge for such a time as each may need it; a resting-place where weakened souls or bodies may be brought back into conditions of life and service, or where young forces may be preserved and strengthened and trained. It should be a home—not simply a place for people to come to die in. Life ought to go out from it in the person of every inmate, to bless and purify the world. It may seem a foolish and impracticable plan, and doubtless would be thought so by a Board of trustees, but I have always been bringing home one and another of the stricken in body and soul, and the house has rarely been without the presence of several friends who have found it a refuge and rest. They are my 'friends' all the same, whether outwardly strangers or not. I want this home to go on, with the understanding that all who come shall be made to know what a Christian home is like."

"And you will arrange for Gretta to do this work? You will leave it a trust to her?"

"To her or to you. I do not like to put upon her what might be a burden of care, but I would leave it to you, if you would consent to carry the care for her. If otherwise, it might be better to separate it from the rest of the estate, and put it in the hands of a Board of managers. Frankly I prefer to leave it to an individual whom I can trust. In any event," she went on, "I hope the dear old place will be your home, Mrs. Gray. You have no ties closer than those which bind you to Gretta, though," her voice softened, "I learned from Deborah that once you lost a little girl." Katharine's head sank lower. "Forgive me," said the tender old voice, "I have never dared touch that sorrow and I will not now"; the lowered head suddenly lifted, Katharine was very pale and a defiant bitterness rang in her tone as she said :

"There is nothing else in the wide world so near or dear to me as my own Gretta."

"Then you will stay and let me plan as I proposed?   I am only asking you to make for some of God's suffering or forsaken ones a home where they would know he is loved and honored—a home with 'God in the midst.'"   But Katharine's face was lowered from sight again, and the old thin hand just touched it pityingly as she said :

"I am sorry I hurt an unhealed wound, my dear; you must forgive me.   God, you see, is entrusting you with other sore hearts.   If you accept, as I am sure you do, his trust, be very sure he will not leave your own uncomforted."   Again the white, anguished face was lifted; she tried to speak but the aged saint bent down and kissed the quivering lips. "Don't try to talk, dear," she whispered, "I understand.   I trust you with the work; I have seen you trusted with your sister's child and know you would be true to any trust," and she passed within doors leaving the kiss that seemed to her the sign of a solemn compact to serve the suffering children of God; and seemed to Katharine, tempted and tortured, like a kiss of betrayal that marked a depth of dishonor and deceit such as her soul had never touched before.

Katharine did not appear at dinner; she was not well and submitted passively in her darkened room to Gretta's caresses and loving efforts to relieve the throbbing head. In the morning she was as usual but for a deepened pallor of cheek and lip, yet Deborah told her mistress:

"I done scared silly, Miss Marion. Mrs. Gray she jest walk, walk all night long dat back veranda on de ole west wing. She walk, and wring her hands, and cry jest like when Gretta's mother died. I hear de po' thing a moanin' and a moanin', and I steal roun' and sees her jest out de do'. She done stay dar mos' all night, miss. I d'clare, Miss Marion, I'se mighty scared to fotch her in and I'se mighty scared to leave her out."

"Don't mind it, Debby," said Madame Maitland, who minded it very much, however, herself. "I am afraid I grieved her by speaking of her poor little dead child."

"Sho' nuff, Miss Marion. She moighty nice, Miss Gray, but she done take on awful inside her body and bones; I do believe she neber done mournin' 'bout dat dead and gone chile."

"Yes, she must have had a great sorrow, and we must do all we can to help her to bear or to forget it."

"Lors, Miss Marion, she won't let me do nuffin. I's tried to wait on her good. 'Pears like she mos' times don't want me roun'. Sho' nuff, we all's been good to her. She kep' our baby and love it more'n sufficient for two chillen. She greedy 'bout her, jes' reg'lar mother greed. I has hard work to wait on Miss Gretta. Her aunt do it all, or make Gretta do for herself. No way to fotch young miss up in dis fambly while Debby got legs to go and hands to work," and suddenly drawing nearer, her black eyes glittering, and glancing furtively around as if she feared she might be overheard, she went on: "When I see how she look sometimes when Miss Gretta's lovin' you, or foolin' roun' me, I's mighty scared. I done believe she kinder conjure Miss Gretta ever since she get her. She boun' to have dat chile all to herself and she don't nebber say 'de Lawd willin',' she don't. She boun' to hev her! She send me off wheder or no and break my heart. She fotch her up all alone on dat crazy farm. She try make Gretta be shet up like her, nebber tell nuffin. 'Pears like she conjure her till she make dat baby over jest like her is herself. Whatever else make dem blue eyes our baby had get brown like Miss Gray's? What make dat little nose dat had little hump jes' like Massa Larry's get straight like Miss Gray's? I done tell you, Miss Marion, I's stedied on it, and stedied on it, and believe dar's a way if we human folks only gits it by de handle, to git eberyt'ing we want. Its all in lovin', Miss Marion. Didn't ole miss love Massa Larry into de kingdom? and didn't dis yer aunt jest git dat baby by lovin' her so much? She jest boun' to hev her! Couldn't nuffin stop her, and now she jest lovin' her into thinkin' same as her and actin' jest same, walkin' jest same, and talkin' and lookin' jest like her too. She done los' de fambly nose, and I tell you, Miss Marion, Miss Gray she done jest love de fambly nose right off dat precious chile."

"But, Deborah, how foolish! Babies' eyes often darken from blue to brown, and no one can prophesy from their faces how they will look when older."

"Dunno 'bout prophesyin', Miss Marion, but

eberybody can reckon, and I's reckoned how de Wild fambly gwine look and gwine act when dey don't nobody meddle wid dere noses or dere souls. And I'm dat sho' Miss Gretta's been conjured. Miss Gray she jis got her own self twisted all in and out dar 'mongst dat chile's idees. Idees dey's like de measles or de ragin' red rash; when dey breaks out dey shows what kind er pisen was bottled up inside de chile."

"Stop, stop, Deborah! I cannot hear you talk so. Whatever is like Mrs. Gray in Gretta is like her own mother; and she could not be sweeter to me if she were altogether like the Wilds. I did not know you kept such thoughts in your heart."

"She done send me away from Massa Larry's baby, and my heart done broke. I don' never git over it, miss."

"But think, Deborah; if she had not sent you back, who would have cared for me? And she has done better by Gretta than we could have done, and now you have her back again."

"I knows, I knows," said Debby, throwing herself on her knees by Mrs. Maitland's sofa. "I's bad, Miss Marion, I is wicked sho', but I's prayed fo' de Lawd. But dat Miss Gray she don't love Debby, and Gretta she don't love me like de fambly always did; and if you's gone, Miss Marion, dey two won't want me roun'. I feels it in my bones; I knows it. I won't be no 'count. Now if Miss Gray she let me wait on Miss Gretta, I get her so she love ole Debby like Massa Larry did. And mebby I get back de Wild look out'n dat chile's eyes, 'cos I's sho' its de love make de looks ebery time, miss."

"Then we will keep on loving her with all our hearts, Debby, for you know there must never be anything but love in this home. You remember once upon a time the dear Lord came with his arms open, and called his children to come and rest on his heart, and they did not understand how much he loved them, and they did not come, and did not know how his heart ached to do loving things for them. When it seems as if Gretta didn't know or seem to feel your love for her, I want you to try to remember him." And the poor old, aching heart just sobbed out its pain, while a gentle, white hand stroked the black one, till ashamed of her weakness Debby rose and stole away, comforted as we all are comforted by the ministry of love. Pausing a minute at the door, hiding her eyes in her apron like a child penitent and ashamed, she said:

"Don't you be noways unheartened 'bout old Debby, Miss Marion; you's tried and tried to make me good, now I's boun' to be good. I's gwine love eberybody, I's gwine love Miss Gray till she jest divide our baby and give me back my share."

CHAPTER XII

GRADUALLY increasing feebleness marked the next two years for Mrs. Maitland, and they were marked also by a constant strengthening of Mrs. Gray's position in the dear old lady's heart and home. These were also Gretta's last years of school life, interrupted now and then by the alarming attacks that characterized the illness of the aged friend who, as her activity diminished, clung more and more dependently to these two who had come to fill the place of all the dear ones lost before.

Meantime Mrs. Gray had continued to live near, or at times for weeks together quite within, the school-family of one hundred girls at Castleton until she became a recognized factor, and without specific responsibility, to share the influence of the many instructors who guarded and guided the students with a love and wisdom not always found in institutional life.

Whenever Gretta was summoned home Katharine went also, but each time she lingered longer, for though Mrs. Maitland scrupulously avoided making any selfish claim, it became more and more evident that she looked upon Katharine as quite the natural sharer of her life.

As for Gretta, her eager young mind and heart stirred by constant contact with Mrs. Maitland, who held her steadily to the Christian standard of the true woman, stimulated by inspiring teachers, themselves all alive to the noblest that woman might be or do, with companions and friends, responsive as herself to the stimulation of the student atmosphere, and, last of all, with Katharine urging her on, and keeping pace with her in a kind of fever of desire to know, it was not strange that she came to feel that the college course was the only one that could ever satisfy or properly fit her for life.

But when the time for decision came, and she knew it meant still more years away from Mrs. Maitland, she showed in this, her first decision for herself, the quality and fiber of her nature. She settled it once for all, in the quiet night-time, in the dear room set apart as her special home-nest, and held ready for her, years before she ever came. It was a tower room which Lawrence had occupied in his boyhood, and Debby had left his books, his fishing rods and gun, his dumb-bells, and all the photographs of himself as baby, youth, and man about the walls. It was here that he had knelt one solemn midnight when he laid down his boyish dreams of battles with the world as a soldier or a statesman, and, putting on the whole armor of God, became a soldier of the Cross. It was here that Gretta, home for the Easter holiday with her head and heart full of college plans, had come to lay them all down after one look at a patient, fading face.

Of her great hope that her schooldays might be supplemented by a college course, and of her longing for the utmost and best equipment and training that woman could secure, she had talked rarely, except to Mrs. Maitland, who had sympathized with her desire, but who must, on no account, have it obtruded upon her now. To her mother in these later years, notwithstanding Katharine's persistence in sharing her work and plans, she found it more and more difficult to open her innermost thought, though she constantly blamed herself for the shrink-. ing shyness that, without meaning to do so, kept the best away from such lovingly watchful eyes. Now that this decision was reached it would be easy enough to say to her that she had given up the hope of college, but hard enough to reveal that she had done so only after struggle and earnest prayer. Though she blamed herself often for this unwilling, almost unconscious reticence, she never guessed that Katharine felt it sorely, or suffered when she saw how naturally the nobler side of Gretta's nature turned to Mrs. Maitland, and throve best in the atmosphere of her saintly presence and life.

The subtle, inward separation that made them both avoid any allusions to religious motive or purpose, that passed as reserve in the older and timidity in the younger woman, was a part of Katharine's penalty of pain. And she accepted it and trusted to her love to divine what Gretta could not say. She had too many conflicts herself, to fail to know the signs on Gretta's face as they sat over their breakfast the day after their arrival, with the breath of the waving honeysuckle drifting in at the open window. They made a pleasant home picture, the lovely young girl and Mrs. Gray, whose pale, proud face, and manner of gentle reserve were well suited to the place she held, which had come to be virtually that of mistress in the beautiful home.

Mrs. Maitland was not down. The respectful man-servant, one of those whom Debby said she "fotched up way down Souf," had left the room, and Katharine, watching Gretta's drooping eyes, yet careful to be looking some other way if the lids lifted, said quietly:

"I see you have given up the college plan?"

"Yes, auntie," said the girl, with a smile, "of course after I saw grandmamma I knew it could not be right to go."

"I am not so sure of it," said Katharine. "She is not strong, but then she is not young, and the physician says she may be with us many years. Her danger is in some sudden and violent attack. Without these, and with care, she has another long term of years."

"But if that is true, and she is happier all these years for having me home, I would not go."

"She is happy when you are away, and interested in all you learn or do. She lets the care all come to me now, and——"

"That is another reason for staying. You could not be there and study with me as you have done all the way so far."

"But I could read at home, and we could share it all together afterward. I want you to go, Gretta —I want you to have all, all, all," she added with some excitement, "that the world, the whole wide world can give, for with such a home and health, and so many friends, you can make life whatever you will—can lead the women of the nation if you choose."

"Auntie dear, you often speak like that to me.

Why should one care to lead? It seems to me there are always leaders enough, too many. I would like to be intelligent enough to know what and whom to follow."

Katharine lifted her brows impatiently.

"You would be content to follow?"

"Yes, auntie dear, I would; but you—you were made for a leader. Not a teacher at Castleton could have done with the girls what you could have done in the place of any one of them. You could have led them into any line of thought and life you wished, auntie, and the girls felt it, and the teachers felt it. Once Madame Crozier told me that if you had been free, and grandmamma had not needed you so often, she would have tried to induce you to take some position in the management that would let your influence reach every one of the girls."

"Stop, stop," said Katharine, her strong face contracting with pain. Yet, even in the shame was mingled a triumph—her child was not ashamed, and if life lasted long enough, she should yet be proud of her. She had paid an awful price. Why should she abate one jot or tittle of that which it could bring? For one moment she forgot herself as the cowardly creature who should grovel in very shame, and saw herself only as a heroine wresting from the world that which was her right—that of which she had been wrongfully deprived. " A leader "— why not? She had not been studying the world of women and of work without seeing the lack of leadership and everywhere the blind following the blind. On every hand she saw the impulsive, ill-regulated, undisciplined forces of womanhood rising to battle with the world's sore problems of misery and sin. She saw the spasmodic, the boastful, the showy surface struggles carried on under flaunting flags of personal vanity, upheld by interchanges of flatteries, or cloaked in borrowed raiment. She saw grand endeavors sink, plunging helplessly in sloughs of simple ignorance. She saw aspiration and enthusiasm dying for lack of guidance as to practical purpose and method, and on the other hand, noble work dying for lack of aspiration and enthusiasm.

She followed with keen eyes the threads of personal ambition, the love of prominence, the vanity, the envy, the self-seeking that women went on weaving consciously or unconsciously into their "garments of praise"; and she knew, none better, that every such thread would find its way, soon or late, into the sackcloth that awaited them in the sure coming day of their shame. And yet she kept in her heart a kind of feverish sense that the good she might do with the power she might win could be made to offset, if it could not overcome, the evils that had conquered her. Gretta's words, the comment of the teachers, she knew they were true. Give her her position, the home, the knowledge of affairs, and the needs of the people which the bravest women souls seemed to be gaining, and she would justify by her use of them the means she had taken to gain them all. Like a flash there came upon her the full realization of how much she had secured already. Years of study and books, this lovely home at whose head she seemed more and more to belong, the means that surely would be forthcoming from Mrs. Maitland to further any grand work, and whatever Gretta might gain of influence would also be her own.

It takes long to tell it, it took but one moment—while she sat in quiet dignity at the head of the table watching the young girl's face half hidden by the white plumes of the lilacs that nodded between them—for her soul to pass over a borderland where her sin and thought and hope had all been for love of her child, into a "worse place than the first," a place where her soul no longer shrank back regretfully, but leaped forward to enjoy, for herself and in herself, the fruits of her wrongdoing. "I think you should decide on the college course," she said.

"But I have already decided, Aunt Katharine; I have given it up once for all."

"Then it seems that the woman who could influence 'all the girls,' fails to influence the one she loves the best."

"No, no," said Gretta, eagerly, coming swiftly over to Katharine's side and taking both her hands. For a moment she searched the elder face with troubled, questioning eyes. "The whole thing is in a word, auntie; I love you for wanting me to have every chance, I hate to disappoint you, but I am not very clever. I shall never be a great woman such as you could have made, or such as you really are," she added, with a kiss; "but I·want to be good, auntie, and I don't think a good woman could take four more years out of this precious old life that has given me everything. I am sorry; I shall do my best to learn with you, auntie; I shall study with you all the ways of women's work, and try to

learn all one ought to know in order to do it, in—"
her voice faltered and fell, "in His way, auntie."
Katharine winced. "I don't believe any of our
ways can be so very great or wise or important in
results. I want to find out the ways in which he
would have us deal with all those things if he dwelt
here now, in the midst of them. I can learn so
much of grandmamma, and of you too, auntie."

"We need not talk of it," said Katharine, sadly,
a faint touch of frigidity in the tone; "I have been
thinking that college was what you longed for, I
see I was mistaken," and she gently and coldly
withdrew her hands. A deep flush swept to
Gretta's forehead; should she tell her how much
she longed? Should she tell her of the victory
over her desire won by her bedside in the silent
night? She tried, but the words would not come.

"I do want it, auntie," she whispered, quick tears
springing to her eyes, "but, most of all, I want to do
the thing that is right."

And after that the subject was utterly dropped
between them. The two who were always struggling to draw nearer and nearer together, had
drifted still farther apart.

These Easter days were Gretta's last at home,
and Mrs. Maitland was anxious to fill them with
delight if possible. She was still able to bear the
part of a kindly presiding genius over many of the
gayeties that revived in the old house the hospitality of its earlier time.

Gretta had always been encouraged to bring
home for the holidays her favorite schoolmates or
others who might enjoy the visit, and many a home-

sick girl had written glowing letters to her parents, in the far South or distant West, telling of the lovely welcome of Wildholm, where Mrs. Maitland and Mrs. Gray and Gretta united to fill the house with everything that was attractive and dear to the young.

And no woman better knew what young people would enjoy, or provided pleasures with more lavish hand. Mrs. Maitland had a gift amounting almost to genius for comprehension and sympathy, and, after the first visit, it seemed as if every young person was her guest and a sharer with Gretta of her motherly love and care.

The young girls told her freely about their homesickness and their lessons, their bonnets and their beaux; and the young men, before they knew it, had confided to her their ambitions and aspirations, their love affairs, their struggles, and, in more than one case, their failures and their sins; for the woman's character created an atmosphere in which the noblest things in human nature sprang upward toward the light.

It was a lovely sight, at the end of a day of joyous festivity, to see the group of strong men and lovely maidens that gathered for a few minutes in the twilight, joining like boys and girls of one household, in even-song and prayer.

At this hour came old Debby, in scarlet turban and kerchief, leading the procession of maids, and the gardener and the coachman and old 'Lijah, whose fringe of white wool was like a silver halo about his bald, bronze head.

And at this hour too came the weary and aged

ones, the mothers with little children clinging timidly to their gowns, the people who might be at the time among the homeless or overworked with whom Mrs. Maitland kept the west wing filled. And blending with the soft minor of the dark-faced worshipers, and the timid, quaking notes of those the music of whose hearts was silenced long ago, rose the fresh voices of these young and happy souls who forgot it for a moment if they were not in truth devout.

Some of them knew quite well what it was "to skip church" and college chapel, but this was different somehow, and yet it was only the old-fashioned Southern home, a Christian home that had set "God in the midst," and included him, as a matter of course, in its pleasures as well as its pain.

These home gatherings of young people had always been made the occasion of delightful entertainments, whether for purely social and festive purposes or for the furtherance of some charity dear to Mrs. Maitland, who could not devise ways enough to give all the pleasure her heart desired to the child of her old age. At this time the house was not only well filled with girls, but many of them had brought, by Mrs. Maitland's invitation, a brother or a cousin, or a brother's or a cousin's friend.

The house party was so large that it overflowed even into the old west wing, filling all the vacant rooms though not allowed, even temporarily, to dislodge the favored inmates, whom Mrs. Maitland called "the wayfarers of God." The guests made not only a very merry but a very happy group as the rustle of arrival and greetings over they came together in the parlor before dinner on Easter eve.

"Grandmamma is not able to be with us through dinner," said Gretta, as she passed from group to group; "but she always tries to meet us for prayers in the library," and there the old friends and the new crowded around the woman on whose face neither sorrow, nor care, nor time could quench the love, which is after all the secret of eternal youth.

She sat in the high-backed carved oak chair that her father had used in the Southern home when she was a little child, her white hair indeed a crown of glory, and her kind welcome scarcely less warm for the old friends than for those whom Gretta now brought to her for the first time.

On the outskirts of the group, waiting till Gretta could present her, was a dark, slender girl with a face that was such a strange combination of reserve and pride and tender sweetness as made one inevitably look again to see which she really was of the two women she seemed to be. "It is one face in the shadow, another in the light," said Mrs. Maitland, as her old friend Dr. Moore called her attention to its swift-changing beauty. "I fancy she is the new teacher about whom Gretta has been raving."

"Here she is, grandmamma. This is our dear Miss Graham, who has come to take the place of our old singing teacher who married last term. I am so glad she could escape, and that we can have her here away from all that crowd of schoolgirls."

"And I am glad too, my dear," she said, holding out both hands to Gretta, and including both in her

smile. "If Miss Graham knew how the house had
rung with praises from an enthusiastic girl, she
would hear them echoing from the very walls.
Stay here by me, my child, till after prayers, I want
to make sure you have really come. Gretta feared
you would escape."

"Indeed I have thought of little else since your
lovely invitation," said the girl, dropping into a low
seat almost at Mrs. Maitland's feet. "I only hesitated because——"

"Because what, my dear?" asked the old lady,
softly, for the old butler had laid the open Bible on
her lap, and the company was quietly disposing itself for worship.

"Why I am the youngest teacher at Castleton,
and have been there so few months that I feared
the others might resent my coming for the week,
the whole week, when they are only invited for the
night of the party."

"Ah, my dear, you gave yourself trouble for nothing. It is better to believe that people rejoice with
us than that they envy us."

"But I haven't found that true," said the girl,
her face clouding.

"But in this case it is so. The teachers, in ac-
cepting my invitation, have several of them said
how glad they were that we could have you. We
know them and love them all, but our Gretta seems
to have lost her heart entirely to you."

"You are both so good to me," murmured the
girl, and then her eyes caught the group of servants filing in, and after them the little group of
friends, tidy and silent, who looked as if they might

be the poor relations of the other guests out of one generation farther back. It was such an unusual sight that Miss Graham watched it fascinated. She knew that Mrs. Maitland used a portion of her home for those who would be homeless without it, but this was so strange, this meeting of rich and poor together, that she hardly gave heed to the voice that read on and on, until it ended with :

"'The Lord' thy God in the midst of thee is mighty; he will save, he will rejoice over thee with joy; he will rest in his love, he will joy over thee with singing.'"

Her eyes lifted to meet Gretta's fixed on her with great gratification that she had her here at last near grandmamma, in the very seat at her feet where no one had ever sat save Gretta herself before. She was so happy to have it so for Gretta, who having Mrs. Gray as the companion for her mind and Mrs. Maitland for her heart, had escaped hitherto the intimacies with other girls that sometimes fill a girl's life full to the brim, until the time when it is filled with the one great love of her life.

Suddenly, Gretta too became conscious of the words that fell reverently from Mrs. Maitland's lips : " The Lord thy God in the midst of thee is mighty; he will save, he will rejoice over thee with joy; he will rest in his love."

Why should he not? It was such a glorious thing to love, to have some one to love. Why should not God rest and rejoice when he loved so much? Surely she was rejoicing and resting in her love. Then, all through the brief evening prayer she was asking the same question :

"How could one love and not rejoice?" Just then she heard the voice of Doctor Moore, who had been asked to pray, saying, "For all whom we love, who are in sickness, sorrow, temptation, danger, or sin——"

Why, yes: there was the secret. That changed everything of course, if the one beloved was in sorrow, or pain, or sin. Then how could God rejoice and rest when almost all of those he loved were in one trouble or another? A little thankful thrill went through her heart: "Her own dear grandmamma was surely looking better, and auntie and this new friend, Margaret Graham, were neither of them in sore trouble." These were the three she loved most, and all was well with them. She could both rest and rejoice in her love. There was no time to question whether he, the God she tried to love with all her heart, could find her so free from evil and pain that he could have joy in his love before the prayer was at an end.

They were singing now, and Miss Graham's voice, clear and sweet, was soaring away up and out, and the other voices all seemed to rest and float upward upon it, as if it were a winged thing that could bear their praises to the very gate of heaven.

As they passed out to dinner Gretta had the comfort of seeing more than one young man glance at Miss Graham as if he were glad of the good fortune that brought him within sound of her voice.

It had not fallen to one of these youths to take her out, however; but to Dr. Moore, a friend of Mrs. Maitland, a physician already well known among scientists as a specialist in diseases of the brain and nervous system.

Mrs. Maitland had seen much of him in her recent years abroad while he was still studying in the hospitals in Paris and Germany. On one occasion she believed his prompt and devoted attention and rapid and exhausting journey to come to her had saved her in an illness that had overtaken her in Rome. She still loved to call him "my doctor," and no matter how hurried his trips to Washington, he never left without spending some time with her. Now he had come to remain, and Mrs. Maitland claimed him whenever there was respite from his always engrossing work, as one she had come to know and to trust, as she felt sure everybody must who understood the heart that revealed itself in face and voice and touch.

Broad-shouldered, long-limbed, his dark hair tossed back loosely in German fashion, he was a contrast to the slender youths around the board, and made them seem like boys. With Miss Graham, who had not been long home from musical studies in Germany, he was soon over the water, telling her of some of the strange psychological cases that had interested him in his student life, and had led him to choose as special studies diseases of the brain and nerves.

"But I must be forgiven for professional talk," he said, turning to Mrs. Gray; "the fact that the subject becomes absorbing makes no excuse for its intrusion."

"Nothing could be more interesting," said Miss Graham, who had been listening intently. "What were you saying of a case you had just brought to Washington?" she added, and thus encouraged he went on:

"I was saying that Mrs. Maitland had become much interested in a case I discovered in a Western hospital. I was talking to her about it when I was on here last, and she told me I might bring the patient here. I wanted to try change of air and scene, and to see if they would produce any mental change. I brought the poor thing on with me, and she is comfortably asleep by this time in that blessed old west wing."

"A woman?" asked Mrs. Gray, with interest.

"Yes, a little white, thin woman with a gentle face, and such lovely, longing eyes as make one's heart ache. We arrived this evening, and the west wing nurse put her to bed; and after a rest, as she seemed none the worse for the journey and I wanted to see the effect of new faces upon her, I let her come down to prayers."

"She is not insane I hope?" asked Mrs. Gray, "though really I do not know as Mrs. Maitland would hesitate, if she thought the poor thing needed a home, to turn the west wing into an asylum."

"Oh, no," said the doctor gently, but with a long, slow, puzzled look at Mrs. Gray, "I am sure she could be trusted not to let her goodness overcome her judgment; but I should be surely inexcusable if I let any temptation of that sort come in her way." Katharine changed color slightly, but he went on as if he did not see. "She suffered from a blow on the head that would naturally have resulted in paralysis of the nerves of motion. It did not; but she was unconscious for days, and when she came to herself everything seemed wiped out of her mind between her early womanhood and the time of her accident, and she has remained almost silent ever since, though the organs of speech are not in the least impaired.

"She recalls her child, her marriage, her husband's death, will talk to or about children, but when you repeat the very names she uses they do not seem to convey any meaning to her mind, and she does not seem to know whether people we bring to her are the same she has been talking of and calling for herself."

"Poor thing! how could she be cared for?" asked Margaret, her sympathy making her dark face radiant.

"She has been kept on and on in the hospital; has made a lovely nurse for little children. A friend of mine who studied with me abroad was in charge there, and he wanted me to see her. I want to leave her here and see what effect new impressions will produce upon her brain."

"You will go away and leave her?" asked Mrs. Gray.

"Yes, but only for a few days. When I return I hope to remain in Washington permanently. I count myself happy to have struck this holiday time," he said. "In a life like mine that constantly sees suffering in one form or another, one almost forgets the world is not old and all awry. It does one good to see people young and happy and gay. Miss Gretta has promised me another gallop over the hills, and Mrs. Maitland says I may come often and bring a friend of mine, another fellow who works too hard and plays too little, to see if we cannot grow young again, seeing how festive you all will be at the party she tells me she will give next week. By the way, is this to be Miss Gretta's introduction into the social life of Washington?"

"Not at all," said Mrs. Gray, promptly. "Gretta is still in school, and will, I trust, decide on some years yet in college."

Harold Moore glanced at her as she sat at the table dividing her merry words and smiles between two youths with close cropped heads and the highest of collars and the latest cut of evening attire.

"She looks too good to waste herself on books and boys," he added under his breath. "I really know of but one man in the world who is worthy of a girl like that, and that's the friend I am going to bring to her *festa*."

"It is not her *festa*, though Mrs. Maitland has always made her holidays lovely for Gretta. This year, I think, doctor," she added in a lower tone, "that she feared she might not be here in the autumn at the proper time for introducing Gretta to her friends. I think she constantly measures her own strength to see how long she can make it last. She has not said it, but I can tell by the character of the invitations that she means Gretta to meet many of her old friends at the same time that she gives her the old pleasant holiday time with her companions. The party occurs upon her own birthday."

"Ah, indeed?" he said with an air of extreme

interest. "I should be sorry to have Mrs. Maitland come to limit her stay in her own mind. I have seen her a good deal in illness, and I hope and believe she has many years of life. God grant it, surely," he added, fervently, "for the sake of this suffering world. It does not hold another like her !"

CHAPTER XIII

THE Easter was a radiant day. After the morning service came the old-fashioned midday dinner. The afternoon was warm enough for tea to be served on the broad western veranda. Through the trees could be seen a gleam of the distant river and the towers and domes of the city, aglow in the evening sun. This veranda, partially enclosed by glass, was Mrs. Maitland's favorite resting-place, and here they gathered once more after the tea service was removed, for evening prayer. Again Harold Moore was asked to conduct the service, and again Miss Graham's voice led the singing, which no one seemed willing should cease. Hymn after hymn floated out upon the air, while the sunset deepened into twilight, until, led by Mrs. Maitland, one after another announced his or her favorite hymn, and there drifted out upon the night the old familiar plantation strains which Debby loved, followed by " Rock of Ages," " Jesus, Lover of My Soul," and ending after an hour that was verily one of peace, with " Lead, kindly Light! amid the encircling gloom."

And all the while there sat in the shadow of one of the great white pillars, among the friends who had come in from the west wing, a little white, thin woman, with hungry, longing eyes, that watched Mrs. Maitland's face, as if she saw in its large lovingness some likeness to the ideal of the Mother of Sorrows, which she always carried in her heart. Through her thin fingers slipped nervously all the time the beads of her rosary, and her lips murmured, as if she were beseeching all the saints in turn to forgive her for being so peaceful and so at rest in the heart of this Protestant home.

When she came in she had separated herself from the other women, and had taken a seat as close to Doctor Moore as possible, looking up confidingly into his face, as if she saw there assurance of protection and strength. His eyes kept kindly watch upon her, when he could take them from the face of the singer, on whose voice seemed to be floating out the religious fervor and feeling concerning which his lips, though not his life, were dumb.

His mind was conscious of a threefold process, one part of which watched and enjoyed with a new and eager delight the face and voice of the singer, while the strong religious life that was at the basis of his almost limitless goodness to everything that suffered, found keen enjoyment in this simple mode of musical worship; and the professional side of the man was yet conscious of watching all the while the effect of the hour and the change upon the withered little woman by his side.

As the group broke up, and a murmur of pleasant talk began to fill the place, the servants and the west wing people withdrew, the silent little woman following with the rest. But as she passed down the steps, Mrs. Gray ascended them, coming up from the seat under the trees, where she had been listening in silence to the hymns. At this point the bright light of the hall lamp streamed out across the veranda, and in its glare the faces of the two women shone each upon the other, and in that flash the white face grew whiter, and the old woman lifted her hand to her head, as if suddenly overcome by the helplessness and horror of some frightful dream.

The doctor saw it all, and saw also the swift change that swept in a wave of deathly pallor across the face of Mrs. Gray. Shaken with a strange shuddering, she grasped the railing, and then, as she saw Dr. Moore moving with outstretched hand to support her, she suddenly turned her back to the light and moved steadily down the garden path into the gathering gloom.

Once in the shadow she grasped the back of a rustic seat and clung, for an instant, as if the shuddering soul had shaken all strength from her limbs. In that instant Dr. Moore had caught a glimpse of the waiting figure. He was by her side as she sank upon the bench, and bending over her, he said :

" You must pardon my following you, but you looked so ill ; you might faint here all alone."

" Thank you, it was very kind," she murmured. " I was faint, but it is passing now."

" But let me do something for you, let me help you to the house," he said, at the same time laying his fingers gently upon her hand, and touching the fluttering wrist. " Here, take this," and he gave her a small vial from his pocket. " Drink it all," he added, seeing that she hesitated, " I keep it about me for just such little emergencies as this. Come now, or if you like the fresh air, let me send Miss Wild to you."

"No, no, I will go to my room. This way, doctor, not through the library," and leaning on him she yet guided him through the conservatory to a door which opened into the large hall.

"I can go alone now, thank you," she said, pausing at the top of the staircase. "I do not like to spoil their pleasure by having any one notice that I am ill," but he stood by the door and watched her as, tottering and feeble, like one suddenly stricken with age, she went slowly down the corridor and closed the door of her room.

"She has had a blow of some kind, that's certain," muttered the doctor, as he made his way back toward the library, "and, if I'm not mistaken, so did my patient also," and acting on that second thought, he turned back and walked with resolute step down the green aisles of the conservatory.

For a moment only he lingered within sound of the tinkle of the fountains, within sight of the moonlit sky, showing through an arabesque of green vine leaves that had strayed to the very summit of the glass dome. The air was heavy with the fragrance of flowers; the whole spot resting in a peaceful Sabbath hush that so touched and stirred his soul as to make him wish the beauty and the silence and the sweetness might be shared. And the woman with whom he would have been glad to share it—whose presence would have doubled its sweetness was back there on the veranda, singing her heart out into the radiant night.

Brief as was the moment of rest and charm, it was long enough for a revelation of himself to himself, long enough for him to know, that between the rough sea of labor on which he had been tossing so many years, and the wider sea of service to humanity stretching before him, there was one difference that meant all the world to him. On the sea just passed it had mattered little that he breasted the breakers alone; he had scarcely realized that he was alone; but now he felt with a sudden pang how hard it would be to go on to the end without another face, another voice, another form to go down into the depths, or to ride the crest of the waves with him. And as he stood there dreaming, the moon smiled down, and the blossoms gave out their breath of fragrance, and the fountains tinkled, and the singing voice went on and on. Nothing without was changed, and yet for this strong man nothing henceforth could ever be quite the same. He was not much given to dreams, and from this one moved forward after a moment to the little porch that led to the entrance of the west wing.

If everything in the old part of the house at Wildholm was substantial and a little somber, everything here in the west wing made up for it in the fresh brightness of the surroundings provided for the weary and suffering lives. A charming living room, with cages of bright-winged birds and flowering plants in the windows, with bright pictures of sunny landscapes and of happy children at their play, upon the walls; and on beyond this, pleasant room after pleasant room, each with its occupant free and happy and at home. It was a home within a home. Gentle nurses moved quietly about, and the atmosphere, even in the evening light, seemed full of a blessed peace.

In the sunny room assigned to his white-haired patient, the doctor found her, not asleep as he hoped, but awake and tossing restlessly upon her pillow, the beads continually slipping on and on in her ever-restless hands. He spoke gently to her, as if she had been a child, laid his large, cool hand upon her head, and she sank down quietly as if in his very presence there were protection and rest.

"What troubles you to-night, little mother?" he asked. "This is the time when I wanted you to be asleep."

"I could not sleep," she said, sinking her voice to a whisper, and clasping both her thin hands around the doctor's sleeve. "I could not sleep until she told me whether she had found the little girl."

"Who told you?" he asked, gently passing one of his hands soothingly over her own.

"The lady, the beautiful lady. Has she found the little girl?"

"What little girl, mother? I did not know she had lost any little girl," he added, trying to follow the gleam of light that seemed to have come into her darkened mind.

"Oh yes," she whispered, confidentially. "She lost her once, she found her once, and I lost her again. Tell me, has she ever found her?"

"Of whom are you talking, and who was the little girl? What did you call her?"

Then he watched her intently while her troubled

mind seemed wandering in an abyss of shadows, searching for something that should guide her through the misty labyrinth of her thought.

"Who was the little girl, and what was her name?" he repeated, distinctly.

Suddenly her face brightened. "Which one do you mean?" she asked. "There were two of them."

"Tell me what their names were, can you not?"

"Oh, Baby, only Baby."

"And whose baby was it? Was it yours?"

"Oh, no," she answered, sadly. "My baby was a little boy."

"Where is he?" asked the doctor, still soothing her hand, and trying to help her to the thought which her memory seemed striving to grasp. "Was your baby boy lost too?"

"He wasn't a baby boy," she answered, quickly. And then, with a rush of tears, she pulled away from him suddenly, and buried her face in the pillow.

Feeling that the experiment had gone as far as she could well bear, he soothed and quieted her as if he were a mother and she a little child, and after a while saw her, under his gentle ministration, fall away into a quiet sleep. But before she slept he knew, from her incoherent talk, that the new-found impressions had been again partially effaced from her mind, and that she had no recollection of one word that she had said.

With the true scientist's spirit of investigation, on the alert for any change in his patient's condition, he had yet gained one point only, that there was, in the darkness of this clouded mind, some chord of association that had vibrated at the sight of Mrs. Gray.

After this Sabbath night there followed a week of delightful planning for the party to occur on Mrs. Maitland's birthday, that fell on one of the last days of Easter week. These preparations were varied by lounging upon the piazza, loitering in the garden, boat excursions upon the Potomac, drives to points of interest in the vicinity of Washington, and best of all, riding parties, leaving in the afterpart of the day, and scouring every beautiful region around Washington, returning in the quiet of the moonlight nights.

In all of these it was Gretta's horse that led the rest, and Gretta's face and voice that, ever in advance, seemed to cheer the others on. It was as if the spirit of hospitality, so marked in Mrs. Maitland, had descended upon her, and she felt it her special pleasure to see that the strangers among their guests should leave nothing unseen and unenjoyed.

Led, as they supposed, by his watchfulness over his new patient, Dr. Moore came every day to the house, and on more than one occasion joined them in their rides, finding his way without much difficulty straight to Margaret Graham's side.

Mrs. Gray, though able to superintend the preparations, kept her room much of the time during the week, sharing the festivities only when her chaperonage was necessary. If possible, she was more quiet and reserved than ever, and though Harold Moore sought opportunities to speak with

her, he found her invariably too much engaged.
She had been a good deal disturbed by the encounter which he had noticed, but she had long
ago passed the time when every breath of remorse-
ful memory could stir her soul to its very depths.
She had become familiar with herself, and the fact
that it was not such a self as she could approve no
longer rent and tore the spirit. She had been
shaken by surprise, and overcome with terror of
discovery, but her memories had lost the element
of regret and sorrow, and kept only that of shame.
More than once she repeated to herself that she
had paid her price, and did not propose to relinquish
that which had been so dearly bought. Least of
all was it her purpose now to abandon the ease and
comfort, position and association, which it had secured, and which, as she whispered to herself,
would never have come to her by any other means.

And when the gala night came that was to show
her beautiful child to the world of Washington, in
her heart there was not only joy in Gretta's youth
and beauty, but unexpected satisfaction in the
thought that she too stood there, in the midst of
this Washington world, as the cherished friend on
whom the honors and the duties of the hostess
came. There was pleasure too, in the fact that not
one woman of all who came and went, and smiled
and talked, was statelier in presence, prouder in
face, or more gracious in bearing than herself.

Mrs. Maitland was unable to stand, and her arm-
chair had been raised until her guests could look
straight into her eyes, and Gretta was like a tall,
fair lily as she stood beside her, in her white robes,

with a face as pure as a flower. But the eyes of the strangers turned oftenest and lingered longest upon the stately woman, who stood in her floating draperies of black lace, with the sweet pallor of moonlight on her face, and eyes that glowed with the beauty and fervor of the stars. And no one gazed upon her with greater admiration than did Mrs. Maitland and Gretta, who whispered to each other that they never knew before what a beautiful woman she was. And those who came and went felt that Mrs. Maitland was favored to have such a representative as they knew this woman would be in the social world, and Gretta to be congratulated on such a chaperone and friend.

And happy as were all the young people on that night, during the hours that were gay with music and laughter and song, and delightful as all found the festival, yet all their gratification was trifling to the pleasure that filled the heart of Katharine Gray.

To Mrs. Maitland, with her old friends and her brother's friends about her, it was like the last page of the book of outward pleasures, of which she had tasted many in a long and brilliant life. To Gretta it was the first page of the same book, but to Katharine, as she talked with the most charming women and the most distinguished men that could be gathered from the city that holds the best, it was like a concentration of the pleasures she felt she ought to have had during all the past years—a full cup, of which she resolved to drink henceforth, until she had tasted the lowest drop. Heretofore she had been a silent woman. She was startled at herself to see how, under the attrition of wits, her own thoughts sparkled and glowed. She had almost forgotten to be merry, and she found the laughter and the light word come springing to her lips as if they had only waited for the touch of some such time as this. Deprived, starved, denied, taking what delights had come to her heretofore as if she had no right to touch them, she let the hard past go, and tested to the full her unused power of enjoyment. In the mirror opposite she saw her face, with the flush of all this new excitement upon it, and hardly recognized herself in the stately beautiful woman against whose breast the scarlet roses gleamed.

It was her life's first moment of conscious triumph, and just as she felt it most keenly the crowd parted, and between the billows of floating drapery of every lovely hue came Harold Moore, and behind him a tall, broad-chested man, over whose forehead there tossed a mass of brown hair, with a glint of gold gleaming in every curl. It was a face of quiet and almost somber strength, if one failed to see the rippling humor that twinkled in the eyes and played around the corners of the mouth; the face of an unquestionably strong man, lighted by the trustful eyes of a child. Mrs. Gray did not notice it until after it had bowed low over Mrs. Maitland's hand, and when it was lifted, and she looked straight into those calm eyes, there suddenly came before her the vision of a child standing in the shadow of a vine-clad church, and watching while she turned her back on him and bore his heart away. Her face turned white to the lips, but

Harold Moore was there; and he was never again to see her quiver or quail. She was tasting her first cup of life's red wine; she did not choose to have it dashed from her lips by the coming of any ghosts out of her horrible past. It was only a week since she had flinched, had been shaken by such a ghost. Now she did not flinch and not a sign, save that of sudden pallor, not a quiver of voice made her greeting to this man other than that which had met the homage of the senators and statesmen and savants who one by one had come to her from out this moving throng.

For one brief second his eyes sent their question into the depths of hers, and he knew her, and knew also that she did not choose to show that he was known. Her mind had acted like lightning. He was a gentleman, as one glance showed. He could not presume upon her ever having had a past if there was no answering gleam to meet his questioning eyes. Almost unconsciously she paid him the highest tribute that woman could pay to the honor of any man. If she was silent, she knew no earthly power could make him speak. What right had he to know her if she did not choose to be known? His eyes answered every question as if her lips had uttered it, and though he might despise her, she knew that she was safe.

"I believe you promised me the pleasure of taking you to the supper room," said a pleasant voice near her.

"Ah, General North, I am glad you have come for her," said Mrs. Maitland. "She is looking pale; she has been standing too long. And do not bring her back again until she has been in the conservatory, or on the veranda for a breath of air," she added, as Katharine laid her hand upon the general's arm.

"I shall be in no haste to bring her back," was the answer, and as they passed out of sight, Harold Moore said, "Will you not trust Miss Graham to me, Mrs. Maitland? And, really, if you would be so good, we would like to carry away Miss Gretta also," he added, speaking for Mr. Conrad, whose eyes had turned from Katharine's vanishing figure to rest in great content on Gretta's face.

"No, no," said Gretta, "I am not going to leave grandmamma alone."

"Then Theodore is to stay with you here until I bring Miss Graham back."

"Nothing will make me happier, if Mrs. Maitland allows ; but, better still, let me bring you both some refreshments." And before they could reply, the shining head had disappeared in the crowd.

"What did you say his name was ?" said Gretta.

"Conrad, Theodore Conrad. He is one of my oldest friends and dearest. We were classmates in college and have been comrades all through so far. I am delighted that they have sent him to Congress, for it is like having a brother come home to me."

He was not gone long, but long enough, in passing down the crowded rooms to get a glimpse of Mrs. Gray, as she sat in the center of a brilliant group, the one apparently most at ease and certainly the one most elegant and charming woman of them all.

As if she felt his gaze, her eyes lifted and he

knew, notwithstanding her seeming ease, that her confidence had deserted her. In their depths he saw such a horror of terror and trouble as was there years ago when she was nearly maddened at the loss of her little girl; and as of old, his great, tender heart pitied her.

" Whither away so fast?" said Colonel Holt, laying his hand on Theodore's arm ; " stay and make one of us. It's an age since I have seen you."

" A little later, perhaps. Your group is perfect and I have permission to serve some ladies."

" Well, we know you," said Senator Nelson, a white-bearded man with a cheery face; " no man can serve them better."

" No man is more loyal to them certainly, if that is what you mean," and his old smile flashed like a promise down upon Katharine's face. Then he passed on and she breathed more freely.

" You seem to admire the new judge, senator," said Colonel Holt.

" Yes, and well I may. He comes from our section. He's a glorious fellow, and he's going straight to the top."

" He looks young for the bench."

" Yes, but he has earned it. This is his first term in Congress, but we'll keep him here straight along now. There's nobody in whose hands our interests are so safe."

" You seem especially enthusiastic," said Mrs. Gray, languidly.

" I do not wonder," said another lady. " There's something about him that makes one think of the knights of the old Crusades."

"Who is it you are lauding in this extravagant fashion?" said Harold Moore, pausing on the outside of the group, "is it our friend Theodore?"

"Yes," answered Mrs. Nelson, a sweet-faced, elderly lady; "I was about to say he was a true knight, not of the olden but of our later time. There isn't a wrong in our State that that man has not been after ever since he was a lad. Why, his father wanted him to take his business, and there was a fortune in it, and he did try to do it, to please the old gentleman after he came out of college; but one day he went to him and said: 'Now, father, I am glad you have the money, and I want to help the business to go on and to grow for what the money can do, but there are too many things that money alone can never set right that I want to learn all about, away down to the bottom. I want to take some time to fit myself for a fight that will call for money, but call a good deal louder for men.'

"And old Mr. Conrad, who was so fond of him that he couldn't bear to have him out of his sight, left him free and gave him his chance, and the fellow just gave himself up to practical examination of what he calls 'the problems of the people.'"

"He was always at it, even in college," said Dr. Moore, who had taken a little turn with Miss Graham on his arm, and returned to the rear of the group. "It was easy enough for him to take honors, and he was away ahead in athletics, but really the only thing he cared for was humanity. I believe he studied law because he fancied justice and protection for the poor were in it."

"Well, he has been a regular John the Baptist since he settled down to the law in our State. We sent him to the legislature, and he was a 'voice crying in the wilderness.'"

"Seems to me you are making your hero out a first-class crank," said a little fat man with a round, bald head, "'Crying in the wilderness' is easy enough. What we want is men to lead us out of the woods, not men to raise a hue and cry because we are in."

"Trust Judge Conrad for that too, friends. The man has a genius for making crooked things straight. I wouldn't like to fall into his hands if I had mountains of iniquity to be brought low."

Mrs. Gray changed color.

"I fear I am allowing your very interesting account of your hero to take the attention that belongs to all our guests," she said rising, with a faint chill in her manner that at once checked all enthusiasm. "Miss Wild said he reminded her of Guido's St. Michael. Evidently," she added, with a little touch of scorn in her voice, for fear and anger were battling in her for mastery, "evidently his mission is to trample out the dragons. He will find enough of them in our legislative halls and in our slums; he will hardly need to drive them out of our salons," and she moved slowly, with gracious word and smiles to those she met, to Mrs. Maitland's side.

Dr. Moore and Miss Graham were there before her. Judge Conrad had lingered with them while they took the ices he had brought, with a manner so unlike that of the young society man, and yet so deferential and gentle to Mrs. Maitland, that Gretta, to whom he said little, felt he found a pleasure in being near the loving mother-heart.

"They have been having a great talk about Mr. Conrad, Dr. Moore's friend," said Miss Graham to Gretta, "and your aunt told them you said he reminded you of St. Michael. They grew quite eloquent in his praise. It seems he has distinguished himself in his own State, but Mrs. Gray appeared to think the praise a little excessive, for she said something about his not needing to hunt for dragons in our drawing rooms."

"St. Michael did not trample, as I remember," said Gretta. "The dragon crouched and shrank as he came; he scarcely touched him."

"It always seemed to me," said Mrs. Maitland, "that the evil shrank before the coming of the light; that it was the light, the moral revelation, before which the darkness sped rather than the indications of physical power to harm."

"Yet," said Gretta, "the drawn sword was there in the uplifted hand. It swung, as if just stayed by some thought of mercy, above the dragon's head." She turned, and Katharine stood beside her. For the first time in all her life Gretta saw, through the half-drooped lids, the eyes blazing on her in anger.

"It may all be very artistic and sentimental," she said in a low voice, that cut like an icicle upon the flower-scented air, "but really I would have preferred one of you young girls as the belle of the evening. I cannot see that we have special use for angels with flaming swords," and she turned with a gracious smile to greet a late-comer at that moment announced.

Gretta bent hastily over Mrs. Maitland, readjusting the light lace wrap that had fallen from her shoulders, keeping her face out of sight lest she should show some sign of the sting of this first sharp word. Mrs. Maitland just prisoned for a moment the little trembling hand and held it close, and though their eyes did not meet, Gretta knew she too had heard and understood.

"It is Mrs. Gray who is the belle of the evening, Gretta," she said playfully, after a moment's pause, "though she does not seem to know it. Every one seems anxious to know her."

"Yes, did you ever see her look so lovely?" said Gretta eagerly, her love at once getting the mastery of her pain. "I am so glad to see her happy, and ashamed that I should vex her."

"I have been fearing your life, when school is over, would lose much that is delightful socially, since my health has so decidedly failed," she said, taking no notice of Gretta's last words, "but with such a chaperon as your auntie, I do not see why you should not be really gay. Would you like to see a good deal of Washington society next winter?"

"Oh, if I might, yes indeed I would. I never thought of it, that is, I never supposed I could."

"Well, we shall see," said Mrs. Maitland, turning to respond to the adieux of some of her own old friends.

"It has been so lovely to see the dear house open once more," they said, "it seems like the old times. By-the-way, how the old judge, your brother, would have enjoyed our young friend Conrad. He's from our State you know; we'll make him governor yet."

"We hope not, since that would take him from Washington," said Harold promptly.

"True," answered the colonel, as he passed on, "the State may need such men, but the country needs them more."

"Mr. Conrad seems to have no lack of friends," said Mrs. Maitland to Gretta. "It is enough for me to know he is a friend of our dear Doctor Moore, who brought him here to-night. We shall hope to see him often," and somehow a great weight was lifted from Gretta's heart. It did not matter so much that her aunt had spoken sharply to her, if only the aversion to the stranger did not keep him forever away. And when he came to make his farewells Mrs. Maitland was so cordial, and her aunt so kind, that her pain and fear departed, nor was it revived during the bedtime talk with Miss Graham which, late as it was before they retired, neither of the girls could resist.

It had been of all Gretta's short life the " merriest, maddest day." But for that one little pang of her aunt's displeasure it had been without a cloud. As usual Mrs. Gray came in in her dressing-gown to see if all was well with the child for the night, but Miss Graham was there in the full flow of girlish talk, so she said good-night pleasantly, and turned away.

And when Gretta was all ready for bed, she went softly into Katharine's room. She was not there. Then she passed on to Mrs. Maitland's bedside for a good-night kiss, and kneeling by the pillow prayed her thankful prayers with a thin white hand upon her head. And Katharine, wandering restlessly up and down the house, saw the white figure kneeling there in the dim light, and knew that, even in a sadder, sorer sense than when Robert Gray had taken her, she had lost her little child.

Pausing in her restless walk at the wide window at the end of the corridor, she gazed across the courtyard to a room where a light was burning feebly in the old west wing. There in the silence lay the old head that had parted with its wits in her service, the old heart that had been robbed of its only child. Down yonder somewhere in the sleeping city was the son robbed of his mother. These two had risen already, as from the dead, to confront her with her sin, and out of the great world it might be that another still would rise to chide her with the memory of even a deeper wrong. For this old woman the years had been a time " of peace and of forgetting," far better for her than years of continued struggle and toil. Therefore no real harm to her lay at Katharine's door. As for Ted, successful and beloved, with a conquered world of difficulties and temptations behind him, and new worlds of service, influence, and honors before, what right had he to haunt her with eyes of question or reproof? He ought to thank her, for indeed he owed it all to her. She would tell him so too, in that hour when she would outpour upon him the dislike and scorn that were hot and seething in her heart. " St. Michael," indeed! She would show him that she feared no shining sword. And, after all, what did these terrors mean?

She pushed up the casement, and kneeling on the low window seat, drew the heavy curtains about her, and watched the stars and the low scudding clouds that now revealed and now obscured the moon. What could Ted know that should make her afraid? Why nothing, save that once there were two. And if he never told it, which, since he smiled into her eyes, she knew he would not do, all would be well. If he dared tell it, if he dared speak of it even to her, she had ready the vials of wrath. Was not he as well as Gretta bearing a name and living on a wealth not his own? Would he like the world to know the depths from which he sprang? the tenement house top floor? the wash-tubs and the brogue? Of course he was ashamed of his old mother, or why had he dropped the name that mother bore? Why had he not searched the wide world over instead of leaving her to be a pauper in a stranger's care?

Ah, how greatly she had changed! How mightily had the evil dwellers that had crept in one by one grown, until they held possession of her soul! What a viper's nest it had become of fierce rebellion, ambition, and anger and envy and hate! They hissed their tempting whispers in her ears. They twisted their foul coils about all that was left that made her long even now for innocence and peace. Even that new passion to help, if by helping she might atone, seemed for the time being at least, poisoned by their scorpion sting.

No wonder that she wandered while others slept. If only she could have known that the heart that reverenced and loved her was a boy's heart still, in so far as its thought of her was concerned; that he wondered as he walked home why she seemed afraid to know him ; that nothing had ever come to his knowledge that had shaken his trust in her ; that his boyish hurt had died with his boyish years. If she had known all this she might have slept that night, since only outward terrors stirred her now. She had grown used to sleeping when she had only her own sick soul to face.

On the day following the party, the morning passed in restful idleness and merry chat on the veranda, when the younger members of the household talked everything and everybody over with Mrs. Maitland, as if she were only another girl. She did not seem the worse for her birthday festival, nor did any one except perhaps Mrs. Gray, who kept her room in the morning in order to be rested to chaperone the young ladies in the afternoon, for which several pleasant engagements had been accepted. Desiring to give a forgotten order to one of the maids, Katharine threw on her wrapper, and stepped through Gretta's room into the hall, while the family were at breakfast. Returning, as she passed through Gretta's chamber, her eye fell upon something that glittered like gold upon the rug, half hidden by the table scarf. Thinking it Gretta's watch, she stooped and rose with such a look of startled wonder upon her face as she would not have cared to have another see. It was a gold locket held by an old-fashioned slender chain, such as in her girlhood she had often seen her mother wear.

She only paused for one look, and hastily concealing the treasure in the folds of her dress, she hurried to her room and locked the door. Opened by trembling hands, the locket revealed on one side a coil of soft brown hair, and on the other her gentle sister's face. And the eyes looked out at her with the same questioning, pleading gaze they wore that night when, dying, she gave into her care her only little child. Like a flood the memory of all her words swept over her. She remembered the pledge she herself had silently given to rear the little one in the faith her mother loved. She had failed in all, yet even now the sweet eyes did not seem to chide, but only to trust and plead with her again.

She closed the locket hurriedly, and almost impatiently put it among her own private treasures deep out of sight in her desk.

Whose was it? She did not know—she hardly cared—she remembered seeing it once at her sister's home. Perhaps Debby kept it for herself, or brought it home to her mistress? Or possibly she packed it with the child's apparel and, without knowing it, might herself have taken it to Chicago and transferred it to Mrs. Burke, in whose care she placed the clothing and the child. This seemed not unlikely, though she could not remember seeing it after she left the parsonage. But Biddy was here now, Gretta saw her daily, and she had doubtless received the locket from her. Or old Debby or Mrs. Maitland might have given it to her; but let it have come as it might, why had Gretta concealed it? For the second time in her life she felt like blaming Gretta, and was conscious of a feeling of irritation that she, for whom she had borne so much, should be the means of bringing to her tormenting memories. She had enough of them, and they embittered rather than softened her heart. She resolved to shake off their influence upon her, and yet the morning was gone, and the face and voice were pleading with her still.

There was a *musicale* at Senator D——'s and a charming out-of-door festival in another quarter, and she must go with Gretta and her girl friends, and she was late. Already she could hear their merry talk and laughter, as they called from room to room, in the happy bustle of preparation; and struggle for control as she would, again she knew she must go forth with white face and quivering hands.

"We are just wearing you out, auntie," said Gretta, as she came at last to find the carriage waiting. "You are not rested at all, and it is cruel of us to let you go."

"Yes, I fear it is too true," said Miss Graham, "you are looking so white and ill. Why not let us stay at home this afternoon? I am sure we all need rest."

"No, indeed," said Mrs. Gray, laughing. "I am quite too eager to go myself to consent to give it up."

"Well, I confess I would give it up cheerfully," said Miss Graham; "for I have lost my pleasure this afternoon in the sense of my other loss."

"Oh, you will be sure to find it," said Gretta, cheerily. "I am very careless, but I always find my things."

"What is it?" asked Katharine from behind her veil. "What have you lost?"

"A locket, the dearest thing I have in the world, a keepsake that I have worn and prized so many years."

"When do you remember seeing it last?"

"Well, last night, you know, I stayed and talked, and partly undressed in Gretta's room. I had it then, for I showed it to her."

"It's her mother's face," broke in Gretta, "or Margaret feels quite sure it is. She never saw her mother. Her grandmother took her when she was a baby, and she kept this picture for her. She never told her whose face it was, but she did tell her it was about her neck under the little frock when she was brought to her. But after her grandmother died she took it, and has always felt sure it was her mother's face."

"And you wore it on your ride yesterday?" asked Katharine, in a tone of earnest sympathy.

"I thought I did; I am so accustomed to wear it that I take for granted that I put it on. The picture was everything to me," she said. "It was a pure face, and I could not feel it about my neck and not at least try to be good."

And all the time, behind her veil, Katharine was struggling to keep her own face and voice under control; and struggling too, to find in that troubled young face opposite, the proof that she was indeed her sister's child.

"I came near losing it once before," Miss Graham added. "I was visiting the dear old lady in the west wing, Dr. Moore's patient you know, and as I was bathing her face, the chain slipped and the locket swung from my neck. She saw it, and thinking to please her, I opened it and kissed it, and she seemed overjoyed like a child, and kissed it herself and watched me, and finally fell to embracing me and patting my head and kissing my hands, until I felt quite emotionally dramatic, as if I were a long-lost daughter or a wandering child returned."

Gretta laughed, saying as the carriage stopped at the end of a long line, " That dear old soul seems to have a fund of unexpended devotion sufficient to run through our list of acquaintances. She has spells of adoring me and devouring me with her eyes. I only wish she would talk. When she does she has the most delightful brogue, and I fancy she must have been a jovial, cheery soul before this dreadful change."

There was no time for answer. The next minute they were at the door of the crowded mansion. A pompous voice announced them in stentorian tones, that had the effect of bringing a host of friends about them, almost before their greetings with the hostess were over.

CHAPTER XIV

THEY filled the next few days with out-of-door gayeties, in which, to Katharine's dismay, both Dr. Moore and Mr. Conrad were constantly included. She would have been still more dismayed if she had been the chaperon of every boating and riding party, and seen how frequently these two gentlemen became the special escorts of Gretta and Miss Graham. But she availed herself of every opportunity to confide her charge to one or another of their matronly friends, and, during the hours when the gentlemen were in the house, succeeded in avoiding a meeting.

On Conrad's part he accepted the place of a new acquaintance, in which she had placed him; but, when the holidays were over, and the house emptied of the bright young faces that had made the brief season like one long festival, the young girls all back at school, the young men scattered, he came to see Mrs. Maitland, and, after an hour spent by the lovely and lonely lady's arm-chair on the veranda, asked if he might see Mrs. Gray and see her alone.

Mrs. Maitland, in whose heart the thought of Gretta's happiness and welfare was ever uppermost, could not help interpreting this request as significant of his having something to say of Gretta; and so accustomed had she grown to thinking of the child as her own, that a little shade of wonder crossed her mind that, if he wanted to speak of Gretta, he should not have broached the subject to herself. They had had more than one quiet talk in the brief time since she had known him, and she had come fully to endorse the high opinion of his friend and classmate, Dr. Moore. She felt that here indeed was a man in whom a woman's heart might safely rest, a man noble in himself, and yet with an ideal and practice of life that counted everybody better than himself. Strong, he gave himself unsparingly to the succor of the weak. Young, his tenderness and deference and care of everything that was aged was such as to stir the affection of every woman's heart. Knowing the world, he yet lived in a range of principles and ideas which did not enter into the ordinary man's scheme of life. Dealing with men and affairs with energy and promptitude, yet with all his strength, a man to win and hold the love of every little child. Surely, if Gretta must sometime be left alone, how could this loving old heart help wishing that she might find the protection of such a soul as this.

No wonder her eyes followed him kindly, as he entered the library where Mrs. Gray, with the same air of impenetrable coldness and reserve, stood waiting for him to come. Instinctively divining her preference, he led her to a sofa where the light would fall full in his face and not upon her own. The frank directness of his gaze was emphasized in his words.

"I have asked to see you, my dear Mrs. Gray, not only because I want to thank you for having allowed me to share in the delights of this home, and to take, with all these lovely young people, rest and recreation such as has not been mine since I was a lad; but, having shared the pleasures and accepted the hospitality of the home, I am not willing to go away feeling that I am a stranger to either of my hostesses, or without at least making an effort to be recognized by my dear old friend."

Almost at the very first word her face relaxed. There was no accusation in his eyes, no rebuke or scorn; nothing but the old loyal gentleness in voice and word. Was it possible that he was not going to condemn her after all?

"I am not going to ask you to talk to me, Mrs. Gray, for I have realized by the very fact of your shunning me on all occasions, how difficult it would be for you to refer to the past. I can easily guess all that I have any right to know." She colored and her eyes fell. "But it is due to you that I should not come to your home, and come in contact with this young girl who is so dear to you, without letting you know more of me than you have yet been told."

He was not going to question her then. The set, strained look of resistance relaxed.

"In that terrible railway accident," he went on, "when I lost my mother, I was one of those who went down with the wreck of the bridge into the water below. As I was struck by fragments of the broken car as I fell, I knew nothing of my descent into what might have been a watery grave. Neither did I know it when, rising to the surface, I was drawn into the boat of one of the rescuers, and taken to the opposite bank. I knew nothing either during much of the terrible illness that followed, as the result of the blow and the shock and the chill. I waked to find myself in the hospital connected with the Catholic Convent in Edholm. I saw the gentle figures in black gliding about the ward. ·I heard low tones and saw kind faces looking out upon me from under their bands of white. I did not know how long I had been there. I hardly knew how long I stayed. I only knew the strength came back slowly, and that I had tender care and the kind ministry of priest and sister of mercy; and I could hear, as I lay on my cot, the voices of the choristers in the little church connected with the convent.

"By-and-by I became able to work in the garden, and to tend the flowers. They were willing to keep me, and, but for two things, I could have been content. The kind priest talked with me of the wickedness of the great world into which I was impatient to go back, of the poverty and struggle and temptation that would meet me there. He offered to rear me in the church and for the church, and it meant home, and protection, and kindness, and a chance—after I should have received my training—to go out into the world, not to fight its battles, but as a helper and comforter of the wounded.

"Of course, Mrs. Gray, you know why I could not stay. But when I pleaded that I must find my mother, every search was made in my behalf, with the result that a woman answering her description had died of her injuries, and had been laid away with the rest on that dreadful day when they buried the other dead. They assured me that their search was far more thorough than any that I, a helpless boy, could make ; but even then I was not content. I had promised you that I would care for the child, and feeling that nothing excused me from that trust, I turned away, really mourning to grieve these, the only friends I had in the world. But, taking the clothing they had so kindly provided for me, and the little fund of money which they had given on condition that I might return it, I made my way back to the place of the accident.

" As you may judge, a child could follow but feebly the traces of such a tragedy. And yet I made inquiry of the officials of the railroad, both at the place of the disaster, and later at their general headquarters. The files of the newspapers, giving accounts of the accident, were searched. The physicians who were said to have come on the rescue trains from a distance were interviewed, and the people in the neighborhood of the disaster had cause to remember the little red-headed boy who tramped from place to place, questioning if a little baby or an elderly woman had been brought, after the accident, to any of their homes.

" Of course it was a failure, and of course I used up all my money in the search. But the people would give me little jobs of work for a meal and a night's lodging, and sometimes for a few days I stayed at work upon some farm until I had earned money to let me go on to the next point. Thus I worked my way back to Chicago, where, homeless, friendless, and alone, I crept back, from very homesickness and heartsickness, to the place where we had lived. The house was torn down. A new business block was rising on the very spot. Even the old policeman had gone from his accustomed beat. A more desolate and helpless little soul you never knew, as I stood on the corner that day. The miles I walked, the doorways and empty carts in which I slept, the appeals for work that I made, the hunger—for never once did I come to where I was tempted to steal"—Mrs. Gray shuddered, as she lifted her eyes to the face of the man before her; "no," he repeated, "never once was I tempted to steal, and never once did I beg, but the struggle to live honestly made a poor little freckled-face, scrawny, red-headed scarecrow of me.

"When sick and faint for lack of food, and too utterly desolate to care whether I lived or died, I had one consolation. If I could creep to the corner where stood that old ivy-mantled church and sit on the steps, or stand with my back against the wall, and hear them singing within, or feel the throb of the great bell as it rang in the high church tower, it somehow gave me a feeling of being nearer home. And from that point I went around and around the square, living over and over again that hour when I had wheeled your baby on that day when you found her, and when I lost her," he added, in a lower tone.

"I do not think in my weakness and weariness that it once occurred to me that I might be known and held responsible for the stealing of the child; but one day, as I stood gazing up at the door out of which I had wheeled that little wagon so many times, it opened, and the woman beckoned me to come in. ˙ I must have remembered the woodpile and the weeding of the garden, and the small chores, for there sprang up in me a great hope that she would let me work for her again. I ran over to the door, and once in the hall she closed it behind me. She took me by the shoulders, and drawing me into the little sitting room, all dark and shadowy, because the blinds were closed to keep out the heat of the midday sun, she seated herself, and while I stood before her with my old cap in my hand, she said, 'You are the boy who once did errands for me. You are the boy who weeded the garden, and helped me to take care of that little child.'

" My heart stood in my mouth, but she went on rapidly, putting her hand on mine. I drew it away with the feeling that my hand was too dirty for her to touch. She then clasped her fingers about my ragged sleeve.

" 'Where have you been hiding?' she said, not unkindly. 'Why did you not come back and tell me that some one stole the child away from you? You brought the wagon back, but you ought to have come and told me how it was that the child was taken from you. Did you think that I should blame you? Other people told me all about it. They said a woman pushed you aside, and snatched the child from the carriage, and went faster than you could follow.' And that was all true in a way, as you know, Mrs. Gray."

Katharine nodded assent. She was all breathless attention now.

"But of course I never dreamed that every one who saw it did not know that the child was taken with my consent.

"'You should have run back here at once and told us,' said the old woman, 'so that we might have followed. Then they would not have blamed me as they did. They would have known that it was not my fault. As it was, the child's father and old Mrs. Gray held me responsible for the loss of the child, and kept back all the money that they should have paid for taking care of it.' And here the old voice quivered a little. And I, who had known all about the frugal fare and the poverty of this old soul, felt suddenly as if I had wronged her, and I put my dirty hand on hers as it rested on my sleeve.

"'I did not know that, indeed I did not know that,' I said; 'but I am going to get work, and just as quick as I can get the money, you shall be paid for taking care of the child.'

"'It isn't that alone,' she answered, 'although, of course, in losing the Grays I lost my only friends, and everything has gone wrong with me since. It is a bad season. There are no lodgers in the rooms. I must have the rent, or I shall be turned away from the house. And when I saw you waiting outside, and remembered what a good boy you were, and how you helped me with the chickens and the flowers and the yard, I thought perhaps you would take this letter for me. I knew I could trust you.'

"Think of that, Mrs. Gray, after I had deliberately stolen the child. And after I saw the letter that she had given me, and saw that it was addressed to Mrs. Gray, I confess that for a moment I was a coward. I was afraid that if I went to that house I would be recognized, arrested, and lodged in prison by those who knew that I was not so innocent as this poor woman thought. I was such a coward, Mrs. Gray, that I even asked her if she did not think the landlord would wait for the rent until I could earn it, and when she looked at me, soiled and tattered and wasted, I did not wonder that she mournfully shook her head.

"'No,' she said, 'it must be done at once. I have pleaded with them in the letter, as one of their old servants, to pay me enough of what I earned by the care of the baby-girl, so many weeks, to meet my rent, and let me keep my home. And you will take the letter for me?' she asked, and I felt her old hand trembling on my arm.

"Really, Mrs. Gray," laughing and tossing back his hair with a shake of his head, as she had often seen him do when a child, "there was no withstanding a need like that. Of course I said I would go, but when I held out my hand for the letter, I think she shrank from putting it in such a dirty little paw. At any rate she took me out through the kitchen, where I had had many a meal, and where on the table was a part of a loaf of bread, into the woodshed. She gave me a tin basin, and shut the door and left me to myself. And such a scrub as I got, filling the basin again and again from the pump, was better than the baths of the old Romans to the young athletes preparing for their games. There was no help for it, the old clothes had to go on again, and so with the preparation of clean hands, and what I think was a pure purpose in my heart, and my soiled rags for armor, I went forth to meet my first fight, and to resist the first temptation to be a coward of which I had ever been conscious in my life."

" Quickly, tell me quickly," said Mrs. Gray, almost gasping out the words. "It moves too slowly. I cannot wait to hear."

" Oh, well then," he answered; "I feared I might be wearying you. You know the fine old house, you know the grounds, you know the pillar by the gate. When I reached the pillar my heart failed me, and I slunk behind it like a beggar. I think that even then, if I had not recollected that I had promised to earn the money, if Mrs. Gray would not pay it, that I would have run up to the piazza, and thrown the note upon it, and have ignominiously fled the field. But I remembered in time that it was I who had brought this trouble upon her; it was I who must protect her now; and strong in that thought, I rang the kitchen bell. It was answered by a smart serving maid, who was polishing a basket of gleaming silver at a table at the farther end of the room. She looked at my ragged garments and said, 'What are you here for, boy? No tramps allowed.'

" 'I am not a tramp,' I said; 'a lady sent me with this note for Mrs. Gray. I was to wait for an answer.'

" She looked at me, she looked toward the silver, and then came to the door and called, 'Towser, Towser,' over my head, and there came bounding toward her a large dog from the region of the stables.

" ' Here, Towser, take care of the silver,' she said, pointing to me, and leaving the dog with his head raised, watching as if ready to spring at my throat.

" You know I always loved animals, Mrs. Gray, animals and babies, and they were never afraid of me, and I looked this great dog straight in the face. When she came down again she was very much surprised to find Towser licking my clean hands, and putting one paw in a friendly way upon my shoulder.

" ' Down, Towser,' she said, ' let him alone.'

" ' Oh, he is not hurting me, we are only playing,' I answered, and she gave me a sealed note to take away. And all this time how hungry I was ! And just inside that door stood a tray of cold meat and bread and fruit, somebody's luncheon prepared to be taken from the room.

" She turned, and taking a large piece of meat and another of bread, held them out in her hand, ' Here, Towser, good dog, here is something to reward you,' and the dog snapped eagerly at the food.

" Whether or not she saw the hungry look in my eyes I do not know, but she turned again ; ' Here boy,' she said, holding out another portion like that which she had already given the dog. ' Don't you want a bit of something to eat ? '

" Oh, how I wanted it ! My hand was lifted to take it ; but Mrs. Gray, I remembered that that was the home of the man who had treated you so badly, and in a moment the very thought of the food choked me; I do not think I thanked her. I turned away lest I should not be able to resist the temptation, and ran as fast as ever I could. I was back before Mrs. Brown expected me, and while she devoured the letter, my eyes were devouring the remnants of the loaf of bread from which, since I had been gone, she had already taken her meal.

"Seeing how absorbed she was, I was slinking away, when she caught my movements.

"'Do not go boy. I have no money, but I must try to find something to pay you with.'

"'No, no,' I said, 'I could not take your money if you had it. I am glad to do the errand for you. I should like it very much though if you had some work for me to do.'

"'Well, I have—no I haven't, for you see I have no money to pay for the work; but there is the garden waiting to be weeded, and there is the wood to be cut, and if only you were a girl, I could get you to help me sweep and clean the lodgers' rooms. They need it sorely.'

"'Let me stay, let me help you. You can pay me by-and-by when the rent comes in. And perhaps,' I said, 'as the work goes on, you could give me something to eat.'

"She opened her eyes wide and stared at me. 'Are you hungry, boy?' she asked suddenly, starting toward the table. 'Now that your hands are clean you may help yourself to a piece of that loaf.'

"I eyed it greedily and put my hands behind me.

"'Why don't you take a piece, boy?' she said, wonderingly.

"'I can't,' I gasped. 'I am afraid—if I touch it—that I shall eat the whole.'

" And then you ought to have seen that dear old creature bustle around. She set a chair for me as if I were a king. She actually broke that loaf in pieces, so that I could eat it faster; and, greedy little thing that I was, Mrs. Gray, I never looked up again until I had swallowed it all. In my selfishness I had not even noticed how startled she was by the letter that she had read ; but, when I did lift my eyes to her face, she had gone back to it, and was reading it over and over again.

" 'The Lord has been merciful to me,' she said solemnly. 'I had it on my heart and conscience that I had been the means of letting a child be stolen away from its father, who had a rightful claim upon it, and Mrs. Gray writes me that the child has been restored to her, and because of that she sends me the amount that Robert told her was my due. He did not tell her right, my boy. It is only half what was my due. But I know him. No doubt he told her he had paid the rest, and this is enough for my rent. I am more than content. The home is saved, and you, my dear boy, shall have a resting-place in it so long as I have a roof over my head.'

" Mrs. Gray, in these later years, I have wondered how, in that time, I had the sense and the discretion to hold my tongue ; but I never said a word except to ask her how they got your child.

" 'I do not know,' she answered. 'Robert Gray told me the mother had once deserted it. Perhaps she did so again. I know that Mrs. Gray had

offered to take it, and to relieve the mother of its
support.   Probably life grew hard for her and she
let them have the child.'

"At any rate, I learned that the little one so
dear to you and so dear to me was there.   I also
learned afterward that the father was away, to be
gone three years, and so I had no longer a terror
lest he should not be kind to Gretta.   But while I
could understand that you might be driven to allow
Mrs. Gray to have the child during his absence, I
never for a moment felt as if I was excused from
the trust you had reposed in me to watch and care
for her, nor that I ever could be excused until such
time as you should set me free."

He paused.   During all the latter part of this re-
cital Mrs. Gray's head had dropped lower and lower,
until now the face was entirely hidden in her hands.
She could not understand it.   There was but one
explanation.   Robert, unwilling to admit himself
defeated, had either prevailed upon his mother to
take some other child, or the old lady herself, after
Robert's departure, had supplied the loneliness of
her life by taking some little one to rear in the
place of the true granddaughter of the house.   In
either case the result to her was the same.   Here
was this strong man as loving and loyal to her, and
as ready to serve her as had been her little Ted.

"This is giving you too much pain," he said, gently.
"Knowing how you felt to be parted from your
child, I can judge that to give her up to Mrs. Gray,
whatever may have forced you to do it,"—Katharine lifted her head with a defiant denial written
on every feature of her face; he, intent upon his

own thoughts, did not observe the look,—"was too hard a thing for you to remember without pain. Let me leave the rest of the story, for I want you to know every step of the way I have taken since those days. I am sure you have had more than you can bear," and he rose as if to go.

"Do not leave me," she said, pleadingly, laying her hand upon his arm, and lifting a very white and haggard face to his.

"I do not think we should talk more now. I could not forgive myself for touching an unhealed wound. Whatever led you to give her up, I know you did what you felt was right, and I want you to know how, above all things, I rejoice that you have her back again."

Katharine shuddered, and once more hid her face.

"She is very lovely, and to have her with you now in her beautiful girlhood is, I am sure, worth all you have suffered. I suppose she came back to you after old Mr. Gray's loss of fortune. One thing only puzzles me, that, as an old friend, I would like to know; but even that I have thought out for my-self."

"What is it?" she whispered, with lips that were white with a new terror.

"As I make out the story it looks to me as if, the other child having died in that terrible accident, must have left this beautiful home and this dear old heart of Mrs. Maitland desolate too, and Mrs. Maitland told me that she looked upon Gretta as her very own child. I thought that meant that she had made her her own, and put her in the place of the lost little girl; and that you, remembering how her father had dishonored his name, had consented to have her take this family name."

And while he waited, once more the angel of truth and life battled with the angel of deceit and death in this perjured woman's soul, and made her long to cry out so that even the heavens might hear, against this added lie. Whether the truthful eyes that looked down upon her bent head, and the strong, true soul of the man helped to rouse once more within her the impulse to tell the truth and take whatever came, she did not know. She did know that her soul was once more a battlefield. And when he said gently, "You need not talk about it. I see how the whole thing wrings your heart; I see what it must mean to you, even though you can see her face and hear her voice, to be obliged to relinquish your daughter first to Mrs. Gray, next to Mrs. Maitland, and to live here the life that for her sake, never claims her," she lifted her heavy eyelids for a moment with such a look of anguish as went to his heart. Between her white lips came the words, "No one remembers, no one ever thinks of it but you."

"And from this day, unless you desire it, I too will forget. You cannot question that your secret is safe with me, and that I honor you all the more for yielding up your claim that she may have the larger, richer life."

And she had not said a word to confirm or to deny, yet he went away believing he knew the truth, and she hugged to her soul still closer her awful, living lie.

CHAPTER XV

AND while this talk was going on in the library, in the drawing room to which Mrs. Maitland's arm-chair had been drawn from the veranda, sat three of her friends in earnest conversation.

" She seems to me so eminently fitted for the work," said Mrs. Dougall.

" Yes, for any position of prominence, surely," said Mrs. Maitland ; " but you will have difficulty in persuading her of the fact."

" My husband said he had a charming talk with her at your party, and found her really a scholarly woman," said Mrs. Bird, the wife of a college professor.

" She has watched her niece's education very carefully, and participated in most of her work, and is indeed well-read—a thoroughly well-bred and intelligent woman."

" Quite up in all the questions of the day, I presume," said Mrs. Jennings, a pretty and dainty young matron well known in Washington society.

" Of course," said Mrs. Maitland, gently. " That is a part of being an intelligent woman in this day. It was not so, unfortunately, in mine. And Mrs. Gray has given more than usual thought and study to problems that, even now, are too little considered either by women or men."

" She cares for temperance ? " asked Mrs. Bird, eagerly.

"Most assuredly. What good woman does not? I have heard her express herself strongly on that point; and though her life here has been retired, and devoted to her niece and myself, I shall be glad to see it widen out into such good work for the world as I know she is able to do. And I mean that Miss Wild too, when she comes from school, shall also become a student in the world of practical work for others. I want her to know real needs as they exist, to learn what is being done by men and women to alleviate or prevent misery and sin, and then she will be able to judge fairly as to the best methods of help, and how and when and where her own forces can be best applied."

"So you think Mrs. Gray cannot be induced to consent to take the post we are so anxious to see her fill?" asked Mrs. Bird, not willing to let Mrs. Maitland get too far from the point in hand.

"I cannot say. For this morning she is especially engaged; but I will lay it before her, and she will arrange to talk with you later. I can promise you she will think of it. If I were her age, I would help you myself."

That night there was a little dinner party at Wildholm, and Mrs. Maitland chanced to mention her morning visitors, Mrs. Dougall, Mrs. Bird, and Mrs. Jennings.

"Did you see them?" asked Miss Graham of Gretta.

"Not this morning, but I have met them all before. They are old friends of Mrs. Maitland."

"They often come to our house," added Mrs. Nelaton, a pretty blond matron, whose beauty was

Gretta's special admiration ; "and they usually come together as if sent forth on their special mission in threes instead of twos. Papa said one day that they represented to him three different parts of a combination woman."

"How do you mean?" said Mrs. Gray, lifting her eyes with sudden interest.

"Well, I do not know that I can explain ; but they' certainly are three different types, and yet they seem always to embody different phases of the same idea. There is Mrs. Dougall, whose type might be called the solidly sympathetic ; and Mrs. Bird, who might be termed the intensely genuine ; and Mrs. Jennings, who always seems to represent what might be termed the socially serious."

Everybody laughed, for everybody knew the trio.

"They are very noble women," said Mrs. Maitland, gently, "and doing very noble work."

"Now, my dear friend," broke in Mrs. Egbert, in a tone of remonstrance—she was a little woman with a sharp nose, and bright eyes that seemed to be trying to outshine the glitter of her diamonds— "you are always determined to see only the lovely in people. Now I will admit that Mrs. Dougall produces an effect. She just comes in in her wide-winged sleeves, and a wide-winged jet butterfly, that would never be suspected of being a bonnet but for the fact that it has lighted on her back hair. And with her little nods and gurgles and pantings of assent and dissent, and her smiles and her fluttering fan, she keeps up a certain air of activity ; but she never really says anything, and I

have never seen any evidence that she does anything."

The speaker stopped suddenly and dropped her
eyes, like a naughty child, who knew she had said
what she ought not, and yet was encouraged rather
than ashamed by the smiles of her hearers.

"But there is Mrs. Bird. She certainly does
enough for all three," said Gretta, feeling as if
somebody were being attacked, and she would like
to come to the rescue.

" That is true," said Colonel Holt ; "that woman
works like a house afire."

" But what is the use of a woman working like
a house afire," said Shakespeare Potts, a lank young
man, with his hair parted in the middle. " A house
afire does nothing but mischief. Women that work
like a house afire ought to be treated like one."

" How is that ? " asked Mrs. Potts. Her son was
just out of college, and she knew his answer would
be brilliant, and was disappointed that nobody
laughed when he said : " The first thing to do to a
house afire, you know, is to put it out."

" I suppose Potts means that since such women's
work always ends in smoke anyway, that the quicker
it is put out the better," said Elmer Hood, a classmate and admirer of Shakespeare's wit.

Gretta's eyes sought Mrs. Maitland's. Something in the tone and words of the young men
hurt her.

" I have known Mrs. Bird thirty years," said the
old lady, with gentle dignity, "and she has been
helping somebody all that time."

" But to what good ? " asked Mrs. Egbert, her

eyes twinkling. "She has worn herself out, and as far as anybody can judge, the world is just as miserable and just as wicked as if she had let it alone. Now Mrs. Dougall stays fat and comfortable, but the other has grown like a little thin, yellow wasp, with a sting for everything in her way."

"Why, she actually told in a meeting," broke in another lady, "that her husband, the professor, became so tired because she never had any time for reading, that he said, the alphabet had no longer any significance to her in literature; that she had no use for it except in combinations of initials. As W. F. M. S. or Y. W. C. A. or W. C. T. U., it became mystical and mighty in its meaning. He said she put her capital "C" before everything under the sun that she could term a cause; and that he would like to see it put once in a while before Cooking and Children and Comfort. And you can imagine the effect of this story, given with those sharp vibrations of the thin little voice and the swaying of the thin little body, and the waving of the thin little hands."

"Unless I had heard that," said Mrs. Maitland, quietly, "I should be inclined to consider it the effort to be witty of some person who felt a prejudice against some cause with a capital C."

A faint tinge of color crept to the parting of Potts' pale hair.

"Professor Bird is, as I happen to know, in full sympathy with his wife's efforts," she added. "He is the last man to say any such thing as that, and she the last woman to take a family conversation to any meeting of women."

"Well, I didn't hear it myself," said Mrs. Egbert, "but I think it was said, and moreover I understood that it was received as an indication of masculine inability to rightly estimate the work of women."

"Don't you think," said Potts, with a faint smirk that was meant for a conciliatory smile, "that when women work so hard, night and day, that they lose that womanly sweetness that is so—ah—so sweet?"

He didn't care a pin for the whole subject, but he wasn't easily suppressed, and found his inclination to say what he considered witty things hard to control. "It seems to me," he added, "that those who work night and day are apt to be like a barrel of vinegar: the harder and longer that works, the sourer it gets."

"Doesn't that depend upon whether the nature is acid at the outset?" asked Mrs. Gray, quietly.

"I have known Mrs. Bird for thirty years," said Mrs. Maitland, "and her thin little body, and her thin little voice have, I can assure you, not had as a companion a thin little soul. The difference between that woman and the rest of us is, that the horror and misery and sin of the world are a reality to her, and she genuinely cares to have them removed more than she cares for her own comfort. I have heard her talk of the wrongs of working women, the needs of tenement house children, the sorrows of drunkards' wives, until other women wept, and those who never cared before began to care, and to add the weight of their influence to the work she was trying to do."

"But is it the weight of real influence that they

add?" asked Mrs. Holt. "In Mrs. Dougall's case, what weight is added, except "—she went on almost under her breath—"possibly the weight of so many pounds avoirdupois."

"I know she succeeds in making women temporarily ashamed of their indifference," added Mrs. Egbert, "and now and then she attaches one to her, and tugs her about from meeting to meeting. There is Mrs. Jennings, for example. How much is the influence of such a follower worth?"

"Yet you must admit," said Mrs. Holt, looking up into the colonel's kind face for support, "that Mrs. Jennings' life was all fun and farce till Mrs. Bird convinced her that it was a woman's duty to have views, and to believe in things, and to aid in the coming solidarity of her sex; and Mrs. Bird really has developed her out of her jelly-fish existence into a vertebrate creature. She found her mucilaginous. She knew she would stick to something, and she got her to stick to her, and the vertebræ have developed until Mrs. Jennings now really dares speak out her new ideas in the face and eyes, or I should say in the ears, of her fashionable friends. True, it doesn't matter in the least to her hearers or to herself that the ideas she advances are not her own, but Mrs. Bird's. In fact, she doesn't know it; but even that doesn't matter, for I fancy not many of her hearers would ever find it out."

"No," said Mrs. Gray, thoughtfully. "And why should it matter? The idea, if it is of any value, is the only thing that is of consequence, and I have always felt that in women's work, as in men's, there must come a day when the question of who says it or who does it shall sink into insignificance, and the question of the thing said and done shall be the only thing of importance."

"That means the millennium," said Judge Walton, a white-haired senator, and one of Mrs. Maitland's oldest friends. "But every new and right thought is one more mite taken from the great sum of evil and added to the little sum of good. If life is worth having at all, the little mountain of good must some day overtop the other."

"And I suppose the real business of life," said Gretta, who had watched and listened, but had said almost nothing hitherto, "the chief business of life must be the carrying of mites of evil away from one mountain, and the carrying of mites of good to the other."

"That is the reason, perhaps, why we are sent to the ants for an example," said Dr. Moore. "I sometimes wonder if to the higher intelligences of other worlds our small life, and our ways of conducting affairs upon our planet, may not seem as the work of the ant-builders seems to us. If we could find out the laws of our existence, and follow them with the obedience which those little creatures show, we should all build to better purpose."

"But you cannot think," said Mrs. Egbert, returning to the attack, "that the building is to be done by women's banding together in great organizations, and turning the world upside down and wrong side out, and shaking it as hard as they can, to shake the iniquity out of it, fancying that we can then set it upright, and make it go on after an improved scheme of our own. Now I have known, ever since your Easter party, that the eyes of the organized women have been fixed upon our friend, Mrs. Gray, as a possible coming leader in what they call their glorious fields. I am sure Mrs. Gray must see all such efforts from quite another point of view."

For a moment Mrs. Maitland's eyes rested, with some anxiety, on Katharine's face. It was true she had now position, influence, home, and the use of wealth. The brave old soul that would stand by every good work, however feeble, had its inward trembling lest she might have given all these outward advantages to a woman who would not understand that their only value was their power to bless and comfort and heal the suffering of the world. It was only an instant, but in that instant Katharine knew the older heart's desire. There was left in her still something of that vague feeling that the good she might do would atone for the evil she had done. In any case, she was not going to let Mrs. Maitland feel any disappointment in her chosen almoner and friend. Her face glowed with excitement as she answered in a voice that, while it was low, could be distinctly heard about the board : " I have had little observation and less experience, but it seems to me the highest honor that can come to any woman is the privilege of working in any field that means the uplifting and strengthening and comforting of human bodies or souls. I have not yet been asked to help, but be very sure that if I am, I shall not hesitate to try to do my best." And she motioned to the servant to wheel away Mrs. Maitland's chair, while she rose with the gentle dignity that was becoming her habitual manner, and led the way back to the parlor.

The time between that Easter holiday and the June Commencement passed all too quickly, and the little stir of social pleasure, and the interests arising from it, seemed to have given Mrs. Maitland a new lease of life. As the journey was short and could be taken by carriage, it was possible for Gretta to have the desire of her heart, and see the beautiful old lady in the seat of honor in the midst of the throng on the day of her graduation.

Dr. Moore was there too. He was a lover of music, and no mean musician himself, and yet it was not the music so much as the young singing teacher that drew him to Castleton that day.

It was indeed a proud day for Katharine, as any one could see. It was also a bitter day, as no one who observed her would have dreamed. Her disappointment at Gretta's refusal to take the college course was lessened somewhat, for much that it would have brought both to Gretta and herself was coming without it, and the four years more of study made four years longer for them to wait for the life that seemed already crowding upon both.

Gretta had led her class. There had been several conferences concerning the choice of a graduating theme, and on several subjects proposed by Mrs. Gray the girl had labored earnestly and long. Finally, during their last interview, Gretta had said to her: " I cannot write to my satisfaction on either of those topics. It may be that my heart isn't in them. But I have been here all these years, auntie; I know all these young girls, and many of them I love. It is we who are going out into the new life together. There are many things that I would like to say to them. I am going to give up the effort to write a fine essay, and try to put into my little paper some of these things that I know I shall never have an opportunity to say again."

"I see no reason why you should sermonize, Gretta. You have neither the years nor the experience to make you a counselor of other girls. Why should you put yourself in the rôle of a teacher?"

"I never dreamed of that, auntie. It is not as a teacher or as a counselor that I want to speak to them, but simply as another girl. Let me do the thing that is in my heart, auntie. It may not please you so well. It may not seem brilliant or fine; but you know I do not care for brilliant or fine or clever things. I shall fail if I attempt them. I have faithfully tried to carry out the whole course of study as you thought best. Can you not trust me in this, even if I have my way?" And Katharine yielded, only begging her not to inflict upon her audience a prosy and pious talk.

And when the hour came, in the flower-decked chapel of the school, and the low strains of the music had died away, and the exercises were nearly over, and the slender girl, who had sat in her seat half hidden by the platform's waving palms, stood before them and talked, without her paper, with no oratorical effort or effect, but gently and sweetly, as a young girl would speak to other young girls, Mrs. Gray's disappointment changed to a feeling of gratified and exultant pride that for a moment overswept that swelling sorrow in her heart, that must ever and ever be hidden. She could not be the first to put out her arms after it was over, and let the whole world see and know that this beautiful girl, pure and true as she was fair, was every bit her own. This sorrow laid its silent, cold hand upon her, while lips and eyes were smiling and kept her heart weeping hot tears of longing and trouble and shame.

She bent her head that she might not lose one word. When she heard the subject she started nervously, but from that moment never lost a syllable. Gretta was speaking of the power and value of the Christian principle of love and service in human life, and especially in the woman life of our day. Choosing the highest embodiment of that principle, she called her subject "One in the Midst." With rapid and picturesque lines she revealed the effect of the principles embodied in the life of Christ, in the history, the institutions, the governments, the social conditions, the home, and the individual life of the world. With outlines rapid, strong, and vivid, she opened up the conditions in all of these lines resulting from the lack of the principles that, wherever in human lives they have been truly operative, have made for righteousness and peace.

With discrimination that showed how carefully she had thought and read, she traced the development of every phase of human progress that had, as a governing power, set Christ in the midst ; and, on the other hand, showed how the horrors of war, the persecutions of bigotry, the pangs of poverty, ignorance, degradation, and shame had cursed the world and debased human existence wherever the life of Christ had had no place or power. And when from these broader, general considerations she turned to the individual life, and especially to the woman life of the day, and outlined what might be the highest type of Christian womanhood, dwelling pitifully upon what it must be, lacking this vivifying and ennobling force, Katharine, who had followed eagerly every word, began to feel as if the eyes of this child had read and were depicting the condition of things in her own unhappy soul. For a few moments, as the girl went on, she questioned whether the secrets of her inner life and purpose and motives had been read by these purer eyes that had never looked upon her with one shadow of suspicion clouding their smile of trust.

For a moment the whole room swam before her, but rallying with an effort, she listened through all those last words of earnest pleading with these, who were going forth with her into the struggle of life, to touch nothing, to have nothing, to do nothing, to be nothing in which and of which these everlasting principles should not be the center and the soul. Rich, fortunate, educated, influential, yet without Him poor and empty and desolate indeed. With him, having nothing, yet possessing all things. If they had learned this and nothing else as students, the gain outranked the loss, and it mattered little whether into joy or sorrow, into success or failure, into life or death they passed on, if only at the heart of life they kept the living Christ.

It was all very simple and very gentle and very sweet, and yet not a soul there, from the white-haired old lady, who watched her through her tears, to the youngest schoolmate of them all, that did not know that her own life had throned and crowned him, and that he was indeed the living presence in the midst.

Many flowers came to her, and many kind and loving words, and in all that throng there was only one of her friends who uttered never a word, and in whose soul was anguish where no one else was sad.

"Were not the essays excellent?" asked Miss Graham of Dr. Moore and Judge Conrad, who were standing side by side.

"Yes, beautiful," said Moore, heartily; "and Miss Wild's most beautiful of all. Didn't you like it, Conrad?"

"Yes," he answered, with a far-away look in his eyes; "I liked it for its beauty, but most of all, I like it for its truth." And Gretta, who stood within hearing, though he did not know it, felt as if she had received the word above all praise.

CHAPTER XVI

TO the delight of all who knew her, Mrs. Maitland continued stronger, and the following winter was one of such social pleasure as the old house had not known for many and many a year. To this new phase of existence Katharine gave herself with all her powers. She had allowed herself to be made a director and prominent helper in more than one phase of charitable and philanthropic work, and her name rapidly became known as one who might be depended upon for splendid service, that showed all the enthusiasm of the worker, tempered by the wisdom and grace of the woman of the world. Everywhere she was the chaperon and sharer of the social life that came in full measure to Gretta, and in which was included Miss Graham, as often as Gretta could persuade her away for a day or two from her duties at Castleton.

It might have been to Gretta, had she chosen it, a time of absorption in purely social life; but Mrs. Maitland had encouraged the girl's tendency to devote herself, in part, to those subjects and objects that pertained to general warfare. The girl was, therefore, the sharer of every phase of Katharine's philanthropic work. Together they tried to make practical studies of the problems of the poor, and in all their efforts they had the constant aid and stimulus of the experience of Judge Conrad and Doctor Moore.

Other beautiful and wealthy young girls followed readily in the wake of Gretta's pursuits, and the old mansion at Wildholm became a center, not only of social and intellectual life, but of helpful influence in behalf of everything that was uplifting, beneficent, and true.

The west wing kept always its quota of invalids and the aged, and it was well understood that soon or late the wing would become fully, as it was now in a marked degree, a place where theories might be subjected to the test of practical experiment.

In one sense Katharine was happier than she had ever been before. Everybody admired, respected, and looked up to her. She was a recognized power socially as well as in her various fields of labor, and the distance between her heart and Gretta's seemed in a measure bridged by their mutual interests and work.

Among Gretta's special duties and pleasures were watchfulness of Mrs. Maitland and the sharing with Mrs. Maitland of the ministry to all the inmates of the old west wing. Its invalid rooms were always open to patients of Dr. Moore, and as, from time to time, either Gretta or Miss Graham, who was an enthusiast with reference to the interests of children and working girls, or even Mr. Conrad, who had not by any means abandoned his own investigations in fields of practical service, discovered a poor creature needing the sort of kindness and care that Wildholm could offer, they brought the sufferer there.

Katharine was always ready with counsel and suggestion, but it was the younger women who shared more especially with Mrs. Maitland the work of comforting, encouraging, cheering, and coaxing these poor waifs of humanity back into more hopeful ways of life. The children fell more especially to Gretta's care, and it was she who coddled and played with them, guided and chided and, feeling that life would be hard enough for them by-and-by, resolved that they should be happy at least while sheltered by the old west wing.

The place was not large, and those who went out from it to new situations, or back to their homes after recovery from illness, especially the young girls, fell to Miss Graham's care, until there grew to be enough of them to make almost a parish of her own.

And such was her delicacy and skill in dealing with their various dispositions, and in coaxing them out of their discontent and self-pity and rebellion, that Mrs. Maitland sometimes said, "I cannot conceive where you ever learned it, Margaret. One would suppose that you had lived each one of their separate lives yourself."

A sudden shadow swept down over the girl's bright face, and she turned away hurriedly, saying, "I cannot do very much for them, but Gretta says she thinks I sing them into being good. I can sing to them and I can show them that I care."

"But what makes you care? That is what I do not understand."

"One has to care," she answered, softly, "when one knows, and I think everybody does care who really understands. The indifference of women to the suffering of other women is only because they do not comprehend."

" I have sometimes hoped," said Mrs. Maitland, "that this work might develop into something much larger than it can ever be in my lifetime, and I do not see why the knowledge of the life of every young girl who comes here should not lead, ultimately, to the knowledge of her home, and all the conditions, circumstances, surroundings, and influences that might be improved therein. Every young girl who goes away from here ought to be a co-worker of yours, and you ought to become like the leader of a spiritual community, Margaret, with everybody you can help transformed into a worker in her own little field under your guidance and care "

" I have often dreamed of such a life as that," said Gretta, eagerly ; "and one of these days, perhaps Margaret and I can work it out together. Margaret can only leave the school to come to us from Friday until Monday now, and she winds the girls up for me with the pleasures she plans for them on Saturday, and the singing service on Sunday, so that they run beautifully all the next week. I only wish that, instead of a handful, we had a whole army to hear her every Sunday afternoon."

" Well, one of these days,". said Miss Graham, gently, " when we are through with the music teaching, it may be that life will take such shape that I can give it entirely to such work."

" Then we will have a procession of our working girl and tenement house acquaintances and friends, those who will go to walk somewhere on Sunday afternoons, in spite of our advice against it, turning their steps in the direction of Wildholm," said

Gretta; "and we will build a chapel in' that little grove beyond the west wing, and Miss Graham shall talk to them and sing to them and send them back to be good all the next week. Wouldn't that be lovely? and the best of it all would be that we would have Margaret for ourselves every day in the week."

"And wouldn't that be just lovely for me?" said Margaret, with enthusiasm, smiling up into Mrs. Maitland's face.

"Yes, I think that would be just lovely," said a voice behind her, as Dr. Moore came up the steps and took his seat by Mrs. Maitland's side. "That would be just lovely," he repeated, "to have her all the week." But before Gretta could answer, Miss Graham had put her hand in hers, and drawn her within the door.

"To whom does she belong, Mrs. Maitland?' asked Dr. Moore, turning earnestly to his friend. "Not to that school, surely; I am inclined to think more to you than to anybody else. Where would anybody go who wanted her, not only for all the week, but for all the year round; for all his life, in fact?"

Mrs. Maitland smiled back into his eyes, "You have wanted her a long time, haven't you?" she said.

"Yes, indeed; and I am tired of waiting. If she belonged to you, would you not let me have her?"

"With all my heart," she said, fervently. "I can never be grateful enough that Gretta should have made her one intimacy with a friend like that. The two girls are like sisters. They seem to belong together. They are both Christian women. Gretta has come to her faith by very easy paths; sometimes I suspect Miss Graham has had a harder way."

"I know she has," said Dr. Moore. "She told me that she had had years of doubting whether there was any goodness in God, or in any one of his creatures. And she told me too, that you and your way of life had done more to convince her of both than anything else that had ever come to her."

"Poor child," said Mrs. Maitland. "I fancy she was very lonely at the school, and to come out to us has seemed like going home. Indeed she told me once that this was the only Christian home that she had ever seen. You knew, I presume, that she had a hard struggle to secure her education. She has told me as much as that, and I suspect, when I see her in her ministry to other young women, that she has known more of the hardships of the bread-winner's life than she has told."

"Well, however that may be," he answered, with impetuosity, "I think she has had hardship enough, and I would like to take her away from her pupils."

"One pupil is often a severer task upon a teacher than many," said Mrs. Maitland, playfully.

"Yes, but I would be very docile. She should teach me anything she liked."

"Well, I fancy she could teach us all some things. I am sure the girl has had great experience. Her character is to me like her face, all light and brightness and sparkle, but behind it, as if just waiting to drown the light, a great background of shadow.   In one way I feel that she always opens her whole heart to me ; in another that I do not know her at all."

" Well, I know enough," said Dr. Moore, impulsively, " to be satisfied with her as she is in the present.   I have nothing to do with her past.   I am sure that, whatever it has been, it has had nothing but goodness in it, and I would like to carry her off this very afternoon, little crank that she is, with her silver cross and her white ribbon, and all the rest of her badges and pins, and she might reform me and make me over into any kind of member of any kind of circle she liked."

" Really it does seem a desperate situation, Dr. Moore.   I am afraid this is a case in which the physician cannot heal himself."

" Just that, dear Mrs. Maitland.   And it is a contagious disease too.   Conrad has it as bad as I, only he won't tell me and I won't tell him.   I don't imagine he suspects me ; but, of course, as far as he is concerned, it is written all over his face."

" You think he loves Gretta ? " said Mrs. Maitland, with an earnest tender tone, that revealed that of all things earthly this was what she most desired.

" Loves her!   Why the man doesn't know how to live without her.   Has he not told you so ? "

" Not in words," said Mrs. Maitland.   " Have you told Margaret ? "

" Not yet.   How could I till I asked you if I might ? "

" And yet she doesn't, as you say, belong to me."

" No, but you have grown to be a sort of mother to us all. Conrad feels it as I do. By the way, he got tired of hotel life, and he is coming to live with me; and I have grown so fond of my dear old patient, and she is so much improved, that I am going to bring her back to Washington again."

" Back to us?" said Mrs. Maitland.

"No, not back to you. I—" and he hesitated, "well, for one reason it is not so well for her to be here. At the sanitarium where I sent her, she has grown stronger both in mind and body."

"What was the adverse influence here?" said Mrs. Maitland. "You know I was very feeble when she was in the west wing, and did not see her much. Mrs. Gray told me she thought it was better for her to go."

"Well, frankly, Mrs. Maitland, it was Mrs. Gray who suggested that she should go."

"What! You surprise me," said Mrs. Maitland, bending forward eagerly.

"Well, speaking professionally and psychologically, I can only say that the action and reaction of each upon the other did not seem to be well for either. The fact is, Mrs. Maitland, my old lady was always agitated and troubled whenever she saw Mrs. Gray. On her part, Mrs. Gray always avoided seeing the patient, if possible, and if by chance they met, my old lady was always in a strange state of excitement thereafter; such an excitement," he said, watching Mrs. Maitland, "as in other cases people similarly afflicted have shown when there is a partial recognition and an association with their past life. This is not the only case of this kind that I have had, and, judging from its effect, I should say that the two had known each other in that stage of my patient's existence before she came into her present state."

" Impossible ! " said Mrs. Maitland.   " And yet, where did you say you found her ? "

" In a hospital in Detroit."

" But Mrs. Gray never lived in Detroit.   She lived in Chicago."

" But the accident by which this woman's brain was injured occurred on a train coming from Chicago to Detroit.   May they not have known each other in Chicago ? "

" In that case wouldn't Mrs. Gray remember the woman ? She never said one word or gave one sign of having recognized her."

Moore was silent.   His interest in the case was that of the scientist simply, but he had the type of mind that could never let go a clue.   He believed it would be in his power to nurse the spark of recollection until from it he might kindle to a flame the embers of thought smouldering in the woman's mind.   In Mrs. Gray he had found his only clue. No other influence had seemed to arouse the woman to any agitation of pleasure or of pain.   Gentle and helpful and active, but strangely silent, a dear old body with kind heart and willing hands, he felt that she would be a comfort in his bachelor home, at the same time that he could study, as a scientist, the peculiar phase of her infirmity.

As he rose, thinking to find Margaret in the garden, whither she had escaped with Gretta, Mrs. Gray came on to the veranda dressed for a drive.

As she passed down to the carriage, Mrs. Maitland called, "Stop a moment, Katharine. I want to ask you a question. Dr. Moore has been speaking to me about the silent old lady who was in the west wing for a while."

Katharine neither shivered, colored, nor paled, as once she would have done at mention of the woman.

"Dr. Moore says that she never has given any sign of recollection of anybody, unless her agitation whenever she had seen you was an indication of some association with you in her mind. Did you ever know anything about her?"

"What was her name?" asked Mrs. Gray, quietly.

"That is one of the things I do not know, and one of the things she seems utterly to have forgotten. They never knew at the hospital."

"Where did you find her?" asked Katharine.

"In a hospital in Detroit."

"I have never been in Detroit except to pass directly through upon an Eastern or Western-bound train."

."But they say she was injured in an accident in coming from Chicago to Detroit, somewhere about fifteen or sixteen years ago."

"It is longer than that, as you know, Mrs. Maitland, since I have been in Chicago."

"Oh, of course then, it is only the fancy of a clouded mind," Mrs. Maitland said.

All this time Dr. Moore had said nothing; he only watched Katharine's face. As she turned to go away, he said, "Did her face suggest any association to you, Mrs. Gray?"

A flash of anger came to her eyes. Did he think that he could entrap her?

"Certainly not; why should it?" she answered, quietly; and then resuming her cordial manner, "I am going to drive your way, Dr. Moore. Will you drive with me, and let me set you down at your door?"

"I am going to indulge myself for a few minutes longer here." But he walked by her side to the carriage, and lifted his hat as she drove away. And Harold, turning back, caught a glimpse of a white frock between the leaves of the shrubbery, and straightway forgot patients and science and everything but a dark face, with eyes that, notwithstanding their changing gleams and shadows, were to him like the stars of a quiet night.

"Do not run away from me, Miss Graham," he said, with characteristic eagerness, as Margaret turned toward the path that led to the house. "I wonder what makes you always do that."

"Do what?" she asked, a little glow of consciousness creeping into her eyes.

"Turn away when I am coming."

"I do not always know you are coming," she answered, demurely.

"You did know to-day. It seems to me that I have been coming a year and more, always trying to get nearer, and always feeling that you are trying to escape."

She picked the petals from a flowering shrub by the wayside.

"Lift up your eyes," he said, impetuously. "The light goes out of your face, and out of the world for me, when you hide them. Listen to me, little one. You know me. I am a hard-working, serious man. My youth is gone. I have behind me a life of struggle." She glanced swiftly up into his face. "Yes," he went on, answering the question her eyes asked, "a life of struggle. Every man who is good for anything must fight with himself, with circumstances, with the world, the flesh, and the devil. By God's help," he added, reverently, "I have not been always and utterly defeated. But in all my struggles I have been alone, and I have walked much of the way in the dark."

He paused suddenly. Over his head a long, low bird-note thrilled the summer air.

"Look up, Margaret," he said, gently. "Let me go on in the light." He waited. "Only look," he whispered, "I shall find my answer in your eyes."

And he found it, though when she lifted them the light seemed drowned in happy tears.

From her arm-chair on the veranda, Mrs. Maitland saw two figures arm in arm, go slowly up and down the myrtle walk. It was a very punctual household, but when the old butler came to announce dinner, she said, "Let it wait awhile, 'Lijah. We are not ready to dine just yet;" and she added, as he departed, "see that a cover is laid for Dr. Moore."

And they waited till, when they came she saw on Margaret's breast a cluster of white roses from the farthest hedge, and she held out her hands to them, and drew Margaret's face down and kissed her. Harold's face was radiant. He was walking in the light.

And as the succeeding weeks sped on, these two, loving with all the strength of mature manhood and womanhood, seemed to have gone back into the full glow of early youth. Margaret continued to do beautiful service, having charge of the singing in the Castleton Institute, and Harold worked hard at his profession, busying himself in the intervals fitting up the new house which was to be his home, which, at least while he maintaind bachelor quarters, was to be shared by Theodore Conrad. Yet through all the girl's singing ran the undertone of the new song that her heart had been learning, and through all his work ran the fervor of the love and light that had come into his life. She never sang so well, and his patients never before found him so tender and so strong. And every Friday afternoon, by special arrangement, she came away from duties at the school to take up duties that seemed even more congenial to her, among the poor and the sick and the suffering who were Mrs. Maitland's special charge.

The winter that followed Gretta's graduation found Mrs. Maitland still in comfortable health, happy herself and ready to fill the days with every pleasure for those she loved. It was altogether a wonderful season for opportunity and enjoyment. Wildholm took on the old open-house aspect of Mrs. Maitland's earlier days. Mrs. Gray made a charming hostess, meeting every social demand with such native tact as kept the older woman always in everybody's mind, yet relieved her from all care.

Gretta was not only the light and life of the house, but a great favorite in the large circle of young friends with whom she shared her pleasures, and who, drawn by the influence of her sunny, loving spirit, came to share the work and plans for others which made her own young life such a blessing to the poor.

She had drawn them to each other and to herself, singly or in their pet groups and cliques, caring little whether they put on yellow ribbon, or white, or purple, whether they wore Maltese cross or cross *fleurie*, or no cross at all, so that they came to think and feel and work in accord with the spirit that led her not only to work, but to wear, unhesitatingly, anything that showed the world she belonged in its working force.

With these influences permeating its circles as never before, there was no lack of the elements representing the social as well as the religious and charitable life at the "Conference of Women Workers" in all charitable lines, that took place at midwinter.

The meetings were held in one of the most beautiful churches, where the light falling through the stained glass windows was saved from too somber and subdued a tone by countless flowers that nodded and smiled and filled the air with an incense of their own.

Here were gathered from all sections of the country the thinkers, the writers, the careful students of one phase or another of human need, and the earnest seekers of the wisest and surest ways to help.

The gentleness and dignity and earnestness of the entire proceedings suited the place and the topics.   The power of motherhood as a strong factor in training citizens and patriots was emphasized by women who knew what they meant when they talked of what was needed to uplift the nation from degradation and redeem it from its shame. These were followed by women who had proven by years of labor for women and children in foreign lands, or by searching out and saving the little ones from the degradation of our great cities, that they were ready to make of their outstretched arms an orphanage for the world's childhood, and of their beating hearts a bulwark against its ever-rising tide of misery and sin.

Starting out with strong emphasis of all home influence and all motherly responsibility, the range of topics widened, including the causes and cure of the pauperism, intemperance, and crime that crowd out from our individual and national life "whatsoever things are true and whatsoever things are pure."

There were many thoughtful and well-considered papers; one now and then that showed heart with little thought, or others that showed research without zeal.   Statistics, sentiments, and sympathies sometimes got in each other's way, and now and then an intemperate and intolerant plea for temperance and tolerance found a place for utterance, and gave perhaps a little ground for criticism.

But as a whole the press was patronizingly patient, condescendingly consenting that women should vary their excitements by this sort of play at public service if they chose.   It spoke of the conferences with the good-natured air of the strong man who did not object to his wife's beating him, on the ground that she was such a little thing that it did not hurt him, while it always diverted her.

Once or twice an earnest divine, one on whose lips women hung admiringly, or a glorious reformer at whose shrine they were proud to worship, felt it his duty to whet his pen point to the sharpness of the dissecting knife, and to cut all so-called "women's movements" into infinitesimal bits which were divided among the sermons that aimed at saving the souls of the misguided sex, and the columns of journals for women which paid for the results of the vivisection at so many dollars a column.

Yet with strange lack of appreciation of all such self-sacrificing efforts for their redemption, the women went on, doing some things well, some ill. They were a school of learners, just awakened to the conviction that they were under solemn obligation to know the real conditions of other human lives and to help to make them better if they might.

To Gretta and the young women she had brought with her, much that was seen and heard was like glimpses into an unknown world. None listened more earnestly than these young society girls to the needs as outlined by those older and wiser than themselves, none were more eager and enthusiastic in their desire to learn practical methods of using their own best forces for relief. They were in their seats all day, and Mrs. Gray, who had been urged to preside at the evening session, was already in her seat against the background of nodding palms. The light was not yet fully on as she looked out over the gathering audience, but she caught a picture of

Gretta's bright eager face as the center of this group of lovely girls.

In a pew a little farther back sat Theodore, and farther still, near the door, was Dr. Moore, and beside him a gentle-faced old woman in a close bonnet and soft gray dress of Quaker style and hue. Two days since, Harold had gone to the sanitarium where he took her when she left Wildholm, and he had returned with her only to-night and installed her in his new home.

There was no time for him to flee away to get a look at Margaret, but he knew by her letters that she was to sing at the great convention. He must hear her. Theodore was away at Wildholm no doubt. The old lady seemed restless and tired in her new surroundings and he feared she would be nervous and unhappy without him, yet he must hear Margaret sing. Ready with expedients, he took his patient with him. He would see the face and hear the voice he loved; and she would be happy, and diversion was one of the remedies from which he hoped a cure.

Notwithstanding the prominence Katharine had taken in recent years in charitable work, she had heretofore resisted any appearance upon a public platform, and had only consented to preside to-night at Mrs. Maitland's request and promise to be with her. As she sat there for the first time, the charm of her proud, reserved face deepened by the beauty of her iron-gray hair, Gretta glanced backward to find repeated in Theodore's face her own sense of gratified pride. How graceful and gracious! How thoroughly suited to the occasion and the place she seemed! On her right sat Mrs. Maitland, whose infirmities rarely allowed her to leave home, but who could not on an occasion like this withhold the sanction of her presence. Near her was Miss Graham, who had consented to lighten the more serious programme with her songs. Behind them on the platform were statesmen, clergymen, representatives of science and philanthropy, and distinguished and beautiful women. Forgetting that she was before the eyes of all the people, Katharine waited and gazed out upon the picture like one in a pleasant dream. She felt the softened light, the low strains of the organ, the fragrance of the flowers, and watched the slow procession of people, among whom she recognized a host of friends, as they moved down the aisle and were lost in the audience like a stream swallowed up in the sea. The sense of comfort and well-being was all new and delicious to her. The old harassed and tortured existence seemed to have slipped away into the background and in its place was this new life of ease, and pleasant words and smiles, the every-day and simple pleasures that are the common experience. Now they were hers. She had never before been allowed to feel that they were hers. She had been able to know these simple things only as the result of labor and struggle and shame. Now there was no need to struggle any longer for herself or for her child. It was delicious to cease to fight and watch, and to have things come of themselves.

Suddenly the light deepened, as when the sun moves out from under a cloud, and tossing plumes, and waving fans, and gay attire, and fair faces, and bright eyes, lay illuminated before her. The organ notes softened, and then out upon the beauty and the radiance floated Miss Graham's voice. Under its spell the people held their breath, and as the strains rose and fell, bearing all hearts upon their melody, Katharine knew that Mrs. Maitland must have chosen the music, for these were the words that Margaret sang:

"The Lord thy God—in the midst—in the midst of thee is mighty; he will save, he will rejoice over thee with joy; he will rest in his love." And as she sang, Mrs. Gray's eyes wandered over the throng, seeing Theodore, whose face reflected reverently the singer's words, and Mrs. Maitland's eyes shining through grateful tears, and Gretta's face gleaming like a star, and farther on her gaze rested upon a face that suddenly gleamed out from the standing group under a stained glass window— a man's face, haggard and scarred with marks of wasted years and unrepented sin — the face of Robert Gray.

Then the great throng rocked and swung before her, and her deathly white face stared straight on beyond all to that other face that stood still though everything else swayed, while above it, in the stained glass window's mosaic of crimson and blue and gold was a figure of St. Michael above the cringing form of the dragon, poising the glittering sword.

It was her place as presiding officer to announce the next item on the programme. The music ceased. Not a word of what she meant to say would come, but written on her brain as she had heard it sung over and over, were the words that made her first public testimony uttered unconsciously and quite against her will. In a clear, solemn tone she said, reverently: "The Lord thy God in the midst of thee is mighty—he is here, in the midst. The Rev. Bishop Reynolds will lead us in prayer;" and while their heads were bowed, she passed swiftly through the door that led to the pastor's study. Neither Mrs. Maitland nor Margaret had taken special note of her words, but Gretta's heart gave a great throb of gratitude to hear the lips that heretofore had always seemed to shrink from uttering the "name that is above every name," that never, even at home, joined audibly in hymn or prayer, thus make their first public utterance a word that turned all hearts toward Him. She prayed earnestly, but even through her prayer she was conscious of a movement, a step, a presence, and she lifted her head to see Theodore passing noiselessly forward down the aisle. She followed. Katharine was sitting bolt upright in the pastor's study chair, like a woman of stone, her face set as in the gray pallor of death. "It's nothing," she gasped feebly as Gretta lifted her head to her breast; "I will go back in a moment;" but, opening her eyes she saw Mr. Conrad gazing down upon her with the old pitying look that had marked his face in his boyhood.

"You are not to go back," he said, with his air of masterful tenderness. "Go in quietly, Gretta, and whisper to Mrs. Maitland that the heat and excitement are too much for Mrs. Gray, and we will take her home."

"Shall Margaret come with us?" said Gretta.

"No, she is to sing again, and she will stay with Mrs. Maitland. I will come back for them both. There are plenty of ladies to preside."

When Gretta stole in with her message she found Mrs. Maitland, who had never done such a thing in her life before, filling with ease and grace the president's chair, and the programme going on as if nothing had occurred. "Brave old soul," murmured Theodore, when Gretta came back; "she will stand by her colors every time."

Dr. Moore, from the distant seat, had noticed the change and movement on the platform. Tucking the little mother's arm in his, he drew her gently out at the door and round the corner to the pastor's study, and unseen, there crept after him the tall, pale man whose eyes had darkened with fierce anger and hate as he saw the woman's face.

"Wait a moment for me here," said Harold, placing her on a bench in the vestibule. "I want to run upstairs; I fear some one is ill; it will only be a moment."

But in that moment the baize-covered doors had swung noiselessly open, and in the dim light, the poor trembling old woman stood face to face with the one human being whose hate she had reason to fear. He sprang toward her with a curse that was more like the snarl of an angry dog than like a human sound. She saw the face, the lifted hand, and the shock and the terror startled her long-numbed faculties to action, and wakened the long slumbering memories and fears. With a cry of "Ted! Ted! Help me, Ted!" she sprang toward the staircase, escaping the blow that fell heavily upon the bench where she sat. The cry to Theodore, like a voice from the dead, reached his ears. With one swift bound he cleared the steps, and gathering her in one strong arm, grasped her assailant with the other, and pressed him writhing and panting back against the wall. For one instant he held them there, and the lion that could have torn the man to pieces battled with the child that could have hid his head upon the wrinkled neck of this old woman to sob out his grief and be comforted. She trembled and clung to him with all her strength.

"Don't let him get me," she muttered, beside herself with fear.

"No, no, little mother, he shall not hurt you. I am here. I will take care of you. Don't you know Ted, your own little Ted? Where have you kept her hidden from me all these years?" he asked, turning fiercely upon the man, who, cowed and panting for breath, made no effort to resist or to escape.

"He did not hide her," said Dr. Moore, coming swiftly down the stairs. "I left her here a moment ago. This is my little patient that I brought home to-night. Can you not understand?"

"Yours, your patient, Harold? She is mine—my mother; and she knows me too; and this man is her enemy and mine."

A rustle on the stairs above and Gretta appeared. "Is the carriage ready?" she called; "auntie is able to go home now."

"Wait a minute, Harold," said Theodore. "Here,

little mother, stay with our good doctor," and he loosened her arms tenderly. " You take her home to Wildholm, doctor. We must not let either of the sick ones have more excitement. Come, the carriage is waiting." Never loosing the hand from Robert's collar he led his mother gently to the street. Mrs. Maitland's carriage was waiting. "Take the ladies and the doctor home, Thomas, and come back for Miss Graham and· myself. We shall be here when the meeting is over." Then he hurried Robert around the corner so quickly that he did not see the white-faced woman who came out with Harold and took her seat in the carriage, and was driven away with Gretta and Mrs. Burke.

All the way the doctor was very silent, but he kept a finger of one hand on Mrs. Gray's pulse, and another on that of Mrs. Burke. Gretta tried to throw her arms protectingly about her aunt, and was touched to see that she did not want to be held, but tried to draw the girl down to her breast and held her tight as if she feared she might never have her again. In the darkness she felt for the girl's face and covered the brow and cheeks with tender, passionate kisses. Whatever the blow that had come to her, it had unlocked the fountain's tenderness, so long sealed up apparently beneath her reserve and pride.

As for the Widow Burke, she sat as one dazed and dumb. The doctor had not recovered from his astonishment, but if Theodore was right and she had recognized him, he had new evidence that his own theory that the heart held the key to the brain was true. His own heart rejoiced for Theodore and his mother, but to him the old creature was still a "case," and the wonder of the scientist had hardly yet yielded to the interest of the friend. If she knew him she would know others, so he reasoned. She evidently had known her assailant, and as if to prove he was right she suddenly reached over to the corner where Mrs. Gray sat with Gretta's head on her arm, and said, "Are ye going back wid the carriage for my Ted, lady dear?"

"Yes," answered Dr. Moore, for he noticed that Mrs. Gray seemed to shrink from her companion.

"Whilst he's coming, darlin', ye must let me get you to shlape. Ye're needin' rest, God help ye, if that thafe of a man has been shtalin' yer childer all the toime. No wonder yer hair is white, dear, and ye won't lave her out of your arms. Whin I gets me Ted, I'll rock him and hould him too, like he was a little boy."

Dr. Moore quieted her, and bade her not to disturb the lady, for he thought the excited brain wandered, and Katharine answered never a single word. She had known nothing of the encounter and could only hope that Robert had not seen her or known her if he had seen.

Theodore once in the street relaxed his hold and taking the stranger by the arm, they turned away from the church. Robert walked tottering, whether from feebleness or drink Theodore could not tell, but he took him into the restaurant of the nearest hotel, and ordering a good supper was surprised to find the man ate like one who had fasted long. His clothing was worn but decent; and his face showed the ravages of illness or of drink.

Until they were at the table not a word was said. Then Ted, whose hot anger had given place to the problem as to how to protect his mother and Mrs. Gray, said quietly, "Once you invaded her home, and she humiliated you." A great oath burst from the man's lips. "You deserved all you got and more, and you shall not harm her now, for I can protect her."

The man half rose and angrily pushed back his plate. "Will you not take something more?" asked Theodore.

Robert sneered, "Yes, if you please."

"What shall I order?"

"Whisky."

"Not a drop from me," said Theodore. "Not one drop."

"You need not be so mean as that to me; I never did you any harm."

"Your conduct cost me my mother, and cost her her reason, and we have only just found each other after being each eighteen years alone."

"And I would have killed her if I had got my hands at her throat," he broke in, with a curse that could only have had its origin in a long-nursed hate.

"You will never attempt to touch her again," said Ted, his eyes gleaming like cold steel. The man sneered. "And, more than that, you will keep away from your wife. Understand, I suffered too much in protecting her from you when I was a boy to have you trouble her again. They must be absolutely left alone by you, now and forever."

"Who made you their guardian, I would like to know?"

Ted waited a moment, and then said reverently, "God."

The old man laughed a sneering laugh. "I have never lost trace of her, the beggar. Living in luxury instead of clinging as a wife should to her husband. Leaving me to wander over the earth with no one to do the first thing for me sick or well. Even my own child deserted me; but I'll be even with them yet. I don't want the women. Heaven knows I have no use for them; but I want money, and I'm not going to see them live in luxury and not be able to get a drop of whisky when I need it. I am a sick man," he added in a whining tone, "I ought to have medical advice and care."

"I think that is true," said Theodore; "but it will not come through tormenting women and girls. That part of your life has come to an end."

"Whose business is it but my own?"

"Mine," answered Ted, his eyes blazing.

"Look here," said Robert, "I'm no beggar. All I want is an advance on my own property. When my old governor sent me abroad I was so temperate and so honest, don't you see, that after a while I persuaded him to let me have a little money to develop the business here and there. And when I got it I enlarged after my own ideas. I made the most of it fly, I assure you; but I *did* make some investments, just enough to keep the supplies coming. When my daughter left me to go to the dogs, I went, but I wandered back over the old ground last year, and these investments that we thought a dead loss, some of them had begun to pay. I sold some land and the proceeds I ate up and drank up; but I tell you there is more and better for those that can afford to wait. There is land in California and in Australia that cost a song and cannot be sold now, but that means a fortune by-and-by."

And Theodore did not believe a word of it; but he gave him money for a lodging, told him he would devise some plan to keep him from want, on *one* condition, that he go away and never trouble any of his family more. They parted to lunch at the same place on the next day, and Theodore did not notice as he took his way back to the church that this shuffling, bent figure was following close behind.

The meeting had been long. The audience was standing. The last hymn was being sung. The shivering old man edged his way between the people till he stood where he could see and hear. Mrs. Maitland stood in the foreground, stately and noble, her face glowing with this unwonted experience of a great multitude of women pledged each to do her share of Christ's unfinished work, each eager to unite service and worship, and all standing together, daring to think and to speak and to act for the uplifting of the children of men. It made her feel like saying, " Lord, now lettest thou thy servant depart." Close beside her, her glorious voice leading all the rest, was her young friend, Margaret Graham, whose life was already a power for untold good; and down there, gazing up to them, as from hades one might gaze at the beauty and listen to the music of paradise, was this weak and wicked wreck of what God meant should be a man. And Margaret went on singing, singing up into heaven, when suddenly her eyes fell upon that sneering, wasted face. She bowed her head with the rest at the benediction. The crowd was great. There were many pressing for greetings and hand grasps. How should she get to him or he to her? How could she bear to make him known to those who would see her greet the stranger? All the time, though she did not look, she felt him coming closer. The look she had seen on his face said he would claim her before all the world, and she, like a fascinated bird drawn nearer and nearer every moment to the serpent's fangs, heard congratulations, felt friendly hand grasps, said her little pleasant words to one and another, coming closer and closer to this sneering, leering creature all the time. Suddenly a tall form stood between them, and Theodore said, abruptly, " I am very sorry, Miss Graham, but Mrs. Maitland begs you will not wait one minute longer. Indeed, I fear she is already feeling the effect of the excitement and the chill of the night air. This way; allow me." And he wrapped her mantle about her, keeping his broad figure between her and the crowd, and hastily taking her through the rear door, in another minute they were gone.

As the carriage turned the corner, Theodore caught a glimpse of Robert Gray's angry and disappointed face as he emerged from the church, and thought he had probably returned hoping for one more glance at his wife and child. Robert asked a coachman waiting on the pavement whose coach it was that had just passed, and was told it was "the Maitland carriage from Wildholm."   "And where is Wildholm?"   "Out on the boundary; any one will tell you," answered the man; "and the street car will take you within a hundred yards."

When they reached home, Katharine was reported as resting quietly in the care of Gretta and Debby, who, contradictory as it seemed, was never quite so happy as when somebody had a pain, for then she had a chance to nurse and coddle and pet. Harold hoped a night's rest would relieve the attack, whose cause, if it were fatigue only, seemed to his practised medical eye wholly inadequate to the effect.

He had not succeeded in inducing the "little mother" to go to rest, for unfortunately he had said on the way up that Ted would come and take her to his home.   And when Ted came, she lifted her tired eyes, and said, as he bent over her, "Ah, yere at yer old ways, Teddy; I never could cure ye of runnin' out at night."   And when they were in the carriage, she laid her head down on his shoulder, and in one minute was asleep.

CHAPTER XVII

CONSIDÉRATE of Katharine's condition and watchful lest some new excitement overtake Mrs. Burke, Harold had foreborne all allusion in the presence of Mrs. Gray and Gretta to the outbreak that had occurred in the vestibule of the church. Theodore, with equal caution, had said nothing of it to Mrs. Maitland or Margaret as they drove back to Wildholm. The next day found Katharine better, and Mrs. Maitland none the worse for her exertions. Indeed, but for her solicitude for Mrs. Gray, she would have felt rather triumphant over her unexpected opportunity to bear testimony to her sympathy with the objects of the convention, and with the effort of women to meet their full share of responsibility for the welfare of the world.

Overwhelmed by the encounter in the church and anxious for solitude that she might face her new trial, Margaret fled to her room without the usual bedroom talk with Gretta. She threw herself on her knees by the window, and as the carriage drove away with Theodore and his mother, she saw Harold's face lifted eagerly in the moonlight and knew that he had waited for a word and smile from her, and the sight of his disappointed face made all the sorer the struggle of the bitter night.

Too sleepless and excited in the morning to remain quiet in bed she came down much earlier than usual and went to her usual rounds, looking in upon one or two of the sick ones in the west wing and wandering thence away through the garden paths, lingering a few moments at the spot where Harold had told her of his love and won her to share his life. As if the thoughts that came there were those from which she could not too speedily hasten, she rose and walked forward rapidly as if trying to escape from herself, never pausing until she had reached the gate that opened to the road.

A hundred yards away ran the street car line from the city, and as she saw the yellow cars go rapidly by, a great impulse seized her to take one and go somewhere, anywhere, to escape the trouble that she knew was near at hand. While she lingered, a car stopped. A man descended, hesitated a moment, and then obeying the conductor's hand that pointed toward the gate of Wildholm, came staggering forward with a shambling gait that might mean feebleness or worse. At the first glance she knew him and, obeying a sudden impulse, she turned and walked hurriedly toward the house. But at her second thought she paused. Why should she bring to the friends, and worse, to the servants of the home that had sheltered her, a knowledge of this man? He was her own disgrace and sorrow; surely she ought to bear it alone. And, though she would have given worlds to meet him if she must, with Harold, or Mrs. Maitland, to prove to him that she had friends, she yet turned back. Seated on a bench near the gate, half hidden by a clump of shrubbery from the road, she waited for the coming of the man who had been the burden and blight of her life. He shuffled forward slow'y, and overwhelmed as she was that his coming meant death to all her hopes of happiness, she yet noted pitifully the signs of feebleness and age. He started at sight of her, but anger seemed at once to oversweep all pleasure or surprise.

"So you lie in wait for me here?" he said. "You turned your back on me last night when I appeared among your fine friends, and now you stand between them and me again. I am going on up to that house yonder. I'll show them who you belong to," he added, quivering with drunken rage. "You will find I can give you trouble enough."

For a moment she felt powerless, but only for a moment. "You will only make trouble for yourself in that way," she answered, quietly. "Come and sit down here by me," she added, moving to make room for him. "Unless I go to the house with you, there is no one to receive you there. The servants would not admit you, and no one would listen to your story."

"I would shout it under the windows," he said, gesticulating wildly. "I would tell them how you have broken your promise."

"Then they will think you intoxicated or a lunatic. You are reeling already," she said. "Stop here and I will listen to you. I am sorry to see you looking so ill. Go there and I shall not go with you, but I will go away while you are gone, where you will not find me. What is it that you want of me?"

For a moment her strong and steady will held him from his purpose, and he began to grow maudlin and to weep with sudden self-pity. "You promised to come back if I needed you, and I am old and very poor and very sick. I want a home and you in it to take care of me. I want to stay with you. Haven't I slaved all my life to take care of my dear family?" he said, growing tragic; "am I a man to be deserted?"

Something like the shadow of a smile played for a moment over her look of well-controlled disgust, but she answered calmly: "You are not deserted, you shall be cared for; I will keep every promise, but not here. Go away, go back to Chicago, anywhere but here, and I will see that you do not lack for care."

He drew himself nearer to her side, tears still standing in his watery eyes, and put out his arms as if to embrace her, but she drew herself away. "Just as you please," he said, with an air of grieved affection. "You are my long-lost darling, and now to find you so beautiful, so kind. I would like to go to Chicago," he said, wiping his eyes, "the scene of my happy boyhood, the last resting-place of my beloved parents; but, alas——"

"You are going to say you have no money," she said, cutting short his sentimental outburst. "I will furnish you with just enough to take you to Chicago and supply your needs on the way. Stop," as he would have thrown himself upon his knees before her; "I know you will go, and go at once, for I shall send some money on to Mrs. ——, your old nurse, who lives in the house you know so well, with instructions to give you her best room and care for you and to give you the money if you apply for it not later than three days from this. That will enable you to go to-night. If you are not there on the third day, then the funds are to be returned at once to me."

There was still more protest, still more declaration that he could not leave without her, still more complaint that was hard to answer or to listen to, but it ended in his waiting for her while she went to the house, returning with the funds for a journey which he promised to take that night. And while she was gone his muddled brain recalled that he had come to Wildholm as much or more to seek Katharine as to find Miss Graham. Fortunately for the former there was enough of native cunning left him to decide that he would not risk the unexpected good luck that had come to him by any further effort to-day. It would be soon enough to come back upon his wife when he had gotten out of Margaret all he could. Yes, yes, he would go ; with money awaiting him there he would go ; but there was no law that would forbid his coming back again some day and renewing his acquaintance with Katharine Gray. For the present he took the money, and five minutes later took the car that bore him once more out of Margaret's sight.

Some hours later, having visited a barber, a clothing store, and in a measure recovered from the effect of his cheap morning dram, he sauntered with an air of easy insolence into the restaurant where he had promised to meet Theodore, who was already there looking over the morning papers. He nodded to the waiter to bring the meal already ordered, and noticing the change for the better in his guest's appearance, added to his "Good morning, Mr. Gray, I hope you found a comfortable rest last night."

"Yes," answered the other. "I went back to the church and heard the last of the music, though church-going hasn't been very much in my line of late."

"I presume not," said Theodore, as he led the way to their table in a quiet alcove.

"I do not mind telling you," said the man, with an air half-insolent and half-conciliatory, "that I went back for a purpose. I read in the paper that Mrs. Katharine Gray was to preside at that meeting. I presume they hadn't heard *I* was in town, or they would have made it Mrs. *Robert* Gray."

Theodore watched him closely. "You saw her?" he asked quietly.

"No, I didn't get in until the singing, and I confess, though my eyes are not of the strongest, that I saw only the singer. A white-haired lady was in the chair. But it doesn't matter that I did not meet her. It was hardly a place for a conjugal interview after an absence of so many years. I shall find her at home at Wildholm, no doubt."

"At Wildholm?" said Theodore, with astonishment.

"Yes, I have naturally traced her movements, and I knew last night that she went to Wildholm. I saw her daughter drive away and I learned it was the Wildholm carriage, and you may be very sure that where the daughter is, the mother can be found. Besides, I looked for her in that old parsonage in Massachusetts, where her father used to live, and they told me that she was living at Wildholm with Mrs. Maitland. I intend some day to seek her there."

Theodore rested his arms upon the table and bent forward until his face came close to that of his neighbor. "You will never find her there," he said, between his teeth.

"And what shall hinder me?" said the man, insolently.

"I will hinder you. Look here, Mr. Gray, we are here for business. You told me last night that you wanted money. You told me you had still some property. I have a proposition to make to you. Nothing but misery can come to Mrs. Gray by your coming back into her life. Furthermore, she will not have you in it, after your brutal treatment of her; and further still, you have no right in it. You have no claim upon her whatever. More than that, I will see that she is guarded against you day and night. But it is true, as you have told me, that you are old and ill. It is true that you must suffer if you have not proper care and comforts. Make over to me in trust for your wife and your daughter your claim to the property you say still remains in California and in Australia—property that must be worthless to you and probably would be worthless to anybody— and I will supply you with an annuity that, paid monthly as long as you live, shall be sufficient for your support. Stop!" as the man was about to speak, "there is one condition, that you never again make an attempt to see Mrs. Gray, and that you make your home away from Washington."

The man began to bluster, but was sharply interrupted.

"We needn't waste one word in talk. You have your choice. Take this offer or your chance of ending your days in suffering and want. I do not imagine that this property of which you speak has any value, but if it has, it should not surely be squandered like the rest."

"What will you do with it?" asked the man, with a sneer.

"See that it is taken care of for the benefit of your wife and child."

"My child; ah, she can take care of herself and me too; and I mean that she shall do it. You are very kind not to demand that I shall never endeavor to see my child. Why do you not include her in your conditions?"

"Simply because I can prevent your seeing her without conditions."

There followed a great deal of bluster and defiance and irritation; but it ended, as Theodore knew it would. The bird in the hand must not be allowed to escape. Robert went with him to the shabby lodgings, for which his own money had paid, and from the old traveling bag there were taken and given over to him whatever papers he possessed. A deed of sale for all right and claim to the properties, of which the papers contained descriptions, was executed, and the first instalment of the annuity paid, the ticket bought, and the man on the way to Chicago without ever once having been allowed to escape from Theodore's sight.

As the train moved out, the stern face relaxed

and he gave an audible sigh of relief, when passing from the door of the station he came face to face with Margaret Graham. She seemed embarrassed, and declined to let him take her home ; so after putting her on the Boundary line car, he turned his face homeward, eager to give to the clinging little mother all that remained of this his first day after the separation of many years. Henceforth, whatever might come into his life, the little, white, silent shadow of the brave, rollicking, hard-working woman who had taught him to speak the truth and not to be afraid to work, was to have all he could do to atone for the desolate years.

It was a very sad heart that Margaret bore back to the house that morning. Neither Mrs. Maitland nor Mrs. Gray came down to breakfast, and Gretta and her friend were too close and dear not to allow each to the other the privilege of silence.

"You went over to the west wing early, I hear," said Gretta. "You should have stayed in bed as I did and taken a good rest after such an excitement as last night. I find I must take better care of my dear ones," she added. "Auntie seems quite prostrated to-day. I believe the dear grandmamma has borne it best of all. I wonder what it is," she went on, noticing that Margaret did not care to talk, "that makes all such public occasions a strain upon the bodies and nerves of women. The nobler and more sensitive the woman the more it seems to wear upon her strength and to rob her of vitality. I have sometimes wondered if the opponents of all such work for women have not one of their strongest arguments there."

"But I do not see why it is harder than teaching or the strain of social life."

"Yet you must admit that it is. I have listened so eagerly when the grand women, who almost all of them are close friends of grandmamma, talk with her, hoping there would be one who would not say she stayed in public life and work from sense of duty, yet longed for the day when she need not, when she could pass it on and feel that her task was done. It seems to me they each and all take too much. Surely God does not mean to lift the burdens of the race by piling them all on the shoulders of a few devoted ones."

"I cannot tell," said Margaret, kissing Gretta, as arm and arm they went up to seek Mrs. Maitland. "It seems to me that women are, and perhaps it is all right that they should be, the scapegoats of the world. I would like to talk that whole matter over with you one of these days, Gretta."

"Yes, dearie, and let us see if we cannot find a better way, if we cannot be of use and yet save our souls alive."

The next few days Harold made Margaret atone for having escaped him on the night of the meeting by claiming a great deal of her time. It was a most joyful day for him until there fell upon it a strange shadow, that seemed to creep up from the very depths of Margaret's heart. He felt it and yet refused to feel it until at evening, in the same sheltered path where she had lifted her eyes to his and let the light of her love shine into his life, she quietly withdrew it again, with no explanation except that it was right, and she had been wrong to admit that she had ever loved him. In desperation he pleaded and talked, until, as the night came down and the stars came out, he put his arm about her and said, "Come with me to Mrs. Maitland. She is like a mother to both of us. I will do anything she says, except," he added under his breath, "to give you up altogether." And, with a gentle hand, he drew her into the old lady's presence, and placing the cushions for her, he led her to Gretta's place at Mrs. Maitland's feet, and placed himself beside her on the step.

"We have come to tell you all about it, mother," he said, with an attempt at cheerfulness. "I had been telling Margaret that the new house is ready, but that I have given up my intention of making bachelor quarters of it; and I have placed there my faithful man-servant, and some good women to take care of it, every one of them people whom I have cured or helped, and to whom I fancy I have given back their lives, and who are ready to serve me and mine upon their knees, if I so wish. I have got my little old patient to keep as a patron saint to smile at us, and say a thousand prayers a day for us, a prayer on every bead, as she slips them continually through her fingers. I have told Conrad that I still have a room for him, though it is not going to be bachelor quarters as we expected, and that I want him to be sure to be home and to stand beside me with Gretta on Easter eve.

"You see, Mrs. Maitland, what an arbitrary fellow I am. I am arranging it all my own way. When we come together for the evening worship here on Easter eve I want to bring that dear old white-haired chaplain, who gave the best part of his life to the sick and wounded in the army, and who is now the comfort of all the poor souls in our city mission.   He is the sort of clergyman who is after our own hearts, and like his Master full of grace and truth.   And I want just there, after the evening prayers are over, to be married to this precious little woman here, and take her away to my home. And I have been telling her all about it, when she tries to break my heart by saying that it is impossible that we should ever marry.   She withdraws, not her love,—I do not believe that is possible,—but she withdraws the promise made to me that other evening when we lingered so long out there under the trees."

"What reason can she give?" asked Mrs. Maitland, laying her cool hand on Margaret's burning cheek.

"I have no right to ask a reason, if she does not offer one."

"No, no," interrupted Margaret, "he has every right, and yet I cannot tell.   The truth is that I did very wrong, Mrs. Maitland.   I—I let myself be tempted.   I forgot my promise."

"Your promise! certainly not your promise to another?" said Harold, fixing upon her a startled gaze.

She hesitated, waited, and hid her face in Mrs. Maitland's lap.

"Certainly you cannot mean that?" said the old lady, softly caressing the brown hair.

There was no answer, but the bowed head moved in assent.

"Am I to understand," said the man, rising, a gray pallor sweeping swiftly over his face, "that a promise to some other man is the obstacle in our way, and that you gave yourself to me without once giving me a hint of such a fact?"

"Gently, gently," said Mrs. Maitland, "there must be some mistake."

"There can be no mistake," he answered, sternly. "Either it is the truth, or it is not."

"Surely, Margaret, there must be some explanation. You would not plunge him into a darkness like this, and leave him there, alone."

The pause was broken only by the girl's low sobs.

"Poor child, poor little girl!" said Harold, gently, "she is excited and overstrained, and we are troubling her, and after all it doesn't matter. Nothing shall separate us in earth or heaven. Let us give her a little time, and she surely will explain," and his hand swept gently down over her tear-stained face, as he turned away.

"No, no, do not let him go!"

"Harold," said Mrs. Maitland, "come back. She will explain."

"No, no, I cannot," moaned the girl.

"And I am to understand there is no explanation then," he said, coldly, as if all the warmth of his tenderness had suddenly been chilled to ice.

There was no answer. "Speak," whispered Mrs. Maitland. "You are wrecking your whole life's peace."

"I cannot," answered the girl.

"Good night, Mrs. Maitland. Good night, Miss

Graham," and in another moment they heard the clang of the gate and the ever-lessening sound of footsteps as he went forth into the dark.

They sat in silence. Old Debbie came to help her mistress to her room.

"Good-night, dear child," said the old lady softly to Margaret. "You said you must go back to Castleton in the morning. If you want to see me at any hour in the night come to my room; I shall be awake."

Margaret and Gretta occupied adjoining rooms. Long after Gretta was asleep, Margaret sat by the window. More than once she left the room and crept softly down the corridor, and waited by Mrs. Maitland's door. Then her resolution failed her, and she crept back again. And every time she went, Katharine, sitting in the arm-chair behind the curtain that swept across the door of her own chamber, saw her go and saw her come. Once, the third time, she had made up her mind, she would surely have gone within, but Katharine's hand swept back the curtain, and she said, rather coldly, "You are restless, Miss Graham. Can I do anything for you? I stayed with Mrs. Maitland until I think she dropped asleep. She is not well to-night, and ought not to be disturbed."

"You are right," the girl said softly, "she shall not be disturbed."

CHAPTER XVIII

IN a few weeks came again the Easter holiday. Harold waited one week. Then the young girls, taking their morning stroll in the grounds of Castleton, saw the stalwart man striding straight toward the door.

He sent in his card to the lady in charge, "I hope I am not trespassing," he said, as Madame Crozier came to the parlor. "I am specially anxious to see Miss Graham, and to see her, if possible, at once. I hope this is not an hour when I shall find her engaged."

Madame Crozier looked for one moment into his earnest face and, seeing the anxiety there, answered with unfeigned regret, "I am so sorry that you should have come too late, Dr. Moore, but Miss Graham is already gone."

"Gone! where?"

"Since last she came back from Washington she has seemed ill, and really unequal to the conduct of her work. As some of her pupils go home early for the Easter vacation, I advised her to leave the remaining lessons to her assistant, and to lengthen the vacation by taking another week at this end. She consented, rather reluctantly I thought, and left yesterday for the West."

"Do you know her destination?"

"She said she should be traveling from place to

place, but she gave me this, giving a teachers' agency in New York, from which point she said her letters would be forwarded from time to time, as she might write for them. I hope she is going to travel, for she greatly needs rest and change. Do you know anything of her future plans, Dr. Moore?"

"Certainly not," he answered, quietly. "Is she not to return to the school?"

"I supposed so until she was gone; but a letter came this morning from New York, in which she said, that since circumstances might arise that would prevent her return, and her duty might call her in other directions, she did not consider it right for me to hold the position open for her, and she would therefore resign it, trusting to secure another, should it be necessary for her to do so. Of course, she can have no difficulty in doing that, for I say to you very frankly, Dr. Moore, that her voice, her training, and her methods are all exceptional. She could easily make her fortune upon the operatic stage."

"I think however, that her inclinations, and possibly her principles, would be averse to such a life," he answered.

"Yes," said Madame Crozier, deprecatingly; "she is a little morbid about those things. She fancies that her voice is a sacred charge, given her to be used for the benefit of the world. I, for my part, do not see why she should not use it in elevating those classes who would hear her elsewhere, as well as to use it in drawing rooms or places where the proceeds are to go for charity; but of course, I have no right to attempt to modify her views concerning purely personal things."

" And the New York letter gave no permanent address?"

" No, she wrote from this same agency, where she was evidently arranging to have her mail received, and said that she was leaving New York almost immediately for the West. You will not leave us, Dr. Moore?" as he rose to go. "This is one of our lecture afternoons, and Mrs. Gray, from Wildholm, whose niece was a favorite and prominent pupil here, is coming to address our girls. We would be glad to have you remain; indeed, we would be only too grateful if you could be persuaded to say a few words to them."

" Thanks, many," said Dr. Moore. "In such able hands as yours and Mrs. Gray's, they will have little need of anything that I could offer. She will say only such words as will do them good."

"It is wonderful how she succeeds in inspiring them," Madame Crozier went on. "No one comes to us who arouses in them such enthusiasm for various lines of helpful work. Why, she has the white ribbon on a whole group of them already, and they are all divided up into little bands and circles, working for one cause or another, and doing every time whatever Mrs. Gray suggests."

" Yes," he answered, thoughtfully, "there is nothing truer than that the young womanhood of the country can be led into every possible good, if only their leaders are true and kind and wise, as I am sure they are here," he added, smiling and bowing low over her outstretched hand. Then he took his way back through the grounds to the little station to wait for the next up-train.

Fortunately the gentle woman did not see the sneer that came to his countenance as he crossed the threshold, a sneer that deepened and deepened as he strode through the wood, setting his face like ice in the expression of stern scorn that really half startled Mrs. Gray, as she met him walking up from the station to the school.

"I congratulate the young ladies on having the benefit of your wisdom this afternoon," he said, lifting his hat as he made way for her to pass.

"Not great wisdom," she answered; "but they are so eager for even the crumbs that I can give them, that it makes me wish that some one would feed them who can really offer bread; but I feel, on the other hand, that if any one of us knows one thing that the others do not know, we are bound to tell it in times like these."

"Ah, well," he answered, lightly, "bread or a stone, one doubts sometimes if it matters much. A good many of them do not know the difference, and a good many of them can draw as much nutriment for brain and soul out of the one as they would be capable of taking out of the other."

She looked at him sharply. Was he reading her and chiding her for preaching what she did not practise, and teaching what she did not know?

"I have sometimes thought," he went on, bitterly, "that much of the slimy sinuosity and wriggling inconsistency of youthful character, feminine as well as masculine, is largely due to the fact that we older people keep on hand for the young a plentiful and persistent diet of serpents and of stones. You see that is contrary to Scripture, and I am coming more and more to believe that the Bible is a true book. Of course, I do not mean to insinuate that *you* are not bearing to them bread enough and fish enough to feed the multitude, and to gather up baskets of fragments for the next company of young women that you will meet. *Au revoir*," he added, lightly, not waiting to give her time to reply.

Without a word Katharine stood and gazed after him as he moved away. What did he mean? She had not answered the question to her satisfaction, when she reached the door and met Madame Crozier, who had seen her coming up the walk, and who said to her at once, " I was so sorry for Dr. Moore. He came to see Miss Graham, and was so disappointed that she was gone."

And then Katharine felt that she had no need to question longer. She knew what had put the bitterness into his voice and made his face like ice.

Harold went to New York, but he did not find her. At the Teachers' Bureau the madame in charge received him politely. " Yes, Miss Graham's address was there. They had arranged to forward the lady's mail." " But where ? " " To such points as she might direct, from time to time, as she sent for it, and as yet she had not sent. They would not be at liberty to give these addresses, but they could forward anything."

And letters went again and again, from Harold, from Mrs. Maitland and Gretta, from Madame Crozier, and many more. And the spring passed into summer, and the autumn leaves came, and the school opened again and Madame Crozier received word, much to her regret, that Miss Graham would not be able to return. So far as all the other friends were concerned, she might as well be dead.

With all her girlish trials, this blow was Gretta's first great grief. To Dr. Moore no one ever mentioned Margaret's name. Gretta and Mrs. Maitland talked lovingly and tenderly of her together, Gretta always insisting that her secret must have been some great sorrow, but could not have been, by any possibility, a sin. As for Mrs. Maitland, when she saw Dr. Moore going about doing his duty with the white, hard face that had become habitual, she found it hard to forgive the girl. "Nothing can excuse a woman for carrying secrets," she said one day with great decision to Gretta, in the presence of Mrs. Gray; "they are invariably unsafe. It is of no use, of course, for any human being to try to hide a sin, or a wrong done to other human beings, for soon or late every hidden thing shall be revealed, and every secret thing made known."

Katharine's head bent lower over her embroidery.

"And as for what women suffer through their morbid sense of duty or their shrinking from the notoriety that makes them live years falsely, because they are carrying and hiding some other person's sin, I am coming to feel that even that is a mistake. In my own work among the suffering and the poor I have seen so many cases where women endured intemperance, brutality, and hardness of every sort, simply because men trusted to this something in a woman that would practise concealment. Those are usually the cases where justice, and not mercy, is the reformatory agent, though justice is contrary to all the old theories and ideas. I was brought up among people who considered that a woman disgraced and degraded herself if she admitted that her husband beat her in his drunken rage. And there were plenty of women who, in such a case, would have blamed the woman for not being able to "get along" with the man whose vices they thought her bound to hide. I suspect this poor child has sacrificed the happiness of her life and the happiness of this noble man to some such wretch as that."

"What leads you to think especially in that direction?" asked Mrs. Gray, lifting her eyes.

"Her interest in the temperance question, to begin with, and her constant urging, in all her talks to the young girls, that they be prayerful, and patient, and silent as to what they have to endure. The tendency of her teaching was to make them feel that whatever man put upon them to bear they were to take as a dispensation sent of God. The theory is all wrong, and my advice to you, Gretta, is this: never, never carry about in your heart or in your life anything that you have to hide."

Gretta looked up smiling, and caught Katharine's eyes fixed upon her with a gaze full of anguish and entreaty, such as Theodore Conrad had seen on that far-back festive night. Something in the look checked the assent to Mrs. Maitland's words, and she said, gently, "But would it not all be different if one loved and forgave the sinner? Isn't that more like the Heavenly Father?" she added, bending over Mrs. Maitland's chair. "He says he puts our iniquities behind his back. That means where he could not see them; that he removes them, as far as the east is from the west; that he wipes them out of his remembrance. We ought to love Margaret only the more if she is doing that."

"I have never taught you any severe doctrines, Gretta; but I think that even God does all that after the sinner repents."

"But, you dear, precious saint," said Gretta, "isn't he heaping love and kindness all the time upon us before we do repent, and assuring us that that is what he will do if we do repent? And isn't that the only course that we could take?" and glancing again toward Katharine, she saw that gentle tears had softened the strained look of terror in her eyes. With a sudden rush of tenderness and pity for she knew not what, she kissed Mrs. Maitland, and moving over to where Mrs. Gray sat, put both her arms around her, and held the weeping face close to her true young heart. A minute more and Katharine had slipped away.

"Your auntie is growing nervous, I see," said Mrs. Maitland. "She ought to have a change."

"Yes, grandmamma; she has been working a little too hard, I fancy, and I find her often looking very sad. So much of this outside work is too heavy a strain upon her. She never seemed very fond of Margaret, and yet she takes her going very much to heart."

"And so do we all, my child," said Mrs. Maitland, sadly.

"Yes, indeed; but then we comfort each other by just loving her on and on, and trusting her and believing that she will come back, and that everything will be well. Mr. Conrad believes that too, and some day we are going on a crusade together to see if we can find her."

"That would hardly be a proper proceeding," said Mrs. Maitland, playfully, glad to escape for a moment from the gloomy subject. "Modern society doesn't admit of a knight and ladye faire setting forth, even with so good an object as to find and restore the ladye love of another knightly heart. Two of you would be too few, and I hardly know where you would get an army of retainers to go on such a quest. I, alas, am too old for a chaperon, but two of you could surely not go alone."

"There wouldn't be two," said Gretta, laughing softly; and standing behind Mrs. Maitland's chair, she put her hands over the old lady's closed eyes, and laid her curly head down softly against the white locks.

"What do you say, Gretta?"

"There wouldn't be two, grandmamma."

"Is that a riddle for me to guess?"

"Yes, guess it in the dark, and I will give you a kiss for your reward."

"Give me the kiss then, for I know the answer," she said, softly: "Is it that you two would be one?" and the hands dropped swiftly, and in a minute Gretta was on her knees by the old lady's side, and the arms were around her, and her blushing face was hidden against the kind old heart.

T

"He didn't want me to tell you, grandmamma, because he said he wanted to ask you for me himself; but when you said I must not have a secret, I knew I must not dare wait another little minute," and the girl's rosy face overflowed with merriment.

"And how long have you been carrying this secret?"

Again Gretta laughed. "Since, well, since long enough for Tom to unsaddle the gray pony."

"What! was it this morning in your ride by the river?"

"Yes, or rather it was after we were home. We rode through the myrtle path, and stopped under that beautiful old tree where Margaret told me Harold said he loved her that beautiful summer night. And we spoke about that, and I told Mr. Conrad,—I am always going to call him Theodore now, for you know, grandmamma, the name means a gift of God,—I told him I was going on a crusade of my own to find Margaret, and bring her back to Harold, and that I wouldn't have Harold go with me because he was too grim and hard, and didn't trust and forgive her beforehand, just as he ought to do. And he said he had long intended himself to go and find her for Harold. And then I laughed and told him he could go over one half of the world, and I could go the other, and we would see which would find her first If I found her I should bring her to him, and if he found her he should bring her to me, and we would clear up all the mysteries, and take her to Harold together. And I asked him when he was willing to start?

and he said, 'Day after to-morrow.' And then, grandmamma, he turned his horse until he looked straight down into my face, and asked me if I didn't think I would be unhappy searching the wide world all alone? And I told him 'Yes, but we must not mind being unhappy, if only we were being good.' And then, grandmamma, he looked all around, up at the sky and through the branches of the trees, and down among the flowers, as earnestly as if he thought he could find Margaret hidden somewhere there. And I was just going to give my pony a little lash and come on, when he looked back into my face, and said :

"'It is a noble crusade, Gretta, and I am going, but I am not going alone. Unless you refuse to allow me, I am going your way.'"

And the girl laughed again from sheer merriment. "It wasn't very sentimental, was it, grandmamma? It wasn't a bit like love-making. He just said, 'I am going your way, always and forever your way.'"

"And what did you say, my child."

"I am ashamed to tell, grandmamma," and the old face and the young one smiled together, and one was scarcely merrier than the other. For a moment they were two children of nearly the same age.

"You needn't be ashamed, dear."

"I think I ought to, for I always thought that when anybody made love to me it must be in the moonlight, and over and over again I have planned what I would say and what I would do, if ever my true love came. And when he looked at me and said, 'I am going your way,' I just gave the pony a little cut and looked up in his face, and said, 'Come on.'"

"And I am coming on," said Theodore's voice, as he stepped from the window opening on the piazza.

"It is true, dear little mother," he said, with a strange, tender light in his clear eyes. "We are going through the world whenever you are ready to send us on our little crusade, to seek and rescue and help Margaret first, and then as many more as we can. I believe we have one purpose, we have long had one heart, and we are going one way."

"Not yet, not yet," said the old lady, as she reached her trembling hand to each of them. She who rarely gave way to any outward emotion found her lips trembling and her eyes filling with tears. "Not yet, you would not take her away from me?"

"Never," he answered, "so long as you want her, nor so long as you have need of her. She belongs to you still, and," he added, bending down and touching his lips with reverence to her forehead, "I belong to her, and so of course I belong to you also."

"And she has never given you a word except 'Come on'?" said Mrs. Maitland, trying to escape from the emotion that overcame her.

"She could not have given me a better word. It is like a challenge. I know that into whatever is true and noble and sweet in life she is the woman to lead me, and every day and hour I shall feel her going like an angel before me, guiding me to everything that is highest and best. And wherever I am, or whatever I do, I shall hear her saying 'Come on.' You see that is going even farther than can be expected even of the obedient modern husband. I am really ready to follow."

And Katharine, who when she left the room had passed to the veranda and seated herself on the bench just outside the window, had been sitting there like one outside the gate of paradise, seeing the joy of heaven. She had seen their faces, and held spellbound by the sight, had listened to every word.

"There is only one shadow on it all," said Mrs. Maitland, trying to recover from the emotion that had nearly overswept her usual calm; "it will be so hard for Dr. Moore to see and feel your joy."

"But I think he has a heart big enough to rejoice in it. He has long known that I loved Gretta. He told me one night, as we were taking a long walk by the river, something about his love for Margaret, and many things about his early life. Among other things he said he had never loved any other woman, and he thought the thing that kept him from loving was a romance that came into his life when he was a little lad. You see we men, when we get together, sometimes talk over our experiences as if we were girls. I had a romance in my boyhood too, and I told him my tale, and he told me his."

There was a little rustle and movement on the veranda outside. Katharine had moved her chair nearer to the window.

"Harold said that his father was a physician, and had found a country practitioner's life a hard one, that gave him little leisure and less money, and he was rather inclined to check his son's disposition, which showed itself as a very young lad, to study medicine. His father had a brother, a successful business man living in a Western city, and it was rather understood between the two men that Harold should go to his brother at the close of his school life, and be brought up in business. His mother had died in his infancy, and his father died when Harold was about twelve years of age. The maiden aunt arranged for him to go to his uncle's home. He traveled alone. On the train with him was a helpless man, who had in charge a dainty little girl scarce out of babyhood who was restless and fretful and refused to be comforted. He said the man put the child on the seat by him, and the little thing went to sleep and he played with it, and it put its hands in his hair and pulled his curls, and altogether was a great delight to him and evidently a great relief to the man who had her in charge, quite to the journey's end. He had his uncle's address and knew his uncle had intended to meet him, but so reluctant was he to lose sight of this little being, that he followed the man who took her into a carriage, and seeing him standing by the door, threw a dollar down on the pavement. He said he had a hole made in it, and that for years he wore it on a string on his neck, although he was so angry that before he picked it up he tried to stamp it into the pavement under his feet.

"The door of the carriage closed, and in his rage and bewilderment and unwillingness to be left behind, he sprang up on the trunk-rack at the rear and rode until they turned in at a gate and approached a beautiful house. He slipped behind the gate-post. He knew that the man left the child there, because he waited until he saw the carriage and the man driving away.

"Then he looked in his little pocket-book for his uncle's address, and arrived in due time, to find them very much exercised because he had failed to meet them at the station. After this there followed his school life, interspersed with such partial training in business as could be given to a boy while in the public school, and as he grew older the business claimed him altogether."

"But was the desire to study medicine so strong that it overmastered the business career?" asked Mrs. Maitland. "He seems to be a born physician."

"Yes, evidently that was the case. His uncle had many children, and at his death there was nothing left for the boy but to carve out his own future for himself. He had a hard time of it, but the bent toward his present profession was so strong that, in one way or another, he fought his way to college. There is where I found him. We were classmates, and we have been chums ever since. He made a grand record, but there was nothing he did not do meantime to pay his expenses. Proud then as he is now, he would not have help, for I would gladly have divided with him everything I had. But he pinched and coached and wrote for the periodicals, and taught in the vacations, and tutored in and out of the university, and got scholarships and fellowships and came out ahead, and has always kept ahead.

"But he told me that in all those years when he ran errands in a store, or stood behind the counter, or in the after-life of student struggle, he always called that little baby-girl his sweetheart. And he vowed a vow to himself that when he grew up, and had become very rich and great, he would go back and marry her, and give her that very dollar that the man had thrown to him. And he said he believed that the dream that stayed in his mind of what the girl would be, and how she would look, and what she would say to him, held him back from failure in many an evil day. He often found himself asking this unknown idol what she would have him do, and he could trace all through his early life the influence of what he called 'his little love.'

"I asked him if he knew what became of her, and he said 'No.' For a year or two he used to hang about the house, and see the little thing sent out with dainty frills and lace about her in the little wagon pushed by a maid in a white cap. He used to stop and look at her, and place flowers in the carriage, and in his heart he always called her his little girl. At one time he determined to go to the business house in which the man who had the child was engaged, and ask him for a position. He fancied that, as he had read sometimes happened to deserving clerks, he would be invited to the house for Sunday dinner, and little by little he would become acquainted with the lady of his heart. But he was retarded from this attempt by learning that the man was old, and was not engaged actively in the business which bore his name. Then his uncle sent him away to school for a time, and when he came back the house had been sold and the family had moved away, and from that time to this, until he saw Margaret, he says he has never loved any one, girl or woman."

"Perhaps he will find that early love yet and marry her, and thus his sad heart will be healed," said Mrs. Maitland, who dearly loved a romance.

"But what would become of Margaret then?" asked Gretta, quickly.

"Oh, yes," said Theodore, "the myth must remain a myth. Margaret is a living reality, and she belongs to Moore."

"But I thought you said you had a romance of your own," said Gretta. "Was that about a girl?"

"Yes, that was about a girl," he said, playfully.

"Was she beautiful?"

"Most beautiful to me. I hardly know which I adored the more, the girl or her mother."

"Was her mother beautiful too?"

"Yes. My mother was a Catholic, and I had been reared to love all the representations of Mary, and to think of her as the ideal mother and ideal woman, and I transferred all my adoration to the mother of my sweetheart."

"How long did you love her?"

"All my life," he said. "I have been faithful to her all my life."

"You mean to say you love her still?" asked Gretta, her eyes widening.

"I am afraid I love her still."

The smile died out from her bright lips for a minute, but there was no mistaking the twinkling in Theodore's clear blue eyes.

"If you love her still then, how can you have another love?"

"I have no other," he said, playfully. "I think she has possession of my heart. I have only transferred all that was beautiful and loving in my thought of her to another, who seems to me to be just what my early love would have been if she had grown up."

"And did you ever tell her that you loved her?" asked Gretta.

"Yes, indeed, over and over again, a hundred times a day."

"Well, why haven't you been going after her all these years," said Gretta, her face showing the coming of a little shadow of fear.

"I would if she had only told me to 'Come on.'"

"What did she tell you?"

"She never answered me once a single word."

"And you told her over and over that you loved her, and she never said a word? She must have been a very cruel girl."

"No, she gave me other signs of loving me." The pout and the shadow grew more decided. "She put her arms tightly around my neck and kissed me, and snuggled her face close to mine."

"Where is Aunt Katharine?" said Gretta, hurriedly. "I am neglecting her all this morning," and she started to go out of the room.

"Here I am," said Katharine, leaning in at the window. "You must excuse me, but I have been hearing this very romantic tale."

"But, auntie, did you ever hear of a man's boasting in such a very bold way about another girl?"

" Have you asked him," said Katharine, quietly, " how old was the other girl ? "

" Why, no indeed ; of course she was old enough— to fall in love with."

" Of course," said Theodore, gravely. " Quite old enough, and pretty enough, and dear and sweet enough."

" But how old ? " said Gretta, coming back and peering down into his face.

" Just one year and a half," he said, rising and drawing her close to his breast, "and if she could have spoken, I am sure she would have said ' Come on.' " And like happy children they went away, leaving these two, for one of whom the light of a true love was gone, and the other to whom it never came, to look into each other's eyes, hardly knowing whether to smile or weep.

CHAPTER XIX

WITH Mrs. Maitland's increasing feebleness, Katharine had come to be more and more essential to her in the conduct of the house, in the care of the west wing, and in many details of her affairs. At first only the letters that made constant appeals to her well-known philanthropic sympathies were passed over to Katharine for consideration and for action, after the decision was reached as to each appeal. But it came to be, after a while, quite a matter of course for all her mail to be laid upon Katharine's desk in the little parlor that stood between Gretta's room and her own. On leaving Mrs. Maitland, as she retired to her room, an unusual parcel of letters awaited her. As was her custom, those that she knew at a glance were for Mrs. Maitland's personal perusal were laid aside unopened. Among the others, appeals for help, household accounts, invitations, and those relating to business, was one from the agency in New York, which she knew at once must contain some news of Margaret. Without hesitation she opened it. Enclosed was a letter sealed and addressed to Mrs. Maitland, which had evidently been forwarded through the agency, showing the writer's wish that no postmark should betray the place whence it came.

For some moments she sat and gazed upon it.

It was a thick packet, large enough to be half a dozen letters returned, large enough to be the story of a life. Who knew what secrets it might contain?

It was a long time since she had done a mean or cowardly thing. Not once, so far as she could remember, since the day when she said " No," to Dr. Moore, in reply to the question as to her knowledge of Mrs. Burke. She shrugged her shoulders. It was the circumstances that were always forcing her into complications. And, while she was hesitating, her fingers twisted one end of the envelope, and it opened, and she read:

" MY DEAR MRS. MAITLAND :

" When I sat at your feet on that day, which it seems to me was the last day of my life, you remember I said that I could give no explanation of my action. In these long months that have passed since, I have been convinced that I was wrong; that I owed it to you, who had been so good to me, and to the noble man who had taken me into his heart, the fullest explanation that it was possible for me to give. But at the time it did not seem to me that I had any right to lay bare to either of you the mistakes and wickedness of another life, especially when I felt that if I had done my duty by that life, the errors might have been overcome and the sins repented and forgiven. In my exaggerated sense of what was due to one, I failed to have a true conception of what was due to others.

" Since coming to this conviction I have felt that I ought to write you fully and freely of all that concerning which I was silent as I sat at your feet. I have not done so, because it seemed to me like asking you to consider me less wrong than I seemed; and in reality my errors have been, as you will see by the following letter, greater than my ingratitude toward both you and Harold would lead you to believe.

"Again, I felt that your love for me would lead you to persuade me to reconsider my decision, even after you knew all, and to reconsider would only be adding sin to sin. But now that I know this letter will not give you any means of tracing me, now that I have entered upon my duty, and am, as far as possible, undoing the errors of the past, I feel that I must relieve the anxiety and doubt lingering in both your minds, as to whether I claimed to love Harold Moore when a promise bound me to some other life.

"Now let me, dear Mrs. Maitland, as if I were sitting there at your feet, tell you what I ought to have told you then, and then try to forgive me for all that I have made you bear.

"I am, although you never knew it, the daughter of a man who has wrecked his life by intemperance. I never knew my mother, and thought that she was dead, until my father, in a fit of drunken anger, told me that she had deserted me when I was a baby, and left me to the care of an old servant, from whom he had rescued me through a man he had employed to watch this nurse. He told me that she was escaping with me on a train, when an accident deprived her of consciousness, and the man whom he had sent to watch and to recapture me, took charge of me and returned me to the home of my grandfather. He told me that my mother was living, was utterly unworthy of my love or thought, and that all my own unworthiness and the faults for which he blamed me were my inheritance from her.

"He was absent during my early years, and I was brought up by his parents. He came home when I was a little girl. There was something wrong about me, for I felt such a repugnance to him. I ought to have loved him, but I not only feared him, but when he tried to fondle me, I almost hated him. I do not want to write about that. He was —well, everything that intemperance makes a man. My grandmother was weak and subservient to him. She died clinging to him, and believing that all his vices were largely my mother's fault. She blamed me for my own feeling toward him, and insisted that if I loved him and was tender to him, and gave my life to making him happy as a true daughter should, that I could save him. Sometimes I tried, but oftener I resisted and rebelled.

"I hated my home, I hated my life. My grandfather was always at war with his son ; but after he became a helpless paralytic, he came more or less to trust him with his affairs, and in a few years the fortune was utterly dissipated and swept away.

"My education was constantly interrupted by these home troubles. My father did not care whether I was taught or not, except in the matter of the training of my voice. He thought it an exceptional voice, and often said to me that I must go on with my singing lessons, for he expected, if his father would not take care of him, that he would have a fortune in my voice, and added that he would find ways to make me understand my duty as a child. The pity of it was that I did understand. If he had been like my poor grandfather, I could have loved him and served him with all my heart. Only the thought that grandmother was gone, and that grandfather had no one else to care for him, enabled me to live the life that came after the fortune was gone. The old home and everything in it was taken by creditors. The little apartment in which my grandfather lived out his last days, and where with my own hands I had to do all that was done, was the scene of bitter upbraiding from the father, and bitter, brutal indifference and neglect on the part of the son.

" The old man softened toward his only child before he died, and on the last day of his life he talked about him, and said when he was gone he would have no friend but me in all the wide, wide world. He implored me to stand by him. He made me promise solemnly that I would not forsake him, that I would make it my life-work to save him.

" You have often asked me how I knew what working girls and working women, and the children of the slums, and the daughters of drunkards, had to endure; how I could work for them as I had done? The truth is, I had lived it all. I tried in every way to support and care for this man. I sang in church, I gave music lessons, I took in sewing in the evenings, I washed and scrubbed and kept our poor rooms clean. I cooked the food and he cursed me while he ate, but I kept my vow until the day when he said he had made an engagement for me to sing in a concert saloon. That night I forsook him, and left him to his life and to his fate.

" I had no refuge except with an old woman who had been my father's nurse. She took me in, but I was not safe from him even there. Some day, if ever I have strength, I can tell you such a story of a girl's struggle to earn support as has never been matched by that of any girl of the many you have helped and cheered. But I found an honest way. Through an employment agency I learned of an aged invalid woman desiring a nurse who would care for her during a long sojourn at German baths and other health resorts. I applied for the situation. The woman, for some reason, seemed to like me. She was paralyzed, and when I told her that I had nursed and cared for a paralytic grandfather for some years, she seemed to feel that I could care for her.

" Within a year from the time I broke my vow to live to save my father, we were settled in Florence. One night, when Mrs. Graham was restless, I sang to her. She seemed delighted with my voice. The next day she called me to her and asked me to tell her all about my past life. I told her, and why, with a voice like mine, I had accepted this position. It ended in her insisting that I should continue my musical studies, but I was so bitter and so proud, and had so little trust in God or in any human being, that I refused the lessons as a gift. I stayed with her all the remaining years of her life. And when she died, she left me, in her will, calling me the 'beloved friend and comforter of her declining years,' enough to complete a musical training that would fit me to support myself by my music. I asked her for the privilege of taking her name, for my life was haunted by the fear that my father should find me, though I was never free from self-condemnation because I had not kept my promise to give my life to him. I never deliberately decided not to go back to him, but I did think that if I sang upon the stage, or in any public way, it was better that the old name should not be known. I thought too, that I could more easily find and care for my father if he did not know where or how to find me, and when I came back to this country I did try to find him, but there was nowhere to look except among his old haunts, and certainly he was not there.

"Then came the comfort and the consolation of your care, dear Mrs. Maitland, and of Gretta's beautiful friendship, and after that the awful temptation of Harold's tenderness and love, and I yielded to them all.

"Do you remember the first night when Gretta brought me home, and you let me sit at your feet, while Harold played and all the others sang, and they read this passage, 'The Lord thy God in the midst of thee is mighty'? Do you know, I hadn't been believing for a long time in any God, or love, or home, or heaven, or in any human kindness. That night was a revelation to me, and I assure you, Mrs. Maitland, I felt like a child that had found a home. Somehow the atmosphere of Wildholm seemed native air to me, and I could never begin to tell you how, from that day on, I clung to my thought of you, and my desire to get back to you whenever I was away.

" You did not heed it much, because your heart was full of Gretta, and though you were very kind to me, you did not know that my heart was always waiting beside yours like a little homesick child. When you looked approvingly at me or smiled upon me, I was always strong to go back to my work, and when you began to show me the ways in which I could carry out my desire to help others who had been as miserable as myself, you really began to put new life into me. Then Gretta's faith and Gretta's sunny, beautiful trust was another teacher for me, and Harold Moore's prayer that Easter evening was the first prayer that I had heard for years that had not been answered by a bitter feeling in my heart. I felt that God could not be good, and let young women suffer as I had suffered, as others suffered, from the brutal degradation of those who ought to protect them from all harm.

" After I began to feel what it was to have God in my heart, I began to feel too, that probably grandmother was right, that it was the utter absence of love in me that made it impossible for me to help or win my father. He was my own, and yet I hated him. You were not my own, and I loved you, and that was pure selfishness of course. I loved you because you were kind to me, and I hated him because he was unkind. If ye love them that love you, what reward have ye?

"You see I gave up the duty that God had given me, and that I had vowed to perform, and tried to atone for my wrong-doing by saying that I would give as much of my life as possible to the helping of others who were unfortunate and sad. You know how I have interested myself in other girls. You do not know how I have always tried to work as much as possible for the daughters of those who had suffered by intemperance. You wonder that my eyes blaze, and that I become excited when men like Shakespeare Potts, and a good many others, laugh at the women who wear the yellow or white ribbon or the little silver cross. It is hard for me to remember that such critics do not know, and cannot know, the blight and wreck that drink is to human lives and homes. Why, Mrs. Maitland, I believe I could become a greater fanatic than has ever been born upon that one question alone, because of my knowledge of its resultant misery and degradation and sin.

"There is nothing more to be told. I had been willing to work, but I would not take the concert singer's life, although I knew I could earn more in that way than I could do by teaching. It seemed to me that I could never stand before an audience without searching in it for my father's angry face. But I taught early and late. I lived frugally. I have saved as much money as I ever received at Mrs. Graham's hands, and am ready to pass it over to some one who will do the good with it that it might have done if it had never come to me. Besides this, I can earn by my teaching more than enough for one.

"You must not feel that my mental struggle was altogether new, dear friend Ever after I allowed myself to be happy in the thought of love and home I was troubled. I had made a dying pillow easy by a vow that I would give my life to saving my father. I knew also, that somewhere in the world was my mother, perhaps an outcast and a sinner too. What right had I to bring the daughter of such parents to any good man's home?

" And how could Harold hope to find a helper in me in doing good work for the families of other drunkards, teaching daughters and mothers that their patience and love should last while life lasts, when I turned my back upon my own ?

" I was such a coward, Mrs. Maitland, that it took me a long time, after I knew the right, to be willing to go back to my duty, to lay down my selfish hopes of happiness and home. And when I had taken my resolve to find my parents, to give myself to them as long as they needed me, I think I comforted myself with a hope that they could not be found, or that if found they might not want me or need me, or might need only the money I could earn. I clung to the hope that I should be able soon to bring back to you, Mrs. Maitland, all my best years and best powers, and offer them to you for the use of the poor and suffering for whom you cared. You see, dear friend, to whom I owe so much of my knowledge and love of the truth, that all this time of my repentance I was 'rebuilding my house of lies.' I constantly gave up my love for Harold, and my joy of being near you all, and as constantly when I saw them escaping, my heart went out after them and hugged them to itself once more.   And you must tell Harold that, had it not been for what I learned of you, and of him, and of Gretta, of a life that 'seeketh not its own,' a life with God in the midst, I would never have been able to resist the temptation to just stay and love you all, and be happy with you forever.

"And do you know, I gave up finally only that night in the church when I stood up and sang for you.   My own heart went out with the words, and for the first time I was willing, heart willing, to seek and to save.   For the first time it seemed ·to me better to 'rescue the perishing, care for the dying' than to live my own life of love and joy. Ever since I have been so grateful that God sent the joy in service before it was forced upon me, for when the music ended, there, in the midst of that throng looking up at me with the old look that I hated when a child, I saw my father's face.   When I fled from him I left him a letter telling him that I was not unmindful of my promise to his father, that I was willing to work for him in all honest and reputable ways ; that if the time ever came in his life that he was sick and in trouble and needed me, I would come to him and take care of him and try to keep my word.   And here he was.   I had only to look at his face to see how ill he looked, what a wreck he was, to know that the time of needing me had come.

"The next morning he came to me in the garden at Wildholm, and though he did not know it, I sent him away fully intending to follow.   · ·

"And I have found him.   I shall never leave

him while he lives. If this work does not take all
the rest of my days, perhaps, dear Mrs. Maitland,
some day you will let me come back to watch beside you after dear Gretta makes a home with Mr.
Conrad who, as you know, has long had possession
of her heart.

"To Harold I can never come back, but some
other woman will be to him what I could not have
been ; but I believe none will ever love him more
than I have loved.

"To me the way is clear—to give my life to my
father, and to my mother, if she may be found. If
not, to give it to others who have suffered or sinned,
and who are needing the love of God as it can
come to them only through the love of one who
can give herself for them."

It was early afternoon when Katharine began to
read. The dusk was falling, and she still sat in her
room with the folded sheets held tightly in her
hand. Her face was white and drawn. Her eyes
had again the same horror-stricken look that Gretta
had so recently kissed away. From the garden below she could hear Gretta's voice, in merry talk with
Conrad. What strange Nemesis was this that pursued her ? What network was this that was weaving itself closer and closer about her life ? Who sent
them, one after another, Harold Moore, and Theodore and his mother, and Robert, and now this
beautiful girl, who had lived day after day under
the same roof, whom she never liked because of a
haunting something in her face that was familiar,
and that always seemed to bear in it a reproach ?

a girl to whom she had been kind for Gretta's sake, but with an intangible reluctance to receive her whenever she came, and a sense of relief when she was gone. She understood it now. She understood that some subtle inward chord between Margaret's heart and that of Mrs. Maitland had made those two understand and love each other. She understood that some unrecognized consciousness of kinship had drawn Margaret's heart and Gretta's close together. She understood the warfare between the conscience and the nature that could not, try as she would, feel any throb of natural love for Robert Gray. She understood why old Debby had so many times come to her, saying, "If Miss Gretta jest let ole Debby take care of her and all her things, like Miss Graham do, 'twould 'pear mighty sight more like Miss Gretta was Massa Larry's own child. Miss Graham she's every bit like our own fambly folks; 'pears like Miss Graham done b'long here jest same's Miss Gretta do."

Mrs. Gray understood also why Theodore treated Margaret with the protective brotherly kindness that had always marked his manner; she thought she knew even why old Biddy, no matter how restless she might be, sank into quiet and comfort when she was near. Between Margaret and every one of these was the subtle link of old association. She, alone—because in her heart had been kept no tender memory of love—she alone felt no throb of this unseen tender tie that bound all the others more or less closely to her sister's child. And even now, no throb of gladness that she lived, and was good and true and brave, as her sister would have been proud to have her be, softened the pang of fear and annoyance that she should have crossed her path again.

She underwent no very extended conflict as to whether she should take the letter to Mrs. Maitland. If Mrs. Maitland read it, Gretta would read it. If Gretta read it Theodore would do so, and if Theodore read it he would know at once that the woman who should be at Wildholm in the place of her own child—the woman to whom should come the wealth and the position and the love that had blessed, and that ought to continue to bless Gretta's life—the woman whom she had deserted as a child, and who would be able to follow step by step the dark road of deceit that she herself had trod, the woman who, if she came back into their lives, would perhaps bring Robert with her, was waiting somewhere to be called to claim her own. Nor was this all. She had sneered at the drawn sword, but she knew too well the sense of justice in the heart of Theodore Burke to believe for a moment that he would take to himself a bride, allowing her to retain a name and an inheritance to which she had no claim. A wild thought took possession of her, of taking the letter to him, revealing all the facts, appealing to him to conceal them, and to save her from Gretta's scorn when she knew who she was, and comprehended what her life had been. But only for one brief moment did the impulse run riot in her mind. She watched them, Theodore and Gretta, as out yonder in the garden they moved up and down in the afternoon shadows, and her knees trembled and her whole frame shook with the thought of having Gretta know. Then the courage of habit came to her rescue. Surely there was no need of this agitation. Mrs. Maitland was not strong. The girl, Margaret, had chosen her own life. It might be years that Robert would keep her nursing and caring for him, and in those years what might not happen? Margaret was not the woman to return and bring that man, nor the woman again to forsake him. Mrs. Maitland was old; Theodore's mother was old. If Margaret got no answer, she would only suppose that the letter widened the breach. To show the letter was folly and madness; and calmly folding it up, she glanced about her room. There was no place of safety. Gretta was in the habit of going constantly to her closets and her desk.

While she hesitated a rap came at the door, and old Debby brought a request from Mr. Conrad that he might see her in the library. Hastily dropping the letter into her pocket, she descended to find him waiting for her, with a face full of such earnest and happy hopefulness as reminded her of the boy she had known long ago.

She took her hand from the letter she was grasping so tightly in her pocket, and wondered, as she put it in his warm grasp, if he would feel how the very touch of that paper was tingling and stinging to the very ends of her fingers. But he felt nothing evidently, except the new happiness that was flooding his life.

"Of course you did not think it strange, dear Mrs. Gray," he began, "that I spoke to Mrs. Maitland first. I could not, as you understand, ask you for Gretta when,"—he added, sadly—" she doesn't seem even to remember that she belongs to you. But I do not forget, and I believe you would be willing to share her love with me. As for me I have always loved her, and have never known an hour in my life when my heart turned away from her toward any other woman. She aroused the manly and protective instinct in me when I was only a child and seemed given me to care for and defend. I can never think of living the rest of my life without her. Indeed, I never have lived without her. She has been in every purpose since I had a purpose, and in every plan and hope and dream she has always had her place. Surely you are not unwilling?" he asked, having in his own eagerness failed to notice the pallor of her troubled face. " You cannot lose her in giving her to me."

" No, not unwilling, only very, very thankful and glad," she said, her lips trembling. "But as for losing her, Teddy," she said, using the old name for the first time and turning to him with more of the old, confiding manner than he had seen before, " I have—" and her voice suddenly choked with sobs— "I have lost her already. I have reared her to think of herself as belonging to some one else, until I have cheated my heart of its child. And, oh, my God !" she added, passionately, "there are times when the mother in me is wild for her. I feel sometimes as if I could take her in my arms and cry out to all the world that she is mine, mine, mine."

" She will be none the less yours for belonging to me," said Theodore, soothingly. " I shall find the child heart in her and bring it back to you. Do you not remember how I found her for you once before ? "

And she suddenly turned upon him, her eyes streaming with tears, and placing both her hands in his, said, with a passionate outbreak of feeling, " You helped me then, dear boy. You stood by me then. I was a weak and foolish, and perhaps a wicked woman. Certainly I was wicked when I married Robert Gray. But it didn't matter to you whether I was weak or strong, evil or good."

He winced a little, and his face grew pale. He remembered the shock that came to him when first he saw something in her that made her seem less than noble and true, but he only held her hands more tightly and listened as she went on.

" I loved my daughter and it didn't matter to you what I did or what I was, for you loved her too, and we two, out of the wide world, are the ones who love her still. And I have lost her," she repeated, with a look of anguish such as might have been on her face if she gazed into an open grave. " She loves me too, but I never feel that she trusts me. She is never able to bring to me her innermost feeling or thought. There is a barrier always between us. Promise me, oh, my friend, that nothing that you ever do, or that you ever say, shall widen this gulf. Promise me that my mistakes, even the things I have done that are wrong, shall never be made known by you to her ; that she shall be kept by you from learning to despise the mother who has lived for her and who would have died for her."

And Theodore, remembering nothing but that in those early days she had been willful and unwise, soothed and chided her for blaming herself over-much for the misfortunes of her life, and readily promised that if it were in human power to help it, life should bring nothing more to rob the mother of her child.

And when she seemed comforted, he added, " I wanted more than your consent to give Gretta to me, Mrs. Gray, this afternoon. I wanted to go on with the little story that I began to tell you in this room so long ago, and that ended with my discovery that Gretta was back at the house of your father-in-law. I was thinking about this strange change of names that has come to both of us. When Gretta comes to me she must come, of course, in her own name, unless she was legally adopted by Mrs. Maitland, and given the name of Wild. I suppose you provided for that, did you not ? " and Katharine, once more feeling the sword of discovery swinging above her head, whispered unhesitatingly, "Yes."

" That is all right then. And it is all right also in my own case. I took the Conrad name with the Conrad fortune, which came to me from the man who, after those early years of battling with hard work and temptation and poverty in Chicago, took me into his business and into his home and into his heart as well. I did not tell you anything beyond the fact that that blessed old nurse, for whom I secured one-half the money due her from Robert Gray, gave me a room in her house, and gave me work among the chickens and the flowers in her yard, and made me her boy of all work until I secured a position in the mercantile house of Conrad & Son.

I did not tell you how I got that first position. Remember, I had nothing to comfort my soul in those days except my memory of yourself and Gretta. I used to pass that little grocery after my work was done, and actually peer in to see if I could get a look at the baby wagon, which must have tumbled to pieces long ere then. My chief pleasure was in sitting on the shady side of the wall of that old stone church where you waited while I wheeled the baby to you. My favorite walk, as I told you, was round and round the square, imagining that I had the little thing before me in the wagon.

"One sunny summer afternoon, I fell asleep sitting upon the steps of that church. My great delight was in listening to the throbbing and swelling of the organ music, as it came out through the half-closed doors. I opened my eyes from a heavy slumber to see a throng of carriages by the door, and to see a long, black coffin, piled high with flowers and wreaths, borne by the arms of strong, young men down the aisle and placed before the altar. Behind it followed a man with a kind face, who walked with head bowed low, as if crushed with an overwhelming grief. The church filled slowly. I watched from my post at the door and heard the service, and bowed my head, and shrank back into the shadows of the porch as they bore the body forth again. They had placed it in the hearse, which was drawn forward a few steps, and the gentleman was entering his carriage with eyes hardly lifted from the ground, when the sudden dash of a fire-engine around the church corner frightened the horses, and he was thrown back upon the pavement, with his body between the wheels. The horses reared and plunged, and I, who stood nearest, sprang to their heads, and though I was such a little fellow that they lifted me from the ground and fairly swung me, I kept my hold until the injured man was lifted to the walk.

" He insisted upon getting into the carriage, declaring he was not hurt; and when a gentleman would have entered with him, he waved him aside, and reaching out his hand to me, said, " Come, my little man, I want you here with me." And all that long, slow, silent ride, while he gazed out at the window and up at the sky, I sat oppressed by the solemn sadness of his face, in the corner of the carriage opposite this sad old man. At the grave he did not beckon me to come, and I waited by the carriage door. When it was all over and he came back and sank into his seat with his face buried in his hands, he seemed to have forgotten me; but as the carriage started he motioned me to come in, and though he never spoke to me and never looked at me, I felt somehow not afraid of him, only afraid of disturbing the great sorrow that seemed to be breaking his heart.

" We stopped at last. It was before the Conrad mansion. I do not know whether he saw the tears in my eyes or not, but he took me in. He questioned me. He offered me money which I could not take, but he found I wanted work. It is a long story. He gave me a place in his counting-room and, after a while he gave me a place in his home. His wife had died years before. The new grave held the remains of his only son, a young man just admitted to his father's business.

" I never shall forget the joy of that day when my savings had amounted to enough to enable me to pay all that Mr. Gray had left unpaid of that old sum for taking care of our little girl. I was the proudest and happiest lad in Chicago. I remember I lingered on the way and stole into the church we both know, and said my prayers in a shadowy corner behind a pillar. My mother took me to church when I was a wee laddie, and I confess that to this day an open church door tempts me to go in and sit in the dim silence and pray. Of course, the good old woman resisted taking the money; declared she did not need it. But to me it was a promise to be kept, a debt to be paid. My first debt," he added, " and I have never made another. Mrs. Brown said her luck turned on the day that I came back to her, ragged and hungry and forlorn. Perhaps it did. I only know she is living there still, and still filling her rooms with people for whom she is sorry, and who frequently do not pay. It doesn't matter, though. I shall be able to see that she never knows want again, and the fact that once she protected and cared for Gretta is reason enough for me to care for her. You know all the rest, Mrs. Gray. You have heard how generously Mr. Conrad gave me a choice of my own career in life, and you know too that before he died he gave me the name and the place in his heart and the place in his fortune that he would have given to the one who died."

" And you deserved it all," said Katharine, who

had listened so intently that for the moment she had forgotten her own sorrow and shame. "You have deserved it all."

"But I have valued it all," he added, "because it has given me the power to help 'the widow and the fatherless in their affliction,' to undo the heavy burdens, and to let the oppressed go free. My mother's early experience, your awful life, the fate of the women who suffer and toil, the degradation in which little children are reared, the pollution by drink of the body that was meant to be the temple of the living God, the self-seeking of human beings, the dishonesty in business, the corruption in politics, the debasement of even our governmental life —everything, everything made me feel that, in so far as one human life put between these evils and their victims could save or help, my one life should be given to that end. Beyond that, my one personal purpose and desire was to find and serve the woman and the child who had won my boyish heart. To find you two, to take my place again in your lives as protector and friend, to bring you all I had been able to wrest from life, this was my dream. Even in the long years before I gave up my search for my mother, I think I was unconsciously seeking also for you, and now that I have found her, I——"

"Found her?" said Katharine, with an involuntary outward movement of her hands, as if she were striving to break free from some horrible network that was tightening about her. "When did you find her, and where?"

"That night when the doctor took you home from the meeting so ill that we dared not excite you. She was in the carriage with you. You had seen her before, when she was here as Harold's patient ; but she is so greatly changed, so thin and silent that of course you did not know her, or you would have been the first to——" Katharine winced.

" She, poor dear," he went on, " knew no one of us I think, until that night. That night, though you did not see him, Robert Gray was in Washington. Do not be troubled," he said, seeing that she trembled ; " he is gone, and will never disturb you again. 'He is only a wreck of a man, but I have arranged that he shall not live in hunger and die in want. You see," he added, playfully, " that I have only been forestalling my duties as your son."

" How can I thank you ? " she murmured. " Did you say your mother saw him ? "

" Yes, and the shock of her sight of him, and of the brutal attack he made upon her, brought the past all back to her."

" All ? " asked Katharine, feelingly, her white face pitiful in its dread.

" Perhaps not all, but she recalls the railway accident. She even arouses in me a hope that after all your sister's child was saved. She knows you perfectly "—Katharine shuddered—" and the last picture left on her brain as she fell was that of a man staggering up the bank with a child in his arms. I know a man caught the child from my own hands. We are not going to rest, Gretta and I, till we have found Margaret and brought her back to Harold, who has saved and kept my mother alive for me. He is a changed man since he lost Miss

Graham, and a part of our life-work is going to be the bringing of her back to him. If only we might also find your sister's child, and bring her back to you, we should indeed be glad."

"It is impossible, impossible," she gasped.

"It seems so, but worth all it can cost to try. Do you know, Mrs. Gray, that when Mr. Conrad made me his heir, I felt at first as if I had been deprived of my right to work and earn my bread. And then I just put his fortune all aside and let it grow, and said to myself that I would live as if it were not mine. It should be used for the poor and oppressed. It has been a trust in my hands, a sword with which I have slain the dragons of distress that were threatening many a life. I would use it freely to find your niece for you."

"Did you care so much for that child? I thought Gretta was the one you loved."

"And so she is, my love and my life," he answered, fervently; "but you remember in your time of sore trouble you entrusted your sister's little one to me to keep for you, and I want to fulfill that trust."

Her head bowed low. She feared her eyes might betray her. Her fingers linked tightly together in her lap, felt that letter. She drew it forth and Theodore saw it, though she clasped her hands around it as if the living, writhing secret were a serpent out of which she would crush all power to coil and sting.

It was a moment of almost mortal anguish; perhaps the final struggle of the outraged truth and honor in her soul. Slowly, surely her life was coming to judgment.   She was as certain of it as are the condemned toward whom the day of doom and darkness creeps.

But here was one more chance of mercy.   In the dim twilight to her excited imagination the somber room with its high carved panels was like some old confessional.   The faces of the old portraits of true men and pure women stood out pale against the shadows, and bent sad eyes upon her that seemed to read her secret through and through. Theodore's noble head outlined against the back of the carved oak chair reminded her more than ever of the angel of the lifted sword.   He, he only had the power to slay her utterly if he persisted in his purpose to find her sister's child.   He only could keep that sword from falling, and he only out of all her world had the heart to pity and protect her if she told him all.   Why not give him the letter, tell him the whole story, cast off in one moment the horrible burden of years, be ever after an outcast and alone, a wanderer, a toiler, living only to undo and atone, but once more, once more, caring only to be good.

Lower and lower the head dropped upon her breast ; the tense fingers relaxed their clasp, a hot rain of tears fell upon the listless hands.   Suddenly stole into the window Gretta's voice singing by some bedside in the old west wing the anthem arranged for the meeting that seemed so long ago :

" The Lord thy God—in the midst—in the midst of thee is mighty.   He will save.   He will rejoice over thee with joy.   He will rest in his love."

Gretta ! Gretta !   At the thought of her the face

hardened to defiance. Was she mad, to do a thing to hasten the day when Gretta should hate and scorn her as she hated and scorned herself? Not even if the shining wings of those who had waited to bear a joy to heaven drooped never to lift again.

Theodore rose, and held out both his hands. She put hers in them, and looked straight into the noble, loving face whose eyes had never changed from their boyish tenderness and truth. One great truth went surging and sweeping through her brain. As ever he was Gretta's and her own. He, by the straight path of justice and right, had brought to Gretta love and wealth and honor and name, all and more than she had been able to give her by the devious and dreadful road her burdened soul had trod. She had lost everything for herself, won nothing for her child that would not have been hers in any case. She had gained the whole world, wresting it out of God's hand only to find that He would have given it to her, if she could have trusted him, without one penny of the awful price.

Ted took her trembling hands, and gazed down, with his old tender, protective smile.

"You have suffered much," he said, "but you have been so faithful and so good. You have taught Gretta everything that is good. The old mother whom I lost long ago is most dear to me still. It is a joy to call her mother. It has cut me to the heart to see your face when Gretta called you by another name. Hereafter you must let me feel that you have some one to call you mother, and remember no act of mine shall ever separate you either from your daughter or your son."

He led her to the door, and as he held the drapery aside for her to pass, stooped down and kissed the white, unyielding face.

Ten minutes after, Debby, shaking the pillows of the sofa and putting them back in place, and re-arranging the books upon the table, picked up a letter from the floor. Poor old Debby, she could not read, but she waddled away with it and laid it open in Mrs. Maitland's hand.

CHAPTER XX

KATHARINE walked steadily till she reached her door, then staggering to her couch, she threw herself upon it with a gesture of despair. Fool, fool of a boy, a sentimental, over-conscientious boy, to search as he would through the world, and bring to her a woman to betray and blight the work of weary years. She knew him ; he would do it soon or late. Meantime there was the letter. She would destroy it without a moment's delay. She rose, and pushing back her hair, glanced at herself in the mirror. She remembered that Harold Moore was to dine with them, and someway, somehow, she must make of that white, maddened face a countenance that could calmly meet them all at dinner; but first let her destroy the letter. She put her hand in her pocket. It was not there. Remembering the hands tightly clasped about it in the library, she flew down the wide staircase. No one was there. Noises sounded from Mrs. Maitland's room.

"Come quickly, auntie," called Gretta. "Grandmamma has such a letter from Madge. Debby picked it up in the library. The man must have dropped it on his way to your room with the mail." They were all much agitated. Mrs. Maitland's old eyes were full of tears. Harold Moore's face was as white as on that night when Margaret took herself away.

"Go back to the first word, Theodore, read it all out once more, from beginning to end. I want to hear it once more myself, and I want Mrs. Gray to hear." And Katharine had to sit and listen, wondering if the stern look in Theodore's face meant that he had seen that letter in her hand. She could not guess and yet she must sit there if she died, while his voice read over again all the tale that brought relief to their hearts, and added a thousand-fold to the burden of her own.

It was a singularly subdued and quiet party that gathered around the table at Wildholm later than usual that night. Before the servants no one wished to speak of that which was uppermost in every mind.

"To think that I should have doubted her," said Harold to Gretta, taking advantage of a moment when old 'Lijah was out of the room.

"But we must not dwell upon that now. The only thing that matters at present is that we find her quickly. How soon can you start, Dr. Moore?"

"I would like to start this minute. I would start to-night, but that I have patients who are critically ill, and whom I cannot leave to others. I suppose," he said inquiringly, "Theodore would not wish to leave his mother or ——" he looked at Gretta and hesitated.

"Or me," she said smiling. "You know Dr. Moore, we meant to go and find her, and bring her back to you before that letter came. It was to be ——" and she smiled up in his face and suddenly dropped her eyes.

"What! your wedding journey?"

"Yes," she whispered.

Theodore had taken Mrs. Gray down to dinner. Mrs. Maitland feeling too fatigued with the excitement and emotion of the afternoon, had preferred to remain in her room. To Theodore, Katharine's silence and weary white face were no surprise. The other two chatted on quietly, and the ladies soon left the table, followed almost immediately by the gentlemen.

"You are looking so white and weary, Mrs. Gray," said Dr. Moore, kindly. "You have never seemed like yourself since that night when you fainted in the church."

"I am quite well again, nevertheless," said Katharine, calmly. "But the night is warm. I was just thinking of asking Theodore to take me into the garden a few moments for the fresh air."

As they strolled down the myrtle walk, Theodore halted almost unconsciously, and drew her to a seat under the very tree where Gretta had spurred her horse and bidden him "Come on."

"There was something you wanted to say to me?" he said, gently. "See how Providence has favored us. We wanted to bring back Margaret for Harold. We wanted to bring back your sister's child for you, and God seems to have sent them both to us, and sent them both in one. I heard Harold say he could not go for her. I know you do not wish any time to be lost. I believe I can trace her readily. I shall find her with Robert Gray, and as I send to him every month, I know just where to look for him. I will go for her at once. But look up, dear friend," he said. "I will go, but I do not wish to go alone. Why may not Gretta go with me?"

"Gretta," she started as if in horror. "Gretta to meet Robert Gray?"

"No, that need not be, necessarily. I can easily keep her from meeting him; and surely you know that I would spare her any pain. But if either of these girls is the one to come in contact with this man, it should not be the one who has already borne so much, the one who has so nobly taken up the daughter's hopeless task. We must think of what is just and right to her. He is not Margaret's father. Her heart has always told her that, and yet she has trained her heart, noble girl that she is, to do what she thought to be her duty, and to practise an affection and tenderness that she could not feel. The poor girl has been greatly wronged, and it is for us to make amends and without a moment's delay."

"Let Gretta go? I cannot," she moaned, pitifully. "I cannot, I cannot be separated from her."

"But surely you would not let your love for her stand between you and an act of justice to your sister's child?"

Suddenly she sprang to her feet, and standing in the path, looked down upon him with her eyes blazing with excitement. "Justice to my sister's child does not require it," she said, fiercely. "It is enough that wreck and ruin come upon myself. Why need they touch my child? Listen to me, Theodore. Mrs. Maitland knows the story of this unfortunate girl's career. She does not know that the man who has cursed her life is the same who has cursed mine. Why need she know? Her whole heart is bound up in Gretta."

"And would you have Gretta keep the name and the fortune and the love that belong to another child? Would you let her live a life that you know to be false, unjust, and wrong?"

"Listen," she said, seizing his arm. "She is utterly innocent and utterly ignorant of any wrong. Let her alone. You and I only know that Margaret Graham is Margaret Wild. You and I only know that her place is here, as the daughter in this home, as the heiress of all this wealth. Why disturb that state of things? Mrs. Maitland cannot linger here many years. Bring Margaret if you will. Let her marry Harold Moore, and by-and-by, when Mrs. Maitland is gone, take Gretta away, and leave Harold and Margaret if you like in this home. And since you have means enough to care for Gretta, let Harold and Margaret share as largely as you will in Mrs. Maitland's wealth. Let them spend her means in doing the good that she would wish to have done. Margaret will not be defrauded. All that would have been her own will come back to her, except the one thing, that, if you give to her, you do it at the risk of breaking the hearts of both Gretta and Mrs. Maitland. Gretta would know that I am her mother, and I should know that she did not love me as a child, or want my mother-love. Mrs. Maitland gives the love of kinship to Gretta. She would not transfer it to Margaret, and Margaret would know that she was not able to take her own. It would only mean misery for all."

"But my friend, my dear friend," said Theodore,

seizing both her hands, and drawing her close to him, and looking earnestly into her face, "you are excited; you could never say such things in your senses. Do you not realize, can I not make you understand, that all you plan means nothing when, in order to accomplish it, you must do the thing that is dishonorable and unjust? What hope have we, Gretta and I, for happiness in a life that held a shameful deceit and wrong like that? No, no, the way of peace is the way of righteousness and truth, and much as I love you, much as I love Gretta, I can travel with you by no other road. There has been a wrong done, Mrs. Gray. Nothing matters to any of us save that we make it right. If, as you say, there is money to be returned, all I have is yours. Let us together undo as speedily as possible all that never should have been done, . and then take together whatever is the result. What does it matter to any of us three, where or how we live? But to be upright, to be just—that is vital; that is imperative."

While he talked her head had dropped upon her breast. She had come to the end. Defeated, discovered, all her life's labor come to naught. And yet in that hour it was all as nothing to her compared to one maddening terror that Gretta, her child, should know she was her mother, and should know that her mother was too vile a thing for her sweet lips ever to touch again with even a good-night kiss.

Theodore watched her. There swept over his soul the great anguish of that far-away night when she fled away from him with Gretta in her arms, and he knew in his inmost soul that she was unworthy of the worship of his childish heart. He had scorned himself for his own suspicions, he had fought one by one as if they were traitors every thought that had ever risen in his heart against her, and he had loved her, been faithful to her through all. But now, as if with a sudden revelation that could not be gainsaid, he knew her for what she was. With a sudden flash of recollection he knew that he had seen that letter in her hands, and that she knew all it contained. And yet this was the woman on whose heart had been cradled the head that was henceforth to find its resting-place upon his breast. But it had not been given to him to mete out justice. His must not be the hand that should strike the light and gladness out of Gretta's heart, for well he knew how straight and true the higher instincts of her soul would lead her to the falseness and shame that had been behind her mother's word and deed.

As these feelings stirred him, his face softened, and Katharine, with that subtle vividness of perception that was able to follow his thoughts as if they had been written in the air, felt and used her advantage.

"Theodore Burke," she said, quietly, "you would see righteousness and justice done. Believe me, if you reveal to Mrs. Maitland or to Gretta that you know anything more of Margaret or of me than they already know, you are doing the greatest cruelty that ever was conceived. Three hours ago, with my hands in yours, you promised me on your honor never to permit word or act of yours to hurt me in the eyes of my own child. Whatever came you vowed to stand by me in it. You desire to guard my honor. You cannot; I will take care of what is left of it myself." And her lip took a scornful curve. "Take you care of your own honor. How much of it will be left when you have betrayed a woman who is at your mercy, and been false to your solemn word?"

"Stop, stop," he said. "I will hear no more. I can guard your secret; I can leave the wrong you are doing to God; I can free this poor girl from the clutches of that man; I can see that out of my own fortune comes to her even more than could have come to her from Mrs. Maitland. It is no question of what I shall do, I am only daring to urge you to do the thing that is just and right."

"Wait there," she said, huskily. "All that could have come to her from the Wild estate shall surely come; but in my way and in my time. All that I have ever expended from that which would have come to her from my father, wrong as it was that it should have gone to her, shall come back to her. Do you fancy I have spent it for myself? I have not. I have lived here, it is true, but my service has more than paid for my home, and nearly all of that which would have been Margaret's can be gathered for her again. Besides, I am not old, and what is lacking may yet be won. I swear to you, Theodore, that if God gives me life, she shall not be defrauded of one penny; but she shall wait a little longer for her inheritance, and you shall not betray me to my child. What right have you?" she went on angrily. "Is it not a family matter?

and who has made you the judge and ruler of us all?"

"Stop, stop," he said. "Do you mean that in your family matters I have no right, no place—that I may not dare, loving you as I do, loving Gretta as I do, even to protect you from yourself?"

"I mean," she added, fiercely, "that you can betray me if you will, but the day you show my daughter that I am her mother, that day I show you what a mother's influence can be, and no power in earth or heaven shall let you have my child. She will need no word of mine to keep her from taking to any man her heritage of shame."

He rose quietly. Heretofore his face had shown a bitter battle with honor and pity and grief and tenderness; but now he drew himself up to his full height, and his eyes took the steely look that made them gleam like an avenging sword. "It is enough," he said. "You have chosen to threaten. I did not need to listen to your pleading. I did not need that you should call upon the pity and the love my heart has known for you, or the pity I have too, for the child who must yet know what it is to have a mother like this. I said no word; I had no thought of betrayal. I only urged you to tell the truth yourself. You will not do it, but"—and he bent low and looked straight into her face, and went on in a tone so low and intense that it was like a death warrant to her courage and her hope—"the truth will be known and justice will be done, though I may never open my lips or look again upon the one face that holds the world's whole joy and hope for me."

He turned away from her, but she sprang after him. "Oh, stop, Theodore, let me beg of you, let me beseech of you not to betray me."

"Did you not understand me? I have had no thought of betraying you," he said, as he turned bitterly upon her. "But I said justice will be done, and so it will. You will betray yourself. Already you carry in your face that which stirs a question and a doubt. Robert Gray is alive. My mother is alive. You need not fear me. I shall keep my words to you. My lips shall never breathe to any human soul that which could make you to your child less lovely or less beloved; but I implore you, for her sake, for yours, for my own, to tell the truth yourself, to make the rough places plain, the crooked paths straight, to prepare "—and his voice sank to a solemn whisper—" the way of the Lord, for verily I believe that he comes to deal with your life and with mine. God help you," he said, with a sudden burst of pitying tenderness; " God help you. He meant you to be as noble a woman as, in spite of you, he has made of your own child."

And as he walked away she turned and threw herself upon the bench, and dropped her head upon her arms. A low, shuddering cry of unutterable anguish broke from her lips. It would have melted any heart to hear it, but the strong man who hastened swiftly away from her did not hear or heed.

Overswept by the tide of his own indignation and distress, he strode forward, almost overthrowing Debby, who, rushing down the steps from the door of the conservatory, staggered straight into his arms.

"Good Lawd, Marse Conrad, go quick! Fetch Doctor Harold; he's jest visitin' Miss Marion round de front porch."

"Stop! stop! What is it?"

"Miss Gretta. She's daid in 'mong de flowers dar. She's all daid."

"Go yourself, Debby, and bring Dr. Moore back with you. For your life don't let Mrs. Maitland be excited. Just tell the doctor that I want to speak with him a moment, at once;" and away she went, her teeth chattering and her eyes shining white against the darkness. She meant to do just as she was told. What she did do was to steal up softly behind her mistress and beckon frantically to the doctor, who sat in his old place on the steps.

He saw Debby and raised a warning finger slowly. "Ah, here's Debby come to carry you off to rest," he said, as he rose slowly to his feet. "It has been an exciting day for all of us," and he kissed Mrs. Maitland's hand reverently, and said "Good-night." One stride and he was inside the window drawing Debby after him by the arm. "Where?" he whispered.

"Dar in the conserbatory; she's daid," she began in a wailing whisper, but he was already gone.

Theodore had lifted her from the seat where Debby found her in the swoon that was indeed like death.

Katharine's room was nearest. They took her there. Theodore could not have expressed his pain to see her, as like a little, helpless child, with life all to live over again, they put her back into her mother's bed.

W

The doctor stayed long, worked hard, and grew very anxious. Once there was a little flutter of life and the eyes opened, and looking past Theodore's face, watching with anxious terror, past the doctor, she saw Katharine, who had entered silently and stood watching in the shadows like a mute statue of despair.

"Leave her to me," she said, in a voice that cut the air like an icicle, so cold and low and controlled that one could never have guessed the volcano that burned within. "She has fainted before, and I know what to do for her"; and she came swiftly forward with a glance that would have swept them both from the room, but a sharp spasm, as of pain, convulsed the poor child's face, and her eyes were lifted to Theodore with helpless, mute appeal.

"Do not agitate her," said the doctor, anxiously; but he was too late, for Katharine bent with outstretched hands as if to gather the girl to her breast, when with a shudder of horror, Gretta drew herself back, and turning her face away, sank senseless on the pillows.

"Go out of the room, Mrs. Gray, I beg of you," said Harold. "I will not be responsible if she sees you. Leave me with Debby"; and both of those who loved her most shrank powerless backward beyond the drapery of the door, and waited in the hall.

"Men talk of sparing and protecting women," said Katharine, in a fierce whisper; "this is the way they do it. I told you it would kill her to know, and before I could get to her side you have told her."

"I have told her nothing," he answered, gently.

"I did not see her till Debby told me she had fallen in a swoon."

"Where?" she asked, sharply.

"In the conservatory. Dr. Moore was with her when we went out. Mrs. Maitland sent for him. I suppose she went to walk or rest among the flowers, and it proved too warm for her," he added, soothingly, for Katharine's face was so white and anguished, and her hands, which she vainly tried to keep quiet, made the chair tremble by which she held.

Indignant as he was, he pitied her. "Do not be frightened," he said, putting his arms about her to lead her to the wide window-seat from which one night she had watched the window of his mother's room; but she drew away from him, and throwing herself upon the couch, burst forth in such a tempest of sobs and tears as never once in all his life had it been his fate to see.

"Frightened. I am not frightened," she said. "She will not die, but, oh, Theodore," she added, with a pitiful little moan, "did you not see that she turned away from me? She would not let me touch her. She will never come back to me." She paused suddenly, and then laying her hand on his arm, as if she had forgotten her anger, she whispered, "If I could take her in my arms, and go out into the world alone, and leave home, and name, and friends, and all, and work for her until I died, and she would love me, I would stand up and tell all the world of all," the whisper sank lower, "all that it does not know; but she would turn from me, she would not touch me. Ah, God, I have lost my little child."

"I think she is conscious again," said Harold, stepping swiftly to Mrs. Gray's side; "but she seems delirious. Do not sob so, Mrs. Gray," he said, pityingly. "She will soon be better, and your voice seemed to disturb her. Tell me, has she had any shock, any excitement, more than Miss Graham's letter gave to us all?"

"I know of none," said Katharine, yet gazing at Theodore with suspicious eyes. Could he have told her? If not, why did she turn away? Yet she knew he did not tell. If all other things crumbled beneath her feet, her belief in his honor and truth could not be shaken. He might be angry with her, despise her, put out no hand to stay the sword that overhung her, but if he said he had not spoken or would not speak, she knew she could believe him. All this went like a flash through her mind as she repeated, "I know of nothing, nor does Mr. Conrad. Neither of us saw her after dinner until she was unconscious."

"It is the beginning of an illness," he said, "and I fear of a serious character. She must have absolute quiet, and only those about her who can control all agitation. Evidently your distress disturbed her," he said, turning to Katharine; "and you must go home to the little mother, Conrad. Poor Debby is shaking with fright—and Mrs. Maitland must not know.

"I shall stay here," he went on, "and if Mrs. Gray's distress can be so hidden that Gretta does not perceive it, she shall be with me; but you should come back and be here just at hand, Theodore, and I think perhaps you would better

bring the little mother with you. There is no presence in the sick-room better than hers. She is
so healthy in body, so tender and sympathetic,
and yet so unshaken, we can rely upon her if Mrs.
Gray's nerves fail us."

"I shall not fail," said Katharine, controlling
every trace of her recent agitation. "I shall not
fail again." Secure in the belief of Gretta's ignorance of the truth, the mother's love and anxiety
reasserted itself, and she begged Harold to let her
go back.

"I will keep in the shadow, and when she sees
me again, if it troubles her I will come away."
Then all together they softly stole back to the room
where Debby was trying vainly to bathe the burning, restless hands. The girl was conscious, but
delirious, and in her incoherent mutterings of that
long night talked of Theodore and grandmamma
and Debby and Margaret, but never once, though
Katharine's strained ears listened for it as the
condemned might listen for the news of a reprieve,
did the sick girl speak her name. And when she
saw her, there was the same shuddering cry, the
same shrinking from a touch or kiss that had
broken the mother's heart. Little by little she
yielded to the girl's evident distress at sight of
her, and while she was always present and always
watching, it was from behind the curtain or the
screen.

The "little mother," as they all called her
now, had slipped quite naturally into all loving
ministry in the sick-room. Gretta yielded to her
gentle care like a tired babe trusting to a nurse

who could quiet her to sleep when no one else could soothe. The old woman knew perfectly well that the stately pallid lady who always spoke gently to her, was the idol of those early days in Chicago, and quite free from the agitation that Katharine's presence once caused, her old heart rested in sweet content in her kindness, and she was at home and happy in nursing Gretta, as if there had never been an interruption in her care.

CHAPTER XXI

AS day succeeded day and the first terror settled
into the certainty of brain fever, all life for
the whole sad household vibrated with hope or fear
according to the news that came from the sufferer.
Day or night Katharine never left her. Mrs. Maitland's chair was wheeled to the great hall window,
and Debby, broken-hearted, stayed close at her side
or haunted the door of the sick-room, rejoicing
when the little mother was forced to rest and she
could take her place. Just outside the heavy curtains that swung before the door sat Theodore, waiting to serve if need arose, and watching constantly
from his shadowed place every flitting shade of
peace or pain that overswept the precious face.

His "little mother," glad as she was to be there,
needed much tenderness and rest, and he gave her
both, taking her into the garden for fresh air, or to
the conservatory, or sitting beside her talking to
her of old times till she slept, and then stealing
back to watch and wait and pray. And through it
all Katharine went in and out, her face hard and
cold as ice, under the strain of her effort to control
her grief.

But she did control it, never once giving way
after that first night, never seeming to know fatigue or to need slumber. All life for her had nar-
rowed to that one room. To be there, to do with

her own hands all that could be done, to let Mrs. Burke or Debby take her place when she saw the dear eyes close as if to shut out the sight of her face, this was all that was left of a world that held so much for her only a week ago.

When forced to meet the others, she asked no sympathy, and as far as coldly gentle words could comfort, tried to comfort Mrs. Maitland. As for Theodore she rarely looked his way. She could not bear that one who knew the fierceness of her struggle, and perhaps the greatness of her sin, should see her humiliation and defeat. Besides, there was something in his very presence that seemed to claim a share in Gretta's heart, and now, at last, whether Gretta knew her or loved her or not, she was determined to have her all to herself.

And thus they moved on to that awful day when, down in the library, the physicians met once more—for Harold, who had never allowed any but most exacting duties to keep him from Gretta, had from the first called to his aid the skill of other specialists and the experience of older practitioners.

Katharine had kept behind the curtains while they lingered by the bedside and watched their faces as they watched her child, and she knew, when they left the room, as well as she would when Harold should creep back after they were gone and whisper their words to her, that they could not save her child. She knew when Mrs. Maitland's chair was wheeled softly nearer the door and Theodore held the curtain aside, that the stricken old heart was taking its last farewell. She saw Theodore creep softly in and stand and gaze as if he would gather her up and hide her in his inmost heart, and she knew that he came now lest later they would not let him come. She knew all when she felt the wheels of the carriage that took the physicians away crunching and grinding her heart, and when Harold stole softly back, had no need to hear him say, "They fear there is nothing more that we can do." She knew it all before. She heard, but it was like a distant voice coming over the sea of beating waves, when Mrs. Maitland answered, "I am not going to rest in their judgment. I am going to hope. You remember the text she always loved, 'The Lord thy God in the midst of thee is mighty'; he is in our midst, in her heart, and in each one of our hearts, and he is mighty. He can and I believe will save. It shall be according to his word." "Amen," said Theodore, fervently; but Katharine never moved or spoke, she only wondered vaguely when they would have done and said all they wished and would go and leave her with her child.

And as the night moved toward midnight, Theodore—who knew her heart's desire by the longing in his own, who would have given years of his life to gather Gretta in his arms and alone in the silence and the shadows, hold her till the new dawn broke upon her eyes—persuaded Mrs. Maitland to go to her room. Then he took the "little mother" to her rest and sat by her till she slept. Then whispering to Katharine that he would be outside and that she had only to speak and he would come, he went out softly and closed the door. She opened it swiftly and taking him by the arm drew him within.

Gretta was moaning and muttering in her troubled sleep.

"Teddy," she said, brokenly, "you remember I said she should never belong to you. I was wrong. She did and she does."

"Yes," he answered, softly; "she does and she will in that other home—where God is in the midst of his people, where," he added, very gently, "his servants shall serve him and his name shall be written on their foreheads, where there shall be no more pain. See how utterly at peace she looks. His name has always been written in her forehead, has it not? She belongs to God—I can wait—I shall find her once more. But now," he added, "she belongs to you, you only. One would be cruel to take her from you for one moment," and before she could answer or detain him he was gone.

The door was shut, the light burned low, the firelight sent strange flickering shadows over the pallid face. Gretta was going away where not she but Theodore would find her again. He did find her once before, and she took her treasure from him and fled. She did not care whether his little heart broke or not. Now when he found her in that other land, would he bring her to her, or would he keep her for himself? She could not think. She could only watch the white face and suffer, suffer God only knew how much. God! Did he care? They called him pitiful. Why should he care or be pitiful to her? She had not cared. She had not been pitiful to any one, not even to her sister's little helpless babe, not even to loving old Debby, who had tried so faithfully to show her that love could conquer; not to the "little mother" and never once, even in his childhood, had she been pitiful to Ted. Ah! if it should be true that God was pitiful as well as "mighty," might it not be that it was his loving kindness—to Gretta, not to herself,—he must of course hate and despise her,—but his love for Gretta that had held back her own punishment all these years, kept the sword from falling because Gretta was his own, and if the sword fell, must have felt the hurt. If it was true that all this time he had waited to let Gretta have joy and comfort in her life then surely he must be good, so good, so pitiful, so kind.

And now if Gretta lived, shame and pain must inevitably come to her. The shadow of her mother's sin and the shame of her penalty must fall upon her too. So he had shown loving kindness again in taking her where she could not suffer if her mother were disgraced. He had shown love for Gretta then and that love, greater far than her own, was saving her daughter now from the effects of that mother-love which she, in her mad selfishness and vanity, had thought so great. She was dying that he might save her from her mother. As the deep consciousness of this truth stole into her heart, hardened as it was, she bowed her head and through her sobs broke the first genuine prayer her lips had prayed for many and many a year. "Yes, Lord God, in the midst of human lives and hearts thou art mighty. I love thee for sparing to my child the knowledge of my sin. I have not been worthy to keep her! I will not try any more to hold her—thou lovest her. I give it all up—the mad struggle to keep her for myself! I give her up to thee, and take from thee the shame and burden of my sin. Because thou hast loved her I give her up to thee."

And while she waited and prayed with her face buried in Gretta's pillow as close as she could lie and not distress the sick one, a strange thing happened. The tones of her low murmuring voice in words of prayer seemed to quiet the restless head and hands. The girl lay quite still. Then the eyes opened and looked steadily into Katharine's, bright with consciousness, sweet with recollection. Her child, her little child, she knew her, and she did not turn away. She only looked long and searchingly into the eyes that gazed down upon her, heavy with their weight of unshed tears.

"Mother, mother," she whispered, "I am your own little girl."

"Yes, yes, my own, my own!" she answered, gathering up the girl so softly that no breath or movement seemed to stir the silence, and, joy of joys, she did not shrink but nestled close and lifted the face a little for the kisses that fell on cheek and brow and lip.

"I love you," whispered Gretta. "Mother, mother," she repeated, in a whisper, but with lips that lingered and seemed to love the word.

"I have been a wicked mother"—for, verily, if this was the lucid interval that comes before the end, she must speak—"I have sinned."

"I know—I went down to the garden to find you and Theodore that night; I was too frightened to go away—I heard every word."

" And you do not hate me ? "

" Hate you ? I love you, love you," the voice died away to a sigh, but its utterance was love.

" But I did wrong, always, all wrong, always, in everything."

As if with one supreme last effort the drooping lids lifted, the fluttering hands, never still these many days and nights, tried to reach the cheeks down which hot tears were falling.

" My whole life was all a sin," she repeated, in a passion of confession.

" I know, I know, God was not in the midst of it, that was all.   But you will make all the wrong right again—you and Theodore."

Ah, there was Theodore—even now at this moment must the thought of him intrude !

Swift and horrible, as if all evil spirits had rallied at sight of her relenting, and were maddened at sound of her confession, a fierce jealousy of Theodore took possession of her soul.   But for him Gretta need not have known, need not have died. If he had kept out of their lives all this anguish would not have come.   She heard the door move gently, and there he was, coming softly to her side. Her eyes blazed under her drooped lids, like those of a wild beast about to be robbed of her young, and she pressed the girl closer to her heart.   Gretta opened her eyes.   One long look into the tender, manly face bending over her, so white and still in its anguish, and she smiled.   Her hands that had fluttered like rose leaves in the wind sought his, and when he held them in his broad, warm palm, the pleading eyes sought her mother's face.

Did she want to go away? Did she turn after all from mother-heart to his? Had she won her back only to give her dying love to him? The child's eyes pleaded.

It was the supreme moment of her life-conflict, and bitter, bitter as death; but God had been pitiful to Gretta in the past, and he had been pitiful to her, for he had made her know that wicked as she was, there was yet love in the world for her. Gretta loved her, even if she loved Theodore more. Gretta loved her, and with such a look of triumph over the supreme anguish as Theodore never forgot, she drew herself up and laid the sick girl in his arms. "No, no," he whispered. "Hush," she answered, softly, "I have given her up—forever."

She turned to the window and left them alone. Outside, the moon was riding serenely in the heavens; the paths stretched white and shining away into the gloom, and across them the shadows of the swaying branches swung, and the light falling through the trees made the ground an arabesque of drifting light and shade; the sky was mottled with just such white feathery clouds, as— yes, she remembered now—as she had seen that day when she waited in the shadow of an ivy-covered church for Teddy to give her back her child. With lightning vividness she saw his face as she hastened away from him. "Poor little Ted," she thought; yet, late as it was, she had made atonement. She had given her back to him now.

A little, troubled, murmuring voice broke through her thoughts. In an instant she was by the bed to see the hands upraised to her, to hear the feeble voice call, "Mother, mother." She bent over her. "Take me, mother, kiss me; I love you; I want you to hold me a long, long time."

She smiled on Theodore as he laid her in her mother's arms, and almost before he turned away her eyelids drooped. Together they waited and watched for the fluttering breath to cease; but it only rose and fell more evenly and quietly than before. Over the face crept a look of comfort and repose. The mother's eyes sought Theodore's. Could it be that penitence and love and heart's content had brought the slumber that science and care had not been able to bring? Theodore had lifted Gretta's hand and placed it in her mother's. Now he took both in his warm clasp and answered the question with a rush of tears that he did not try to hide. In both their souls the dreaded death-angel had given place to the angel of hope.

Harold came in on tiptoe—Katharine's finger was laid to her lip. Gretta was quietly sleeping. "It is her salvation to sleep on and on," he whispered to Theodore, when they had stolen outside the door. "She must not be even moved unless Mrs. Gray can no longer bear the strain."

And the night crept on to morning, and the morning dawn changed to the fullness of day. The birds sang, the bees hummed in the honeysuckle, the yellow sunlight flooded all around, and still the sufferer slept.

Theodore came softly in now and then, asking with his eyes if he might relieve her, but Katharine would not risk a movement. Sometimes her fears grew to anguish lest in her weakness, Gretta should sleep her life away. Again hope stirred as she saw the wan, white face look natural and sweet, yet through hope and fear she ran on and on, as if she were reading from a book, leaf after leaf of which was turned by an unseen hand, the story of her life, with all its awful error and its unrequited sin. And when Gretta awoke and knew them all, though too weak for anything but to smile and sleep again, and the doctors came and declared the awful crisis past, the thrill of a great gratitude to God ran from heart to heart throughout the silent house.

Katharine left her daughter in Debby's care, with Theodore to watch, and went away to Gretta's room to rest. There was everything just as the girl had left it, and on the table her open Bible and the little book of devotions, "The Words and Mind of Jesus." Involuntarily Katharine looked at the Bible. It was the story of the Prodigal Son, and through blinding tears she read, "When he was yet a great way off, his father saw him . . . and fell on his neck and kissed him." O God! It was such a long way back. After one had retraced all one's steps ; gone over all the way ; undoing, restoring, making the wrong right, the crooked straight, the rough places plain ; she could understand that at the end there might be pardon and love ; but to be loved while "a great way off," to be held close to the great Father-heart and forgiven and kissed while " a great way off "—this was not for such as she had been. For her it ought to be enough that she knew her way back, knew what the "making it right" that she had promised Gretta meant. It looked a long and weary and lonely journey, but she had taken the first step, she had given Gretta up, and, thank God, there was even for her as she struggled on, a lamp to her feet and a light to her path, in this Book that Gretta loved. To its guidance and instruction, if not to its promise and its peace, she surely had a claim. This first inward step was all she could take now while Gretta was so ill, but by-and-by she would go back over all the way, atoning and returning everything, four-fold, even as the Book said was right for her to do.

So the day wore on toward evening, and Mrs. Maitland began to be troubled about her lest she should be ill. The old lady had had her chair moved for an hour to its old place on the veranda. Harold was beside her, glad of an opportunity to note the effect of the prolonged anxiety. On the other side sat Theodore, and the little mother watched by Gretta, who, like a baby, was fed and sank again to sleep.

"Do not go, doctor, till I know if Mrs. Gray needs you. If she does not, then all our knowledge as to the limits of human endurance fails. She has taken neither food nor rest and ought to sleep a week."

"I reckon she done ben converted, Miss Marion," broke in Debby, her palsied head shaking with emphasis. "She's up dar in Miss Gretta's room on de sofa huggin' up Miss Gretta's open Bible right in her neck jest like she been huggin' dat sweet chile's hair. Fo' de Lawd, I do b'leve she done got religion."

"Stop," said Mrs. Maitland, sharply. "Debby,

I wish you and I were half as good as Mrs. Gray."

" She's good, sho 'nuff, she mighty good ; and so we all orter be when de Lawd sen' down his bressed angels to live right under our noses in de house all day long. 'Pears like havin' de dear Lawd himself right in de nex' room to have dat sick, patient chile."

" Perhaps," said Mrs. Maitland, " that is one of his own ways of dwelling in our midst, by dwelling in the hearts that love him, and showing his loveliness through their own."

" He's been here, sho 'nuff. He sees we's old, Miss Marion and me. He *couldn't* take Gretta away when he see how much we love her. He jest couldn't."

" Then you don't think the doctor saved her ? " asked Harold, playfully.

" Yes, de doctor and lovin' and prayin'. No, lovin' and prayin' and de doctor; las', but not leas', de doctor."

CHAPTER XXII

ABSORBING as Gretta's illness had been, it did not shut Margaret or her letter out of mind. It kept both Theodore and Harold from seeking her in person, but remonstrance and pleading went to her by mail from every one, even from Katharine herself. Mrs. Maitland kindly pointed out her exaggerated and mistaken sense of duty and begged her, if she had found her father, to bring him back and allow them all to help her in her care of him, offering him quiet rooms in the west wing. Theodore wrote her, unknown to Harold, and yet in Harold's behalf, and, after the crisis had passed, and they were all assured of Gretta's recovery, Katharine wrote, urging that she come back for Gretta's sake, though neither she nor Theodore told her the story that both knew must soon be told. Harold himself wrote that home and her own place were here, and that he was coming speedily to bring her back. And to all these there came in return only the cry of her heart's sorrow and longing to be with Gretta in this time of weakness and pain. And all this time Katharine was making ready for what she called "the first stage of her journey home."

During all the slow convalescence, there had been no sign or look or word from Gretta or from Theodore, that showed they remembered the tempest of shame and distress through which they had passed with Katharine. All was the same in their manner except that they daily broke her heart anew with their gentleness, treating her, whenever alone with her, like the mother to be trusted and counseled with and loved. If they carried a new burden they kept it out of sight. Indeed, for Gretta the new attitude seemed to afford an outlet for a natural loving tenderness which showed toward all her friends, but which in her mother's case had always been held back and restrained. They two never talked of the revelations of the sick-room, but lying awake in the still, sad nights, often and often the mother's listening, waiting heart heard Gretta coming softly from her room, and without a word she would take her in her arms and hold and soothe her till she slept. Once Gretta, coming softly in the darkness, surprised her mother kneeling in the dark by the bedside, and after that, though neither said a word, the two knelt side by side—always in the dark and always silent, save to God, who knew what each endured.

Outwardly Katharine was unchanged, save for a sadder, whiter face, a lowered voice, and a more resolute devotion to Mrs. Maitland, and especially to the "friends," as the old lady always called them, who dwelt in the bright west wing. In the old time that seemed so far away, she did not love the ministry there; but if she did not love it now, she performed it so tenderly that the sick and the aged learned to listen for her footsteps and her voice. The "little mother," whose mind remained much like the mind of a child, content to be in the presence of those she loved, seemed to grow feeble, and as Gretta needed her less she clung to Katharine, who made her more and more her special care. Debby, too old to serve much, but free to love Gretta as much as her old heart dictated, finding that Katharine no longer repulsed and chilled her, was ready to outpour upon her unstinted affection, and Mrs. Maitland also seemed to recognize the new spirit that was in her, and was even more dependent upon her than she had ever been before.

"It grieves me to leave her before Gretta is quite strong," Mrs. Gray said one day to Theodore as they were arranging for her departure, which he had always accepted as a settled thing.

"Why not wait a little longer?" he asked, "or why not let me go for you and represent you in the things you wish to bring to pass? You promised that I should be to you as a son."

"But your own mother surely should not be left now, Theodore, and no one could do my duty for me," she answered, sadly. "If only you could grow happier here when I am gone. I know what you think would make you happy, Ted."

"Yes, and I wish it might be to-morrow," he answered, eagerly.

"And I also wish it might be soon," said Katharine.

"Please, mother, dear mother, do not say it," broke in Gretta. "You wish it might be because you are unwilling to leave me alone. I do not think I ought to be left. I want to go where you go, to live as you live."

"We cannot both leave Mrs. Maitland until Margaret comes, though we have neither of us any right to be here," she added, as if to herself; "yet her heart would break without you, Gretta."

"But by-and-by, when you go permanently, as I know you will, I want to go with you."

"And I mean to go also," said Theodore.

"The duty is mine," she said, bitterly "If only I could do all and suffer all alone."

"The duty is ours," said Gretta, kissing her; "not dear Ted's, but yours and mine, dear mother."

"And am I to be left out?" said Theodore. "Am I not to be allowed to help?"

"Not yet, not now," said Katharine. "Wait till I return. It will not be long. I shall see the next step clearer after the first is taken. I can bear anything but the thought that I have wrecked life for you two. Could you not let me go altogether and you be happy in each other?"

"And leave you to bear your life alone?" said Gretta, earnestly. "We two are happy in each other, and I am happier in you, mother, than I have ever been in all my life; I love you so," she said, the tears starting to her eyes. "Only one thing hurts me now. I want to take our own little place in the world, to be where I can call you 'mother.' I am almost strong again; let me work too. As for Theodore, he knows I am right. How could he trust or honor me if I went to home and shelter and peace, and let you go out to fight the world alone?"

"We will all go together," said Theodore, gently; "but not quite yet."

"No, not yet," answered Katharine. "Let me

go alone now. Do not make it too hard for me to do my duty ; only promise me, Theodore, that you will take care of Gretta till I come back."

" How long ? " said Gretta, clinging to her mother's hand.

" Not long. I may return at Easter, and you shall hear from me every day."

" What shall you say to Mrs. Maitland ? "

" The truth, that I have a duty to perform that has waited too long. She will be willing, and you are to summon me at once if she is ill."

And two days later, Katharine was gone, not as she would have preferred to go, without a word to any one of them, but in the only way she could go, if she did not wish to leave them all with hearts too sore for endurance.

After the date of her departure was fixed, Katharine had written to Margaret, sending as usual through the Teachers' Agency in New York.

" I am going to Chicago," she wrote ; " I believe you are there. I want to see you, not only for my sake, but far more for your own. I shall not go to a hotel, but have written for rooms at the house of Mrs. Brown, an old pensioner of Mr. Conrad's in ———— Street on the north side. If you are unwilling I should know your residence, you can come to me there. My train arrives on Thursday morning. I shall stay indoors all day for you."

It was a sad journey, this of atonement. When last she passed over this road she was young and wretched, fleeing to escape the crosses of her life. Now she was returning to take up the task she hated, in the presence she abhorred.

It was evening when she arrived in the great bustling city. She had stopped in New York at the Teachers' Agency to try once more for Margaret's address ; but beyond the fact that she was in Chicago still, they declined to give her any information.

For the first time, on this journey she had an opportunity to practise the new principle that must henceforth dominate every phase of her personal life. The love of luxury, the delight in pleasant things about her, the ease and comfort to which for years she had been accustomed, these were no longer for her. . She took her place in the throng of the great middle-class travelers, instead of in the drawing-room car with the few fastidious ones who, on this particular journey, had it entirely to themselves. With the great debt of a lifetime behind her, necessity only must determine hereafter the limit of personal expenditures.

She had been greatly interested in hearing Theodore's tale of the dear old lodging-house keeper, from whom he stole the baby, and into whose life, during all these years, he had brought a measure of comfort and repose. And when he gave her the address it only occurred to him, that, with the new-born kindliness of her heart, she desired to take to this old woman some news of him. But for the same reason that at night she slept with her cloak for a pillow, she also avoided the hotel, and sought the little lodging house on the north side, with which she had already so many associations.

An aged woman, bent and slight, with a few faint streaks of yellowish gray hair straggling from under her black lace cap, received her, and taking her up two flights of stairs, explained that the second floor rooms were taken by an invalid gentleman and his daughter, who would gladly have gone to the third floor, but for the fact that the gentleman was too feeble to climb the stairs. " It is well for me," she added, "that they did decide to remain on the first floor, for the daughter has gone East, and now the care of her father has fallen upon me, and since she left he has grown very, very ill."

" That must make you very weary," said Katharine kindly.

" No, not over-weary," said the old woman patiently; " but I am not as young or as strong as I was once. And the daughter only went away last night."

" I thought you would like to know how I chanced to come here," said Katharine, motioning the woman to a seat while she removed her wraps. " Your old friend, Mr. Conrad, is a friend of mine, and he told me that you had taken good care of him when he was a little boy; and farther back than that he told me what beautiful care you took of a little baby that was left in your charge for a time. So I thought that instead of going to a hotel, I would come and ask you to take care of me."

With this introduction, the wrinkled old face brightened, and Katharine knew that hand and heart, and all the little home possessed, were quite at her disposal. As she passed down to the tiny dining room, where these kind old hands had prepared some refreshment for her, she noticed among the letters that lay upon the hat-rack, one addressed to Margaret Graham. Glancing at it a second time, she saw that it was her own letter, sent to New York and re-addressed to this house.

She knew, as she seated herself opposite Mrs. Brown, that the broiled chicken and the toast had been prepared by the trembling old hands, and when she saw that she had put on a fresh print dress and a Sunday cap, that she might sit by her and pour her tea, her heart was touched ; yet she could think of nothing but that letter. Looking her landlady straight in the face, as she passed her cup, she said, " Is there with you a lodger named Margaret Graham ? "

" Yes, indeed ; and beautiful she is too, and such a singer. Her voice is as sweet a one as we can ever hope to hear in heaven. It is her father who is so ill upstairs."

" And she has gone ? "

" Yes, some one she loved very much in the East has been ill, and though they wrote her that she was almost well now, she grew so anxious and so eager to go, that I told her I would take care of her father if she would only be gone a week. I have known the family many, many years. Her father, Mr. Robert Gray——"

" But I thought her name was Graham," said Katharine.

" Yes, many of her friends write to her as Miss Graham, because when she was studying abroad she lived for years with a Mrs. Graham, and many people think that is her name."

" But you were telling me about her father."

" Yes, I was his nurse when he was a little tiny

lad and I was a young woman. He married unfortunately, and took to evil ways. His wife deserted him, and this little daughter of his was in
my care. It is a long story, ma'am, and may tire
you. The family came from wealth to poverty, and
Robert, who is here with me now, went from bad
to worse, and the daughter had to take care of herself. She has been supporting herself teaching
music, and now, because his health is so poor, she
has come back to nurse and watch over him. She
will be back in a week."

"She will not be back so soon, Mrs. Brown,"
said Katharine. "My name is Gray. I am Robert
Gray's wife. I have come back to nurse and care
for him myself. Margaret will stay for a while in
the East."

"I do not think you can keep her away from her
poor father. She is the most dutiful of daughters,"
said the old lady, with a little touch of suspicion
under her great surprise.

"Perhaps we need not say so to her father if he
is very ill, but she will not come back again."

"And you, you—was it you who deserted him
and forsook that lovely child?"

"No, Mrs. Brown; it was he who took the child
away from me; but we need never talk of this. I
know he is sick and in trouble. I have come to see
if I can minister to him."

The old lady gazed at her in astonishment.
"Well, if you would do that, then you could never
have been so bad; you never would have forsaken
your child."

"I never forsook my child," Katharine repeated.

" I was often hard to Robert. I was impatient and angry with all his wretched ways, but I shall be gentle enough with him now. You need not fear that I will not be kind and good to him."

Afterward she went to him, lingering first a moment in her own room, striving to conquer the dislike and reluctant dread that tempted her almost beyond control to fly without a moment's delay out of the house and away, as fast as she could, to the things and the people that she loved. And because the longer she waited the heavier grew the dread, she went almost at once.

He was lying with his face turned toward the window, apparently asleep, his face wasted and sunken far beyond the haggard look it wore when she had seen him last. She bent over him, putting both hands behind her, with the instinctive feeling that no power could ever make her touch him ; and then, remembering her own life, the angels of mercy and pity pleaded for him, and when he looked up at her and knew her, she was able to say, " I am sorry you are suffering so much, Robert. I have come back to see if I cannot take care of you, and help to make you better." And he simply gazed and gazed, looking with a child's wonder in his eyes, at the whitened hair and the pallid face and the pitying eyes, and never said one word.

And as she answered his look, the tears filled her eyes, and for the first time for twenty years, she knew in her heart that she forgave, even as she hoped to be forgiven. A frightful fit of coughing racked his frame. She raised his head, and as tenderly as she would have done it for Gretta.

"Margaret has gone away? When will she come back?" he whispered.

"Not just at present, Robert. I am going to stay and take her place. I can take care of you. Don't you remember I did it a great many times when we were younger and you were ill? You have grown more ill since she went away?"

"Yes," he answered, with difficulty, "a hemorrhage yesterday after she was gone." And then, from very weakness, his mind seemed to let go its wonder and its sense of anything unusual in her presence. That he should be taken care of by some woman if he were ill, this was a matter of course. He had always had this. His surprise would have been greater had no woman appeared to nurse and strive to ease him of his pain.

That very night Katharine sent for the physician, and asked him on the following morning to bring another. Could Robert be moved? Could he be taken to some climate that would be more favorable to his condition? Could his life be saved, or could it be prolonged? And when she found that there was scarce a chance of either, she set herself to making him not only as comfortable, but as happy as it was possible for him to be.

A telegram was sent to Dr. Moore to tell them to keep Margaret when she came, and letters followed, saying she herself was where she ought to be, and where she wished to be, and where she should remain. Robert's condition of weakness was such that he neither missed nor asked for Margaret, who need have no fear that it was her duty to return. As for the story that must be told Margaret by-and-by, they must do as they thought best, tell her now or wait till she, Katharine, should be back among them again ; it could not be very long.

And yet it was longer than they thought. There was time for the ebbing and flowing, again and again, of the poor, wrecked, and wasted life ; there was time for curses and hatred and every evil passion to rage within the sufferer's breast, because of his anger that he must die. There was time for days of maudlin weakness and childish penitence and plenty of tears. Yet through all this, she led him day by day and hour by hour, with such patience and tenderness as won him to be, in her hands, as plastic and as gentle as a child. When he abused her in his hours of rebellion she quieted him by admitting that she had been wrong, in one way as wrong or worse than he or than any one could know. As the weakness grew he clung to her more and more, like a child to its mother, and when at last he fell asleep one peaceful twilight, there was left in her heart all the new pity for his weakness, and there was gone from her all the self-pity for her own great wrongs.

She lingered only one day after the simple burial. All of Margaret's belongings and her own, she had packed and sent away. She bade Mrs. Brown good-bye in the late afternoon, and then went over to that ivy-grown church on the corner, and finding Ted's quiet place behind a column, she listened while the evening service was being held, and the organ notes went wandering through the arches, and the shadows came. She was conscious of all, yet really heard nothing save the voices in her own soul that chided and rebuked and refused to listen to any whisper of peace.

The music ceased. The people went out softly. The figures on the stained glass windows of apostle and martyr and saint, grew dimmer and dimmer as the night came on, and then when the old sexton was ready to close the church, with the burden of all her past life upon her, yet with the first stage of her soul's home-journey over, she went forth once more to take the train to the East.

Believing that Robert might linger for many months, she had in every letter urged Gretta to consent to Theodore's desire that they should be married with Harold and Margaret, in the dear old library on the evening of Easter Monday. She knew that Robert could not be moved, or sometimes she would have been tempted, her longing to go was such, to take him to Wildholm, and let him know Gretta, and live out his life amid the benedictions of that home. Very gently one day, when he was strong enough to bear it, when he was weakly bewailing his own errors, she had opened up to him the iniquity of her own life, and revealed to him that Margaret was not his child. That Gretta was still too feeble to make the journey to see him, he understood; but if only Katharine stayed with him his heart was quite content. But she knew not how long it might be, and she knew also that after the awful secret that must be told to Mrs. Maitland and to Margaret was once known, she herself, however much they might pity her and urge her, could never remain at Wildholm. Only Gretta's marriage would deter the girl from sharing what she knew must henceforth be a wandering and a bitter life. To be there and see this marriage, and know that her own deceit was as yet unconfessed and unatoned, seemed impossible; to be there and see them struggling to be happy, after the truth was known, seemed more impossible still; and yet when Robert was gone she never waited except for that hour of twilight in the church.

If she could have hidden in some silent place until the wedding was over, and know that in deed and truth, as well as in word, she had given up her child, she would have been grateful. She thought of the old Shaker home at Loriston, of the little whitewashed room, furnished with the bare necessaries of existence—of a silence and solitude in which a soul might wrap its own sorrow or immure its own content—and the temptation to hide herself there was very strong. She had not told them at Wildholm of Robert's death. They did not know she was coming, and until it was all over they would never know that she could have come. But while she hesitated, she remembered that for Gretta, her own child, the joy of this wedding-day would not be the same without the sight of her mother's face. And what was she that she should give a pain to save herself a pain? So she went on, reaching home on Saturday night. It was the time of the evening prayer, and she stole in softly, and kneeling in her black dress, buried her white face in her hands.

When they arose Gretta sprang to her arms, and Theodore folded his about them both.

Unconventional as it might seem for the wed-

dings not to be delayed by Robert's death, the
joy of that occasion was a very sacred and solemn joy, that had in it more than one element
of sacrifice. To Mrs. Maitland, while it was like
the gaining of two strong sons, it was in another
way the giving up of two lovely daughters of the
house. To Katharine it was the final submission
and yielding to separation from Gretta's after-life.
After this there could be no lingering hope that she
would have her with her, come what might, as long
as both should live. As she had vowed to do, she
gave her up utterly, knowing that however much
they might keep her in their hearts, henceforth
she was to live her life alone. But perhaps for no
one was the renunciation greater than for Margaret,
who ought, as she believed, to devote her life
utterly to women who suffered and struggled as
she had done, and who, for the great love she bore
to Harold Moore, laid down this career, accepted
his view of duty when he said, " Living for each
other, there are two of us to multiply the good that
we shall do, because we each shall live and work
for that for which the other cares." And for
Gretta to give up her unwillingness that any one
but herself and her mother should have any share
in the work of atonement they meant to do, to yield
the pride that would even have shut Theodore out,
was a triumph indeed for love. Steadily she held
that, even loving him, her first duty until it was performed, was not to him and not to the world, but
to the redemption of her mother's life from any
trace of debt or any shadow of shame. And Theodore's heart held a love large enough to take her,

Y

letting these thoughts have dominion over her, knowing that soon or late, the love that would serve Katharine and help her in carrying out her life, would return full freighted to his own.

What wonder then that the wedding time was as solemn and sad as it was joyful and sweet. From its sacredness they shut out all people except their very own. Mrs. Maitland and the "little mother," and Katharine and Deborah, and two or three of the old servants in the background, made the group in the library. And after it there was a little feast together, in which they were too peaceful to be merry, too tender to be gay. And later still, in the moonlight on the veranda, in the last hours before the young couples went their way, there gathered a group around Mrs. Maitland, with Harold and Margaret on one side, and Theodore on the other, and at her feet Katharine with one arm tightly around Gretta, who rested her head upon her breast, while she told in broken words, interrupted often by sobs, the tale of her early temptation, and yielding, and sin, and penitence, and her resolve of restoration that should be fourfold, and of the consecration of her after-life to the comforting of those who suffer and the rescue of those who sin.

They did not interrupt her as, with low, broken tones, gathering strength as she went on, she made the awful revelation. And when it was over, Gretta only clung closer to her, and Margaret only said, "I knew most of it before. You wrote them to tell me or not, as they thought best, auntie, and of course Harold had to tell me something, or he never could have kept me away from that sick-room in Chicago. And we are both agreed, Harold and I, that perhaps there has been wrought for me less harm than good, for without the hard life that came ·in my youth, how could I ever have helped, as I mean to do, the other working girls?"

"Why should you separate yourself from us now, aunt," he asked, smiling as he used the new name, "when everything is past and forgiven? You must think that you have four children now where you had but one. Why shouldn't everything between us be just forever the same?"

"Not the same," said Mrs. Maitland, her voice trembling with tears. "Not the same; it ought to be infinitely better. The old life dead, the old hard hearts softened and filled with love, and a new life that means, for every one of us, blessing to all who suffer, uplifting for all who sin—a life that has at last God at its very heart, that must be mighty for good because he is mighty and because he is in the midst."

CHAPTER XXIII

THE wedding journey, taken in different directions, ended for both young couples at the old parsonage, which had stood for some time vacant. The old man of business had gone, and to his son had come the care of all. When they arrived they found that Katharine had been there, and had brought old Deborah, lingering herself only long enough to arrange that everything should be put in order for the others.

The man who had charge of the business had been instructed to bring all the books and accounts for all the years to Harold, and he said that Mrs. Gray had taken from him minute record of all that had been spent, and all that had ever passed through her hands for the support of herself and the child.

How Katharine's heart ached for one more indulgence, just to linger and see them when they came; but no, their pleasure must not be marred by the haunting shadow of her presence. They were to come at night. Old Job took her and her trunk to the afternoon train, but she waited till he was gone and then walked back by a quiet road to the churchyard, and lingered there by the graves of her parents and her sister till she heard the rumble of the wheels and the bark of Job's dog, and saw the lights flash out from the windows of the chambers and the old south room. What voices whispered to her in the silence ! What forgiving faces shone upon her out of the shadows ; what she suffered as she stole back in the darkness to the station to take the evening train, no one but God could know ! Perhaps each step that took her farther and farther away from her loved ones took her one step nearer to him. She went straight to Loriston, and while they were at the parsonage, she had her two or three days of silence and solitude in the bare little cell, and there, sitting by the bed of the aged man who had begged her to rear Gretta in the love and fear of God, she told him, as she might have done had he been a monk of mediæval time and she the penitent in the confessional, the story of defeat and shame by which she had learned at last that which he had tried to teach her long ago, that life without God was not life, but anguish and humiliation and shame.

After a time the four went back to Wildholm, Harold and Margaret into the house where it was the hope of all that Gretta would return. Mrs. Maitland's old heart pined for her. Her welcome for Margaret was full of sincerity and affection, yet her nature was broad enough to receive the new love without any sacrifice of the old, and Gretta was simply in her old place, the child of her lovely old age. To be near her, where she could see her every day and help in the west wing ministry, they took a cottage just outside the grounds, where she lived with Theodore and the "little mother" a life of such simplicity as made everybody wonder if the tide of fortune had turned against the handsome young senator, whose advent in Washington society had made a flutter in the breast of more than one mother of marriageable daughters.

Theodore plunged steadily into work, and with his usual insight and sympathy, encouraged and united with Gretta in every economy. The desire to go into the world with her mother, and to share the working woman's life, had been her one objection to the early marriage. She had been eager to apply for a teacher's position at Castleton, and her heart had no stronger proof that she and her husband were truly one than her yielding to his pleading that he might share the son's privilege of toiling and saving for their mutual end. Neither one of them would rest any more than would Katharine until the uttermost farthing went back to the Wild estate.

Though she gave up the teaching, she did not swerve from her purpose to add her earning forces to those of the other two. Her sensitiveness and lack of self-confidence would have inclined her to hide her experiments and failures and partial successes; but she never forgot a warning word of Mrs. Maitland's, or the resolve that followed it, never to have unnecessary secrets, to avoid the habit of concealment or even the shadow of deceit. She could not sit opposite Theodore at table, or in her old seat at Mrs. Maitland's feet, and let them suppose they knew and shared her life, when she was spending hours of her absence from them in thoughts and work of which they never dreamed. So she took to both her bits of verse and her sketches and little stories, and showed the returned manuscripts to them, in spite of her mortification and shame, and carried to them with all the glee of a child the few little checks that, now and then, at rare intervals, gave her courage to try again.

In the little cottage the room she had taken for her study and work was one that was always held in readiness for her mother's use; but Katharine, entered already upon her duty of restitution, very rarely came except for a night. She was making no child's play at penitence. When it was known that she would accept a position that would bring remuneration, Castleton opened its doors both to her and to Gretta, and a prominent philanthropic association offered her a high position in the management of its work. Both were declined, because to hold either implied a character above reproach. She could not publish her unworthiness in the market place, or cry out from the housetops, but she could keep herself from seeming to be what she was not. She might work harder, bear this part of her punishment longer, but it must be honest money this time and earned by honest toil. She found it at first in the care of a children's hospital supported by private funds. There came mother-work without the coveted mother-joy. From this center her life radiated to even wider fields in the homes of the very poor. The physical condition of the little ones under her care was such a revelation of the ignorance of the mothers in such homes as those from which they had come, that she began a work of teaching these mothers in their homes, that could not possibly bring her any credit, but which became the nucleus of a great work resulting ultimately in the redemption of many homes. Her passion for motherhood took the form of helping other women to be good mothers, and no home was too squalid, no task too menial, for her with her own hands to show the mothers how their wretched rooms might be transformed to homes. From tasks like these she gave herself, as long as the old Elder of the Shaker Community lived, now and then a few days' rest in the little white-walled chamber, which was to her like the cell of a convent in which a world-weary penitent hides for the time of "retreat."

To Wildholm she could never freely go back, though only forgiving tenderness met her there, and no one, not even old Deborah, was told the story of her shame. The old creature's heart vibrated between the two young wives, feeling it reasonable enough that Mrs. Maitland, now very infirm, should need to have the doctor in the house, and reasonable that Judge Conrad should want Gretta all to himself. Sometimes when Katharine came to the cottage for a night, she came up through the garden in the dark, and alone in Mrs. Maitland's chamber the soul that had always been true met in solemn converse the other soul that had always been false, and they drew in such times very near to each other and very near to God. Mrs. Maitland had long ago ceased to urge Katharine to abandon her work of restitution, felt that she did right to resign from every position in philanthropic circles that implied worthiness of trust, but held her to her promise to help to develop the work to which Wildholm was consecrated, when her other task was done.

And there came a day when, notwithstanding Mrs. Maitland's unwillingness, shared fully by Harold and Margaret, everything spent in all those years for Gretta and her mother, was brought back in money earned and fourfold measure to the Wild estate, and was promptly passed over to the funds that were to develop the future plans that had their beginning in the old west wing. The young people could not find it in their hearts to give up Wildholm, but the west wing was separated from the main building and extended and developed into an ideal house of rest for the aged and weary, after Mrs. Maitland's own heart and plan, and bearing the name, Marion Wild. It included also a training school for domestic and other service, for girls as poor as Margaret had been, who had no saving gift like hers. And there came a later day when old Mr. Conrad's fortune, which Theodore had always treated as a trust, went far toward founding the home for boys and men, where reading rooms, recreation and instruction for hand, head, and heart, united to supply whatever was not put into their lives by work or home. And still later there came a day when the lands in California and Australia, left by Robert, enabled Gretta to make a beginning of that school of philanthropy and social economics on which her heart was set.

It had always been a theory of Mrs. Maitland, a theory which Gretta had absorbed, that opportunity and privilege and a share in all good work for the world, come faster to women than they are ready for it; that their problem is how to grow and learn fast enough to keep pace with the responsibilities of their lives. She would have all those whose hearts would serve any good cause or enter upon any helpful work, whether missions, or temperance, or education, or social, or economic problems, avoid the spasmodic, misguided, ineffective waste of energy, by placing study and thought before action. To provide place and time and wise instruction in order to open up to those whose hearts were ready to help humanity, the true needs, true conditions, the work already accomplished along all lines, and true and wise methods for future development—this was the purpose and hope.

The plan might in time cover the world's work along all lines and in all times, but at first it aimed only to gather a few of the best and most thoughtful women, to give them knowledge in the hope that each in turn would impart it to those who could not be otherwise taught. It was an effort against ignorance and conceit and wasteful enthusiasm, and in behalf of sincerity in purpose and sound principles in action.

And Mrs. Maitland lived to see the first group gather, eager—before dabbling in all the world's reforms, moral, social, and governmental—to learn the true significance and relation of reform, and how best to develop the woman thought and the woman heart, that it might become a powerful and genuine factor in the salvation of the race.

And in all these new homes, and in all these lines of work and study, there came and went a quiet woman who gave her life to practical experiment of others' plans and methods ; who knew the best thought of the student as well as the saddest

experience of the slums; whose days were a benediction by bedsides of pain; who never spared herself anywhere; but with almost infinite pity and
tenderness, helped everything that was wicked and
spared everything that was weak, and, keeping her
personality always in the background, brought into
these various institutions the results of her experience and her work.   To her unceasing. labors
they owed more, perhaps, than to any other one
person.   There were many influential helpers, a
fine Board of trustees and managers for each
branch of Wildholm work, but this woman, who
spoke in no meetings, served on no committees,
held no position in societies, was the one who never
faltered in her insistence that all the work should
be built upon the one foundation, having God as
the center and source of its life.

And when the day came that other women would
have done her honor, she bowed her head and went
back to the rooms in the heart of the most degraded
section of the city, that had of late been her home,
and sitting in the twilight opened her Bible and
read, as if to strengthen herself against temptation, these lines, written on the fly-leaf on the
night when God gave Gretta back to life:

> Therefore O friend, I would not, if I might,
> Rebuild my house of lies wherein I joyed
> One time to dwell.   My soul shall walk in white,
> Cast down but not destroyed
>
> Therefore in patience I possess my soul,
> Yea, therefore as a flint I set my face
> To cast down—to build up again the whole
> But in a distant place.